William Morris was a staggeringly talented man. He was architect, sculptor, author, musician, artist and translator extraordinary; he designed fabrics, glass, and furniture, musical instruments and, undoubtedly, primitive labor-saving devices. It seems that any activity in which he was interested became at once an area for fresh creation, and of a superlative quality. He was probably the nineteenth century's most protean Renaissance man.

The Well at The World's End is one of William Morris's extraordinary prose romances. Beginning simply in the little kingdom of Upmeads, it traces the story of Ralph, the youngest son of the homely ruling house, who sets out in quest of the Well at the World's End, and tells of his desperate adventures in the Wood Perilous, at the Burg of the Four Friths, with the sinister Fellowship of the Dry Tree, and with many another diversion encountered on the Road. The rhythm of the story moves like the rhythm of life, moments of high and sudden excitement overtaking pools of reflective quiet as Ralph moves steadfastly toward his objective, despite the many side-progressions of idyllic love, jealousy, murder and adventure which seek to deflect him. The fantasy is shot through with the small, human realities of a young man making his way in an utterly strange world, learning and growing in stature as he goes. It is a classic journey, and a classic quest.

Adult
Fantasy

THE WELL AT THE WORLD'S END

Volume 1

a tale by

WILLIAM MORRIS

Introduction by Lin Carter

PAN/BALLANTINE

First published 1896
This edition first published in Great Britain 1971 by
Pan/Ballantine,
33 Tothill Street, London SW1

ISBN 0 330 23845 0

2nd Printing 1973

Introduction © Lin Carter 1970

Cover art by Gervasio Gallardo

Printed in Great Britain by
Cox & Wyman Ltd, London, Reading and Fakenham

Contents.

Utterbol, and the Way Thither

AND so the four sons of the King drew straws to see which of them would rule the little kingdom after their father, and which would ride to the north or the east or the west in quest of adventure. And so the youngest of the four princes set forth on his destrier, Falcon, and departed from the little kingdom of Upmeads in quest of Utterbol which lieth beyond the Wood Perilous, the Castle of Abundance, the Burg of the Four Friths, and the Vale of the Tower, to the place of the miraculous Well . . .

AND thus begins *The Well at the World's End,* one of the first and one of the finest novels of heroic fantasy ever written.

Scholars and historians of fantasy, such as my friend L. Sprague de Camp, agree that it was the English novelist, poet, and artisan William Morris (1834–96) who founded the genre of the heroic fantasy laid in imaginary Medieval lands or worlds where magic works. His first novel in this genre, *The Wood Beyond The World* (1895), has already been revived in our Adult Fantasy Series. It was the first of all such tales of adventurous wanderings through the marvelous landscapes of worlds which have somehow managed to avoid the wear and tear of ever having actually existed. But far better, and nearly twice as long, is this present book, which is Morris' masterpiece.

The Well at the World's End was the second of his fantasy novels, published in 1896. At approximately 228,000 words, it is one of the longest fantasy novels ever written—probably the longest novel in this field before Professor Tolkien wrote *The Lord of the Rings*—and so lengthy that we are forced to publish it in two volumes, of which this is volume one.

Now, when de Camp or I say that William Morris founded the heroic fantasy novel we are of course aware that earlier examples can be found. Even without going all the way back to the Late Middle Ages and such prose romances as *Palmerin of England, Amadis of Gaul,* or *Felixmarte of Hyrcania,* it is possible to find forerunners of Morris. One of them was George MacDonald, whose "faerie romance," *Lilith,* appeared in 1895, the same year as Morris' first great fantasy, *The Wood Beyond The World.* MacDonald also wrote a novel of fantasy, appropriately titled *Phantastes,* published in 1858 when William Morris was twenty-four. And then there was George Meredith, who wrote an Oriental extravaganza called *The Shaving of Shagpat,* published in 1855. And that Prince of Eccentrics, William Beckford, whose astonishing *Vathek* was published in English translation nearly three-quarters of a century earlier, in 1786. (Publication of the French original was preceded by the translation, oddly enough.)

These four famous fantasies came before William Morris, yet we still consider Morris the founder of the genre. There are two reasons for this seemingly contradictory claim. In the first place, Oriental tales like *Vathek* and *The Shaving of Shagpat* are set—not in completely imaginary worlds of their authors' invention, as are the romances of William Morris—but in "literary" versions of the actual Middle East: in exotic Arabian Nights landscapes, real but romanticized. Then again, such novels as *Lilith* and *Phantastes* are set in Dreamland: we are not expected to take their imagined landscapes seriously; over and over MacDonald reiterates that his heroes are wandering through a waking dream. Thus, if we accept MacDonald as the founder of the heroic fantasy laid in invented worlds, we would also have to admit *Alice's Adventures in Wonderland* (1865) to the fold, as well. And, obviously, that would never do. The key element in the imaginary-world romance is that the reader is to assume that the worldscape of the story is *a real place*: that the hero of such a story is in very real danger from the various monsters and magicians he encounters; in a word, you can get *killed* on the road to Utterbol. Not so, in MacDonald's dreamscapes.

The second reason why we consider Morris to be "the man who invented fantasy" is that the tradition of this genre descends from his romances in a direct line. No one ever tried to write another *Vathek* or *Shagpat*, and only a few books (such as the *Perelandra* trilogy of C. S. Lewis and David Lindsay's brilliant and astounding novel *A Voyage to Arcturus*) show to any extent the influence of *Lilith* and *Phantastes*. But the genre of the heroic fantasy laid in an imaginary world descends from William Morris to Lord Dunsany and E. R. Eddison, and from thence to whole generations of writers such as James Branch Cabell, Fletcher Pratt (*The Blue Star*), Robert E. Howard, J. R. R. Tolkien, L. Sprague de Camp (*The Tritonian Ring* and *The Goblin Tower*), Fritz Leiber, Jack Vance, Jane Gaskell, Lloyd Alexander, and my own (as yet incomplete and unpublished) fantasy epic, *Khymyrium*.

No one—to my knowledge, anyway—has ever tried to explain just why Morris began making up the worlds in which he set his tales. It is especially puzzling when you consider that many of his works prior to that first great fantasy, *The Wood Beyond The World*, were set in actual historical or at least legendary settings. Such as his *Sigurd the Volsung*, laid against the scenery of the ancient Rhineland; or his book-length poem *The Life and Death of Jason*, which unfolds in settings borrowed from Greek mythology; or his first novel, *The House of the Wulfings*, published six years before *Wood* and depicting the struggle of the noble but primitive Germanic warriors against the advanced but decadent Roman legions.

Perhaps Morris found his storytelling talents uncomfortably restricted by the necessity of making his tales conform to known historical events or landscapes, and yearned for the completer freedom of the fantasy novelist. If so, his motive was the same as that which impelled the brilliant American novelist James Branch Cabell to turn aside from tales of cavaliers and Elizabethan heroes to his invented quasi-Medieval province of Poictesme and other realms—Antan, Cockaigne, Hell, and Paradise—whose attachments to Reality are even more remote and tenuous.

Most likely, however, Morris was improvising his worlds to a slightly larger extent than that found in the Medieval prose romances whose form and style he was imitating in these novels. He was nostalgically hearkening back to the sort of adventure story set in dim landscapes whose geography is at best, vague and imprecise. As, for example, in the early thirteenth century *Parzival* of Wolfram von Eschenbach, when Gahmuret in Book II journeys overland from Dolet (Toledo) to Waleis (Wales), somehow managing the trip without crossing the English Channel, no one is particularly surprised: that is the way things happen in romances!

The authors of Medieval romance mingled real and made-up geography with a fine contempt for consistency. In the Arthurian romances, the wandering knights appear equally at home in actual places like Scotland, Winchester, or Brittany, as they do in Sarras or Belacane or Avalon, which of course do not and never did exist. In the great *Amadis*, the Knight of the Green Sword finds actual realms such as Greece or France somehow contiguous to purely imaginary places such as the Firm Island or the land of Urganda the Unknown. And the knightly adventurers of *Orlando Furioso* are as likely to be found in Cathay or Tartary as they are in the mysterious kingdom of Prester John or the strange valleys of the Moon. What William Morris did was to go these early romancers one better, and make up a whole world instead of merely parts of one. In so doing, the fantasy novel was born.

This novel, *The Well at the World's End*, was first published by Longmans, Green and Co. in London in 1896. It has been out of print now, insofar as I have been able to discover, for slightly less than a half-century. As you will perhaps agree as you turn the page and set forth on the way to Utterbol and the wondrous Well, it is high time so marvelous a story was revived and once again made available to all of the many thousands of fantasy enthusiasts who have yet to venture in the magic worlds of William Morris, the man who invented fantasy.

—LIN CARTER
Editorial Consultant

Hollis, Long Island, New York

BOOK ONE
The Road
Unto Love

CHAPTER 1
The Sundering of the Ways

Long ago there was a little land, over which ruled a regulus or kinglet, who was called King Peter, though his kingdom was but little. He had four sons whose names were Blaise, Hugh, Gregory and Ralph: of these Ralph was the youngest, whereas he was but of twenty winters and one; and Blaise was the oldest and had seen thirty winters.

Now it came to this at last, that to these young men the kingdom of their father seemed strait; and they longed to see the ways of other men, and to strive for life. For though they were king's sons, they had but little world's wealth; save and except good meat and drink, and enough or too much thereof; house-room of the best; friends to be merry with, and maidens to kiss, and these also as good as might be; freedom withal to come and go as they would; the heavens above them, the earth to bear them up, and the meadows and acres, the woods and fair streams, and the little hills of Upmeads, for that was the name of their country and the kingdom of King Peter.

1

So having nought but this little they longed for much; and that the more because, king's sons as they were, they had but scant dominion save over their horses and dogs: for the men of that country were stubborn and sturdy vavassors, and might not away with masterful doings, but were like to pay back a blow with a blow, and a foul word with a buffet. So that, all things considered, it was little wonder if King Peter's sons found themselves straitened in their little land: wherein was no great merchant city; no mighty castle, or noble abbey of monks: nought but fair little halls of yeomen, with here and there a franklin's court or a shield-knight's manor-house; with many a goodly church, and whiles a house of good canons, who knew not the road to Rome, nor how to find the door of the Chancellor's house.

So these young men wearied their father and mother a long while with telling them of their weariness, and their longing to be gone: till at last on a fair and hot afternoon of June King Peter rose up from the carpet which the Prior of St. John's by the Bridge had given him (for he had been sleeping thereon amidst the grass of his orchard after his dinner) and he went into the hall of his house, which was called the High House of Upmeads, and sent for his four sons to come to him. And they came and stood before his high-seat and he said:

"Sons, ye have long wearied me with words concerning your longing for travel on the roads; now if ye verily wish to be gone, tell me when would ye take your departure if ye had your choice?"

They looked at one another, and the three younger ones nodded at Blaise the eldest: so he began, and said: "Saving the love and honour that we have for thee, and also for our mother, we would be gone at once, even with the noon's meat still in our bellies. But thou art the lord in this land, and thou must rule. Have I said well, brethren?" And they all said "Yea, yea." Then said the king; "Good! now is the sun high and hot; yet if ye ride softly ye may come to some good harbour before nightfall without foundering your horses. So come ye in an hour's space to the Four-want-way, and there and then will I order your departure."

The young men were full of joy when they heard his word;

2

and they departed and went this way and that, gathering such small matters as each deemed that he needed, and which he might lightly carry with him; then they armed themselves, and would bid the squires bring them their horses; but men told them that the said squires had gone their ways already to the Want-way by the king's commandment: so thither they went at once a-foot all four in company, laughing and talking together merrily.

It must be told that this Want-way aforesaid was but four furlongs from the House, which lay in an ingle of the river called Upmeads Water amongst very fair meadows at the end of the upland tillage; and the land sloped gently up toward the hill-country and the unseen mountains on the north; but to the south was a low ridge which ran along the water, as it wound along from west to east. Beyond the said ridge, at a place whence you could see the higher hills to the south, that stretched mainly east and west also, there was presently an end of the Kingdom of Upmeads, though the neighbours on that side were peaceable and friendly, and were wont to send gifts to King Peter. But toward the north beyond the Want-way King Peter was lord over a good stretch of land, and that of the best; yet was he never a rich man, for he had no freedom to tax and tail his folk, nor forsooth would he have used it if he had; for he was no ill man, but kindly and of measure. On these northern marches there was war at whiles, whereas they ended in a great forest well furnished of trees; and this wood was debateable, and King Peter and his sons rode therein at their peril: but great plenty was therein of all wild deer, as hart, and buck, and roe, and swine, and bears and wolves withal. The lord on the other side thereof was a mightier man than King Peter, albeit he was a bishop, and a baron of Holy Church. To say sooth he was a close-fist and a manslayer; though he did his manslaying through his vicars, the knights and men-at-arms who held their manors of him, or whom he waged.

In that forest had King Peter's father died in battle, and his eldest son also; therefore, being a man of peace, he rode therein but seldom, though his sons, the three eldest of them, had both ridden therein and ran therefrom valiantly. As for

3

Ralph the youngest, his father would not have him ride the Wood Debateable as yet.

So came those young men to the Want-ways, and found their father sitting there on a heap of stones, and over against him eight horses, four destriers, and four hackneys, and four squires withal. So they came and stood before their father, waiting for his word, and wondering what it would be.

Now spake King Peter: "Fair sons, ye would go on all adventure to seek a wider land, and a more stirring life than ye may get of me at home: so be it! But I have bethought me, that, since I am growing old and past the age of getting children, one of you, my sons, must abide at home to cherish me and your mother, and to lead our carles in war if trouble falleth upon us. Now I know not how to choose by mine own wit which of you shall ride and which abide. For so it is that ye are diverse of your conditions; but the evil conditions which one of you lacks the other hath, and the valiancy which one hath, the other lacks. Blaise is wise and prudent, but no great man of his hands. Hugh is a stout rider and lifter, but headstrong and foolhardy, and over bounteous a skinker; and Gregory is courteous and many worded, but sluggish in deed; though I will not call him a dastard. As for Ralph, he is fair to look on, and peradventure he may be as wise as Blaise, as valiant as Hugh, and as smooth-tongued as Gregory; but of all this we know little or nothing, whereas he is but young and untried. Yet may he do better than you others, and I deem that he will do so. All things considered, then, I say, I know not how to choose between you, my sons; so let luck choose for me, and ye shall draw cuts for your roads; and he that draweth longest shall go north, and the next longest shall go east, and the third straw shall send the drawer west; but as to him who draweth the shortest cut, he shall go no whither but back again to my house, there to abide with me the chances and changes of life; and it is most like that this one shall sit in my chair when I am gone, and be called King of Upmeads.

"Now, my sons, doth this ordinance please you? For if so be it doth not, then may ye all abide at home, and eat of my

4

meat, and drink of my cup, but little chided either for sloth or misdoing, even as it hath been aforetime."

The young men looked at one another, and Blaise answered and said: "Sir, as for me I say we will do after your commandment, to take what road luck may show us, or to turn back home again." They all yeasaid this one after the other; and then King Peter said: "Now before I draw the cuts, I shall tell you that I have appointed the squires to go with each one of you. Richard the Red shall go with Blaise; for though he be somewhat stricken in years, and wise, yet is he a fierce carle and a doughty, and knoweth well all feats of arms.

"Lancelot Longtongue shall be squire to Hugh; for he is good of seeming and can compass all courtesy, and knoweth logic (though it be of the law and not of the schools), yet is he a proper man of his hands; as needs must he be who followeth Hugh; for where is Hugh, there is trouble and debate.

"Clement the Black shall serve Gregory: for he is a careful carle, and speaketh one word to every ten deeds that he doeth; whether they be done with point and edge, or with the hammer in the smithy.

"Lastly, I have none left to follow thee, Ralph, save Nicholas Long-shanks; but though he hath more words than I have, yet hath he more wisdom, and is a man lettered and far-travelled, and loveth our house right well.

"How say ye, sons, is this to your liking?"

They all said "yea." Then quoth the king; "Nicholas, bring hither the straws ready dight, and I will give them my sons to draw."

So each young man came up in turn and drew; and King Peter laid the straws together and looked at them, and said:

"Thus it is, Hugh goeth north with Lancelot; Gregory westward with Clement." He stayed a moment and then said: "Blaise fareth eastward and Richard with him. As for thee, Ralph my dear son, thou shalt back with me and abide in my house and I shall see thee day by day; and thou shalt help me to live my last years happily in all honour; and thy love shall be my hope, and thy valiancy my stay."

Therewith he arose and threw his arm about the young man's neck; but he shrank away a little from his father, and his face grew troubled; and King Peter noted that, and his countenance fell, and he said:

"Nay nay, my son; grudge not thy brethren the chances of the road, and the ill-hap of the battle. Here at least for thee is the bounteous board and the full cup, and the love of kindred and well-willers, and the fellowship of the folk. O well is thee, my son, and happy shalt thou be!"

But the young man knit his brows and said no word in answer.

Then came forward those three brethren who were to fare at all adventure, and they stood before the old man saying nought. Then he laughed and said: "O ho, my sons! Here in Upmeads have ye all ye need without money, but when ye fare in the outlands ye need money; is it not a lack of yours that your pouches be bare? Abide, for I have seen to it."

Therewith he drew out of his pouch three little bags, and said; "Take ye each one of these; for therein is all that my treasury may shed as now. In each of these is there coined money, both white and red, and some deal of gold uncoined, and of rings and brooches a few, and by estimation there is in each bag the same value reckoned in lawful silver of Upmeads and the Wolds and the Overhill-Countries. Take up each what there is, and do the best ye may therewith."

Then each took his bag, and kissed and embraced his father; and they kissed Ralph and each other, and so got to horse and departed with their squires, going softly because of the hot sun. But Nicholas slowly mounted his hackney and led Ralph's war-horse with him home again to King Peter's House.

CHAPTER 2

Ralph Goeth Back Home to the High House

Ralph and King Peter walked slowly home together, and as they went King Peter fell to telling of how in his young days he rode in the Wood Debateable, and was belated there all alone, and happed upon men who were outlaws and wolfheads, and feared for his life; but they treated him kindly, and honoured him, and saw him safe on his way in the morning. So that never thereafter would he be art and part with those who hunted outlaws to slay them. "For," said he, "it is with these men as with others, that they make prey of folk; yet these for the more part prey on the rich, and the lawful prey on the poor. Otherwise it is with these wolfheads as with lords and knights and franklins, that as there be bad amongst them, so also there be good; and the good ones I happed on, and so may another man."

Hereto paid Ralph little heed at that time, since he had heard the tale and its morality before, and that more than once; and moreover his mind was set upon his own matters, and these was he pondering. Albeit perchance the words abode with him. So came they to the House, and Ralph's mother, who was a noble dame, and well-liking as for her years, which were but little over fifty, stood in the hall-door to see which of her sons should come back to her, and when she saw them coming together, she went up to them, and cast her arms about Ralph and kissed him and caressed him,— being exceeding glad that it was he and not one of the others who had returned to dwell with them; for he was her best-beloved, as was little marvel, seeing that he was by far the fairest and the most loving. But Ralph's face grew troubled again in his mother's arms, for he loved her exceeding well; and forsooth he loved the whole house and all that dwelt

7

there, down to the turnspit dogs in the chimney ingle, and the swallows that nested in the earthen bottles, which when he was little he had seen his mother put up in the eaves of the out-bowers: but now, love or no love, the spur was in his side, and he must needs hasten as fate would have him. However, when he had disentangled himself from his mother's caresses, he enforced himself to keep a cheerful countenance, and upheld it the whole evening through, and was by seeming merry at supper, and went to bed singing.

CHAPTER 3

Ralph Cometh to the Cheaping-Town

He slept in an upper chamber in a turret of the House, which chamber was his own, and none might meddle with it. There the next day he awoke in the dawning, and arose and clad himself, and took his war-gear and his sword and spear, and bore all away without doors to the side of the Ford in that ingle of the river, and laid it for a while in a little willow copse, so that no chance-comer might see it; then he went back to the stable of the House and took his destrier from the stall (it was a dapple-grey horse called Falcon, and was right good,) and brought him down to the said willow copse, and tied him to a tree till he had armed himself amongst the willows, whence he came forth presently as brisk-looking and likely a man-at-arms as you might see on a summer day. Then he clomb up into the saddle, and went his ways splashing across the ford, before the sun had arisen, while the throstle-cocks were yet amidst their first song.

Then he rode on a little trot south away; and by then the sun was up he was without the bounds of Upmeads; albeit in the land thereabout dwelt none who were not friends to King Peter and his sons: and that was well, for now were folk stirring and were abroad in the fields; as a band of carles

8

going with their scythes to the hay-field; or a maiden with her milking-pails going to her kine, barefoot through the seeding grass; or a company of noisy little lads on their way to the nearest pool of the stream that they might bathe in the warm morning after the warm night. All these and more knew him and his armour and Falcon his horse, and gave him the sele of the day, and he was nowise troubled at meeting them; for besides that they thought it no wonder to meet one of the lords of Upmeads going armed about his errands, their own errands were close at home, and it was little likely that they should go that day so far as to Upmeads Water, seeing that it ran through the meadows a half-score miles to the northward.

So Ralph rode on, and came into the high road, that led one way back again into Upmeads, and crossed the Water by a fair bridge late builded between King Peter and a house of Canons on the north side, and the other way into a good cheaping-town hight Wulstead, beyond which Ralph knew little of the world which lay to the south, and seemed to him a wondrous place, full of fair things and marvellous adventures.

So he rode till he came into the town when the fair morning was still young, the first mass over, and maids gathered about the fountain amidst the market-place, and two or three dames sitting under the buttercross. Ralph rode straight up to the house of a man whom he knew, and had often given him guesting there, and he himself was not seldom seen in the High House of Upmeads. This man was a merchant, who went and came betwixt men's houses, and bought and sold many things needful and pleasant to folk, and King Peter dealt with him much and often. Now he stood in the door of his house, which was new and goodly, sniffing the sweet scents which the morning wind bore into the town; he was clad in a goodly long gown of grey welted with silver, of thin cloth meet for the summer-tide: for little he wrought with his hands, but much with his tongue; he was a man of forty summers, ruddy-faced and black-bearded, and he was called Clement Chapman.

When he saw Ralph he smiled kindly on him, and came and held his stirrup as he lighted down, and said: "Welcome, lord! Art thou come to give me a message, and eat and drink in a poor huckster's house, and thou armed so gallantly?"

Ralph laughed merrily, for he was hungry, and he said: "Yea, I will eat and drink with thee and kiss my gossip, and go my ways."

Therewith the carle led him into the house; and if it were goodly without, within it was better. For there was a fair chamber panelled with wainscot well carven, and a cupboard of no sorry vessels of silver and latten: the chairs and stools as fair as might be; no king's might be better: the windows were glazed, and there were flowers and knots and posies in them; and the bed was hung with goodly web from over sea such as the soldan useth. Also, whereas the chapman's warebowers were hard by the chamber, there was a pleasant mingled smell therefrom floating about. The table was set with meat and drink and vessel of pewter and earth, all fair and good; and thereby stood the chapman's wife, a very goodly woman of two-score years, who had held Ralph at the font when she was a slim damsel new wedded; for she was come of no mean kindred of the Kingdom of Upmeads: her name was Dame Katherine.

Now she kissed Ralph's cheek friendly, and said: "Welcome, gossip! thou art here in good time to break thy fast; and we will give thee a trim dinner thereafter, when thou hast been here and there in the town and done thine errand; and then shalt thou drink a cup and sing me a song, and so home again in the cool of the evening."

Ralph seemed a little troubled at her word, and he said: "Nay, gossip, though I thank thee for all these good things as though I had them, yet must I ride away south straightway after I have breakfasted, and said one word to the goodman. Goodman, how call ye the next town southward, and how far is it thither?"

Quoth Clement: "My son, what hast thou to do with riding south? As thou wottest, going hence south ye must presently ride the hill-country; and that is no safe journey for a lonely man, even if he be a doughty knight like to thee, lord."

Said Ralph, reddening withal: "I have an errand that way."

10

"An errand of King Peter's or thine own?" said Clement.

"Of King Peter's, if ye must wot," said Ralph.

Clement were no chapman had he not seen that the lad was lying; so he said:

"Fair lord, saving your worship, how would it be as to the speeding of King Peter's errand, if I brought thee before our mayor, and swore the peace against thee; so that I might keep thee in courteous prison till I had sent to thy father of thy whereabouts?"

The young man turned red with anger; but ere he could speak Dame Katherine said sharply: "Hold thy peace, Clement! What hast thou to meddle or make in the matter? If our young lord hath will to ride out and see the world, why should we let him? Yea, why should his father let him, if it come to that? Take my word for it that my gossip shall go through the world and come back to those that love him, as goodly as he went forth. And hold! here is for a token thereof."

Therewith she went to an ark that stood in the corner, and groped in the till thereof and brought out a little necklace of blue and green stones with gold knops betwixt, like a pair of beads; albeit neither pope nor priest had blessed them; and tied to the necklace was a little box of gold with something hidden therein. This gaud she gave to Ralph, and said to him: "Gossip, wear this about thy neck, and let no man take it from thee, and I think it will be salvation to thee in peril, and good luck to thee in the time of questing; so that it shall be to thee as if thou hadst drunk of the WELL AT THE WORLD'S END."

"What is that water?" said Ralph, "and how may I find it?"

"I know not rightly," she said, "but if a body might come by it, I hear say that it saveth from weariness and wounding and sickness; and it winneth love from all, and maybe life everlasting. Hast thou not heard tell of it, my husband?"

"Yea," said the chapman, "many times; and how that whoso hath drunk thereof hath the tongue that none may withstand, whether in buying or selling, or prevailing over the hearts of men in any wise. But as for its whereabouts, ye shall not find it in these parts. Men say that it is beyond the

11

Dry Tree; and that is afar, God wot! But now, lord Ralph, I rede thee go back again this evening with Andrew, my nephew, for company: forsooth, he will do little less gainful than riding with thee to Upmeads than if he abide in Wulstead; for he is idle. But, my lord, take it not amiss that I spake about the mayor and the tipstaves; for it was but a jest, as thou mayest well wot."

Ralph's face cleared at that word, and he stood smiling, weighing the chaplet in his hand; but Dame Katherine said:

"Dear gossip, do it on speedily; for it is a gift from me unto thee: and from a gossip even king's sons may take a gift."

Quoth Ralph: "But is it lawful to wear it? is there no wizardry within it?"

"Hearken to him!" she said, "and how like unto a man he speaketh; if there were a brawl in the street, he would strike in and ask no word thereof, not even which were the better side: whereas here is my falcon-chick frighted at a little gold box and a pair of Saracen beads."

"Well," quoth Ralph, "the first holy man I meet shall bless them for me."

"That shall he not," said the dame, "that shall he not. Who wotteth what shall betide to thee or me if he do so? Come, do them on, and then to table! For seest thou not that the goodman is wearying for meat? and even thine eyes will shine the brighter for a mouthful, king's son and gossip."

She took him by the hand and did the beads on his neck, and kissed and fondled him before he sat down, while the goodman looked on, grinning rather sheepishly, but said nought to them; and only called on his boy to lead the destrier to stable. So when they were set down, the chapman took up the word where it had been dropped, and said: "So, Lord Ralph, thou must needs take to adventures, being, as thou deemest, full grown. That is all one as the duck taketh to water despite of the hen that hath hatched her. Well, it was not to be thought that Upmeads would hold you lords much longer. Or what is gone with my lords your brethren?"

Said Ralph: "They have departed at all adventure, north, east, and west, each bearing our father's blessing and a bag of pennies. And to speak the truth, goodman, for I perceive I

12

am no doctor at lying, my father and mother would have me stay at home when my brethren were gone, and that liketh me not; therefore am I come out to seek my luck in the world: for Upmeads is good for a star-gazer, maybe, or a simpler, or a priest, or a worthy good carle of the fields, but not for a king's son with the blood running hot in his veins. Or what sayest thou, gossip?"

Quoth the dame: "I could weep for thy mother; but for thee nought at all. It is good that thou shouldest do thy will in the season of youth and the days of thy pleasure. Yea, and I deem that thou shalt come back again great and worshipful; and I am called somewhat foreseeing. Only look to it that thou keep the pretty thing that I have just given thee."

"Well," said the chapman, "this is fine talk about pleasure and the doing of one's will; nevertheless a whole skin is good wares, though it be not to be cheapened in any market of the world. Now, lord, go thou where thou wilt, whether I say go or abide; and forsooth I am no man of King Peter's, that I should stay thee. As for the name of the next town, it is called Higham-on-the-Way, and is a big town plenteous of victuals, with strong walls and a castle, and a very rich abbey of monks: and there is peace within its walls, because the father abbot wages a many men to guard him and his, and to uphold his rights against all comers; wherein he doth wisely, and also well. For much folk flocketh to his town and live well therein; and there is great recourse of chapmen thither. No better market is there betwixt this and Babylon. Well, Sir Ralph, I rede thee if thou comest unhurt to Higham-on-the-Way, go no further for this time, but take service with the lord abbot, and be one of his men of war; thou may'st then become his captain if thou shouldest live; which would be no bad adventure for one who cometh from Upmeads."

Ralph looked no brighter for this word, and he answered nought to it: but said presently:

"And what is to be looked for beyond Higham if one goeth further? Dost thou know the land any further?"

The carle smiled: "Yea forsooth, and down to the Wood Perilous, and beyond it, and the lands beyond the Wood; and far away through them. I say not that I have been to the Dry Tree; but I have spoken to one who hath heard of him who

13

hath seen it; though he might not come by a draught of the Well at the World's End."

Ralph's eyes flashed, and his cheeks reddened as he listened hereto; but he spake quietly:

"Master Clement, how far dost thou make it to Higham-on-the-Way?"

"A matter of forty miles," said the Chapman; "because, as thou wottest, if ye ride south from hence, ye shall presently bring your nose up against the big downs, and must needs climb them at once; and when ye are at the top of Bear Hill, and look south away. Ye shall see nought but downs on downs with never a road to call a road, and never a castle, or church, or homestead: nought but some shepherd's hut; or at the most the little house of a holy man with a little chapel thereby in some swelly of the chalk, where the water hath trickled into a pool; for otherwise the place is waterless." Therewith he took a long pull at the tankard by his side, and went on:

"Higham is beyond all that, and out into the fertile plain; and a little river hight Coldlake windeth about the meadows there; and it is a fair land; though look you the wool of the downs is good, good, good! I have foison of this year's fleeces with me. Ye shall raise none such in Upmeads."

Ralph sat silent a little, as if pondering, and then he started up and said: "Good master Clement, we have eaten thy meat and thank thee for that and other matters. Wilt thou now be kinder, and bid thy boy bring round Falcon our horse; for we have far to go, and must begone straight-away."

"Yea, lord," said Clement, "even so will I do." And he muttered under his breath; "Thou talkest big, my lad, with thy 'we'; but thou art pressed lest Nicholas be here presently to fetch thee back; and to say sooth I would his hand were on thy shoulder even now."

Then he spake aloud again, and said:

"I must now begone to my lads, and I will send one round with thy war-horse. But take my rede, my lord, and become the man of the Abbot of St. Mary's of Higham, and all will be well."

Therewith he edged himself out of the chamber, and the dame fell to making a mighty clatter with the vessel and

14

trenchers and cups on the board, while Ralph walked up and down the chamber his war-gear jingling upon him. Presently the dame left her table-clatter and came up to Ralph and looked kindly into his face and said: "Gossip, hast thou perchance any money?"

He flushed up red, and then his face fell; yet he spake gaily: "Yea, gossip, I have both white and red: there are three golden crowns in my pouch, and a little flock of silver pennies: forsooth I say not as many as would reach from here to Upmeads, if they were laid one after the other."

She smiled and patted his cheek, and said:

"Thou art no very prudent child, king's son. But it comes into my mind that my master did not mean thee to go away empty-handed; else had he not departed and left us twain together."

Therewith she went to the credence that stood in a corner, and opened a drawer therein and took out a little bag, and gave it into Ralph's hand, and said: "This is the gift of the gossip; and thou mayst take it without shame; all the more because if thy father had been a worser man, and a harder lord he would have had more to give thee. But now thou hast as much or more as any one of thy brethren."

He took the bag smiling and shame-faced, but she looked on him fondly and said:

"Now I know not whether I shall lay old Nicholas on thine heels when he cometh after thee, as come he will full surely; or whether I shall suffer the old sleuth-hound nose out thy slot of himself, as full surely he will set on to it."

"Thou mightest tell him," said Ralph, "that I am gone to take service with the Abbot of St. Mary's of Higham: hah?"

She laughed and said: "Wilt thou do so, lord, and follow the rede of that goodman of mine, who thinketh himself as wise as Solomon?"

Ralph smiled and answered her nothing.

"Well," she said, "I shall say what likes me when the hour is at hand. Lo, here! thine horse. Abide yet a moment of time, and then go whither thou needs must, like the wind of the summer day."

Therewith she went out of the chamber and came back again with a scrip which she gave to Ralph and said: "Herein

15

is a flask of drink for the waterless country, and a little meat for the way. Fare thee well, gossip! Little did I look for it when I rose up this morning and nothing irked me save the dulness of our town, and the littleness of men's doings therein, that I should have to cut off a piece of my life from me this morning, and say, farewell gossip, as now again I do."

Therewith she kissed him on either cheek and embraced him; and it might be said of her and him that she let him go thereafter; for though as aforesaid he loved her, and praised her kindness, he scarce understood the eagerness of her love for him; whereas moreover she saw him not so often betwixt Upmeads and Wulstead: and belike she herself scarce understood it. Albeit she was a childless woman.

So when he had got to horse, she watched him riding a moment, and saw how he waved his hand to her as he turned the corner of the market-place, and how a knot of lads and lasses stood staring on him after she lost sight of him. Then she turned her back into the chamber and laid her head on the table and wept. Then came in the goodman quietly and stood by her and she heeded him not. He stood grinning curiously on her awhile, and then laid his hand on her shoulder, and said as she raised her face to him:

"Sweetheart, it availeth nought; when thou wert young and exceeding fair, he was but a little babe, and thou wert looking in those days to have babes of thine own; and then it was too soon: and now that he is such a beauteous young man, and a king's son withal, and thou art wedded to a careful carle of no weak heart, and thou thyself art more than two-score years old, it is too late. Yet thou didst well to give our lord the money. Lo! here is wherewithal to fill up the lack in thy chest; and here is a toy for thee in place of the pair of beads thou gavest him; and I bid thee look on it as if I had given him my share of the money and the beads."

She turned to Clement, and took the bag of money, and the chaplet which he held out to her, and she said: "God wot thou art no ill man, my husband, but would God I had a son like to him!"

She still wept somewhat; but the chapman said: "Let it rest there, sweetheart! let it rest there! It may be a year or twain before thou seest him again: and then belike he shall be come back with some woman whom he loves better than any other; and who knows but in a way he may deem himself our son. Meanwhile thou hast done well, sweetheart, so be glad."

Therewith he kissed her and went his ways to his merchandize, and she to the ordering of her house, grieved but not unhappy.

CHAPTER 4

Ralph Rideth the Downs

As for Ralph, he rode on with a merry heart, and presently came to an end of the plain country, and the great downs rose up before him with a white road winding up to the top of them. Just before the slopes began to rise was a little thorp beside a stream, and thereby a fair church and a little house of Canons: so Ralph rode toward the church to see if therein were an altar of St. Nicholas, who was his good lord and patron, that he might ask of him a blessing on his journey. But as he came up to the churchyard-gate he saw a great black horse tied thereto as if abiding some one; and as he lighted down from his saddle he saw a man coming hastily from out the church-door and striding swiftly toward the said gate. He was a big man, and armed; for he had a bright steel sallet on his head, which covered his face all save the end of his chin; and plates he had on his legs and arms. He wore a green coat over his armour, and thereon was wrought in gold an image of a tree leafless: he had a little steel axe about his neck, and a great sword hung by his side. Ralph stood looking on him with his hand on the latch of the gate, but when the man came thereto he tore it open roughly and shoved through at once, driving Ralph back, so that he well-nigh overset him, and so sprang to his horse and swung himself into the saddle, just as Ralph steadied himself and ruffled up to him, half drawing his sword from the scabbard the while. But the man-at-arms cried out, "Put it back, put it back! If thou must needs deal with every man that shoveth thee in his haste, thy life is like to be but short."

He was settling himself in his saddle as he spoke, and now he shook his rein, and rode off speedily toward the hill-road. But when he was so far off that Ralph might but see his face but as a piece of reddish colour, he reined up for a moment of time, and turning round in his saddle lifted up his sallet and left his face bare, and cried out as if to Ralph, "The first time!" And then let the head-piece fall again, and set spurs to his horse and gallopped away.

Ralph stood looking at him as he got smaller on the long white road, and wondering what this might mean, and how the unknown man should know him, if he did know him. But presently he let his wonder run off him, and went his ways into the church, wherein he found his good lord and friend St. Nicholas, and so said a paternoster before his altar, and besought his help, and made his offering; and then departed and gat to horse again, and rode softly the way to the downs, for the day was hot.

The way was steep and winding, with a hollow cup of the hills below it, and above it a bent so steep that Ralph could see but a few yards of it on his left hand; but when he came to the hill's brow and could look down on the said bent, he saw strange figures on the face thereof, done by cutting away the turf so that the chalk might show clear. A tree with leaves was done on that hill-side, and on either hand of it a beast like a bear ramping up against the tree; and these signs were very ancient. This hill-side carving could not be seen from the thorp beneath, which was called Netherton, because the bent looked westward down into the hollow of the hill abovesaid; but from nigher to Wulstead they were clear to see, and Ralph had often beheld them, but never so nigh: and that hill was called after them Bear Hill. At the top of it was an earth-work of the ancient folk, which also was called Bear Castle. And now Ralph rode over the hill's brow into it; for the walls had been beaten down in places long and long ago.

Now he rode up the wall, and at the topmost of it turned

and looked aback on the blue country which he had ridden through stretching many a league below, and tried if he could pick out Upmeads from amongst the diverse wealth of the summer land: but Upmeads Water was hidden, and he could see nothing to be sure of to tell him whereabouts the High House stood; yet he deemed that he could make out the Debateable Wood and the hills behind it well enough. Then he turned his horse about, and had the down-country before him; long lines of hills to wit, one rising behind the other like the waves of a somewhat quiet sea: no trees thereon, nor houses that he might see thence: nought but a green road that went waving up and down before him greener than the main face of the slopes.

He looked at it all for a minute or two as the south-west wind went past his ears, and played a strange tune on the innumerable stems of the bents and the hard-stalked blossoms, to which the bees sang counterpoint. Then the heart arose within him, and he drew the sword from the scabbard, and waved it about his head, and shook it toward the south, and cried out, "Now, welcome world, and be thou blessed from one end to the other, from the ocean sea to the uttermost mountains!"

A while he held the white steel in his fist, and then sheathed the blade, and rode down soberly over the turf bridge across the ancient fosse, and so came on to the green road made many ages before by an ancient people, and so trotted south along fair and softly.

Little is to be told of his journey through the downs: as he topped a low hill whereon were seven grave-mounds of the ancient folk in a row, he came on a shepherd lying amidst of his sheep: the man sprang to his feet when he heard horse-hoofs anigh him and saw the glint of steel, and he set his hand to a short spear which lay by him; but when he saw nought but Ralph, and heard how he gave him the sele of the day, he nodded his head in a friendly way, though he said nought in salutation; for the loneliness of the downs made the speech slow within him.

Again some two miles further on Ralph met a flock of sheep coming down a bent which the road climbed, and with them were three men, their drovers, and they drew nigh him

19

as he was amidst of the sheep, so that he could scarce see the way. Each of these three had a weapon; one a pole-axe, another a long spear, and the third a flail jointed and bound with iron, and an anlace hanging at his girdle. So they stood in the way and hailed him when the sheep were gone past; and the man with the spear asked him whither away. "I am turned toward Higham-on-the-Way," quoth he; "and how many miles shall I ride ere I get there?"

Said one of them: "Little less than twenty, lord." Now it was past noon two hours, and the day was hot; so whereas the faces of the men looked kind and friendly, albeit somewhat rugged, he lighted down from his horse and sat down by the way-side, and drew his bottle of good wine from out of his wallet, and asked the men if they were in haste. "Nay, master," said he of the pole-axe, while all eyes turned to the bottle, "HE has gone by too long; and will neither meddle with us, nor may we deal with him."

"Well then," quoth Ralph, "there is time for bever. Have ye ought of a cup, that we may drink to each other?"

"Yea," said the carle with the anlace, "that have I." Therewith he drew from his pouch a ram's horn rimmed with silver, and held it up, and said as if he were speaking to it: "Now, Thirly, rejoice! for ye shall have lord's wine poured into thy maw."

Therewith he held it out toward Ralph, who laughed and filled it up, and filled for himself a little silver cup which he carried, and said: "To you, shepherds! Much wool and little cry!" And he drank withal.

"And I," quoth the man with the horn, "call this health; Much cry and little wool!"

"Well, well, how mean ye by that, Greasy Wat?" said the man with the spear, taking the horn as he spake; "that is but a poor wish for a lord that drinketh out of our cup."

Said Wat: "Why, neighbour, why! thy wit is none too hasty. The wool that a knight sheareth is war and battle; that is wounding and death; but the cry is the talk and boasting and minstrelsy that goeth before all this. Which is the best wish to wish him? the wounds and the death, or the fore-rumour and stir thereof which hurteth no man?"

Ralph laughed thereat, and was merry and blithe with them; but the spearman, who was an old man, said:

"For all Wat sayeth, lord, and his japes, ye must not misdeem of us that we shepherds of the Downs can do nought but run to ales and feasts, and that we are but pot-valiant: maybe thou thyself mayst live to see things go otherwise: and in that day may we have such as thee for captain. Now, fair lord, I drink to thy crown of valour, and thy good luck; and we thank thee for the wine and yet more for the blithe fellowship."

So Ralph filled up the ram's horn till Dame Katherine's good island wine was well-nigh spent; and at last he said:

"Now, my masters, I must to horse; but I pray you tell or we depart, what did ye mean when ye said that HE had gone past? Who is HE?"

The merry faces of the men changed at his word, and they looked in each other's faces, till at last the old spearman answered him:

"Fair lord, these things we have little will to talk about: for we be poor men with no master to fleece us, and no lord to help us: also we be folk unlearned and unlettered, and from our way of life, whereas we dwell in the wilderness, we seldom come within the doors of a church. But whereas we have drunk with thee, who seemest to be a man of lineage, and thou hast been blithe with us, we will tell thee that we have seen one riding south along the Greenway, clad in a coat as green as the way, with the leafless tree done on his breast. So nigh to him we were that we heard his cry as he sped along, as ye may hear the lapwing whining; for he said: 'POINT AND EDGE, POINT AND EDGE! THE RED WATER AMIDST OF THE HILLS!' In my lifetime such a man hath, to my knowledge, been seen thrice before; and after each sight of him followed evil days and the death of men. Moreover this is the Eve of St. John, and we deem the token the worse therefor. Or how deemest thou?"

Ralph stood silent awhile; for he was thinking of the big man whom he had met at the churchyard gate, and all this tale seemed wonderful to him. But at last he said:

"I cannot tell what there is in it; herein am I no help to you. To-day I am but little; though I may one day be great.

21

Yet this may I do for you; tomorrow will I let sing a mass in St. Mary's Church on your behoof. And hereafter, if I wax as my will is, and I come to be lord in these lands, I will look to it to do what a good lord should do for the shepherds of the Downs, so that they may live well, and die in good hope. So may the Mother of God help me at need!"

Said the old shepherd: "Thou hast sworn an oath, and it is a good oath, and well sworn. Now if thou dost as thou swearest, words can but little thanks, yet deeds may. Wherefore if ever thou comest back hither, and art in such need that a throng of men may help thee therein; then let light a great fire upon each corner of the topmost wall of Bear Castle, and call to mind this watch-word: 'SMITE ASIDE THE AXE, O BEAR-FATHER,' and then shalt thou see what shall betide thee for thy good-hap: farewell now, with the saints to aid!"

Ralph bade them live well and hail, and mounted his horse and rode off down the Greenway, and as he rode the shepherds waved their weapons to him in token of good-will.

CHAPTER 5

Ralph Cometh to Higham-on-the-Way

Nought more befell Ralph to tell of till he came to the end of the Downs and saw Higham lying below him overlooked by a white castle on a knoll, and with a river lapping it about and winding on through its fair green meadows even as Clement had told. From amidst its houses rose up three towers of churches above their leaden roofs, and high above all, long and great, the Abbey Church; and now was the low sun glittering on its gilded vanes and the wings of the angels high upon the battlements.

So Ralph rode down the slopes and was brisk about it, for it was drawing toward sunset, and he knew not at what hour they shut their gates. The road was·steep and winding, and it was the more part of an hour ere he came to the gate, which was open, and like to be yet, for many folk were thronging in, which throng also had hindered him soon after he came into the plain country. The gate was fair and strong, but Ralph saw no men-at-arms about it that evening. He rode into the street unquestioned, and therein was the throng great of people clad in fair and gay attire; and presently Ralph called to mind that this was St. John's Eve, so that he knew that there was some feast toward.

At last the throng was so thick that he was stayed by it; and therewithal a religious who was beside him and thrust up against his horse, turned to him and gave him good even, and said: "By thy weapons and gear thou art a stranger here in our burg, Sir Knight?"

"So it is," said Ralph.

"And whither away?" said the monk; "hast thou some kinsman or friend in the town?"

"Nay," said Ralph, "I seek a good hostelry where I may abide the night for my money."

The monk shook his head and said: "See ye the folk? It is holiday time, and midsummer after haysel. Ye shall scarce get lodging outside our house. But what then? Come thou thither straightway and have harbour of the best, and see our prior, who loveth young and brisk men-at-arms like to thee. Lo now! the throng openeth a little; I will walk by thy bridle and lead thee the shortest road thither."

Ralph gainsaid him not, and they bored through the throng of the street till they came into the market-square, which was very great and clean, paved with stones all over: tall and fair houses rose up on three sides of it, and on the fourth was the Great Church which made those houses seem but low: most of it was new-built; for the lord Abbot that then was, though he had not begun it, had taken the work up from his forerunner and had pushed it forward all he might; for he was very rich, and an open-handed man. Like dark gold it showed under the evening sun, and the painted and gilded imagery shone like jewels upon it.

"Yea," said the monk, as he noted Ralph's wonder at this

23

wonder; "a most goodly house it is, and happy shall they be that dwell there."

Therewith he led Ralph on, turning aside through the great square. Ralph saw that there were many folk therein, though it was too big to be thronged thick with them. Amidst of it was now a great pile of wood hung about with flowers, and hard by it a stage built up with hangings of rich cloth on one side thereof. He asked the monk what this might mean, and he told him the wood was for the Midsummer bale-fire, and the stage for the show that should come thereafter. So the brother led Ralph down a lane to the south of the great west door, and along the side of the minster and so came to the Abbey gate, and there was Ralph well greeted, and had all things given him which were due to a good knight; and then was he brought into the Guest-hall, a very fair chamber, which was now full of men of all degrees. He was shown to a seat on the daïs within two of the subprior's, and beside him sat an honourable lord, a vassal of St. Mary's. So was supper served well and abundantly: the meat and drink was of the best, and the vessel and all the plenishing was as good as might be; and the walls of that chamber were hung with noble arras-cloth picturing the Pilgrimage of the Soul of Man.

Every man there who spoke with Ralph, and they were many, was exceeding courteous to him; and he heard much talk about him of the wealth of the lands of St. Mary's at Higham, and how it was flourishing; and of the Abbot how mighty he was, so that he might do what he would, and that his will was to help and to give, and be blithe with all men: and folk told of turmoil and war in other lands, and praised the peace of Higham-on-the-Way.

Ralph listened to all this, and smiled, and said to himself that to another man this might well be the end of his journey for that time; but for him all this peace and well-being was not enough; for though it were a richer land than Upmeads, yet to the peace and the quiet he was well used, and he had come forth not for the winning of fatter peace, but to try what new thing his youth and his might and his high hope and his good hap might accomplish.

So when the supper was over, and the wine and spices had been brought, the Guest-hall began to thin somewhat, and the brother who had brought Ralph thither came to him and said:

"Fair lord, it were nowise ill if ye went forth, as others of our guests have done, to see the deeds of Midsummer Eve that shall be done in the great square in honour of Holy John; for our manner therein at Higham has been much thought of. Look my son!"

He pointed to the windows of the hall therewith, and lo! they grew yellow and bright with some fire without, as if a new fiery day had been born out of the dusk of the summer night; for the light that shone through the windows out-did the candle-light in the hall. Ralph started thereat and laid his right hand to the place of his sword, which indeed he had left with the chamberlain; but the monk laughed and said: "Fear nothing, lord; there is no foeman in Higham: come now, lest thou be belated of the show."

So he led Ralph forth, and into the square, where there was a space appointed for the brethren and their guests to see the plays; and the square was now so full of folk that it seemed like as if that there were no one man in the streets which were erewhile so thronged.

There were rows of men-at-arms in bright armour also to keep the folk in their places, like as hurdles pen the sheep up; howbeit they were nowise rough with folk, but humble and courteous. Many and many were the torches and cressets burning steadily in the calm air, so that, as aforesaid, night was turned into day. But on the scaffold aforesaid were standing bright and gay figures, whose names or what they were Ralph had no time to ask.

Now the bells began to clash from the great tower of the minster, and in a little while they had clashed themselves into order and rang clear and tuneably for a space; and while they were ringing, lo! those gay-clad people departed from the scaffold, and a canvas painted like a mountain-side, rocky and with caves therein, was drawn up at the back of it. Then came thereon one clad like a king holding a fair maiden by the hand, and with him was a dame richly clad and with a crown on her head. So these two kissed the maiden, and lamented over her, and went their ways, and the maiden left alone sat down upon a rock and covered up her face and wept; and while Ralph wondered what this might mean, or what grieved the maiden, there came creeping, as it were from out of a cranny of the rocks, a worm huge-headed and covered over with scales that glittered in the torch-light. Then Ralph sprang up in his place, for he feared for the maiden that the worm would devour her: but the monk who sat by him pulled him down by the skirt, and laughed and said: "Sit still, lord! for the champion also has been provided."

Then Ralph sat down again somewhat abashed and looked on; yet was his heart in his mouth the while. And so while the maiden stood as one astonied before the worm, who gaped upon her with wide open mouth, there came forth from a cleft in the rocks a goodly knight who bore silver, a red cross; and he had his sword in his hand, and he fell upon the worm to smite him; and the worm ramped up against him, and there was battle betwixt them, while the maiden knelt anigh with her hands clasped together.

Then Ralph knew that this was a play of the fight of St. George with the worm; so he sat silent till the champion had smitten off the worm's head and had come to the maiden and kissed and embraced her, and shown her the grisly head. Then presently came many folk on to the scaffold, to wit, the king and queen who were the father and mother of the maiden, and a bishop clad in very fair vestments, and knights withal; and they stood about St. George and the maiden, and with them were minstrels who fell to playing upon harps and fiddles; while other some fell to singing a sweet song in honour of St. George, and the maiden delivered.

So when it was all done, the monk said: "This play is set forth by the men-at-arms of our lord Abbot, who have great devotion toward St. George, and he is their friend and their good lord. But hereafter will be other plays, of wild men and their feasting in the woods in the Golden Age of the world; and that is done by the scribes and the limners. And after that will be a pageant of St. Agnes ordered by the clothiers and the webbers, which be both many and deft in this good town. Albeit thou art a young man and hast ridden far to-day belike, and mayhappen thou wilt not be able to endure it: so it may be well to bring thee out of this throng straightway.

Moreover I have bethought me, that there is much of what is presently to come which we shall see better from the minster roof, or even it may be from the tower: wilt thou come then?"

Ralph had liefer have sat there and seen all the plays to the end, for they seemed to him exceeding fair, and like to ravish the soul from the body; howbeit, being shamefaced, he knew not how to gainsay the brother, who took him by the hand, and led him through the press to the west front of the minster, where on the north side was a little door in a nook. So they went up a stair therein a good way till they came into a gallery over the western door; and looking forth thence Ralph deemed that he could have seen a long way had daylight been, for it was higher than the tops of the highest houses.

So there they abode a space looking down on the square and its throng, and the bells, which had been ringing when they came up, now ceased a while. But presently there arose great shouts and clamour amongst the folk below, and they could see men with torches drawing near to the pile of wood, and then all of a sudden shot up from it a great spiring flame, and all the people shouted together, while the bells broke out again over their heads.

Then the brother pointed aloof with his finger and said: "Lo you! fair lord, how bale speaks to bale all along the headlands of the down-country, and below there in the thorps by the river!"

Forsooth Ralph saw fire after fire break out to the westward; and the brother said: "And if we stood over the high altar and looked east, ye would see more of such fires and many more; and all these bales are piled up and lighted by vassals and villeins of my lord Abbot: now to-night they are but mere Midsummer bale-fires; but doubt ye not that if there came war into the land each one of these bales would mean at least a half-score of stout men, archers and men-at-arms, all ready to serve their lord at all adventure. All this the tyrants round about, that hate holy Church and oppress the poor, know full well; therefore we live in peace in these lands."

Ralph hearkened, but said nought; for amidst all this

27

flashing of fire and flame, and the crying out of folk, and the measured clash of the bells so near him, his thought was confused, and he had no words ready to hand. But the monk turned from the parapet and looked him full in the face and said to him:

"Thou art a fair young man, and strong, and of gentle blood as I deem; and thou seemest to me to have the lucky look in thine eyes: now I tell thee that if thou wert to take service with my lord thou shouldest never rue it. Yea, why shouldest thou not wax in his service, and become his Captain of Captains, which is an office meet for kings?"

Ralph looked on him, but answered nought, for he could not gather his thoughts for an answer; and the brother said: "Think of it, I bid thee, fair young lord; and be sure that nowhere shalt thou have a better livelihood, not even wert thou a king's son; for the children of my lord Abbot are such that none dareth to do them any displeasure; neither is any overlord as good as is Holy Church."

"Yea," said Ralph, "doubtless thou sayest sooth; yet I wot not that I am come forth to seek a master."

Said the brother: "Nay, do but see the lord Abbot, as thou mayst do to-morrow, if thou wilt."

"I would have his blessing," said Ralph.

"No less shalt thou have," said the brother; "but look you down yonder; for I can see tokens that my lord is even now coming forth."

Ralph looked down and beheld the folk parting to right and left, and a lane made amidst the throng, guarded by men-at-arms mingled with the cross-bearers and brethren; and the sound of trumpets blared forth over the noises of the throng.

"If the lord Abbot cometh," said Ralph, "I were fain of his blessing to-night before I sleep: so go we down straightway that I may kneel before him with the rest."

"What!" said the monk, "Wilt thou, my lord, kneel amongst all these burgesses and vavassors when thou mightest see the Abbot in his own chamber face to face alone with him?"

"Father," said Ralph, "I am no great man, and I must needs depart betimes to-morrow; for I perceive that here are things too mighty and over-mastering for such as I be."

"Well," said the monk, "yet mayst thou come back again; so at present I will make no more words about it."

So they went down, and came out amidst the throng, above which the bale still flared high, making the summer night as light as day. The brother made way for Ralph, so that they stood in the front row of folk: they had not been there one minute ere they heard the sound of the brethren singing, and the Abbot came forth out of the lane that went down to the gate. Then all folk went down upon their knees, and thus abode him. Right so Ralph deemed that he felt some one pull his sleeve, but in such a throng that was nought of a wonder; howbeit, he turned and looked to his left, whence came the tug, and saw kneeling beside him a tall man-at-arms, who bore a sallet on his head in such wise that it covered all his face save the point of his chin. Then Ralph bethought him of the man of the leafless tree, and he looked to see what armoury the man bore on his coat; but he had nothing save a loose frock of white linen over his hauberk. Nevertheless, he heard a voice in his ear, which said, "The second time!" whereon he deemed that it was verily that same man: yet had he nought to do to lay hold on him, and he might not speak with him, for even therewith came the Abbot in garments all of gold, going a-foot under a canopy of baudekyn, with the precious mitre on his head, and the crozier borne before him, as if he had been a patriarch: for he was an exceeding mighty lord.

Ralph looked hard on him as he passed by, blessing the folk with upraised hand; and he saw that he was a tall spare man, clean-shaven, and thin-faced; but no old man, belike scarce of fifty winters. Ralph caught his eye, and he smiled on the goodly young man so kindly, that for a moment Ralph deemed that he would dwell in St. Mary's House for a little while; for, thought he, if my father, or Nicholas, hear of me therein, they must even let me alone to abide here.

Therewith the Abbot went forth to his place, and sat him down under a goodly cloth of estate, and folk stood up again; but when Ralph looked for the man in the sallet he could see nought of him. Now when the Abbot was set down, men made a clear ring round about the bale, and there came into the said ring twelve young men, each clad in

29

nought save a goat-skin, and with garlands of leaves and flowers about their middles: they had with them a wheel done about with straw and hemp payed with pitch and brimstone. They set fire to the same, and then trundled it blazing round about the bale twelve times. Then came to them twelve damsels clad in such-like guise as the young men: then both bands, the young men and the maidens, drew near to the bale, which was now burning low, and stood about it, and joined hands, and so danced round it a while, and meantime the fiddles played an uncouth tune merrily: then they sundered, and each couple of men and maids leapt backward and forward over the fire; and when they had all leapt, came forward men with buckets of water which they cast over the dancers till it ran down them in streams. Then was all the throng mingled together, and folk trod the embers of the bale under foot, and scattered them hither and thither all over the square.

All this while men were going about with pitchers of wine and ale, and other good drinks; and every man drank freely what he would, and there was the greatest game and joyance.

But now was Ralph exceeding weary, and he said: "Father, mightest thou lead me out of this throng, and show me some lair where I may sleep in peace, I would thank thee blithely."

As he spake there sounded a great horn over the square, and the Abbot rose in his place and blessed all the people once more. Then said the monk:

"Come then, fair field-lord, now shalt thou have thy will of bed." And he laughed therewith, and drew Ralph out of the throng and brought him into the Abbey, and into a fair little chamber, on the wall whereof was pictured St. Christopher, and St. Julian the lord and friend of wayfarers. Then he brought Ralph the wine and spices, and gave him good-night, and went his ways.

As Ralph put the raiment from off him he said to himself: a long day forsooth, so long that I should have thought no day could have held all that has befallen me. So many strange things have I seen, that surely my dreams shall be full of them; for even now I seem to see them, though I waken.

30

So he lay down in his bed and slept, and dreamed that he was fishing with an angle in a deep of Upmeads Water; and he caught many fish; but after a while whatsoever he caught was but of gilded paper stuffed with wool, and at last the water itself was gone, and he was casting his angle on to a dry road. Therewith he awoke and saw that day was dawning, and heard the minster clock strike three, and heard the thrushes singing their first song in the Prior's garden. Then he turned about and slept, and dreamed no more till he woke up in the bright sunny morning.

CHAPTER 6

Ralph Goeth His Ways From the Abbey of St. Mary at Higham

It was the monk who had been his guide the day before who had now waked him, and he stood by the bedside holding a great bowl of milk in his hand, and as Ralph sat up, and rubbed his eyes, with all his youthful sloth upon him, the monk laughed and said:

"That is well, lord, that is well! I love to see a young man so sleepy in the morning; it is a sign of thriving; and I see thou art thriving heartily for the time when thou shalt come back to us to lead my lord's host in battle."

"Where be the bale-fires?" said Ralph, not yet fully awake.

"Where be they!" said the brother, "where be they! They be sunken to cold coals long ago, like many a man's desires and hopes, who hath not yet laid his head on the bosom of the mother, that is Holy Church. Come, my lord, arise, and drink the monk's wine of morning, and then if ye must need ride, ride betimes, and ride hard; for the Wood Perilous beginneth presently as ye wend your ways; and it were well for thee to reach the Burg of the Four Friths ere thou be benighted. For, son, there be untoward things in the wood; and though some of them be of those for whom Christ's

31

Cross was shapen, yet have they forgotten hell, and hope not for heaven, and their by-word is, 'Thou shalt lack ere I lack.' Furthermore there are worse wights in the wood than they be—God save us!—but against them have I a good hauberk, a neck-guard which I will give thee, son, in token that I look to see thee again at the lovely house of Mary our Mother."

Ralph had taken the bowl and was drinking, but he looked over the brim, and saw how the monk drew from his frock a pair of beads, as like to Dame Katherine's gift as one pea to another, save that at the end thereof was a little box shapen crosswise. Ralph emptied the bowl hastily, got out of bed, and sat on the bed naked, save that on his neck was Dame Katherine's gift. He reached out his hand and took the beads from the monk and reddened therewith, as was his wont when he had to begin a contest in words: but he said:

"I thank thee, father; yet God wot if these beads will lie sweetly alongside the collar which I bear on my neck as now, which is the gift of a dear friend."

The monk made up a solemn countenance and said: "Thou sayest sooth, my son; it is most like that my chaplet, which hath been blessed time was by the holy Richard, is no meet fellow for the gift of some light love of thine: or even," quoth he, noting Ralph's flush deepen, and his brow knit, "or even if it were the gift of a well-willer, yet belike it is a worldly gift; therefore, since thy journey is with peril, thou wert best do it off and let me keep it for thee till thou comest again."

Now as he spake he looked anxiously, nay, it may be said greedily, at the young man. But Ralph said nought; for in his heart he was determined not to chaffer away his gossip's gift for any shaveling's token. Yet he knew not how to set his youthful words against the father's wisdom; so he stood up, and got his shirt into his hand, and as he did it over his head he fell to singing to himself a song of eventide of the High House of Upmeads, the words whereof were somewhat like to these:

Art thou man, art thou maid, through the long grass a-going?
    For short shirt thou bearest, and no beard I see,

And the last wind ere moonrise about thee is blowing.
    Would'st thou meet with thy maiden or look'st thou for me?

Bright shineth the moon now, I see thy gown longer;
    And down by the hazels Joan meeteth her lad:
But hard is thy palm, lass, and scarcely were stronger
    Wat's grip than thine hand-kiss that maketh me glad.

And now as the candles shine on us and over,
    Full shapely thy feet are, but brown on the floor,
As the bare-footed mowers amidst of the clover
    When the gowk's note is broken and mid-June is o'er.

O hard are mine hand-palms because on the ridges
    I carried the reap-hook and smote for thy sake;
And in the hot noon-tide I beat off the midges
    As thou slep'st 'neath the linden o'er-loathe to awake.

And brown are my feet now because the sun burneth
    High up on the down-side amidst of the sheep,
And there in the hollow wherefrom the wind turneth,
    Thou lay'st in my lap while I sung thee to sleep.

O friend of the earth, O come nigher and nigher,
    Thou art sweet with the sun's kiss as meads of the May,
O'er the rocks of the waste, o'er the water and fire,
    Will I follow thee, love, till earth waneth away.

The monk hearkened to him with knitted brow, and as one that liketh not the speech of his fellow, though it be not wise to question it: then he went out of the chamber, but left the pair of beads lying in the window. But Ralph clad himself in haste, and when he was fully clad, went up to the window and took the beads in his hand, and looked into them curiously and turned them over, but left them lying there. Then he went forth also, and came into the forecourt of the house, and found there a squire of the men-at-arms with his weapons and horse, who helped him to do on his war-gear.

So then, just as he was setting his foot in the stirrup, came the Brother again, with his face once more grown smiling

33

and happy; and in his left hand he held the chaplet, but did not offer it to Ralph again, but nodded his head to him kindly, and said: "Now, lord, I can see by thy face that thou art set on beholding the fashion of this world, and most like it will give thee the rue."

Then came a word into Ralph's mouth, and he said: "Wilt thou tell me, father, whose work was the world's fashion?"

The monk reddened, but answered nought, and Ralph spake again:

"Forsooth, did the craftsman of it fumble over his work?"

Then the monk scowled, but presently he enforced himself to speak blithely, and said: "Such matters are over high for my speech or thine, lord; but I tell thee, who knoweth, that there are men in this House who have tried the world and found it wanting."

Ralph smiled, and said stammering:

"Father, did the world try them, and find them wanting perchance?"

Then he reddened, and said: "Are ye verily all such as this in this House? Who then is it who hath made so fair a lordship, and so goodly a governance for so many people? Know ye not at all of the world's ways?"

"Fair sir," said the monk sternly, "they that work for us work for the Lord and all his servants."

"Yea," said Ralph, "so it is; and will the Lord be content with the service of him whom the devil hath cast out because he hath found him a dastard?"

The monk frowned, yet smiled somewhat withal, and said: "Sir, thou art young, but thy wits are over old for me; but there are they in this House who may answer thee featly; men who have read the books of the wise men of the heathen, and the doctors of Holy Church, and are even now making books for the scribes to copy." Then his voice softened, and he said: "Dear lord, we should be right fain of thee here, but since thou must needs go, go with my blessing, and double blessing shalt thou have when thou comest back to us." Then Ralph remembered his promise to the shepherds and took a gold crown from his pouch, and said: "Father, I pray thee say a mass for the shepherd downsmen; and this is for the offering."

34

The monk praised the gift and the bidding, and kissed Ralph, who clomb into his saddle; and the brother hospitalier brought him his wallet with good meat and drink therein for the way. Then Ralph shook his rein, and rode out of the abbey-gate, smiling at the lay-brethren and the men-at-arms who hung about there.

But he sighed for pleasure when he found himself in the street again, and looked on the shops of the chapmen and the booths of the petty craftsmen, as shoe-smiths and glovers, and tinsmiths and coppersmiths, and horners and the like; and the folk that he met as he rode toward the southern gate seemed to him merry and in good case, and goodly to look on. And he thought it pleasant to gaze on the damsels in the street, who were fair and well clad: and there were a many of them about his way now, especially as he drew nigh the gate before the streets branched off: for folk were coming in from the countryside with victual and other wares for the town and the Abbey; and surely as he looked on some of the maidens he deemed that Hall-song of Upmeads a good one.

CHAPTER 7

The Maiden of Bourton Abbas

So went he through the gate, and many, both of men and maids gazed at him, for he was fair to look on, but none meddled with him.

There was a goodly fauburg outside the gate, and therein were fair houses, not a few, with gardens and orchards about them; and when these were past he rode through very excellent meadows lying along the water, which he crossed thrice, once by a goodly stone bridge and twice by fords; for the road was straight, and the river wound about much.

After a little while the road led him off the plain meads

into a country of little hills and dales, the hill-sides covered with vineyards and orchards, and the dales plenteous of corn-fields; and now amongst these dales Higham was hidden from him.

Through this tillage and vine-land he rode a good while, and thought he had never seen a goodlier land; and as he went he came on husbandmen and women of the country going about their business: yet were they not too busy to gaze on him, and most greeted him; and with some he gave and took a little speech.

These people also he deemed well before the world, for they were well clad and buxom, and made no great haste as they went, but looked about them as though they deemed the world worth looking at, and as if they had no fear either of a blow or a hard word for loitering.

So he rode till it was noon, and he was amidst a little thorp of grey stone houses, trim enough, in a valley wherein there was more of wild-wood trees and less of fruit-bearers than those behind him. In the thorp was a tavern with the sign of the Nicholas, so Ralph deemed it but right to enter a house which was under the guard of his master and friend; therefore he lighted down and went in. Therein he found a lad of fifteen winters, and a maiden spinning, they two alone, who hailed him and asked his pleasure, and he bade them bring him meat and drink, and look to his horse, for that he had a mind to rest a while. So they brought him bread and flesh, and good wine of the hill-side, in a little hall well arrayed as of its kind; and he sat down and the damsel served him at table, but the lad, who had gone to see to his horse, did not come back.

So when he had eaten and drunk, and the damsel was still there, he looked on her and saw that she was sad and drooping of aspect; and whereas she was a fair maiden, Ralph, now that he was full, fell to pitying her, and asked her what was amiss. "For," said he, "thou art fair and ailest nought; that is clear to see; neither dwellest thou in penury, but by seeming hast enough and to spare. Or art thou a servant in this house, and hath any one misused thee?"

She wept at his words, for indeed he spoke softly to her; then she said: "Young lord, thou art kind, and it is thy kindness that draweth the tears from me; else it were not well to weep before a young man: therefore I pray thee pardon me. As for me, I am no servant, nor has any one misused me: the folk round about are good and neighbourly; and this house and the croft, and a vineyard hard by, all that is mine own and my brother's; that is the lad who hath gone to tend thine horse. Yea, and we live in peace here for the most part; for this thorp, which is called Bourton Abbas, is a land of the Abbey of Higham; though it be the outermost of its lands and the Abbot is a good lord and a defence against tyrants. All is well with me if one thing were not."

"What is thy need then?" said Ralph, "if perchance I might amend it." And as he looked on her he deemed her yet fairer than he had done at first. But she stayed her weeping and sobbing and said: "Sir, I fear me that I have lost a dear friend." "How then," said he, "why fearest thou, and knowest not? doth thy friend lie sick between life and death?" "O Sir," she said, "it is the Wood which is the evil and disease."

"What wood is that?" said he.

She said: "The Wood Perilous, that lieth betwixt us and the Burg of the Four Friths, and all about the Burg. And, Sir, if ye be minded to ride to the Burg to-day, do it not, for through the wood must thou wend thereto; and ye are young and lovely. Therefore take my rede, and abide till the Chapmen wend thither from Higham, who ride many in company. For, look you, fair lord, ye have asked of my grief, and this it is and nought else; that my very earthly love and speech-friend rode five days ago toward the Burg of the Four Friths all alone through the Wood Perilous, and he has not come back, though we looked to see him in three days' wearing: but his horse has come back, and the reins and the saddle all bloody."

And she fell a-weeping with the telling of the tale. But Ralph said (for he knew not what to say): "Keep a good heart, maiden; maybe he is safe and sound; oft are young men fond to wander wide, even as I myself."

She looked at him hard and said: "If thou hast stolen thyself away from them that love thee, thou hast done amiss. Though thou art a lord, and so fair as I see thee, yet will I tell thee so much."

37

Ralph reddened and answered nought; but deemed the maiden both fair and sweet. But she said: "Whether thou hast done well or ill, do no worse; but abide till the Chapmen come from Higham, on their way to the Burg of the Four Friths. Here mayst thou lodge well and safely if thou wilt. Or if our hall be not dainty enough for thee, then go back to Higham: I warrant me the monks will give thee good guesting as long as thou wilt."

"Thou art kind, maiden," said Ralph, "but why should I tarry for an host? and what should I fear in the Wood, as evil as it may be? One man journeying with little wealth, and unknown, and he no weakling, but bearing good weapons, hath nought to dread of strong-thieves, who ever rob where it is easiest and gainfullest. And what worse may I meet than strong-thieves?"

"But thou mayest meet worse," she said; and therewith fell a-weeping again, and said amidst her tears: "O weary on my life! And why should I heed thee when nought heedeth me, neither the Saints of God's House, nor the Master of it; nor the father and the mother that were once so piteous kind to me? O if I might but drink a draught from the WELL AT THE WORLD'S END!"

He turned about on her hastily at that word; for he had risen to depart; being grieved at her grief and wishful to be away from it, since he might not amend it. But now he said eagerly:

"Where then is that Well? Know ye of it in this land?"

"At least I know the hearsay thereof," she said; "but as now thou shalt know no more from me thereof; lest thou wander the wider in seeking it. I would not have thy life spilt."

Ever as he looked on her he thought her still fairer; and now he looked long on her, saying nought, and she on him in likewise, and the blood rose to her cheeks and her brow, but she would not turn her from his gaze. At last he said: "Well then, I must depart, no more learned than I came: but yet am I less hungry and thirsty than I came; and have thou thanks therefor."

Therewith he took from his pouch a gold piece of Upmeads, which was good, and of the touch of the Easterlings, and held it out to her. And she put out her open hand and he put the money in it; but thought it good to hold her hand a while, and she gainsayed him not.

Then he said: "Well then, I must needs depart with things left as they are: wilt thou bid thy brother bring hither my horse, for time presses."

"Yea," she said (and her hand was still in his), "Yet do thine utmost, yet shalt thou not get to the Burg before nightfall. O wilt thou not tarry?"

"Nay," he said, "my heart will not suffer it; lest I deem myself a dastard."

Then she reddened again, but as if she were wroth; and she drew her hand away from his and smote her palms together thrice and cried out: "Ho Hugh! bring hither the Knight's horse and be speedy!"

And she went hither and thither about the hall and into the buttery and back, putting away the victual and vessels from the board and making as if she heeded him not: and Ralph looked on her, and deemed that each way she moved was better than the last, so shapely of fashion she was; and again he bethought him of the Even-song of the High House at Upmeads, and how it befitted her; for she went barefoot after the manner of maidens who work afield, and her feet were tanned with the sun of hay harvest, but as shapely as might be; but she was clad goodly withal, in a green gown wrought with flowers.

So he watched her going to and fro; and at last he said: "Maiden, wilt thou come hither a little, before I depart?"

"Yea," she said; and came and stood before him: and he deemed that she was scarce so sad as she had been; and she stood with her hands joined and her eyes downcast. Then he said:

"Now I depart. Yet I would say this, that I am sorry of thy sorrow: and now since I shall never see thee more, small would be the harm if I were to kiss thy lips and thy face."

And therewith he took her hands in his and drew her to him, and put his arms about her and kissed her many times, and she nothing lothe by seeming; and he found her as sweet as May blossom.

Thereafter she smiled on him, yet scarce for gladness, and

said: "It is not all so sure that I shall not see thee again; yet shall I do to thee as thou hast done to me."

Therewith she took his face between her hands, and kissed him well-favouredly; so that the hour seemed good to him.

Then she took him by the hand and led him out-a-doors to his horse, whereby the lad had been standing a good while; and he when he saw his sister come out with the fair knight he scowled on them, and handled a knife which hung at his girdle; but Ralph heeded him nought. As for the damsel, she put her brother aside, and held the stirrup for Ralph; and when he was in the saddle she said to him:

"All luck go with thee! Forsooth I deem thee safer in the Wood than my words said. Verily I deem that if thou wert to meet a company of foemen, thou wouldest compel them to do thy bidding."

"Farewell to thee maiden," said Ralph, "and mayst thou find thy beloved whole and well, and that speedily. Farewell!"

She said no more; so he shook his rein and rode his ways; but looked over his shoulder presently and saw her standing yet barefoot on the dusty highway shading her eyes from the afternoon sun and looking after him, and he waved his hand to her and so went his ways between the houses of the Thorp.

CHAPTER 8

Ralph Cometh to the Wood Perilous. An Adventure Therein

Now when he was clear of the Thorp the road took him out of the dale; and when he was on the hill's brow he saw that the land was of other fashion from that which lay behind him. For the road went straight through a rough waste, no pasture, save for mountain sheep or goats, with a few bushes scattered about it; and beyond this the land rose into a long ridge; and on the ridge was a wood thick with trees, and no break in them. So on he rode, and soon passed that waste, which was dry and parched, and the afternoon sun was hot on it; so he deemed it good to come under the shadow of the thick trees (which at the first were wholly beech trees), for it was now the hottest of the day. There was still a beaten way between the tree-boles, though not overwide, albeit, a highway, since it pierced the wood. So thereby he went at a soft pace for the saving of his horse, and thought but little of all he had been told of the perils of the way, and not a little of the fair maid whom he had left behind at the Thorp.

After a while the thick beech-wood gave out, and he came into a place where great oaks grew, fair and stately, as though some lord's wood-reeve had taken care that they should not grow over close together, and betwixt them the greensward was fine, unbroken, and flowery. Thereby as he rode he beheld deer, both buck and hart and roe, and other wild things, but for a long while no man.

The afternoon wore and still he rode the oak wood, and deemed it a goodly forest for the greatest king on earth. At last he came to where another road crossed the way he followed, and about the crossway was the ground clearer of trees, while beyond it the trees grew thicker, and there was some underwood of holly and thorn as the ground fell off as towards a little dale.

There Ralph drew rein, because he doubted in his mind which was his right road toward the Burg of the Four Friths; so he got off his horse and abode a little, if perchance any might come by; he looked about him, and noted on the road that crossed his, and the sward about it, the sign of many horses having gone by, and deemed that they had passed but a little while. So he lay on the ground to rest him and let his horse stray about and bite the grass; for the beast loved him and would come at his call or his whistle.

Ralph was drowsy when he lay down, and though he said to himself that he would nowise go to sleep, yet as oft happens, he had no defence to make against sleepiness, and presently his hands relaxed, his head fell aside, and he slept quietly. When he woke up in a little space of time, he knew at once that something had awaked him and that he had not had his sleep out; for in his ears was the trampling of horse-hoofs and the clashing of weapons and loud speech of men. So he leapt up hastily, and while he was yet scarce awake, took to whistling on his horse; but even therewith those men were upon him, and two came up to him and laid hold of him; and when he asked them what they would, they bade him hold his peace.

Now his eyes cleared, and he saw that those men were in goodly war-gear, and bore coats of plate, and cuir-bouilly, or of bright steel; they held long spears and were girt with good swords; there was a pennon with them, green, whereon was done a golden tower, embattled, amidst of four white ways; and the same token bore many of the men on their coats and sleeves. Unto this same pennon he was brought by the two men who had taken him, and under it, on a white horse, sat a Knight bravely armed at all points with the Tower and Four Ways on his green surcoat; and beside him was an ancient man-at-arms, with nought but an oak wreath on his bare head, and his white beard falling low over his coat: but behind these twain a tall young man, also on a white horse and very gaily clad, upheld the pennon. On one side of these three were five men, unarmed, clad in green coats, with a leafless tree done on them in gold: they were stout carles, bearded and fierce-faced: their hands were bound behind their backs and their feet tied together under their horses' bellies. The company of those about the Knight, Ralph deemed, would number ten score men.

So when those twain stayed Ralph before the Knight, he turned to the old man and said:

"It is of no avail asking this lither lad if he be of them or no: for no will be his answer. But what sayest thou, Oliver?"

The ancient man drew closer to Ralph and looked at him up and down and all about; for those two turned him about as if he had been a joint of flesh on the roasting-jack; and at last he said:

"His beard is sprouting, else might ye have taken him for a maid of theirs, one of those of whom we wot. But to say sooth I seem to know the fashion of his gear, even as Duke Jacob knew Joseph's tabard. So ask him whence he is, lord, and if he lie, then I bid bind him and lead him away, that we may have a true tale out of him; otherwise let him go and take his chance; for we will not waste the bread of the Good Town on him."

The Knight looked hard on Ralph, and spake to him somewhat courteously:

"Whence art thou, fair Sir, and what is thy name? for we have many foes in the wildwood."

Ralph reddened as he answered: "I am of Upmeads beyond the down country; and I pray thee let me be gone on mine errands. It is meet that thou deal with thine own robbers and reivers, but not with me."

Then cried out one of the bounden men: "Thou liest, lad, we be no robbers." But he of the Knight's company who stood by him smote the man on the mouth and said: "Hold thy peace, runagate! Thou shalt give tongue to-morrow when the hangman hath thee under his hands."

The Knight took no heed of this; but turned to the ancient warrior and said: "Hath he spoken truth so far?"

"Yea, Sir Aymer," quoth Oliver; "And now meseems I know him better than he knoweth me."

Therewith he turned to Ralph and said: "How fareth Long Nicholas, my lord?"

Ralph reddened again: "He is well," said he.

Then said the Knight: "Is the young man of a worthy house, Oliver?"

But ere the elder could speak, Ralph brake in and said: "Old warrior, I bid thee not to tell out my name, as thou lovest Nicholas."

Old Oliver laughed and said: "Well, Nicholas and I have been friends in a way, as well as foes; and for the sake of the old days his name shall help thee, young lord." Then he said to his Knight: "Yea, Sir Aymer, he is of a goodly house and an ancient; but thou hearest how he adjureth me. Ye shall let his name alone."

The Knight looked silently on Ralph for a while; then he said: "Wilt thou wend with us to the Burg of the Four Friths, fair Sir? Wert thou not faring thither? Or what else dost thou in the Wood Perilous?"

Ralph turned it over in his mind; and though he saw no

cause why he should not join himself to their company, yet something in his heart forbade him to rise to the fly too eagerly; so he did but say: "I am seeking adventures, fair lord."

The Knight smiled: "Then mayst thou fill thy budget with them if thou goest with us," quoth he. Now Ralph did not know how he might gainsay so many men at arms in the long run, though he were scarce willing to go; so he made no haste to answer; and even therewith came a man running, through the wood up from the dale; a long, lean carle, meet for running, with brogues on his feet, and nought else but a shirt; the company parted before him to right and left to let him come to the Knight, as though he had been looked for; and when he was beside him, the Knight leaned down while the carle spake softly to him and all men drew out of ear-shot. And when the carle had given his message the Knight drew himself straight up in his saddle again and lifted up his hand and cried out:

"Oliver! Oliver! lead on the way thou wottest! Spur! spur, all men!"

Therewith he blew one blast from a horn which hung at his saddle-bow; the runner leapt up behind old Oliver, and the whole company went off at a smart trot somewhat south-east, slantwise of the cross-roads, where the wood was nought cumbered with undergrowth; and presently they were all gone to the last horse-tail, and no man took any more note of Ralph.

CHAPTER 9

Another Adventure in the Wood Perilous

Ralph left alone pondered a little; and thought that he would by no means go hastily to the Burg of the Four Friths. Said he to himself; This want-way is all unlike to the one near our house at home: for belike adventures shall befall here: I will even abide here for an hour or two; but will have my horse by me and keep awake, lest something hap to me unawares.

Therewith he whistled for Falcon his horse, and the beast came to him, and whinnied for love of him, and Ralph smiled and tied him to a sapling anigh, and himself sat down on the grass, and pondered many things; as to what folk were about at Upmeads, and how his brethren were faring; and it was now about five hours after noon, and the sun's rays fell aslant through the boughs of the noble oaks, and the scent of the grass and bracken trodden by the horse-hoofs of that company went up into the warm summer air. A while he sat musing but awake, though the faint sound of a little stream in the dale below mingled with all the lesser noises of the forest did its best to soothe him to sleep again: and presently had its way with him; for he leaned his head back on the bracken, and in a minute or two was sleeping once more and dreaming some dream made up of masterless memories of past days.

When he awoke again he lay still a little while, wondering where in the world he was, but as the drowsiness left him, he arose and looked about, and saw that the sun was sinking low and gilding the oakboles red. He stood awhile and watched the gambols of three hares, who had drawn nigh him while he slept, and now noted him not; and a little way he saw through the trees a hart and two hinds going slowly from grass to grass, feeding in the cool eventide; but presently he saw them raise their heads and amble off down the slope of the little dale, and therewith he himself turned his face sharply toward the north-west, for he was fine-eared as well as sharp-eyed, and on a little wind which had just arisen came down to him the sound of horse-hoofs once more.

So he went up to Falcon and loosed him, and stood by him bridle in hand, and looked to it that his sword was handy to him: and he hearkened, and the sound drew nigher and nigher to him. Then lightly he got into the saddle and gathered the reins into his left hand, and sat peering up the trodden wood-glades, lest he should have to ride for his life suddenly. Therewith he heard voices talking roughly and a man whistling, and athwart the glade of the wood from the northwest, or thereabout, came new folk; and he saw at once that there went two men a-horseback and armed; so he drew his sword and abode them close to the want-ways. Presently they saw the shine of his war-gear, and then they came but a little nigher ere they drew rein, and sat on their horses looking toward him. Then Ralph saw that they were armed and clad as those of the company which had gone before. One of the armed men rode a horse-length after his fellow, and bore a long spear over his shoulder. But the other who rode first was girt with a sword, and had a little axe hanging about his neck, and with his right hand he seemed to be leading something, Ralph could not see what at first, as his left side was turned toward Ralph and the want-way.

Now, as Ralph looked, he saw that at the spearman's saddle-bow was hung a man's head, red-haired and red-bearded; for this man now drew a little nigher, and cried out to Ralph in a loud and merry voice: "Hail, knight! whither away now, that thou ridest the green-wood sword in hand?"

Ralph was just about to answer somewhat, when the first man moved a little nigher, and as he did so he turned so that Ralph could see what betid on his right hand; and lo! he was leading a woman by a rope tied about her neck (though her hands were loose), as though he were bringing a cow to market. When the man stayed his horse she came forward and stood within the slack of the rope by the horse's head, and Ralph could see her well, that though she was not to say naked, her raiment was but scanty, for she had nought to cover her save one short and strait little coat of linen, and shoes on her feet. Yet Ralph deemed her to be of some degree, whereas he caught the gleam of gold and gems on her hands, and there was a golden chaplet on her head. She stood now by the horse's head with her hands folded, looking on, as if what was tiding and to betide, were but a play done for her pleasure.

So when Ralph looked on her, he was silent a while; and the spearman cried out again: " 'Ho, young man, wilt thou speak, or art thou dumb-foundered for fear of us?"

But Ralph knit his brows, and was first red and then pale; for he was both wroth, and doubtful how to go to work; but he said:

46

"I ride to seek adventures; and here meseemeth is one come to hand. Or what will ye with the woman?"

Said the man who had the woman in tow: "Trouble not thine head therewith; we lead her to her due doom. As for thee, be glad that thou art not her fellow; since forsooth thou seemest not to be one of them; so go thy ways in peace."

"No foot further will I go," said Ralph, "till ye loose the woman and let her go; or else tell me what her worst deed is."

The man laughed, and said: "That were a long tale to tell; and it is little like that thou shalt live to hear the ending thereof."

Therewith he wagged his head at the spearman, who suddenly let his spear fall into the rest, and spurred, and drave on at Ralph all he might. There and then had the tale ended, but Ralph, who was wary, though he were young, and had Falcon well in hand, turned his wrist and made the horse swerve, so that the man-at-arms missed his attaint, but could not draw rein speedily enough to stay his horse; and as he passed by all bowed over his horse's neck, Ralph gat his sword two-handed and rose in his stirrups and smote his mightiest; and the sword caught the foeman on the neck betwixt sallet and jack, and nought held before it, neither leather nor ring-mail, so that the man's head was nigh smitten off, and he fell clattering from his saddle: yet his stirrups held him, so that his horse went dragging him on earth as he gallopped over rough and smooth betwixt the trees of the forest. Then Ralph turned about to deal with his fellow, and even through the wrath and fury of the slaying saw him clear and bright against the trees as he sat handling his axe doubtfully, but the woman was fallen back again somewhat.

But even as Ralph raised his sword and pricked forward, the woman sprang as light as a leopard on to the saddle behind the foeman, and wound her arms about him and dragged him back just as he was raising his axe to smite her, and as Ralph rode forward she cried out to him, "Smite him, smite! O lovely creature of God!"

Therewith was Ralph beside them, and though he were loth to slay a man held in the arms of a woman, yet he feared lest the man should slay her with some knife-stroke unless he made haste; so he thrust his sword through him, and the man died at once, and fell headlong off his horse, dragging down the woman with him.

Then Ralph lighted down from his horse, and the woman rose up to him, her white smock all bloody with the slain man. Nevertheless was she as calm and stately before him, as if she were sitting on the daïs of a fair hall; so she said to him:

"Young warrior, thou hast done well and knightly, and I shall look to it that thou have thy reward. And now I rede thee go not to the Burg of the Four Friths; for this tale of thee shall get about and they shall take thee, if it were out of the very Frith-stool, and there for thee should be the scourge and the gibbet; for they of that Burg be robbers and murderers merciless. Yet well it were that thou ride hence presently; for those be behind my tormentors whom thou hast slain, who will be as an host to thee, and thou mayst not deal with them. If thou follow my rede, thou wilt take the way that goeth hence east away, and then shalt thou come to Hampton under Scaur, where the folk are peaceable and friendly."

He looked at her hard as she spake, and noted that she spake but slowly, and turned red and white and red again as she looked at him. But whatever she did, and in spite of her poor attire, he deemed he had never seen woman so fair. Her hair was dark red, but her eyes grey, and light at whiles and yet at whiles deep; her lips betwixt thin and full, but yet when she spoke or smiled clad with all enticements; her chin round and so wrought as none was ever better wrought; her body strong and well-knit; tall she was, with fair and large arms, and limbs most goodly of fashion, of which but little was hidden, since her coat was but thin and scanty. But whatever may be said of her, no man would have deemed her aught save most lovely. Now her face grew calm and stately again as it was at the first, and she laid a hand on Ralph's shoulder, and smiled in his face and said:

"Surely thou art fair, though thy strokes be not light." Then she took his hand and caressed it, and said again: "Dost thou deem that thou hast done great things, fair child? Maybe. Yet some will say that thou hast but slain two butchers: and if thou wilt say that thou hast delivered me;

48

yet it may be that I should have delivered myself ere long. Nevertheless hold up thine heart, for I think that greater things await thee."

Then she turned about, and saw the dead man, how his feet yet hung in the stirrups as his fellow's had done, save that the horse of this one stood nigh still, only reaching his head down to crop a mouthful of grass; so she said: "Take him away, that I may mount on his horse."

So he drew the dead man's feet out of the stirrups, and dragged him away to where the bracken grew deep, and laid him down there, so to say hidden. Then he turned back to the lady, who was pacing up and down near the horse as the beast fed quietly on the cool grass. When Ralph came back she took the reins in her hand and put one foot in the stirrup as if she would mount at once; but suddenly lighted down again, and turning to Ralph, cast her arms about him, and kissed his face many times, blushing red as a rose meantime. Then lightly she gat her up into the saddle, and bestrode the beast, and smote his flanks with her heels, and went her ways riding speedily toward the south-east, so that she was soon out of sight.

But Ralph stood still looking the way she had gone and wondering at the adventure; and he pondered her words and held debate with himself whether he should take the road she bade him. And he said within himself: "Hitherto have I been safe and have got no scratch of a weapon upon me, and this is a place by seeming for all adventures; and little way moreover shall I make in the night if I must needs go to Hampton under Scaur, where dwell those peaceable people; and it is now growing dusk already. So I will abide the morning hereby; but I will be wary and let the wood cover me if I may."

Therewith he went and drew the body of the slain man down into a little hollow where the bracken was high and the brambles grew strong, so that it might not be lightly seen. Then he called to him Falcon, his horse, and looked about for cover anigh the want-way, and found a little thin coppice of hazel and sweet chestnut, just where two great oaks had been felled a half score years ago; and looking through the

49

leaves thence, he could see the four ways clearly enough, though it would not be easy for anyone to see him thence.

Thither he betook him, and he did the rein off Falcon, but tethered him by a halter in the thickest of the copse, and sat down himself nigher to the outside thereof; he did off his helm and drew what meat he had from out his wallet and ate and drank in the beginning of the summer night; and then sat pondering awhile on what had befallen on this second day of his wandering. The moon shone out presently, little clouded, but he saw her not, for though he strove to wake awhile, slumber soon overcame him, and nothing waked him till the night was passing, nor did he see aught of that company of which the lady had spoken, and which in sooth came not.

CHAPTER 10

A Meeting and a Parting
in the Wood Perilous

When the first glimmer of dawn was in the sky he awoke in the fresh morning, and sat up and hearkened, for even as he woke he had heard something, since wariness had made him wakeful. Now he hears the sound of horse-hoofs on the hard road, and riseth to his feet and goeth to the very edge of the copse; looking thence he saw a rider who was just come to the very crossing of the roads. The new comer was much muffled in a wide cloak, but he seemed to be a man low of stature. He peered all round about him as if to see if the way were clear, and then alighted down from horseback and let the hood fall off his head, and seemed pondering which way were the best to take. By this time it was grown somewhat lighter and Ralph, looking hard, deemed that the rider was a woman; so he stepped forward lightly, and as he came on to the open sward about the way, the new comer saw him and put a foot into the stirrup to mount, but yet looked at him over the shoulder, and then presently left the saddle and came forward a few steps as if to meet Ralph, having cast the cloak to the ground.

Then Ralph saw that it was none other than the damsel of the hostelry of Bourton Abbas, and he came up to her and reached out his hand to her, and she took it in both hers and held it and said, smiling: "It is nought save mountains that shall never meet. Here have I followed on thy footsteps; yet knew I not where thou wouldst be in the forest. And now I am glad to have fallen in with thee; for I am going a long way."

Ralph looked on her and himseemed some pain or shame touched his heart, and he said: "I am a knight adventurous; I have nought to do save to seek adventures. Why should I not go with thee?"

She looked at him earnestly awhile and said: "Nay, it may not be; thou art a lord's son, and I a yeoman's daughter." She stopped, and he said nothing in answer.

"Furthermore," said she, "it is a long way, and I know not how long." Again he made no answer, and she said: "I am going to seek the WELL AT THE WORLD'S END, and to find it and live, or to find it not, and die."

He spake after a while: "Why should I not come with thee?"

It was growing light now, and he could see that she reddened and then turned pale and set her lips close.

Then she said: "Because thou willest it not: because thou hadst liefer make that journey with some one else."

He reddened in his turn, and said: "I know of no one else who shall go with me."

"Well," she said, "it is all one, I will not have thee go with me." "Yea, and why not?" said he. She said: "Wilt thou swear to me that nought hath happed to thee to change thee betwixt this and Bourton? If thou wilt, then come with me; if thou wilt not, then refrain thee. And this I say because I see and feel that there is some change in thee since yesterday, so that thou wouldst scarce be dealing truly in being my fellow in this quest: for they that take it up must be single-hearted, and think of nought save the quest and the fellow that is with them."

She looked on him sadly, and his many thoughts tongue-

51

tied him a while; but at last he said: "Must thou verily go on this quest?" "Ah," she said, "now since I have seen thee and spoken with thee again, all need there is that I should follow it at once."

Then they both kept silence, and when she spoke again her voice was as if she were gay against her will. She said: "Here am I come to these want-ways, and there are three roads besides the one I came by, and I wot that this that goeth south will bring me to the Burg of the Four Friths; and so much I know of the folk of the said Burg that they would mock at me if I asked them of the way to the Well at the World's End. And as for the western way I deem that that will lead me back again to the peopled parts whereof I know; therefore I am minded to take the eastern way. What sayest thou, fair lord?"

Said Ralph: "I have heard of late that it leadeth presently to Hampton under the Scaur, where dwelleth a people of goodwill."

"Who told thee this tale?" said she. Ralph answered, reddening again, "I was told by one who seemed to know both of that folk, and of the Burg of the Four Friths, and she said that the folk of Hampton were a good folk, and that they of the Burg were evil."

The damsel smiled sadly when she heard him say 'She,' and when he had done she said: "And I have heard, and not from yesterday, that at Hampton dwelleth the Fellowship of the Dry Tree, and that those of the fellowship are robbers and reivers. Nevertheless they will perchance be little worse than the others; and the tale tells that the way to the Well at the World's End is by the Dry Tree; so thither will I at all adventure. And now will I say farewell to thee, for it is most like that I shall not see thee again."

"O, maiden!" said Ralph, "why wilt thou not go back to Bourton Abbas? There I might soon meet thee again, and yet, indeed, I also am like to go to Hampton. Shall I not see thee there?"

She shook her head and said: "Nay, since I must go so far, I shall not tarry; and, sooth to say, if I saw thee coming in at one gate I should go out by the other, for why should I dally with a grief that may not be amended. For indeed I wot that thou shalt soon forget to wish to see me, either at Bourton Abbas or elsewhere; so I will say no more than once again farewell."

Then she came close to him and put her hands on his shoulders and kissed his mouth; and then she turned away swiftly, caught up her cloak, and gat lightly into the saddle, and so shook her reins and rode away east toward Hampton, and left Ralph standing there downcast and pondering many things. It was still so early in the summer morning, and he knew so little what to do, that presently he turned and walked back to his lair amongst the hazels, and there he lay down, and his thoughts by then were all gone back again to the lovely lady whom he had delivered, and he wondered if he should ever see her again, and, sooth to say, he sorely desired to see her. Amidst such thoughts he fell asleep again, for the night yet owed him something of rest, so young as he was and so hard as he had toiled, both body and mind, during the past day.

CHAPTER 11

Now Must Ralph Ride For It

When he awoke again the sun was shining through the hazel leaves, though it was yet early; he arose and looked to his horse, and led him out of the hazel copse and stood and looked about him; and lo! a man coming slowly through the wood on Ralph's right hand, and making as it seemed for the want-way; he saw Ralph presently, and stopped, and bent a bow which he held in his hand, and then came towards him warily, with the arrow nocked. But Ralph went to meet him with his sword in his sheath, and leading Falcon by the rein, and the man stopped and took the shaft from the string: he had no armour, but there was a little axe and a wood-knife in his girdle; he was clad in homespun, and looked like a carle of the country-side. Now he greeted Ralph, and Ralph gave him the sele of the day, and saw that the new-comer was both tall and strong, dark of skin and black-haired, but of a cheerful countenance. He spake frank and free to Ralph, and said: "Whither away, lord, out of the woodland hall, and the dwelling of deer and strong-thieves? I would that the deer would choose them a captain, and gather head and destroy the thieves—and some few others with them."

Said Ralph: "I may scarce tell thee till I know myself. Awhile ago I was minded for the Burg of the Four Friths; but now I am for Hampton under Scaur."

"Yea?" said the carle, "when the Devil drives, to hell must we."

"What meanest thou, good fellow?" said Ralph, "Is Hampton then so evil an abode?" And indeed it was in his mind that the adventure of the lady led captive bore some evil with it.

Said the carle: "If thou wert not a stranger in these parts I need not to answer thy question; but I will answer it presently, yet not till we have eaten, for I hunger, and have in this wallet both bread and cheese, and thou art welcome to a share thereof, if thou hungerest also, as is most like, whereas thou art young and fresh coloured."

"So it is," said Ralph, laughing, "and I also may help to spread this table in the wilderness, since there are yet some crumbs in my wallet. Let us sit down and fall to at once."

"By your leave, Sir Gentleman," said the carle, "we will go a few yards further on, where there is a woodland brook, whereof we may drink when my bottle faileth."

"Nay, I may better that," said Ralph, "for I have wherewithal." "Nevertheless," said the carle, "we will go thither, for here is it too open for so small a company as ours, since this want-way hath an ill name, and I shall lead thee whereas we shall be somewhat out of the way of murder-carles. So come on, if thou trusteth in me."

Ralph yeasaid him, and they went together a furlong from the want-way into a little hollow place wherethrough ran a clear stream betwixt thick-leaved alders. The carle led Ralph to the very lip of the water so that the bushes covered them; there they sat down and drew what they had from their wallets, and so fell to meat; and amidst of the meat the carle said:

"Fair Knight, as I suppose thou art one, I will ask thee if any need draweth thee to Hampton?"

Said Ralph: "The need of giving the go-by to the Burg of the Four Friths, since I hear tell that the folk thereof be robbers and murderers."

"Thou shalt find that out better, lord, by going thither; but I shall tell thee, that though men may slay and steal there time and time about, yet in regard to Hampton under Scaur, it is Heaven, wherein men sin not. And I am one who should know, for I have been long dwelling in Hell, that is Hampton; and now am I escaped thence, and am minded for the Burg, if perchance I may be deemed there a man good enough to ride in their host, whereby I might avenge me somewhat on them that have undone me: some of whom meseemeth must have put in thy mouth that word against the Burg. Is it not so?"

"Maybe," said Ralph, "for thou seemest to be a true man." No more he spake though he had half a mind to tell the carle all the tale of that adventure; but something held him back when he thought of that lady and her fairness. Yet again his heart misgave him of what might betide that other maiden at Hampton, and he was unquiet, deeming that he must needs follow her thither. The carle looked on him curiously and somewhat anxiously, but Ralph's eyes were set on something that was not there; or else maybe had he looked closely on the carle he might have deemed that longing to avenge him whereof he spoke did not change his face much; for in truth there was little wrath in it.

Now the carle said: "Thou hast a tale which thou deemest unmeet for my ears, as it well may be. Well, thou must speak, or refrain from speaking, what thou wilt; but thou art so fair a young knight, and so blithe with a poor man, and withal I deem that thou mayest help me to some gain and good, that I will tell thee a true tale: and first that the Burg is a good town under a good lord, who is no tyrant nor oppressor of peaceful men; and that thou mayest dwell there in peace as to the folk thereof, who be good folk, albeit they be no dastards to let themselves be cowed by murder-carles.

And next I will tell thee that the folk of the town of Hampton be verily as harmless and innocent as sheep; but that they be under evil lords who are not their true lords, who lay heavy burdens on them and torment them even to the destroying of their lives: and lastly I will tell thee that I was one of those poor people, though not so much a sheep as the more part of them, therefore have these tyrants robbed me of my croft, and set another man in my house; and me they would have slain had I not fled to the wood that it might cover me. And happy it was for me that I had neither wife, nor chick, nor child, else had they done as they did with my brother, whose wife was too fair for him, since he dwelt at Hampton; so that they took her away from him to make sport for them of the Dry Tree, who dwell in the Castle of the Scaur, who shall be thy masters if thou goest thither.

"This is my tale, and thine, I say, I ask not; but I deem that thou shalt do ill if thou go not to the Burg either with me or by thyself alone; either as a guest, or as a good knight to take service in their host."

Now so it was that Ralph was wary; and this time he looked closely at the carle, and found that he spake coldly for a man with so much wrath in his heart; therefore he was in doubt about the thing; moreover he called to mind the words of the lady whom he had delivered, and her loveliness, and the kisses she had given him, and he was loth to find her a liar; and he was loth also to think that the maiden of Bourton had betaken her to so evil a dwelling. So he said:

"Friend, I know not that I must needs be a partaker in the strife betwixt Hampton and the Burg, or go either to one or the other of these strongholds. Is there no other way out of this wood save by Hampton or the Burg? or no other place anigh, where I may rest in peace awhile, and then go on mine own errands?"

Said the Carle: "There is a thorp that lieth somewhat west of the Burg, which is called Apthorp; but it is an open place, not fenced, and is debateable ground, whiles held by them of the Burg, whiles by the Dry Tree; and if thou tarry there, and they of the Dry Tree take thee, soon is thine errand sped; and if they of the Burg take thee, then shalt thou be led into the Burg in worse case than thou wouldest be if thou go thereto uncompelled. What sayest thou, therefore? Who shall hurt thee in the Burg, a town which is under good and strong law, if thou be a true man, as thou seemest to be? And if thou art seeking adventures, as may well be, thou shalt soon find them there ready to hand. I rede thee come with me to the Burg; for, to say sooth, I shall find it somewhat easier to enter therein if I be in the company of thee, a knight and a lord."

So Ralph considered and thought that there lay indeed but little peril to him in the Burg, whereas both those men with whom he had striven were hushed for ever, and there was none else to tell the tale of the battle, save the lady, whose peril from them of the Burg was much greater than his; and also he thought that if anything untoward befel, he had some one to fall back on in old Oliver: yet on the other hand he had a hankering after Hampton under Scaur, where, to say sooth, he doubted not to see the lady again.

So betwixt one thing and the other, speech hung on his lips awhile, when suddenly the carle said: "Hist! thou hast left thy horse without the bushes, and he is whinnying" (which indeed he was), "there is now no time to lose. To horse straightway, for certainly there are folk at hand, and they may be foemen, and are most like to be."

Therewith they both arose and hastened to where Falcon stood just outside the alder bushes, and Ralph leapt a-horse-back without more ado, and the carle waited no bidding to leap up behind him, and pointing to a glade of the wood which led toward the highway, cried out, "Spur that way, thither! they of the Dry Tree are abroad this morning. Spur! 'tis for life or death!"

Ralph shook the rein and Falcon leapt away without waiting for the spur, while the carle looked over his shoulder and said, "Yonder they come! they are three; and ever they ride well horsed. Nay, nay! They are four," quoth he, as a shout sounded behind them. "Spur, young lord! spur! And thine horse is a mettlesome beast. Yea, it will do, it will do."

Therewith came to Ralph's ears the sound of their horse-hoofs beating the turf, and he spurred indeed, and Falcon flew forth.

"Ah," cried the carle! "but take heed, for they see that thy horse is good, and one of them, the last, hath a bent Turk bow in his hand, and is laying an arrow on it; as ever their wont is to shoot a-horseback: a turn of thy rein, as if thine horse were shying at a weasel on the road!"

Ralph stooped his head and made Falcon swerve, and heard therewith the twang of the bowstring and straightway the shaft flew past his ears. Falcon galloped on, and the carle cried out: "There is the highway toward the Burg! Do thy best, do thy best! Lo you again!"

For the second shaft flew from the Turkish bow, and the noise of the chase was loud behind them. Once again twanged the bow-string, but this time the arrow fell short, and the woodland man, turning himself about as well as he might, shook his clenched fist at the chase, crying out in a voice broken by the gallop: "Ha, thieves! I am Roger of the Rope-walk, I go to twist a rope for the necks of you!"

Then he spake to Ralph: "They are turning back: they are beaten, and withal they love not the open road: yet slacken not yet, young knight, unless thou lovest thine horse more than thy life; for they will follow on through the thicket on the way-side to see whether thou wert born a fool and hast learned nothing later."

"Yea," said Ralph, "and now I deem thou wilt tell me that to the Burg I needs must."

"Yea, forsooth," said the carle, "nor shall we be long, riding thus, ere we come to the Burg Gate."

"Yea, or even slower," said Ralph, drawing rein somewhat, "for now I deem the chase done: and after all is said, I have no will to slay Falcon, who is one of my friends, as thou perchance mayest come to be another."

Thereafter he went a hand-gallop till the wood began to thin, and there were fields of tillage about the highway; and presently Roger said: "Thou mayst breathe thy nag now, and ride single, for we are amidst friends; not even a score of the Dry Tree dare ride so nigh the Burg save by night and cloud."

So Ralph stayed his horse, and he and Roger lighted down, and Ralph looked about him and saw a stone tower builded on a little knoll amidst a wheatfield, and below it some simple houses thatched with straw; there were folk moreover working, or coming and going about the fields, who took little heed of the two when they saw them standing quiet by the horse's head; but each and all of these folk, so far as could be seen, had some weapon.

Then said Ralph: "Good fellow, is this the Burg of the Four Friths?" The carle laughed, and said: "Simple is the question, Sir Knight: yonder is a watch-tower of the Burg, whereunder husbandmen can live, because there be men-at-arms therein. And all round the outskirts of the Frank of the Burg are there such-like towers to the number of twenty-seven. For that, say folk, was the tale of the winters of the Fair Lady who erewhile began the building of the Burg, when she was first wedded to the Forest Lord, who before that building had dwelt, he and his fathers, in thatched halls of timber here and there about the clearings of the wild-wood. But now, knight, if thou wilt, thou mayest go on softly toward the Gate of the Burg, and if thou wilt I will walk beside thy rein, which fellowship, as aforesaid, shall be a gain to me."

Said Ralph: "I pray thee come with me, good fellow, and show me how easiest to enter this stronghold." So, when Falcon was well breathed, they went on, passing through goodly acres and wide meadows, with here and there a homestead on them, and here and there a carle's cot. Then came they to a thorp of the smallest on a rising ground, from the further end of which they could see the walls and towers of the Burg. Thereafter right up to the walls were no more houses or cornfields, nought but reaches of green meadows plenteously stored with sheep and kine, and with a little stream winding about them.

CHAPTER 12

Ralph Entereth Into the Burg
of the Four Friths

When they came up to the wall they saw that it was well builded of good ashlar, and so high that they might not see the roofs of the town because of it; but there were tall towers on it, a many of them, strong and white. The road led up straight to the master-gate of the Burg, and there was a bailey before it strongly walled, and manned with weaponed men, and a captain going about amongst them. But they entered it along with men bringing wares into the town, and none heeded them much, till they came to the very gate, on the further side of a moat that was both deep and clean; but as now the bridge was down and the portcullis up, so that the market-people might pass in easily, for it was yet early in the day. But before the door on either side stood men-at-arms well weaponed, and on the right side was their captain, a tall man with bare grizzled head, but otherwise all-armed, who stopped every one whom he knew not, and asked their business.

As Ralph came riding up with Roger beside him, one of the guard laid his spear across and bade them stand, and the captain spake in a dry cold voice: "Whence comest thou, man-at-arms?" "From the Abbey of St. Mary at Higham," said Ralph. "Yea," said the captain, smiling grimly, "even so I might have deemed: thou wilt be one of the Lord Abbot's lily lads." "No I am not," quoth Ralph angrily. "Well, well," said the captain, "what is thy name?"

"Ralph Motherson," quoth Ralph, knitting his brow. Said the captain "And whither wilt thou?" Said Ralph, "On mine own errands." "Thou answerest not over freely," quoth the captain. Said Ralph, "Then is it even; for thou askest freely enough." "Well, well," said the captain, grinning in no unfriendly wise, "thou seemest a stout lad enough; and as to my asking, it is my craft as captain of the North Gate: but now tell me friendly, goest thou to any kinsman or friend in the Burg?"

Then Ralph's brow cleared and he said, "Nay, fair sir." "Well then," said the captain, "art thou but riding straight through to another gate, and so away again?" "Nay," said Ralph, "if I may, I would abide here the night over, or may-happen longer." "Therein thou shalt do well, young man," said the captain; "then I suppose thou wilt to some hostelry? tell me which one."

Said Ralph, "Nay, I wot not to which one, knowing not the town." But Roger close by him spake and said: "My lord shall go to the Flower de Luce, which is in the big square."

"Truly," said the captain, "he goes to a good harbour; and moreover, fair sir, to-morrow thou shalt see a goodly sight from thine inn; thou mayst do no better, lord. But thou, carle, who art thou, who knowest the inside of our Burg so well, though I know thee not, for as well as I know our craftsmen and vavassors?"

Then Roger's words hung on his lips awhile, and the knight bent his brow on him, till at last he said, "Sir Captain, I was minded to lie, and say that I am this young knight's serving-man." The captain broke in on him grimly, "Thou wert best not lie."

"Yea, sir," quoth Roger, "I deemed, as it was on my tongue's end, that thou wouldst find me out, so I have nought to do but tell thee the very sooth: this it is: I am a man made masterless by the thieves of the Dry Tree. From my land at Hampton under Scaur have I been driven, my chattels have been lifted, and my friends slain; and therefore by your leave would I ride in the host of the Burg, that I may pay back the harm which I had, according to the saw, 'better bale by breeding bale.' So, lord, I ask thee wilt thou lend me the sword and give me the loaf, that I may help both thee, and the Burg, and me?"

The captain looked at him closely and sharply, while the carle faced him with open simple eyes, and at last he said: "Well, carle, thou wert about to name thyself this young knight's serving-man; be thou even so whiles he abideth in the Burg; and when he leaveth the Burg then come back to me here any day before noon, and may be I shall then put a sword in thy fist and horse between thy thighs. But," (and he wagged his head threateningly at Roger) "see that thou art at the Flower de Luce when thou art called for."

Roger held his peace and seemed somewhat abashed at this word, and the captain turned to Ralph and said courteously: "Young knight, if thou art seeking adventures, thou shalt find them in our host; and if thou be but half as wise as thou seemest bold, thou wilt not fail to gain honour and wealth both, in the service of the Burg; for we be overmuch beset with foemen that we should not welcome any wight and wary warrior, though he be an alien of blood and land. If thou thinkest well of this, then send me thy man here and give me word of thy mind, and I shall lead thee to the chiefs of the Port, and make the way easy for thee."

Ralph thanked him and rode through the gate into the street, and Roger still went beside his stirrup.

Presently Ralph turned to Roger and spake to him somewhat sourly, and said: "Thou hadst one lie in thy mouth and didst swallow it; but how shall I know that another did not come out thence? Withal thou must needs be my fellow here, will I, nill I; for thou it was that didst put that word into the captain's mouth that thou shouldst serve me while I abide in the Burg. So I will say here and now, that my mind misgives me concerning thee, whether thou be not of those very thieves and tyrants whom thou didst mis-say but a little while ago."

"Yea," said Roger, "thou art wise indeed to set me down as one of the Dry Tree; doubtless that is why I delivered thee from their ambush even now. And as for my service, thou mayst need it; for indeed I deem thee not so safe as thou deemest thyself in this Burg."

"What!" said Ralph, "Dost thou blow hot and cold? why even now, when we were in the wood, thou wert telling me that I had nought at all to fear in the Burg of the Four Friths, and that all was done there by reason and with justice. What is this new thing then which thou hast found out, or what is that I have to fear?"

Roger changed countenance thereat and seemed somewhat

confused, as one who has been caught unawares; but he gat his own face presently, and said: "Nay, Sir Knight, I will tell thee the truth right out. In the wood yonder thy danger was great that thou mightest run into the hands of them of the Dry Tree; therefore true it is that I spake somewhat beyond my warrant concerning the life of the folk of the Burg, as how could I help it? But surely whatever thy peril may be here, it is nought to that which awaited thee at Hampton."

"Nay, but what is the peril?" said Ralph. Quoth Roger, "If thou wilt become their man and enter into their host, there is none; for they will ask few questions of so good a man-at-arms, when they know that thou art theirs; but if thou naysay that, it may well be that they will be for turning the key on thee till thou tellest them what and whence thou art." Ralph answered nought, thinking in his mind that this was like enough; so he rode on soberly, till Roger said:

"Anyhow, thou mayst turn the cold shoulder on me if thou wilt. Yet were I thee, I would not, for so it is, both that I can help thee, as I deem, in time to come, and that I have helped thee somewhat in time past."

Now Ralph was young and could not abide the blame of thanklessness; so he said, "Nay, nay, fellow, go we on together to the Flower de Luce."

Roger nodded his head and grumbled somewhat, and they made no stay except that now and again Ralph drew rein to look at goodly things in the street, for there were many open booths therein, so that the whole street looked like a market. The houses were goodly of building, but not very tall, the ways wide and well-paved. Many folk were in the street, going up and down on their errands, and both men and women of them seemed to Ralph stout and strong, but not very fair of favour. Withal they seemed intent on their business, and payed little heed to Ralph and his fellow, though he was by his attire plainly a stranger.

Now Ralph sees a house more gaily adorned than most, and a sign hung out from it whereon was done an image of St. Loy, and underneath the same a booth on which was set out weapons and war-gear exceeding goodly; and two knaves of the armourer were standing by to serve folk, and crying their wares with "what d'ye lack?" from time to time. So he stayed and fell to looking wistfully at the gleam and glitter of those fair things, till one of the aforesaid knaves came to his side and said:

"Fair Sir, surely thou lackest somewhat; what have we here for thy needs?" So Ralph thought and called to mind that strong little steel axe of the man whom he had slain yesterday, and asked for the sight of such a weapon, if he might perchance cheapen it. And the lad brought a very goodly steel axe, gold-inlaid about the shaft, and gave him the price thereof, which Ralph deemed he might compass; so he brought round his scrip to his hand, that he might take out the money. But while his hand was yet in the bag, out comes the master-armourer, a tall and very stark carle, and said in courteous wise: "Sir Knight, thou art a stranger to me and I know thee not; so I must needs ask for a sight of thy license to buy weapons, under the seal of the Burg."

"Hear a wonder," said Ralph, "that a free man for his money shall not buy wares set out to be bought, unless he have the Burg-Reeve's hand and seal for it! Nay, take thy florins, master, and give me the axe and let the jest end there." "I jest not, young rider," quoth the armourer. "When we know thee for a liegeman of the Burg, thou shalt buy what thou wilt without question; but otherwise I have told thee the law, and how may I, the master of the craft, break the law? Be not wrath, fair sir, I will set aside thine axe for thee, till thou bring me the license, or bid me come see it, and thou shalt get the said license at the Town Hall straightway, when they may certify thee no foeman of the Burg."

Ralph saw that it availed nothing to bicker with the smith, and so went his way somewhat crestfallen, and that the more as he saw Roger grinning a little.

Now they come into the market-place, on one side whereof was the master church of the town, which was strongly built and with a tall tower to it, but was not very big, and but little adorned. Over against it they saw the sign of the Flower de Luce, a goodly house and great. Thitherward they turned; but in the face of the hostelry amidmost the place was a thing which Roger pointed at with a grin that spoke as well as words; and this was a high gallows-tree furnished with four forks or arms, each carved and wrought in the fashion of the very bough of a tree, from which dangled four nooses, and above them all was a board whereon was written in big letters THE DRY TREE. And at the foot of this gallows were divers folk laughing and talking.

So Ralph understood at once that those four men whom he had seen led away bound yesterday should be hanged thereon; so he stayed a franklin who was passing by, and said to him, "Sir, I am a stranger in the town, and I would know if justice shall be done on the four woodmen to-day." "Nay," said the man, "but to-morrow; they are even now before the judges."

Then said Roger in a surly voice, "Why art thou not there to look on?" "Because," quoth the man, "there is little to see there, and not much more to hearken. The thieves shall be speedily judged, and not questioned with torments, so that they may be the lustier to feel what the hangman shall work on them to-morrow; then forsooth the show shall be goodly. But far better had it been if we had had in our hands the great witch of these dastards, as we looked to have her; but now folk say that she has not been brought within gates, and it is to be feared that she hath slipped through our fingers once more."

Roger laughed, and said: "Simple are ye folk of the Burg, and know nought of her shifts. I tell thee it is not unlike that she is in the Burg even now, and hath in hand to take out of your prison the four whom ye have caught."

The franklin laughed scornfully in his turn and said: "If we be simple, thou art a fool merely: are we not stronger and more than the Dry Tree? How should she not be taken? How should she not be known if she were walking about these streets? Have we no eyes, fool-carle?" And he laughed again, for he was wroth.

Ralph hearkened, and a kind of fear seemed griping his heart, so he asked the franklin: "Tell me, sir, are ye two speaking of a woman who is Queen of these strong-thieves?" "Yea," said he, "or it might better be said that she is their goddess, their mawmet, their devil, the very heart and soul of their wickedness. But one day shall we have her body and soul, and then shall her body have but an evil day of it till she dieth in this world."

"Yea, forsooth, if she can die at all," quoth Roger.

The franklin looked sourly on him and said: "Good man, thou knowest much of her, meseemeth—Whence art thou?" Said Roger speedily: "From Hampton under Scaur; and her rebel I am, and her dastard, and her runaway. Therefore I know her forsooth."

"Well," the Franklin said "thou seemest a true man, and yet I would counsel thee to put a rein on thy tongue when thou art minded to talk of the Devil of the Dry Tree, or thou mayst come to harm in the Burg."

He walked away towards the gallows therewith; and Roger said, almost as if he were talking to himself; "A heavy-footed fool goeth yonder; but after this talk we were better hidden by the walls of the Flower-de-Luce." So therewith they went on toward the hostel.

But the market place was wide, and they were yet some minutes getting to the door, and ere they came there Ralph said, knitting his brows anxiously: "Is this woman fair or foul to look on?" "That is nought so easy to tell of," said Roger, "whiles she is foul, whiles very fair, whiles young and whiles old; whiles cruel and whiles kind. But note this, when she is the kindest then are her carles the cruellest; and she is the kinder to them because they are cruel."

Ralph pondered what he said, and wondered if this were verily the woman whom he had delivered, or some other. As if answering to his unspoken thought, Roger went on: "They speak but of one woman amongst them of the Dry Tree, but in sooth they have many others who are like unto her in one way or other; and this again is a reason why they may not lay hands on the very Queen of them all."

Therewithal they came unto the hostel, and found it fair enough within, the hall great and goodly for such a house, and with but three chapmen-carles therein. Straightway they called for meat, for it was now past noon, and the folk of the house served them when the grooms had taken charge of Falcon. And Roger served Ralph as if he were verily his man. Then Ralph went to his chamber aloft and rested a while, but came down into the hall a little before nones, and found Roger there walking up and down the hall floor, and no man else, so he said to him: "Though thou art not of the

66

Burg, thou knowest it; wilt thou not come abroad then, and show it me? for I have a mind to learn the ways of the folk here."

Said Roger, and smiled a little: "If thou commandest me as my lord, I will come; yet I were better pleased to abide behind; for I am weary with night-waking and sorrow; and have a burden of thought, one which I must bear to the end of the road; and if I put it down I shall have to go back and take it up again."

Ralph thought that he excused himself with more words than were needed; but he took little heed of it, but nodded to him friendly, and went out of the house afoot, but left his weapons and armour behind him by the rede of Roger.

CHAPTER 13

The Streets of the Burg of the Four Friths

He went about the streets and found them all much like to the one which they had entered by the north gate; he saw no poor or wretched houses, and none very big as of great lords; they were well and stoutly builded, but as aforesaid not much adorned either with carven work or painting: there were folk enough in the streets, and now Ralph, as was like to be, looked specially at the women, and thought many of them little better-favoured than the men, being both dark and low; neither were they gaily clad, though their raiment, like the houses, was stout and well wrought. But here and there he came on a woman taller and whiter than the others, as though she were of another blood; all such of these as he saw were clad otherwise than the darker women: their heads uncoifed, uncovered save for some garland or silken band: their gowns yellow like wheat-straw, but gaily embroidered; sleeveless withal and short, scarce reaching to the ancles, and whiles so thin that they were rather clad with the embroidery than the cloth; shoes they had not, but sandals bound on their naked feet with white thongs, and each bore an iron ring about her right arm.

The more part of the men wore weapons at their sides and had staves in hand, and were clad in short jerkins brown or blue of colour, and looked ready for battle if any moment should call them thereto; but among them were men of different favour and stature from these, taller for the most part, unarmed, and clad in long gowns of fair colours with cloths of thin and gay-coloured web twisted about their heads. These he took for merchants, as they were oftenest standing in and about the booths and shops, whereof there were some in all the streets, though the market for victuals and such like he found over for that day, and but scantily peopled.

Out of one of these markets, which was the fish and fowl market, he came into a long street that led him down to a gate right over against that whereby he had entered the Burg; and as he came thereto he saw that there was a wide way clear of all houses inside of the wall, so that men-at-arms might go freely from one part to the other; and he had also noted that a wide way led from each ort out of the great place, and each ended not but in a gate. But as to any castle in the town, he saw none; and when he asked a burgher thereof, the carle laughed in his face, and said to him that the whole Burg, houses and all, was a castle, and that it would turn out to be none of the easiest to win. And forsooth Ralph himself was much of that mind.

Now he was just within the south gate when he held this talk, and there were many folk thereby already, and more flocking thereto; so he stood there to see what should betide; and anon he heard great blowing of horns and trumpets all along the wall, and, as he deemed, other horns answered from without; and so it was; for soon the withoutward horns grew louder, and the folk fell back on either side of the way, and next the gates were thrown wide open (which before had been shut save for a wicket) and thereafter came the first of a company of men-at-arms, foot-men, with bills some, and some with bows, and all-armed knights and sergeants a-horseback.

So streamed in these weaponed men till Ralph saw that it was a great host that was entering the Burg; and his heart rose within him, so warrior-like they were of men and array, though no big men of their bodies; and many of them bore signs of battle about them, both in the battering of their armour and the rending of their raiment, and the clouts tied about the wounds on their bodies.

After a while among the warriors came herds of neat and flocks of sheep and strings of horses, of the spoil which the host had lifted; and then wains filled, some with weapons and war gear, and some with bales of goods and household stuff. Last came captives, some going afoot and some for weariness borne in wains; for all these war-taken thralls were women and women-children; of males there was not so much as a little lad. Of the women many seemed fair to Ralph despite their grief and travel; and as he looked on them he deemed that they must be of the kindred and nation of the fair white women he had seen in the streets; though they were not clad like those, but diversely.

So Ralph gazed on this pageant till all had passed, and he was weary with the heat and the dust and the confused clamour of shouting and laughter and talking; and whereas most of the folk followed after the host and their spoil, the streets of the town there about were soon left empty and peaceful. So he turned into a street narrower than most, that went east from the South Gate and was much shaded from the afternoon sun, and went slowly down it, meaning to come about the inside of the wall till he should hit the East Gate, and so into the Great Place when the folk should have gone their ways home.

He saw no folk in the street save here and there an old woman sitting at the door of her house, and maybe a young child with her. As he came to where the street turned somewhat, even such a carline was sitting on a clean white door-step on the sunny side, somewhat shaded by a tall rose-laurel tree in a great tub, and she sang as she sat spinning, and Ralph stayed to listen in his idle mood, and he heard how she sang in a dry, harsh voice:

Clashed sword on shield
In the harvest field;
And no man blames
The red red flames,
War's candle-wick
On roof and rick.
Now dead lies the yeoman
unwept and unknown
On the field he hath furrowed,
the ridge he hath sown:
And all in the middle
of wethers and neat
The maidens are driven
with blood on their feet;
For yet 'twixt the Burg-gate
and battle half-won
The dust-driven highway
creeps uphill and on,
And the smoke of the beacons
goes coiling aloft,
While the gathering horn bloweth
loud, louder and oft.

Throw wide the gates
For nought night waits;
Though the chase is dead
The moon's o'erhead
And we need the clear
Our spoil to share.
Shake the lots in the helm then
for brethren are we,
And the goods of my missing
are gainful to thee.
Lo! thine are the wethers,
and his are the kine;
And the colts of the marshland
unbroken are thine,
With the dapple-grey stallion
that trampled his groom;
And Giles hath the gold-blossomed

rose of the loom.
Lo! leaps out the last lot
and nought have I won,
But the maiden unmerry,
by battle undone.

Even as her song ended came one of those fair yellow-gowned damsels round the corner of the street, bearing in her hand a light basket full of flowers: and she lifted up her head and beheld Ralph there; then she went slowly and dropped her eyelids, and it was pleasant to Ralph to behold her; for she was as fair as need be. Her corn-coloured gown was dainty and thin, and but for its silver embroidery had hidden her limbs but little; the rosiness of her ancles showed amidst her white sandal-thongs, and there were silver rings and gold on her arms along with the iron ring.

Now she lifted up her eyes and looked shyly at Ralph, and he smiled at her well-pleased, and deemed it would be good to hear her voice; so he went up to her and greeted her, and she seemed to take his greeting well, though she glanced swiftly at the carline in the doorway.

Said Ralph: "Fair maiden, I am a stranger in this town, and have seen things I do not wholly understand; now wilt thou tell me before I ask the next question, who will be those war-taken thralls whom even now I saw brought into the Burg by the host? of what nation be they, and of what kindred?"

Straightway was the damsel all changed; she left her dainty tricks, and drew herself up straight and stiff. She looked at him in the eyes, flushing red, and with knit brows, a moment, and then passed by him with swift and firm feet as one both angry and ashamed.

But the carline who had beheld the two with a grin on her wrinkled face changed aspect also, and cried out fiercely after the damsel, and said: "What! dost thou flee from the fair young man, and he so kind and soft with thee, thou jade? Yea, I suppose thou dost fetch and carry for some mistress who is young and a fool, and who has not yet learned how to deal with the daughters of thine accursed folk. Ah! if I had but money to buy some one of you, and a good one, she

71

should do something else for me than showing her fairness to young men; and I would pay her for her long legs and her white skin, till she should curse her fate that she had not been born little and dark-skinned and free, and with heels un-bloodied with the blood of her back."

Thus she went on, though the damsel was long out of ear-shot of her curses; and Ralph tarried not to get away from her spiteful babble, which he now partly understood; and that all those yellow-clad damsels were thralls to the folk of the Burg; and belike were of the kindred of those captives late-taken whom he had seen amidst the host at its entering into the Burg.

So he wandered away thence thinking on what he should do till the sun was set, and he had come into the open space underneath the walls, and had gone along it till he came to the East Gate: there he looked around him a little and found people flowing back from the Great Place, whereto they had gathered to see the host mustered and the spoil blessed; then he went on still under the wall, and noted not that here and there a man turned about to look upon him curiously, for he was deep in thought, concerning the things which he had seen and heard of, and pondered much what might have befallen his brethren since they sundered at the Want-way nigh to the High House of Upmeads. Withal the chief thing that he desired was to get him away from the Burg, for he felt himself unfree therein; and he said to himself that if he were forced to dwell among this folk, that he had better never have stolen himself away from his father and mother; and whiles even he thought that he would do his best on the morrow to get him back home to Upmeads again. But then when he thought of how his life would go in his old home, there seemed to him a lack, and when he questioned himself as to what that lack was, straightway he seemed to see that Lady of the Wildwood standing before the men-at-arms in her scanty raiment the minute before his life was at adventure because of them. And in sooth he smiled to himself then with a beating heart, as he told himself that above all things he desired to see that Lady, whatever she might be, and that he would follow his adventure to the end until he met her.

Amidst these thoughts he came unto the North Gate,

whereby he had first entered the Burg, and by then it was as dark as the summer night would be; so he woke up from his dream, as it were, and took his way briskly back to the Flower de Luce.

CHAPTER 14

What Ralph Heard of the Matters of the Burg of the Four Friths

There was no candle in the hall when he entered, but it was not so dark therein but he might see Roger sitting on a stool near the chimney, and opposite to him on the settle sat two men; one very tall and big, the other small; Roger was looking away from these, and whistling; and it came into Ralph's mind that he would have him think that he had nought to do with them, whether that were so or not. But he turned round as Ralph came up the hall and rose and came up to him, and fell to talking with him and asking him how he liked the Burg; and ever he spake fast and loud, so that again it came on Ralph that he was playing a part.

Ralph heeded him little, but ever looked through the hall-dusk on those twain, who presently arose and went toward the hall door, but when they were but half-way across the floor a chamberlain came in suddenly, bearing candles in his hands, and the light fell on those guests and flashed back from a salade on the head of the big man, and Ralph saw that he was clad in a long white gaberdine, and he deemed that he was the very man whom he had seen last in the Great Place at Higham, nigh the church, and before that upon the road. As for the smaller man Ralph had no knowledge of him, for he could see but little of his face, whereas he was wrapped up in a cloak, for as warm as the evening was, and wore a slouch hat withal; but his eyes seemed great and wondrous bright.

But when they were gone Ralph asked Roger if he knew

aught of them, or if they had told him aught. "Nay," said Roger, "they came in here as I sat alone, and had their meat, and spake nought to me, and little to each other. I deem them not to be of the Burg. Nay, sooth to say, I doubt if they be true men."

As he spake came in a sort of the townsmen somewhat merry and noisy, and called for meat and drink and more lights; so that the board was brought and the hall was speedily astir. These men, while supper was being dight, fell to talking to Ralph and Roger, and asking them questions of whence and whither, but nowise uncourteously: to whom Roger answered with the tale which he had told Ralph, and Ralph told what he would, and that was but little.

But when the board was dight they bade them sit down with them and eat. Ralph sat down at once, and Roger would have served him, but Ralph bade him do it not, and constrained him to sit by his side, and they two sat a little apart from the townsmen.

So when they had eaten their fill, and wine was brought, and men were drinking kindly, Ralph began to ask Roger concerning those women whom he had seen in the street, and the captives whom he had seen brought in by the host, and if they were of one kindred, and generally how it was with them: and he spake somewhat softly as if he would not break into the talk of the townsmen: but Roger answered him in a loud voice so that all could hear:

"Yea, lord, I will tell thee the tale of them, which setteth forth well both the wise policy and the great mercy of the folk of the Burg and their rulers."

Said Ralph: "Are these women also of the Dry Tree? For I perceive them to be born of the foes of the Burg."

Now the townsmen had let their talk drop a while to listen to the talk of the aliens; and Roger answered still in a loud voice: "Nay, nay, it is not so. These queens are indeed war-taken thralls, but not from them of the Dry Tree, or they would have been slain at once, like as the carles of those accursed ones. But these are of the folk of the Wheat-wearers, even as those whom thou sawest brought to-day amidst the other spoil. And to this folk the Burg showeth mercy, and whenso the host goeth against them and overcometh (and that is well-nigh whenever they meet) these worthy lords slay no woman of them, but the men only, whether they be old or young or youngest. As for their women they are brought hither and sold at the market-cross to the highest bidder. And this honour they have, that such of them as be fair, and that is the more part of the younger ones, fetch no ill penny. Yet for my part I were loth to cheapen such wares: for they make but evil servants, being proud, and not abiding stripes lightly, or toiling the harder for them; and they be somewhat too handy with the knife if they deem themselves put upon. Speak I sooth, my masters?" quoth he, turning toward them of the town.

Said a burgher somewhat stricken in years, "Nought but sooth; peaceable men like to me eschew such servants; all the more because of this, that if one of these queens misbehave with the knife, or strayeth from her master's bed, the laws of the Burg meddle not therein. For the wise men say that such folk are no more within the law than kine be, and may not for their deeds be brought before leet or assize any more than kine. So that if the master punish her not for her misdoings, unpunished she needs must go; yea even if her deed be mere murder."

"That is sooth," said a somewhat younger man; "yet whiles it fareth ill with them at the hands of our women. To wit, my father's brother has even now come from the war to find his thrall all spoilt by his wife: and what remedy may he have against his wife? his money is gone, even as if she had houghed his horse or his best cow."

"Yea," said a third, "we were better without such cattle. A thrust with a sword and all the tale told, were the better way of dealing with them."

Said another; "Yet are the queens good websters, and, lacking them, figured cloth of silk would be far-fetched and dear-bought here."

A young man gaily clad, who had been eyeing the speakers disdainfully, spake next and said: "Fair sirs, ye are speaking like hypocrites, and as if your lawful wives were here to hearken to you; whereas ye know well how goodly these thralls be, and that many of them can be kind enough withal; and ye would think yourselves but ill bestead if ye might not cheapen such jewels for your money. Which of you will go to the Cross next Saturday and there buy him a fairer wife than he can wed out of our lineages? and a wife withal of whose humours he need take no more account of than the dullness of his hound or the skittish temper of his mare, so long as the thong smarts, and the twigs sting."

One or two grinned as he spake, but some bent their brows at him, yet scarce in earnest, and the talk thereover dropped, nor did Ralph ask any more questions; for he was somewhat down-hearted, calling to mind the frank and free maidens of Upmead, and their friendly words and hearty kisses. And him seemed the world was worse than he had looked to find it.

Howsoever, the oldest and soberest of the guests, seeing that he was a stranger and of noble aspect, came unto him and sat by him, and fell to telling him tales of the wars of the men of the Burg with the Wheat-wearers; and how in time past, when the town was but little fenced, the Wheat-wearers had stormed their gates and taken the city, and had made a great slaughter; but yet had spared many of the fighting-men, although they had abided there as the masters of them, and held them enthralled for three generations of men: after which time the sons' sons of the old Burg-dwellers having grown very many again, and divers of them being trusted in sundry matters by the conquerors, who oppressed them but little, rose up against them as occasion served, in the winter season and the Yule feast, and slew their masters, save for a few who were hidden away.

"And thereafter," quoth he, "did we make the Burg strong and hard to win, as ye see it to-day; and we took for our captain the Forest Lord, who ere-while had dwelt in the clearings of the wildwood, and he wedded the Fair Lady who was the son's daughter of him who had been our lord ere the Wheat-wearers overcame us; and we grew safe and free and mighty again. And the son of the Forest Lord, he whom we call the War-smith, he it was who beheld the Burg too much given to pleasure, and delighting in the softness of life; and he took order to harden our hearts, and to cause all freemen to learn the craft of war and battle, and let the women and thralls and aliens see to other craftsmanship and to chaffer;

and even so is it done as he would; and ye shall find us hardy of heart enough, though belike not so joyous as might be. Yet at least we shall not be easy to overcome."

"So indeed it seemeth," said Ralph. "Yet will I ask of you first one question, and then another."

"Ask on," said the burgher.

Said Ralph: "How is it that ye, being so strong, should still suffer them of the Dry Tree, taking a man here and a man there, when ye might destroy them utterly?"

The Burgher reddened and cleared his throat and said: "Sir, it must be made clear to you that these evil beasts are no peril to the Burg of the Four Friths; all the harm they may do us, is as when a cur dog biteth a man in the calf of the leg; whereby the man shall be grieved indeed, but the dog slain. Such grief as that they have done us at whiles: but the grief is paid for thus, that the hunting and slaying of them keeps our men in good trim, and pleasures them; shortly to say it, they are the chief deer wherewith our wood is stocked."

He stopped awhile and then went on again and said: "To say sooth they be not very handy for crushing as a man crushes a wasp, because sorcery goes with them, and the wiles of one who is their Queen, the evilest woman who ever spat upon the blessed Host of the Altar: yet is she strong; a devouring sea of souls, God help us!" And he blessed himself therewith.

Said Ralph: "Yet a word on these Wheat-wearers; it seemeth that ye never fail to overcome them in battle?"

"But seldom at least," quoth the Burgher.

Said Ralph: "Then it were no great matter for you to gather a host overwhelming, and to take their towns and castles, and forbid them weapons, and make them your thralls to till the land for you which now they call theirs; so that ye might have of their gettings all save what were needful for them to live as thralls."

"I deem it were an easy thing," said the burgher.

Quoth Ralph: "Then why do ye not so?"

"It were but a poor game to play," said the burgher. "Such of their wealth as we have a mind to, we can have now at the cost of a battle or two, begun one hour and ended the next: were we their masters sitting down amidst of their hatred, and amidst of their plotting, yea, and in the very place where that were the hottest and thickest, the battle would be to begin at every sun's uprising, nor would it be ended at any sunset. Hah! what sayest thou?"

Said Ralph: "This seemeth to me but the bare truth; yet it is little after the manner of such masterful men as ye be. But why then do ye slay all their carles that are taken; whereas ye bear away the women and make thralls of them at home, that is to say, foes in every house?"

"It may be," said the Burgher, "that this is not amongst the wisest of our dealings. Yet may we do no otherwise; for thus we swore to do by all the greatest oaths that we might swear, in the days when we first cast off their yoke, and yet were not over strong at the first; and now it hath so grown into a part of our manners, yea, and of our very hearts and minds, that the slaying of a Wheat-wearer is to us a lighter matter than the smiting of a rabbit or a fowmart. But now, look you, fair sir, my company ariseth from table; so I bid thee a good night. And I give thee a good rede along with the good wish, to wit, that thou ask not too many questions in this city concerning its foemen: for here is the stranger looked upon with doubt, if he neither will take the wages of the Burg for battle, nor hath aught to sell."

Ralph reddened at his word, and the other looked at him steadily as he spoke, so that Ralph deemed that he mistrusted him: he deemed moreover that three or four of the others looked hard at him as they went towards the door, while Roger stood somewhat smiling, and humming a snatch of an old song.

But when the other guests had left the hostelry, Roger left his singing, and turned to Ralph and said: "Master, meseems that they mistrust us, and now maybe is that peril that I spake of nigher than I deemed when we came into the Burg this morning. And now I would that we were well out of the Burg and in the merry greenwood again, and it repents me that I brought thee hither."

"Nay, good fellow," quoth Ralph, "heed it not: besides, it was me, not thee, that they seemed to doubt of. I will depart hence to-morrow morning no worser than I came, and leave thee to seek thy fortune here; and good luck go with thee."

Roger looked hard at him and said: "Not so, young lord; if thou goest I will go with thee, for thou hast won my heart, I know not how: and I would verily be thy servant, to follow thee whithersoever thou goest; for I think that great deeds will come of thee."

This word pleased Ralph, for he was young and lightly put faith in men's words, and loved to be well thought of, and was fain of good fellowship withal. So he said: "This is a good word of thine, and I thank thee for it; and look to it that in my adventures, and the reward of them thou shalt have thy due share. Lo here my hand on it!"

Roger took his hand, yet therewith his face seemed a little troubled, but he said nought. Then spoke Ralph: "True it is that I am not fain to take the wages of the Burg; for it seems to me that they be hard men, and cruel and joyless, and that their service shall be rather churlish than knightly. Howbeit, let night bring counsel, and we will see to this to-morrow; for now I am both sleepy and weary." Therewith he called the chamberlain, who bore a wax light before him to his chamber, and he did off his raiment and cast himself on his bed, and fell asleep straightway, before he knew where Roger was sleeping, whether it were in the hall or some place else.

CHAPTER 15

How Ralph Departed From the Burg of the Four Friths

Himseemed he had scarce been asleep a minute ere awoke with a sound of someone saying softly, "Master, master, awake!" So he sat up and answered softly in his turn: "Who is it? what is amiss, since the night is yet young?"

"I am thy fellow-farer, Roger," said the speaker, "and this thou hast to do, get on thy raiment speedily, and take thy weapons without noise, if thou wouldst not be in the prison of the Burg before sunrise."

Ralph did as he was bidden without more words; for already when he lay down his heart misgave him that he was in no safe place; he looked to his weapons and armour that they should not clash, and down they came into the hall and found the door on the latch; so out they went and Ralph saw that it was somewhat cloudy; the moon was set and it was dark, but Ralph knew by the scent that came in on the light wind, and a little stir of blended sounds, that it was hard on dawning; and even therewith he heard the challenge of the warders on the walls and their crying of the hour; and the chimes of the belfry rang clear and loud, and seeming close above him, two hours and a half after midnight. Roger spake not, and Ralph was man-at-arms enough to know that he must hold his peace; and though he longed sore to have his horse Falcon with him, yet he wotted that it availed not to ask of his horse, since he durst not ask of his life.

So they went on silently till they were out of the Great Place and came into a narrow street, and so into another which led them straight into the houseless space under the wall. Roger led right on as if he knew the way well, and in a twinkling were they come to a postern in the wall betwixt the East Gate and the South. By the said postern Ralph saw certain men standing; and on the earth near by, whereas he was keen-eyed, he saw more than one man lying moveless.

Spake Roger softly to the men who stood on their feet: "Is the rope twined?" "Nay, rope-twiner," said one of them. Then Roger turned and whispered to Ralph: "Friends. Get out thy sword!" Wherewithal the gate was opened, and they all passed out through the wall, and stood above the ditch in the angle-nook of a square tower. Then Ralph saw some of the men stoop and shoot out a broad plank over the ditch, which was deep but not wide thereabout, and straightway he followed the others over it, going last save Roger. By then they were on the other side he saw a glimmer of the dawn in the eastern heaven, but it was still more than dusk, and no man spoke again. They went on softly across the plain fields outside the wall, creeping from bush to bush, and from tree to tree, for here, if nowhere about the circuit of the Burg, were a few trees growing. Thus they came into a little wood and passed through it, and then Ralph could see that the men were six besides Roger; by the glimmer of the growing dawn he saw before them a space of meadows with high hedges about them, and a dim line that he took for the roof of a barn or grange, and beyond that a dark mass of trees.

Still they pressed on without speaking; a dog barked not far off and the cocks were crowing, and close by them in the meadow a cow lowed and went hustling over the bents and the long, unbitten buttercups. Day grew apace, and by then they were under the barn-gable which he had seen aloof he saw the other roofs of the grange and heard the bleating of sheep. And now he saw those six men clearly, and noted that one of them was very big and tall, and one small and slender, and it came into his mind that these two were none other than the twain whom he had come upon the last night sitting in the hall of the Flower de Luce.

Even therewith came a man to the gate of the sheep-cote by the grange, and caught sight of them, and had the wits to run back at once shouting out: "Hugh, Wat, Richard, and all ye, out with you, out a doors! Here be men! Ware the Dry Tree! Bows and bills! Bows and bills!"

With that those fellows of Ralph made no more ado, but set off running at their best toward the wood aforesaid, which crowned the slope leading up from the grange, and now took no care to go softly, nor heeded the clashing of their armour. Ralph ran with the best and entered the wood alongside the slim youth aforesaid, who stayed not at the wood's edge but went on running still: but Ralph stayed and turned to see what was toward, and beheld how that tall man was the last of their company, and ere he entered the wood turned about with a bent bow in his hand, and even as he nocked the shaft, the men from the Grange, who were seven in all, came running out from behind the barn-gable, crying out: "Ho thieves! ho ye of the Dry Tree, abide till we come! flee not from handy strokes." The tall man had the shaft to his ear in a twinkling, and loosed straightway, and nocked and loosed another shaft without staying to note how the first had sped. But Ralph saw that a man was before each of the shafts, and had fallen to earth, though he had no time to see

81

aught else, for even therewith the tall man caught him by the hand, and crying out, "The third time!" ran on with him after the rest of their company; and whereas he was long-legged and Ralph lightfooted, they speedily came up with them, who were running still, but laughing as they ran, and jeering at the men of the Burgh; and the tall man shouted out to them: "Yea, lads, the counterfeit Dry Tree that they have raised in the Burg shall be dry enough this time." "Truly," said another, "till we come to water it with the blood of these wretches."

"Well, well, get on," said a third, "waste not your wind in talk; those carles will make but a short run of it to the walls, long as it was for us, creeping and creeping as we behoved to."

The long man laughed; "Thou sayest sooth," said he, "but thou art the longest winded of all in talking: get on, lads."

They laughed again at his word and sped on with less noise; while Ralph thought within himself that he was come into strange company, for now he knew well that the big man was even he whom he had first met at the churchyard gate of the thorp under Bear Hill. Yet he deemed that there was nought for it now but to go on.

Within a while they all slacked somewhat, and presently did but walk, though swiftly, through the paths of the thicket, which Ralph deemed full surely was part of that side of the Wood Perilous that lay south of the Burg of the Four Friths. And now Roger joined himself to him, and spake to him aloud and said: "So, fair master, thou art out of the peril of death for this bout."

"Art thou all so sure of that?" quoth Ralph, "or who are these that be with us? meseems they smell of the Dry Tree."

"Yea, or rebels and runaways therefrom," said Roger, with a dry grin. "But whosoever they may be, thou shalt see that they will suffer us to depart whither we will, if we like not their company. I will be thy warrant thereof."

"Moreover," said Ralph, "I have lost Falcon my horse; it is a sore miss of him."

"Maybe," quoth Roger, "but at least thou hast saved thy skin; and whereas there are many horses on the earth, there

82

is but one skin of thine: be content; if thou wilt, thou shall win somewhat in exchange for thine horse."

Ralph smiled, but somewhat sourly, and even therewith he heard a shrill whistle a little aloof, and the men stayed and held their peace, for they were talking together freely again now. Then the big man put his fingers to his mouth and whistled again in answer, a third whistle answered him; and lo, presently, as their company hastened on, the voices of men, and anon they came into a little wood-lawn wherein standing about or lying on the grass beside their horses were more than a score of men well armed, but without any banner or token, and all in white armour with white Gaberdines thereover; and they had with them, as Ralph judged, some dozen of horses more than they needed for their own riding.

Great was the joy at this meeting, and there was embracing and kissing of friends: but Ralph noted that no man embraced that slender youth, and that he held him somewhat aloof from the others, and all seemed to do him reverence.

Now spake one of the runaways: "Well, lads, here be all we four well met again along with those twain who came to help us at our pinch, as their wont is, and Roger withal, good at need again, and a friend of his, as it seemeth, and whom we know not. See ye to that."

Then stood forth the big man and said: "He is a fair young knight, as ye may see; and he rideth seeking adventures, and Roger did us to wit that he was abiding in the Burg at his peril, and would have him away, even if it were somewhat against his will: and we were willing that it should be so, all the more as I have a guess concerning what he is; and a foreseeing man might think that luck should go with him." Therewith he turned to Ralph and said: "How say ye, fair sir, will ye take guesting with us a while and learn our ways?"

Said Ralph: "Certain I am that whither ye will have me go, thither must I; yet I deem that I have an errand that lies not your way. Therefore if I go with you, ye must so look upon it that I am in your fellowship as one compelled. To be short with you, I crave leave to depart and go mine own road."

As he spoke he saw the youth walking up and down in

short turns; but his face he could scarce see at all, what for his slouched hat, what for his cloak; and at last he saw him go up to the tall man and speak softly to him awhile. The tall man nodded his head, and as the youth drew right back nigh to the thicket, spake to Ralph again.

"Fair sir, we grant thine asking; and add this thereto that we give thee the man who has joined himself to thee, Roger of the Rope-walk to wit, to help thee on the road, so that thou mayst not turn thy face back to the Burg of the Four Friths, where thine errand, and thy life withal, were soon sped now, or run into any other trap which the Wood Perilous may have for thee. And yet if thou think better of it, thou mayst come with us straightway; for we have nought to do to tarry here any longer. And in any case, here is a good horse that we will give thee, since thou hast lost thy steed; and Roger who rideth with thee, he also is well horsed."

Ralph looked hard at the big man, who now had his salade thrown back from his face, to see if he gave any token of jeering or malice, but could see nought such: nay, his face was grave and serious, not ill-fashioned, though it were both long and broad like his body: his cheek-bones somewhat high, his eyes grey and middling great, and looking, as it were, far away.

Now deems Ralph that as for a trap of the Wood Perilous, he had already fallen into the trap; for he scarce needed to be told that these were men of the Dry Tree. He knew also that it was Roger who had led him into this trap, although he deemed it done with no malice against him. So he said to himself that if he went with Roger he but went a roundabout road to the Dry Tree; so that he was well nigh choosing to go on with their company. Yet again he thought that something might well befall which would free him from that fellowship if he went with Roger alone; whereas if he went with the others it was not that he might be, but that he was already of the fellowship of the Dry Tree, and most like would go straight thence to their stronghold. So he spake as soberly as the tall man had done.

"Since ye give me the choice, fair sir, I will depart hence with Roger alone, whom ye call my man, though to me he seemeth to be yours. Howbeit, he has led me to you once, and belike will do so once more."

"Yea," quoth the big man smiling no whit more than erst, "and that will make the fourth time. Depart then, fair sir, and take this word with thee that I wish thee good and not evil."

CHAPTER 16

Ralph Rideth the Wood
Perilous Again

Now Roger led up to Ralph a strong horse, red roan of hue, duly harnessed for war, and he himself had a good grey horse, and they mounted at once, and Ralph rode slowly away through the wood at his horse's will, for he was pondering all that had befallen him, and wondering what next should hap. Meanwhile those others had not loitered, but were a-horseback at once, and went their ways from Ralph through the wildwood.

Nought spake Ralph for a while till Roger came close up to him and said: "Whither shall we betake us, fair lord? hast thou an inkling of the road whereon lies thine errand?"

Now to Ralph this seemed but mockery, and he answered sharply: "I wot not, thou wilt lead whither thou wilt, even as thou hast trained me hitherward with lies and a forged tale. I suppose thou wilt lead me now by some roundabout road to the stronghold of the Dry Tree. It matters little, since thou durst not lead me back into the Burg. Yet now I come to think of it, it is evil to be alone with a found out traitor and liar; and I had belike have done better to go with their company."

"Nay nay," quoth Roger, "thou art angry, and I marvel not thereat; but let thy wrath run off thee if thou mayest; for indeed what I have told thee of myself and my griefs is not all mere lying. Neither was it any lie that thou wert in peril of thy life amongst those tyrants of the Burg; thou with thy manly bearing, and free tongue, and bred, as I judge, to hate cruel deeds and injustice. Such freedom they cannot away with in that fellowship of hard men-at-arms; and soon hadst thou come to harm amongst them. And further, let alone that it is not ill to be sundered from yonder company, who mayhap will have rough work to do or ever they win home, I have nought to do to bring thee to Hampton under Scaur if thou hast no will to go thither: though certes I would lead thee some whither, whereof thou shalt ask me nought as now; yet will I say thereof this much, that there thou shalt be both safe and well at ease. Now lastly know this, that whatever I have done, I have done it to do thee good and not ill; and there is also another one, whom I will not name to thee, who wisheth thee better yet, by the token of those two strokes stricken by thee in the Wood Perilous before yesterday was a day."

Now when Ralph heard those last words, such strong and sweet hope and desire stirred in him to see that woman of the Want-ways of the Wood Perilous that he forgat all else, except that he must nowise fall to strife with Roger, lest they should sunder, and he should lose the help of him, which he now deemed would bring him to sight of her whom he had unwittingly come to long for more than aught else; so he spake to Roger quietly and humbly: "Well, faring-fellow, thou seest how I am little more than a lad, and have fallen into matters mighty and perilous, which I may not deal with of my own strength, at least until I get nigher to them so that I may look them in the eyes, and strike a stroke or two on them if they be at enmity with me. So I bid thee lead me whither thou wilt, and if thou be a traitor to me, on thine own head be it; in good sooth, since I know nought of this wood and since I might go astray and so come back to the Burg where be those whom thou hast now made my foemen, I am content to take thee on thy word, and to hope the best of thee, and ask no question of thee, save whitherward."

"Fair sir," said Roger, "away from this place at least; for we are as yet over nigh to the Burg to be safe: but as to elsewhither we may wend, thereof we may speak on the road as we have leisure."

Therewith he smote his horse with his heel and they went forward at a smart trot, for the horses were unwearied, and the wood thereabouts of beech and clear of underwood; and Roger seemed to know his way well, and made no fumbling over it.

Four hours or more gone, the wood thinned and the beeches failed, and they came to a country, still waste, of little low hills, stony for the more part, beset with scraggy thorn-bushes, and here and there some other berry-tree sown by the birds. Then said Roger: "Now I deem us well out of the peril of them of the Burg, who if they follow the chase as far as the sundering of us and the others, will heed our slot nothing, but will follow on that of the company: so we may breathe our horses a little, though their bait will be but small in this rough waste: therein we are better off than they, for lo you, saddle bags on my nag and meat and drink therein."

So they lighted down and let their horses graze what they could, while they ate and drank; amidst which Ralph again asked Roger of whither they were going. Said Roger: "I shall lead thee to a good harbour, and a noble house of a master of mine, wherein thou mayst dwell certain days, if thou hast a mind thereto, not without solace maybe."

"And this master," said Ralph, "is he of the Dry Tree?" Said Roger: "I scarce know how to answer thee without lying: but this I say, that whether he be or not, this is true; amongst those men I have friends and amongst them foes; but fate bindeth me to them for a while." Said Ralph reddening: "Be there any women amongst them?" "Yea, yea," quoth Roger, smiling a little, "doubt not thereof."

"And that Lady of the Dry Tree," quoth Ralph, reddening yet more, but holding up his head, "that woman whereof the Burgher spoke so bitterly, threatening her with torments and death if they might but lay hold of her; what wilt thou tell me concerning her?" "But little," said Roger, "save this, that thou desirest to see her, and that thou mayest have thy will thereon if thou wilt be guided by me."

Ralph hearkened as if he heeded little what Roger said; but presently he rose up and walked to and fro in short turns with knit brows as one pondering a hard matter. He spake nought, and Roger seemed to heed him nothing, though in sooth he looked at him askance from time to time, till at last he came and lay down again by Roger, and in a while he spake: "I wot not why ye of the Dry Tree want me, or what ye will do with me; and but for one thing I would even now ride away from thee at all adventure."

Roger said: "All this ye shall learn later on, and shalt find it but a simple matter; and meanwhile I tell thee again that all is for thy gain and thy pleasure. So now ride away if thou wilt; who hindereth thee? certes not I."

"Nay," said Ralph, "I will ride with thee first to that fair house; and afterwards we shall see what is to hap." "Yea," quoth Roger, "then let us to horse straightway, so that we may be there if not before dark night yet at least before bright morn; for it is yet far away."

CHAPTER 17

Ralph Cometh to the House of Abundance

Therewithal they gat to horse and rode away through that stony land, wherein was no river, but for water many pools in the bottoms, with little brooks running from them. But after a while they came upon a ridge somewhat high, on the further side whereof was a wide valley well-grassed and with few trees, and no habitation of man that they might see. But a wide river ran down the midst of it; and it was now four hours after noon. Quoth Roger: "The day wears and we shall by no means reach harbour before dark night, even if we do our best: art thou well used to the water, lord?" "Much as a mallard is," said Ralph. Said Roger: "That is well, for though there is a ford some mile and a half down stream, for that same reason it is the way whereby men mostly cross the water into the wildwood; and here again we are more like to meet foes than well-wishers; or at the least there will be question of who we are, and whence and whither; and we may stumble in our answers." Said Ralph: "There is no need to tarry, ride we down to the water."

So did they, and took the water, which was deep, but not swift. On the further side they clomb up a hill somewhat steep; at the crown they drew rein to give their horses breath, and Ralph turned in his saddle and looked down on to the valley, and as aforesaid he was clear-sighted and far-sighted; now he said: "Fellow-farer, I see the riding of folk down below there, and meseems they be spurring toward the water; and they have weapons: there! dost thou not see the gleam?"

"I will take thy word for it, fair sir," said Roger, "and will even spur, since they be the first men whom we have seen since we left the thickets." And therewith he went off at a hand gallop, and Ralph followed him without more ado.

They rode up hill and down dale of a grassy downland, till at last they saw a wood before them again, and soon drew rein under the boughs; for now were their horses somewhat wearied. Then said Ralph: "Here have we ridden a fair land, and seen neither house nor herd, neither sheep-cote nor shepherd. I wonder thereat."

Said Roger: "Thou wouldst wonder the less didst thou know the story of it." "What story?" said Ralph. Quoth Roger: "A story of war and wasting." "Yea?" said Ralph, "yet surely some bold knight or baron hath rights in the land, and might be free to build him a strong house and gather men to him to guard the shepherds and husbandmen from burners and lifters." "Sooth is that," said Roger; "but there are other things in the tale." "What things?" said Ralph. Quoth Roger: "Ill hap and sorrow and the Hand of Fate and great Sorcery." "And dastards withal?" said Ralph. "Even so," said Roger, "yet mingled with valiant men. Over long is the tale to tell as now, so low as the sun is; so now ride we on with little fear of foemen. For look you, this wood, like the thickets about the Burg of the Four Friths, hath an evil name, and few folk ride it uncompelled; therefore it is the safer for us. And yet I will say this to thee, that whereas awhile agone thou mightest have departed from me with little peril of aught save the stumbling on some of the riders of the Burg of the Four Friths, departing from me now will be a hard matter to thee; for the saints in Heaven only know whitherward thou shouldest come, if thou wert to guide thyself now. This a rough word, but a true one, so help me God and Saint Michael! What sayest thou; art thou content, or wilt thou cast hard words at me again?"

So it was that for all that had come and gone Ralph was light-hearted and happy; so he laughed and said: "Content were I, even if I were not compelled thereto. For my heart tells me of new things, and marvellous and joyous that I shall see ere long."

"And thine heart lieth not," said Roger, "for amidst of this wood is the house where we shall have guesting to-night, which will be to thee, belike, the door of life and many marvels. For thence have folk sought ere now to the WELL AT THE WORLD'S END."

Ralph turned to him sharply and said: "Many times in these few days have I heard that word. Dost thou know the meaning thereof? For as to me I know it not." Said Roger: "Thou mayst well be as wise as I am thereon: belike men seek to it for their much thriving, and oftenest find it not. Yet have I heard that they be the likeliest with whom all women are in love."

Ralph held his peace, but Roger noted that he reddened at the word.

Now they got on horseback again, for they had lighted down to breath their beasts, and they rode on and on, and never was Roger at fault: long with the way and perforce they rested at whiles, so that night fell upon them in the wood, but the moon rose withal. So night being fairly come, they rested a good while, as it would be dawn before moon-set. Then they rode on again, till now the summer night grew old and waned, but the wood hid the beginnings of dawn.

At last they came out of the close wood suddenly into an open plain, and now, as the twilight of the dawn was passing into early day, they saw that wide grassy meadows and tilled fields lay before them, with a little river running through the plain; and amidst the meadows, on a green mound, was a white castle, strong, and well built, though not of the biggest.

Roger pointed to it, and said, "Now we are come home," and cried on his wearied beast, who for his part seemed to see the end of his journey. They splashed through a ford of the river and came to the gate of the castle as day drew on apace; Roger blew a blast on a great horn that hung on the gate, and Ralph looking round deemed he had never seen fairer building than in the castle, what he could see of it, and yet it was built from of old. They waited no long while before they were answered; but whereas Ralph looked to see armed gatewards peer from the battlements or the shot window, and a porter espying them through a lattice, it happened in no such way, but without more ado the wicket was opened to them by a tall old woman, gaunt and grey, who greeted them courteously: Roger lighted down and Ralph did in likewise, and they led their horses through the gate into the court of the castle; the old woman going before them till they came to the hall door, which she opened to them, and taking the reins of their horses led them away to the stable, while those twain entered the hall, which was as goodly as might be. Roger led Ralph up to a board on the dais, whereon there was meat and drink enow, and Ralph made his way-leader sit down by him, and they fell to. There was no serving-man to wait on them nor a carle of any kind did they see; the old woman only, coming back from the horses, served them at table. Ever as she went about she looked long on Ralph, and seemed as if she would have spoken to him, but as often, she glanced at Roger and forbore.

So when they were well nigh done with their meat Ralph spake to the carline and said: "Belike the lord or the lady of this house are abed and we shall not see them till the morrow?"

Ere the carline could speak Roger broke in and said: "There is neither lord nor lady in the castle as now, nor belike will there be to-morrow morning, or rather, before noon on this day; so now ye were better to let this dame lead thee to bed, and let the next hours take care of themselves."

"So be it," said Ralph, who was by this time heartily wearied, "shall we two lie in the same chamber?"

"Nay," said the carline shortly, "lodging for the master and lodging for the man are two different things."

Roger laughed and said nought, and Ralph gave him good

night, and followed the carline nothing loth, who led him to a fair chamber over the solar, as if he had been the very master of the castle, and he lay down in a very goodly bed, nor troubled himself as to where Roger lay, nor indeed of aught else, nor did he dream of Burg, or wood, or castle, or man, or woman; but lay still like the image of his father's father on the painted tomb in the choir of St. Laurence of Upmeads.

CHAPTER 18

Of Ralph in the Castle of Abundance

Broad lay the sun upon the plain amidst the wildwood when he awoke and sprang out of bed and looked out of the window (for the chamber was in the gable of the hall and there was nought of the castle beyond it). It was but little after noon of a fair June day, for Ralph had slumbered as it behoved a young man. The light wind bore into the chamber the sweet scents of the early summer, the chief of all of them being the savour of the new-cut grass, for about the wide meadows the carles and queens were awork at the beginning of hay harvest; and late as it was in the day, more than one blackbird was singing from the bushes of the castle pleasance. Ralph sighed for very pleasure of life before he had yet well remembered where he was or what had befallen of late; but as he stood at the window and gazed over the meadows, and the memory of all came back to him, he sighed once more for a lack of somewhat that came into his heart, and he smiled shamefacedly, though there was no one near, as his thought bade him wonder if amongst the haymaking women yonder there were any as fair as those yellow-clad thrall-women of the Burg; and as he turned from the window a new hope made his heart beat, for he deemed that he had been brought to that house that he might meet some one who should change his life and make him a new man.

So he did on his raiment and went his ways down to the hall, and looked about for Roger, but found him not, nor any one else save the carline, who presently came in from the buttery, and of whom he asked, where was Roger. Quoth she: "He has been gone these six hours, but hath left a word for thee, lord, to wit, that he beseeches thee to abide him here for two days at the least, and thereafter thou art free to go if thou wilt. But as for me" (and therewith she smiled on him as sweetly as her wrinkled old face might compass) "I say to thee, abide beyond those two days if Roger cometh not, and as long as thou art here I will make thee all the cheer I may. And who knoweth but thou mayest meet worthy adventures here. Such have ere now befallen good knights in this house or anigh it."

"I thank thee, mother," quoth Ralph, "and it is like that I may abide here beyond the two days if the adventure befall me not ere then. But at least I will bide the eating of my dinner here to-day."

"Well is thee, fair lord," said the carline. "If thou wilt but walk in the meadow but a little half hour all shall be ready for thee. Forsooth it had been dight before now, but that I waited thy coming forth from thy chamber, for I would not wake thee. And the saints be praised for the long sweet sleep that hath painted thy goodly cheeks." So saying she hurried off to the buttery, leaving Ralph laughing at her outspoken flattering words.

Then he got him out of the hall and the castle, for no door was shut, and there was no man to be seen within or about the house. So he walked to and fro the meadow and saw the neat-herds in the pasture, and the hay-making folk beyond them, and the sound of their voices came to him on the little airs that were breathing. He thought he would talk to some of these folk ere the world was much older, and also he noted between the river and the wood many cots of the husbandmen trimly builded and thatched, and amidst them a little church, white and delicate of fashion; but as now his face was set toward the river because of the hot day. He came to a pool a little below where a wooden foot-bridge crossed the water, and about the pool were willows growing, which had not been shrouded these eight years, and the water was clear as glass with a bottom of fine sand. There then he bathed him, and as he sported in the water he bethought him of the long smooth reaches of Upmeads Water, and the swimming low down amidst the long swinging weeds between the chuckle of the reed sparrows, when the sun was new risen in the July morning. When he stood on the grass again, what with the bright weather and fair little land, what with the freshness of the water, and his good rest, and the hope of adventure to come, he felt as if he had never been merrier in his life-days. Withal it was a weight off his heart that he had escaped from the turmoil of the wars of the Burg of the Four Friths, and the men of the Dry Tree, and the Wheat-wearers, with the thralldom and stripes and fire-raising, and the hard life of strife and gain of the walled town and strong place.

When he came back to the castle gate there was the carline in the wicket peering out to right and left, seeking him to bring him in to dinner. And when she saw him so joyous, with his lips smiling and his eyes dancing for mirth, she also became joyous, and said: "Verily, it is a pity of thee that there is never a fair damsel or so to look on thee and love thee here to-day. Far would many a maiden run to kiss thy mouth, fair lad. But now come to thy meat, that thou mayest grow the fairer and last the longer."

He laughed gaily and went into the hall with her, and now was it well dight with bankers and dorsars of goodly figured cloth, and on the walls a goodly halling of arras of the Story of Alexander. So he sat to table, and the meat and drink was of the best, and the carline served him, praising him ever with fulsome words as he ate, till he wished her away.

After dinner he rested awhile, and called to the carline and bade her bring him his sword and his basnet. "Wherefore?" said she. "Whither wilt thou?"

Said he, "I would walk abroad to drink the air."

"Wilt thou into the wildwood?" said she.

"Nay, mother," he said, "I will but walk about the meadow and look on the hay-making folk."

"For that," said the carline, "thou needest neither sword

nor helm. I was afeard that thou wert about departing, and thy departure would be a grief to my heart: in the deep wood thou mightest be so bestead as to need a sword in thy fist; but what shouldst thou do with it in this Plain of Abundance, where are nought but peaceful husbandmen and frank and kind maidens? and all these are as if they had drunk a draught of the WELL AT THE WORLD'S END."

Ralph started as she said the word, but held his peace awhile. Then he said: "And who is lord of this fair land?" "There is no lord, but a lady," said the carline. "How hight she?" said Ralph. "We call her the Lady of Abundance," said the old woman. Said Ralph: "Is she a good lady?" "She is my lady," said the carline, "and doeth good to me, and there is not a carle in the land but speaketh well of her—it may be over well." "Is she fair to look on?" said Ralph. "Of women-folk there is none fairer," said the carline; "as to men, that is another thing."

Ralph was silent awhile, then he said: "What is the Well at the World's End?"

"They talk of it here," said she, "many things too long to tell of now: but there is a book in this house that telleth of it; I know it well by the look of it though I may not read in it. I will seek it for thee to-morrow if thou wilt."

"Have thou thanks, dame," said he; "and I pray thee forget it not; but now I will go forth."

"Yea," said the carline, "but abide a little."

Therewith she went into the buttery, and came back bearing with her a garland of roses of the garden, intermingled with green leaves, and she said: "The sun is yet hot and over hot, do this on thine head to shade thee from the burning. I knew that thou wouldst go abroad to-day, so I made this for thee in the morning; and when I was young I was called the garland-maker. It is better summer wear than thy basnet."

He thanked her and did it on smiling, but somewhat ruefully; for he said to himself: "This is over old a dame that I should wear a love-token from her." But when it was on his head, the old dame clapped her hands and cried: "O there, there! Now art thou like the image of St. Michael in the Choir of Our Lady of the Thorn: there is none so lovely as thou. I would my Lady could see thee thus; surely the sight of thee should gladden her heart. And withal thou art not ill clad otherwise."

Indeed his raiment was goodly, for his surcoat was new, and it was of fine green cloth, and the coat-armour of Upmead was beaten on it, to wit, on a gold ground an apple-tree fruited, standing by a river-side.

Now he laughed somewhat uneasily at her words, and so went forth from the castle again, and made straight for the hay-making folk on the other side of the water; for all this side was being fed by beasts and sheep; but at the point where he crossed, the winding of the stream brought it near to the castle gate. So he came up with the country folk and greeted them, and they did as much by him in courteous words: they were goodly and well-shapen, both men and women, gay and joyous of demeanour and well clad as for folk who work afield. So Ralph went from one to another and gave them a word or two, and was well pleased to watch them at their work awhile; but yet he would fain speak somewhat more with one or other of them. At last under the shade of a tall elm-tree he saw an old man sitting heeding the outer raiment of the haymakers and their victual and bottles of drink; and he came up to him and gave him the sele of the day; and the old man blessed him and said: "Art thou dwelling in my lady's castle, fair lord?" "A while at least," said Ralph. Said the old man: "We thank thee for coming to see us; and meseemeth from the look of thee thou art worthy to dwell in my Lady's House."

"What sayest thou?" said Ralph. "Is she a good lady and a gracious?" "O yea, yea," said the carle. Said Ralph: "Thou meanest, I suppose, that she is fair to look on, and soft-spoken when she is pleased?"

"I mean far more than that," said the carle; "surely is she most heavenly fair, and her voice is like the music of heaven: but withal her deeds, and the kindness of her to us poor men and husbandmen, are no worse than should flow forth from that loveliness."

"Will you be her servants?" said Ralph, "or what are ye?" Said the carle: "We be yeomen and her vavassors; there is no thralldom in our land." "Do ye live in good peace for the more part?" said Ralph. Said the carle: "Time has been when

96

cruel battles were fought in these wood-lawns, and many poor people were destroyed therein: but that was before the coming of the Lady of Abundance."

"And when was that?" said Ralph. "I wot not," said the old carle; "I was born in peace and suckled in peace; and in peace I fell to the loving of maidens, and I wedded in peace, and begat children in peace, and in peace they dwell about me, and in peace shall I depart."

"What then," said Ralph (and a grievous fear was born in his heart), "is not the Lady of Abundance young?" Said the carle: "I have seen her when I was young and also since I have been old, and ever was she fair and lovely, and slender handed, as straight as a spear, and as sweet as white clover, and gentle-voiced and kind, and dear to our souls."

"Yea," said Ralph, "and she doth not dwell in this castle always; where else then doth she dwell?" "I wot not," said the carle, "but it should be in heaven: for when she cometh to us all our joys increase in us by the half."

"Look you, father," said Ralph, "May it not have been more than one Lady of Abundance that thou hast seen in thy life-days; and that this one that now is, is the daughter's daughter of the one whom thou first sawest—how sayest thou?" The carle laughed: "Nay, nay," said he, "It is not so: never has there been another like to her in all ways, in body and voice, and heart and soul. It is as I say, she is the same as she was always." "And when," said Ralph, with a beating heart, "does she come hither? Is it at some set season?" "Nay, from time to time, at all seasons," said the carle; "and as fair she is when she goeth over the snow, as when her feet are set amidst the June daisies."

Now was Ralph so full of wonder that he scarce knew what to say; but he bethought him of that fair waste on the other side of the forest, the country through which that wide river flowed, so he said: "And that land north-away beyond the wildwood, canst thou tell me the tale of its wars, and if it were wasted in the same wars that tormented this land?" The carle shook his head: "As to the land beyond this wood," quoth he, "I know nought of it, for beyond the wood go we never: nay, most often we go but a little way into it, no further than we can see the glimmer of the open daylight through its trees,—the daylight of the land of Abundance—that is enough for us."

"Well," said Ralph, "I thank thee for the tale thou hast told me, and wish thee more years of peace."

"And to thee, young man," said the carle, "I wish a good wish indeed, to wit that thou mayest see the Lady of Abundance here before thou departest."

His words once more made Ralph's heart beat and his cheek flush, and he went back to the castle somewhat speedily; for he said to himself, after the folly of lovers, "Maybe she will be come even now, and I not there to meet her." Yet when he came to the castle-gate his heart misgave him, and he would not enter at once, but turned about to go round the wall by the north and west. In the castle he saw no soul save the old dame looking out of the window and nodding to him, but in the pasture all about were neatherds and shepherds, both men and women; and at the north-west corner, whereas the river drew quite close to the wall, he came upon two damsels of the field-folk fishing with an angle in a quiet pool of the stream. He greeted them, and they, who were young and goodly, returned his greeting, but were shamefaced at his gallant presence, as indeed was he at the thoughts of his heart mingled with the sight of their fairness. So he passed on at first without more words than his greeting. Yet presently he turned back again, for he longed to hear some word more concerning the Lady whose coming he abode. They stood smiling and blushing as he came up to them again, and heeded their angles little.

Said Ralph: "Fair maidens, do ye know at all when the Lady of the castle may be looked for?" They were slow to answer, but at last one said: "No, fair sir, such as we know nothing of the comings and goings of great folk."

Said Ralph, smiling on her for kindness, and pleasure of her fairness: "Is it not so that ye will be glad of her coming?"

But she answered never a word, only looked at him steadily, with her great grey eyes fixed in wonderment, while the other one looked down as if intent on her angling tools.

Ralph knew not how to ask another question, so he turned

about with a greeting word again, and this time went on steadily round about the wall.

And now in his heart waxed the desire of that Lady, once seen, as he deemed, in such strange wise; but he wondered within himself if the devil had not sown that longing within him: whereas it might be that this woman on whom he had set his heart was herself no real woman but a devil, and one of the goddesses of the ancient world, and his heart was sore and troubled by many doubts and hopes and fears; but he said to himself that when he saw her then could he judge between the good and the evil, and could do or forbear, and that the sight of her would cure all.

Thus thinking he walked swiftly, and was soon round at the castle gate again, and entered, and went into the hall, where was the old dame, busied about some household matter. Ralph nodded to her and hastened away, lest she should fall to talk with him; and he set himself now to go from chamber to chamber, that he might learn the castle, what it was. He came into the guard-chamber and found the walls thereof all hung with armour and weapons, clean and in good order, though there was never a man-at-arms there, nor any soul except the old woman. He went up a stair therefrom on to the battlements, and went into the towers of the wall, and found weapons both for hand, and for cast and shot in each one of them, and all ready as if for present battle; then he came down into the court again and went into a very goodly ambulatory over against the hall, and he entered a door therefrom, which was but on the latch, and went up a little stair into a chamber, which was the goodliest and the richest of all. Its roof was all done with gold and blue from over sea, and its pavement wrought delicately in Alexandrine work. On the dais was a throne of carven ivory, and above it a canopy of baudekin of the goodliest fashion, and there was a foot-carpet before it, wrought with beasts and the hunting of the deer. As for the walls of that chamber, they were hung with a marvellous halling of arras, wherein was wrought the greenwood, and there amidst in one place a pot-herb garden, and a green garth with goats therein, and in that garth a little thatched house. And amidst all this greenery were figured over and over again two women, whereof one old and the other young; and the old one was clad in grand attire, with gold chains and brooches and rings, and sat with her hands before her by the house door, or stood looking on as the young one worked, spinning or digging in the garth, or milking the goats outside of it, or what not; and this one was clad in sorry and scanty raiment.

What all this might mean Ralph knew not; but when he had looked long at the greenery and its images, he said to himself that if he who wrought that cloth had not done the young woman after the likeness of the Lady whom he had helped in the wildwood, then it must have been done from her twin sister.

Long he abode in that chamber looking at the arras, and wondering whether the sitter in the ivory throne would be any other than the thrall in the greenwood cot. He abode there so long that the dusk began to gather in the house, and he could see the images no more; for he was filled with the sweetness of desire when he looked on them.

Then he went back slowly to the hall, and found the carline, who had lighted the waxlights and made meat ready for him; and when she saw him she cried out joyously: "Ah, I knew that thou wouldst come back. Art thou well content with our little land?"

"I like it well, dame," said he; "but tell me, if thou canst, what is the meaning of the halling in the chamber with the ivory throne?"

Said the carline: "Thereof shall another tell thee, who can tell of it better than I; but it is nought to hide that yonder chamber is the chamber of estate of our Lady, and she sitteth there to hear the cases of folk and to give dooms."

The old woman crossed herself as she spoke, and Ralph wondered thereat, but asked no more questions, for he was scarce sorry that the carline would not tell him thereof, lest she should spoil the tale.

So passed the evening, and he went to bed and slept as a young man should, and the next day he was up betimes and went abroad and mingled with the carles and queens afield; but this time he spake not of the Lady, and heard nought to heed from any of that folk. So he went back to the castle and gat him a bow and arrows, and entered the thicket of the

100

wood nigh where he and Roger first came out of it. He had prayed a young man of the folk to go with him, but he was not over willing to go, though he would not say wherefore. So Ralph went himself by himself and wandered some way into the wood, and saw nought worse than himself. As he came back, making a circuit toward the open meadows, he happened on a herd of deer in a lonely place, half wood half meadow, and there he slew a hart with one shaft, for he was a deft bowman. Then he went and fetched a leash of carles, who went with him somewhat less than half willingly, and between them they broke up the hart and carried him home to the castle, where the carline met them. She smiled on Ralph and praised the venison, and said withal that the hunting was well done; "For, as fond and as fair as thou mayst be, it is not good that young men should have their minds set on one thing only." Therewith she led him in to his meat, and set him down and served him; and all the while of his dinner he was longing to ask her if she deemed that the Lady would come that day, since it was the last day of those which Roger had bidden him wait; but the words would not out of his mouth.

She looked at him and smiled, as though she had a guess of his thought, and at last she said to him: "Thy tongue is tied to-day. Hast thou, after all, seen something strange in the wood?" He shook his head for naysay. Said she: "Why, then, dost thou not ask more concerning the Well at the World's End?"

He laughed, and said: "Maybe because I think that thou canst not tell me thereof." "Well," she said, "if I cannot, yet the book may, and this evening, when the sun is down, thou shalt have it."

"I thank thee, mother," said he; "but this is now the last day that Roger bade me wait. Dost thou think that he will come back to-night?" and he reddened therewith. "Nay," she said, "I know not, and thou carest not whether he will come or not. Yet I know that thou wilt abide here till some one else come, whether that be early or late." Again he reddened, and said, in a coaxing way: "And wilt thou give me guesting, mother, for a few more summer days?"

"Yea," she said, "and till summer is over, if need be, and

the corn is cut and carried, and till the winter is come and the latter end of winter is gone." He smiled faintly, though his heart fell, and he said: "Nay, mother, and can it by any chance be so long a-coming?"

"O, fair boy," she said, "thou wilt make it long, howsoever short it be. And now I will give thee a rede, lest thou vex thyself sick and fret thy very heart. To-morrow go see if thou canst meet thy fate instead of abiding it. Do on thy war-gear and take thy sword and try the adventure of the wildwood; but go not over deep into it." Said he: "But how if the Lady come while I am away from this house?"

"Sooth to say," said the carline, "I deem not that she will, for the way is long betwixt us and her."

"Dost thou mean," said Ralph, standing up from the board, "that she will not come ever? I adjure thee not to beguile me with soft words, but tell me the very sooth." "There, there!" said she, "sit down, king's son; eat thy meat and drink thy wine; for to-morrow is a new day. She will come soon or late, if she be yet in the world. And now I will say no more to thee concerning this matter."

Therewith she went her ways from the hall, and when she came back with hand-basin and towel, she said no word to him, but only smiled kindly. He went out presently into the meadow (for it was yet but early afternoon) and came among the haymaking folk and spake with them, hoping that perchance some of them might speak again of the Lady of Abundance; but none of them did so, though the old carle he had spoken with was there, and there also were the two maidens whom he had seen fishing; and as for him, he was over faint-hearted to ask them any more questions concerning her.

Yet he abode with them long, and ate and drank amidst the hay with them till the moon shone brightly. Then he went back to the castle and found the carline in the hall, and she had the book with her and gave it to him, and he sat down in the shot-window under the waxlights and fell to reading of it.

CHAPTER 19

Ralph Readeth in a Book Concerning the Well at the World's End

Fairly written was that book, with many pictures therein, the meaning of which Ralph knew not; but amongst them was the image of the fair woman whom he had holpen at the want-ways of the wood, and but four days ago was that, yet it seemed long and long to him. The book told not much about the Well at the World's End, but much it told of a certain woman whom no man that saw her could forbear to love: of her it told that erewhile she dwelt lonely in the wildwood (though how she came there was not said) and how a king's son found her there and brought her to his father's kingdom and wedded her, whether others were lief or loth: and in a little while, when the fame of her had spread, he was put out of his kingdom and his father's house for the love of her, because other kings and lords hankered after her; whereof befel long and grievous war which she abode not to the end, but sought to her old place in the wildwood; and how she found there another woman a sorceress, who made her her thrall; and tormented her grievously with toil and stripes. And how again there came a knight to that place who was seeking the Well at the World's End, and bore her away with him; and how the said knight was slain on the way, and she was taken by tyrants and robbers of the folk: but these being entangled in her love fought amongst themselves and she escaped, and went seeking that Well, and found it at the long last, and drank thereof, and throve ever after: and how she liveth yet, and is become the servant of the Well to entangle the seekers in her love and keep them from drinking thereof; because there was no man that beheld her, but anon he was the thrall of her love, and might not pluck his heart away from her to do any of the deeds whereby men thrive and win the praise of the people.

Ralph read on and on till the short night waned, and the wax-lights failed one after the other, and the windows of the hall grew grey and daylight came, and the throstles burst out a-singing at once in the castle pleasaunce, and the sun came up over the wood, and the sound of men-folk bestirring themselves a-field came to his ears through the open windows; and at last he was done with the tale, and the carline came not near him though the sun had clomb high up the heavens. As for Ralph, what he had read was sweet poison to him; for if before he was somewhat tormented by love, now was his heart sick and sore with it. Though he knew not for certain whether this tale had to do with the Lady of the Forest, and though he knew not if the Lady who should come to the castle were even she, yet he needs must deem that so it was, and his heart was weary with love. and his manhood seemed changed.

CHAPTER 20

Ralph Meeteth a Man
in the Wood

But the morning began to wear as he sat deep in these thoughts and still the Carline came not to him; and he thought: "She leaveth me alone that I may do her bidding: so will I without tarrying." And he arose and did on his hauberk and basnet, and girt his sword to his side, and went forth, a-foot as before. He crossed the river by a wide ford and stepping stones somewhat below the pool wherein he had bathed on that first day; and already by then he had got so far, what with the fresh air of the beauteous morning, what with the cheerful tinkling of his sword and hauberk, he was somewhat amended of his trouble and heaviness of spirit. A little way across the river, but nigher to the wood, was a house or cot of that country-folk, and an old woman sat spinning in the door. So Ralph went up thither, and greeted her, and craved of her a draught of milk; so the goody turned about and cried out to one within, and there came forth one of the maidens whom Ralph had met fishing that other day, and the old woman bade her bring forth milk and bread. Then the carline looked hard at Ralph, and said: "Ah! I have heard tell of thee: thou art abiding the turn of the days up at the castle yonder, as others have done before thee. Well, well, belike thou shalt have thy wish, though whether it shall be to thy profit, who shall say?"

Thereat Ralph's heart fell again, and he said: "Sayest thou, mother, that there have been others abiding like me in the tower? I know not what thy words mean."

The carline laughed. "Well," said she, "here comes thy morning's bait borne by shapely hands enough; eat and drink first; and then will I tell thee my meaning."

Therewith came the maiden forth with the bowl and the loaf; and indeed she was fair enough, and shy and kind; but Ralph heeded her little, nor was his heart moved by her at all. She set a stool for him beside the door and he sat down and ate and drank, though his heart was troubled; and the maiden hung about, and seemed to find it no easy matter to keep her eyes off him.

Presently the carline, who had been watching the two, said: "Thou askest of the meaning of my words; well, deemest thou that I have had more men than one to love me?" "I know not, mother," said Ralph, who could scarce hold himself patient. "There now!" quoth the carline, "look at my damsel! (she is not my daughter, but my brother's,) there is a man, and a brisk lad too, whom she calleth her batchelor, and is as I verily deem well-pleased with him: yet lo you how she eyeth thee, thou fair man, and doth so with her raiment that thou mayst best see how shapely she is of limb and foot, and toyeth her right hand with her left wrist, and the like.—Well, as for me, I have had more lovers than one or two. And why have I had just so many and no more? Nay, thou needest not make any long answer to me. I am old now, and even before I was old I was not young: I am now

105

foul of favour, and even before I became foul, I was not so fair—well then?"

"Yea, what then?" said Ralph. "This then, fair young fool," said she: "the one whom thou lovest, long hath she lived, but she is not old to look on, nor foul; but fair—O how fair!"

Then Ralph forgot his fear, and his heart grew greedy and his eyes glistened, and he said, yet he spoke faintly: "Yea, is she fair?" "What! hast thou not seen her?" said the carline. Ralph called to mind the guise in which he had seen her and flushed bright red, as he answered: "Yea, I deem that I have: surely it was she." The carline laughed: "Well," said she; "however thou hast seen her, thou hast scarce seen her as I have." Said Ralph, "How was that?" Said she: "It is her way here in the summer-tide to bathe her in yonder pool up the water:" (and it was the same pool wherein Ralph had bathed) "And she hath me and my niece and two other women to hold up the silken cloth betwixt her body and the world; so that I have seen her as God made her; and I shall tell thee that when he was about that work he was minded to be a craftsmaster; for there is no blemish about her that she should hide her at all or anywhere. Her sides are sleek, and her thighs no rougher than her face, and her feet as dainty as her hands: yea, she is a pearl all over, withal she is as strong as a knight, and I warrant her hardier of heart than most knights. A happy man shalt thou be; for surely I deem thou hast not come hither to abide her without some token or warrant of her."

Ralph held down his head, and he could not meet the old woman's eyes as she spake thus; and the maiden took herself out of earshot at the first words of the carline hereof, and was halfway down to the river by now.

Ralph spake after a while and said: "Tell me, is she good, and a good woman?" The dame laughed scornfully and said: "Surely, surely; she is the saint of the Forest Land, and the guardian of all poor folk. Ask the carles else!"

Ralph held his peace, and rose to be gone and turning saw the damsel wading the shallow ford, and looking over her shoulder at him. He gave the dame good day, and departed light-foot but heavy hearted. Yet as he went, he kept saying to himself: "Did she not send that Roger to turn my ways hither? yet she cometh not. Surely she hath changed in these last days, or it may be in these last hours: yea, or this very hour."

Amidst such thoughts he came into the wood, and made his way by the paths and open places, going south and east of the House: Whereas the last day he had gone west and north. He went a soft pace, but wandered on without any stay till it was noon, and he had seen nought but the wild things of the wood, nor many of them. But at last he heard the tinkle of a little bell coming towards him: so he stood still and got the hilt of his sword ready to his hand; and the tinkle drew nearer, and he heard withal the trample of some riding-beast; so he went toward the sound, and presently in a clearer place of the wood came upon a man of religion, a clerk, riding on a hackney, to whose neck hung a horse-bell: the priest had saddle bags beside him and carried in his right hand a book in a bag. When he met Ralph he blessed him, and Ralph gave him the sele of the day, and asked him whither he would. Said the Priest: "I am for the Little Plain and the Land of Abundance; whence art thou, my son, and whither wilt thou?" "From that very land I come," said Ralph, "and as to whither, I seek adventures; but unless I see more than I have this forenoon, or thou canst tell me of them, back will I whence I came: yet to say sooth, I shall not be sorry for a fellow to help me back, for these woodland ways are some-what blind."

Said the Priest: "I will bear thee company with a good will; and I know the road right well; for I am the Vicar appointed by the fathers of the Thorn to serve the church of the Little Plain, and the chapel of St. Anthony yonder in the wood, and to-day I go to the church of the good folk there."

So Ralph turned, and went along with him, walking by his bridle-rein. And as they went the priest said to him: "Art thou one of my lady's lords?" Ralph reddened as he sighed, and said: "I am no captain of hers." Then smiled the priest and said: "Then will I not ask thee of thine errand; for belike thou wouldest not tell me thereof."

Ralph said nought, but waxed shamefaced as he deemed

that the priest eyed him curiously. At last he said: "I will ask thee a question in turn, father." "Yea," said the priest. Said Ralph: "This lady of the land, the Lady of Abundance, is she a very woman?" "Holy Saints!" quoth the priest, blessing himself, "what meanest thou?" Said Ralph: "I mean, is she of those who outwardly have a woman's semblance, but within are of the race of the ancient devils, the gods of the Gentiles?"

Then the priest crossed himself again, and spake as solemnly as a judge on the bench: "Son, I pray that if thou art not in thy right mind, thou will come thereinto anon. Know this, that whatever else she may be, she is a right holy woman. Or hast thou perchance heard any evil tales concerning her?"

Now Ralph was confused at his word, and knew not what to say; for though in his mind he had been piecing together all that he had heard of the lady both for good and for evil, he had no clear tale to tell even to himself: so he answered nothing.

But the priest went on: "Son, I shall tell thee that such tales I have heard, but from whose mouth forsooth? I will tell thee; from a sort of idle jades, young women who would be thought fairer than they be, who are afraid of everything save a naked man, and who can lie easier than they can say their paternoster: from such as these come the stories; or from old crones who live in sour anger with themselves and all else, because they have lived no goodly life in their youth, and have not learned the loveliness of holy church. Now, son, shall the tales of such women, old and young, weigh in thy mind beside the word I tell thee of what I have seen and know concerning this most excellent of ladies? I trow not. And for my part I tell thee, that though she is verily as fair as Venus (God save us) yet is she as chaste as Agnes, as wise as Katherine, and as humble and meek as Dorothy. She bestoweth her goods plentifully to the church, and is merciful to poor men therewith; and so far as occasion may serve her she is constant at the Holy Office; neither doth she spare to confess her sins, and to do all penance which is bidden her, yea and more. For though I cannot say to my knowledge that she weareth a hair; yet once and again have I seen her wending this woodland toward the chapel of her friend St. Anthony by night and cloud, so that few might see her, obedient to the Scripture which sayeth, 'Let not thy right hand know what thy left hand doeth,' and she barefoot in her smock amidst the rugged wood, and so arrayed fairer than any queen in a golden gown. Yea, as fair as the woodwives of the ancient heathen."

Therewith the priest stayed his words, and seemed as if he were fallen into a dream; and he sighed heavily. But Ralph walked on by his bridle-rein dreamy no less; for the words that he had heard he heeded not, save as they made pictures for him of the ways of that woman of the forest.

So they went on soberly till the priest lifted up his head and looked about like one come out of slumber, and said in a firm voice: "I tell thee, my son, that thou mayest set thy love upon her without sin." And therewith suddenly he fell a-weeping; and Ralph was ill at ease of his weeping, and went along by him saying nought; till the priest plucked up heart again, and said, turning to Ralph, but not meeting his eye: "My son, I weep because men and women are so evil, and mis-say each other so sorely, even as they do by this holy woman." As he spake his tears brake out again, and Ralph strode on fast, so as to outgo him, thinking it unmannerly to seem as if he noted not his sorrow; yet withal unable to say aught to him thereof. Moreover it irked him to hear a grown man weeping for grief, even though it were but a priest.

Within a while the priest caught up with him, his tears all staunched, and fell to talk with him cheerfully concerning the wood, and the Little Land and the dwellers therein and the conditions of them, and he praised them much, save the women. Ralph answered him with good cheer in likewise; and thus they came to the cot of the old woman, and both she and the maiden were without the house, the old carline hithering and thithering on some errand, the maiden leaning against a tree as if pondering some matter. As they passed by, the priest blessed them in words, but his eyes scowled on them, whereat the carline grinned, but the damsel heeded him not, but looked wistfully on Ralph. The priest muttered somewhat as he passed, which Ralph caught not the meaning of, and fell moody again; and when he was a little past the ford he drew rein and said: "Now, son, I must to my cell hard by the church yonder: but yet I will say one word to thee ere we sunder; to wit, that to my mind the Holy Lady will love no one but the saints of heaven, save it be some man with whom all women are in love."

Therewith he turned away suddenly, and rode smartly towards his church; and Ralph deemed that he was weeping once more. As for Ralph, he went quietly home toward the castle, for the sun was setting now, and as he went he pondered all these things in his heart.

CHAPTER 21

Ralph Weareth Away Three
Days Uneasily

He read again in the book that night, till he had gotten the whole tale into his head, and he specially noted this of it, that it told not whence that Lady came, nor what she was, nor aught else save that there she was in the wood by herself, and was found therein by the king's son: neither told the tale in what year of the world she was found there, though it told concerning all the war and miseries which she had bred, and which long endured. Again, he could not gather from that book why she had gone back to the lone place in the woods, whereas she might have wedded one of those warring barons who sorely desired her: nor why she had yielded herself to the witch of that place and endured with patience her thralldom, with stripes and torments of her body, like the worst of the thralls of the ancient heathen men. Lastly, he might not learn from the book where in the world was that lone place, or aught of the road to the Well at the World's End. But amidst all his thinking his heart came back to this: "When I meet her, she will tell me of it all; I need be no wiser than to learn how to meet her and to make her love me; then shall she show me the way to the Well at the World's End, and I shall drink thereof and never grow old, even as she endureth in youth, and she shall love me for ever, and I her for ever."

So he thought; but yet amidst these happy thoughts came in this evil one, that whereas all the men-folk spoke well of her and worshipped her, the women-folk feared her or hated her; even to the lecherous old woman who had praised the beauty of her body for his torment. So he thought till his head grew heavy, and he went and lay down in his bed and slept, and dreamed of the days of Upmead; and things forgotten in his waking time came between him and any memories of his present longing and the days thereof.

He awoke and arose betimes in the morning, and when he had breakfasted he bade the carline bring him his weapons. "Wilt thou again to the wood?" said she. "Didst thou not bid me fare thither yesterday?" said he. "Yea," she said; "but to-day I fear lest thou depart and come not back." He laughed and said: "Seest thou not, mother, that I go afoot, and I in hauberk and helm? I cannot run far or fast from thee. Also" (and here he broke off his speech a little) "where should I be but here?"

"Ah," she said, "but who knows what may happen?" Nevertheless she went and fetched his war-gear and looked at him fondly as he did it on, and went his ways from the hall.

Now he entered the wood more to the south than he had done yesterday, and went softly as before, and still was he turning over in his mind the thoughts of last night, and ever they came back. "Might I but see her! Would she but love me! O for a draught of the Well at the World's End, that the love might last long and long!"

So he went on a while betwixt the trees and the thickets, till it was a little past noon. But all on a sudden a panic fear took him, lest she should indeed come to the castle while he was away, and not finding him, depart again, who knows whither; and when this thought came upon him, he cried aloud, and hastened at his swiftest back again to the castle, and came there breathless and wearied, and ran to the old woman, and cried out to her; "Is she come? is she come?"

The carline laughed and said, "Nay, she is not, but thou art come: praise be to the saints! But what aileth thee? Nay, fear not, she shall come at last."

Then grew Ralph shamefaced and turned away from her, and miscalled himself for a fool and a dastard that could not abide the pleasure of his lady at the very place whereto she had let lead him. So he wore through the remnant of the day howso he might, without going out-adoors again; and the carline came and spake with him; but whatever he asked her about the lady, she would not tell aught of any import, so he refrained him from that talk, and made a show of hearkening when she spake of other matters; as tales concerning the folk of the land, and the Fathers of the Thorn, and so forth.

On the next morning he arose and said to himself, that whatever betid, he would bide in the castle and the Plain of Abundance till the lady came; and he went amongst the haymaking folk in the morning and ate his dinner with them, and strove to be of good cheer, and belike the carles and queens thought him merry company; but he was now wearying his heart with longing, and might not abide any great while in one place; so when, dinner over, they turned to their work again, he went back to the Castle, and read in that book, and looked at the pictures thereof, and kept turning his wonder and hope and fear over and over again in his mind, and making to himself stories of how he should meet the Lady and what she would say to him, and how he should answer her, till at last the night came, and he went to his bed, and slept for the very weariness of his longing.

When the new day came he arose and went into the hall, and found the carline there, who said to him, "Fair sir, wilt thou to the wood again to-day?" "Nay," said Ralph, "I must not, I dare not." "Well," she said, "thou mayest if thou wilt; why shouldst thou not go?" Said Ralph, reddening and stammering: "Because I fear to; thrice have I been away long from the castle and all has gone well; but the fourth time she will come and find me gone."

The carline laughed: "Well," she said, "I shall be here if thou goest; for I promise thee not to stir out of the house whiles thou art away." Said Ralph: "Nay, I will abide here." "Yea," she said, "I see: thou trustest me not. Well, no matter; and to-day it will be handy if thou abidest. For I have an errand to my brother in the flesh, who is one of the brethren of the Thorn over yonder. If thou wilt give me leave, it will be to my pleasure and gain."

Ralph was glad when he heard this, deeming that if she left him alone there, he would be the less tempted to stray into the wood again. Besides, he deemed that the Lady might come that day when he was alone in the Castle, and that himseemed would make the meeting sweeter yet. So he yea-said the carline's asking joyously, and in an hour's time she went her ways and left him alone there.

Ralph said to himself, when he saw her depart, that he would have the more joy in the castle of his Lady if he were alone, and would wear away the day in better patience therefor. But in sooth the hours of that day were worse to wear than any day there had yet been. He went not without the house at all that day, for he deemed that the folk abroad would note of him that he was so changed and restless.

Whiles he read in that book, or turned the leaves over, not reading it; whiles he went into the Chamber of Estate, and pored over the woven pictures there wherein the Lady was figured. Whiles he wandered from chamber to chamber, not knowing what to do.

At last, a little after dark, back comes the carline again, and he met her at the door of the hall, for he was weary of his own company, and the ceaseless turning over and over of the same thoughts.

As for her, she was so joyous of him that she fairly threw her arms about him and kissed and clipped him, as though she had been his very mother. Whereof he had some shame, but not much, for he deemed that her goodwill to him was abundant, which indeed it was.

Now she looks on him and says: "Truly it does my heart good to see thee: but thou poor boy, thou art wearing thyself with thy longing, and thy doubting, and if thou wilt do after my rede, thou wilt certainly go into the wood to-morrow and see what may befall; and indeed and in sooth thou wilt leave behind thee a trusty friend."

He looked on her kindly, and smiled, and said, "In sooth, mother, I deem thou art but right; though it be hard for me to leave this house, to which in a way my Lady hath bidden me. Yet I will do thy bidding herein." She thanked him, and he went to his bed and slept; for now that he had made up his mind to go, he was somewhat more at rest.

CHAPTER 22

An Adventure in the Wood

Ralph arrayed himself for departure next morning without more words; and when he was ready the carline said to him: "When thou wentest forth before, I was troubled at thy going and feared for thy returning: but now I fear not; for I know that thou wilt return; though it may be leading a fair woman by the hand. So go, and all luck go with thee." Ralph smiled at her words and went his ways, and came into the wood that lay due south from the Castle, and he went on and on and had no thought of turning back. He rested twice and still went on, till the fashion of the thickets and the woods changed about him; and at last when the sun was getting low, he saw light gleaming through a great wood of pines, which had long been dark before him against the tall boles, and soon he came to the very edge of the wood, and going heedfully, saw between the great stems of the outermost trees, a green strand, and beyond it a long smooth water, a little lake between green banks on either side. He came out of the pinewood on to the grass; but there were thornbushes a few about, so that moving warily from one to the other, he might perchance see without being seen. Warily he went forsooth, going along the green strand to the east and the head of that water, and saw how the bank sloped up gently from its ending toward the pine-wood, in front of whose close-set trees stood three great-boled tall oak-trees on a smooth piece of green sward. And now he saw that there were folk come before him on this green place, and keen-sighted as he was, could make out that three men were on the hither side of the oak-trees, and on the further side of them was a white horse. Thitherward then he made, stealing from bush to bush, since he deemed that he needed not be seen of men who might be foes, for at the first sight he had noted the gleam of weapons there. And now he had gone no long way before he saw the westering sun shine brightly from a naked sword, and then another sprang up to meet it, and he heard faintly the clash of steel, and saw withal that the third of the folk had long and light raiment and was a woman belike. Then he bettered his pace, and in a minute or two came so near that he could see the men clearly, that they were clad in knightly war-gear, and were laying on great strokes so that the still place rang with the clatter. As for the woman, he could see but little of her, because of the fighting men before her; and the shadow of the oak boughs fell on her withal.

Now as he went, hidden by the bushes, they hid the men also from him, and when he was come to the last bush, some fifty paces from them, and peered out from it, in that very nick of time the two knights were breathing them somewhat, and Ralph saw that one of them, the furthest from him, was a very big man with a blue surcoat whereon was beaten a great golden sun, and the other, whose back was towards Ralph, was clad in black over his armour. Even as he looked and doubted whether to show himself or not, he of the sun raised his sword aloft, and giving forth a great roar as of wrath and grief mingled together, rushed on his foe and smote so fiercely that he fell to the earth before him, and the big man fell upon him as he fell, and let knee and sword-pommel and fist follow the stroke, and there they wallowed on the earth together.

Straightway Ralph came forth from the bushes with his drawn sword in his hand, and even therewith what with the two knights being both low upon the earth, what with the woman herself coming from out the shadow of the oak boughs, and turning her toward Ralph, he saw her clearly, and stood staring and amazed—for lo! it was the Lady whom he had delivered at the want-ways. His heart well nigh stood still with joy, yet was he shamefaced also: for though now she was no longer clad in that scanty raiment, yet did he seem to see her body through that which covered it. But now her attire was but simple; a green gown, thin and short, and thereover a cote-hardy of black cloth with orphreys of gold and colours: but on her neck was a collar that seemed to him like to that which Dame Katherine had given him; and the long tresses of her hair, which he had erst seen floating loose about her, were wound as a garland around her head. She looked with a flushed and joyous face on Ralph, and seemed as if she heeded nought the battle of the knights, but saw him only: but he feared her, and his love for her and stood still, and durst not move forward to go to her.

Thus they abode for about the space of one minute: and meanwhile the big man rose up on one knee and steadied him with his sword for a moment of time, and the blade was bloody from the point half way up to the hilt; but the black knight lay still and made no sign of life. Then the Knight of the Sun rose up slowly and stood on his feet and faced the Lady and seemed not to see Ralph, for his back was towards him. He came slowly toward the Lady, scowling, and his face white as chalk; then he spake to her coldly and sternly, stretching out his bloody sword before her.

"I have done thy bidding, and slain my very earthly friend of friends for thy sake. Wherewith wilt thou reward me?"

Then once more Ralph heard the voice, which he remembered so sweet amidst peril and battle aforetime, as she said as coldly as the Knight: "I bade thee not: thine own heart bade thee to strive with him because thou deemedst that he loved me. Be content! thou hast slain him who stood in thy way, as thou deemedst. Thinkest thou that I rejoice at his slaying? O no! I grieve at it, for all that I had such good cause to hate him."

He said: "My own heart! my own heart! Half of my heart biddeth me slay thee, who hast made me slay him. What wilt thou give me?" She knit her brow and spake angrily: "Leave to depart," she said. Then after a while, and in a kinder voice: "And thus much of my love, that I pray thee not to sorrow for me, but to have a good heart, and live as a true knight should." He frowned: "Wilt thou not go with me?" said he. "Not uncompelled," she said: "if thou biddest me go with threats of hewing and mangling the body which thou

116

sayest thou lovest, needs must I go then. Yet scarce wilt thou do this."

"I have a mind to try it," said he; "If I set thee on thine horse and bound thine hands for thee, and linked thy feet together under the beast's belly; belike thou wouldest come. Shall I have slain my brother-in-arms for nought?"

"Thou hast the mind," said she, "hast thou the might?" "So I deem," said he, smiling grimly.

She looked at him proudly and said: "Yea, but I misdoubt me thereof." He still had his back to Ralph and was staring at the lady; she turned her head a little and made a sign to Ralph, just as the Knight of the Sun said: "Thou misdoubtest thee? Who shall help thee in the desert?"

"Look over thy left shoulder," she said. He turned, and saw Ralph drawing near, sword in hand, smiling, but somewhat pale. He drew aback from the Lady and, spinning round on his heel, faced Ralph, and cried out: "Hah! Hast thou raised up a devil against me, thou sorceress, to take from me my grief and my lust, and my life? Fair will the game be to fight with thy devil as I have fought with my friend! Yet now I know not whether I shall slay him or thee."

She spake not, but stood quietly looking on him, not unkindly, while a wind came up from the water and played with a few light locks of hair that hung down from that ruddy crown, and blew her raiment from her feet and wrapped it close round her limbs; and Ralph beheld her, and close as was the very death to him (for huge and most warrior-like was his foeman) yet longing for her melted the heart within him, and he felt the sweetness of life in his inmost soul as he had never felt it before.

Suddenly the Knight of the Sun turned about to the Lady again, and fell down on his knees before her, and clasped his hands as one praying, and said: "Now pardon me all my words, I pray thee; and let this young man depart unhurt, whether thou madest him, or hast but led him away from country and friends and all. Then do thou come with me, and make some semblance of loving me, and suffer me to love thee. And then shall all be well, for in a few days we will go back to thy people, and there will I be their lord or thy servant, or my brother's man, or what thou wilt. O wilt thou not let the summer days be sweet?"

But she spake, holding up her head proudly and speaking in a clear ringing voice: "I have said it, that uncompelled I will not go with thee at all." And therewithal she turned her face toward Ralph, as she might do on any chance-met courteous man, and he saw her smiling, but she said nought to him, and gave no token of knowing him. Then the Knight of the Sun sprang to his feet, and shook his sword above his head and ran furiously on Ralph, who leapt nimbly on one side (else had he been slain at once) and fetched a blow at the Sun-Knight, and smote him, and brake the mails on his left shoulder, so that the blood sprang, and fell on fiercely enough, smiting to right and left as the other gave back at his first onset. But all was for nought, for the Knight of the Sun, after his giving aback under that first stroke drew himself up stark and stiff, and pressing on through all Ralph's strokes, though they rent his mail here and there, ran within his sword, and smote him furiously with the sword-pommel on the side of the head, so that the young man of Upmeads could not stand up under the weight of the blow, but fell to the earth swooning, and the Knight of the Sun knelt on him, and drew out an anlace, short, thick and sharp, and cried out: "Now, Devil, let see whether thou wilt bleed black." Therewith he raised up his hand: but the weapon was stayed or ever it fell, for the Lady had glided up to them when she saw that Ralph was overcome, and now she stretched out her arm and caught hold of the Knight's hand and the anlace withal, and he groaned and cried out: "What now! thou art strong-armed as well as white-armed; (for she had rent the sleeve back from her right arm) and he laughed in the extremity of his wrath. But she was pale and her lips quivered as she said softly and sweetly: "Wilt thou verily slay this young man?"

"And why not?" said he, "since I have just slain the best friend that I ever had, though he was nought willing to fight with me, and only for this, that I saw thee toying with him; though forsooth thou hast said truly that thou hadst more reason to hate him than love him. Well, since thou wilt not have this youngling slain, I may deem at least that he is no

118

devil of thy making, else wouldst thou be glad of his slaying, so that he might be out of the path of thee; so a man he is, and a well-favoured one, and young; and valiant, as it seemeth: so I suppose that he is thy lover, or will be one day—well then—"

And he lifted his hand again, but again she stayed him, and said: "Look thou, I will buy him of thee: and, indeed, I owe him a life." "How is that?" said he. "Why wouldst thou know?" she said; "thou who, if thou hadst me in thine hands again, wouldst keep me away from all men. Yea, I know what thou wouldst say, thou wouldst keep me from sinning again." And she smiled, but bitterly. "Well, the tale is no long one: "five days ago I was taken by them of the Burg: and thou wottest what they would do with me; yea, even if they deemed me less than they do deem me: well, as two of their men-at-arms were leading me along by a halter, as a calf is led to the butcher, we fell in with this goodly lad, who slew them both in manly fashion, and I escaped for that time: though, forsooth, I must needs put my neck in the noose again in delivering four of our people, who would else have been tormented to death by the Burgers."

"Well," said the knight, "perchance thou hast more mercy than I looked for of thee; though I misdoubt thee that thou mayst yet pray me or some other to slay him for thee. Thou art merciful, my Queen, though not to me, and a churl were I if I were less merciful than thou. Therefore will I give his life to him, yet not to thee will I give him if I may help it—Lo you, Sweet! he is just opening his eyes."

Therewith he rose up from Ralph, who raised himself a little, and sat up dazed and feeble. The Knight of the Sun stood up over him beside the lady with his hands clasped on his sword-hilt, and said to Ralph: "Young man, canst thou hear my words?" Ralph smiled feebly and nodded a yea-say. "Dost thou love thy life then?" said the Knight. Ralph found speech and said faintly, "Yea." Said the Knight: "Where dost thou come from, where is thine home?" Said Ralph, "Upmeads." "Well then," quoth the big knight, "go back to Upmeads, and live." Ralph shook his head and knit his brows and said, "I will not." "Yea," said the Knight, "thou wilt not live? Then must I shape me to thy humour. Stand on thy feet

119

and fight it out; for now I am cool I will not slay a swordless man."

Ralph staggered up to his feet, but was so feeble still, that he sank down again, and muttered: "I may not; I am sick and faint;" and therewith swooned away again. But the Knight stood a while leaning on his sword, and looking down on him not unkindly. Then he turned about to the Lady, but lo! she had left his side. She had glided away, and got to her horse, which was tethered on the other side of the oak-tree, and had loosed him and mounted him, and so sat in the saddle there, the reins gathered in her hands. She smiled on the knight as he stood astonished, and cried to him; "Now, lord, I warn thee, draw not a single foot nigher to me; for thou seest that I have Silverfax between my knees, and thou knowest how swift he is, and if I see thee move, he shall spring away with me. Thou wottest how well I know all the ways of the woodland, and I tell thee that the ways behind me to the Dry Tree be all safe and open, and that beyond the Gliding River I shall come on Roger of the Ropewalk and his men. And if thou thinkest to ride after me, and overtake me, cast the thought out of thy mind. For thy horse is strong but heavy, as is meet for so big a knight, and morever he is many yards away from me and Silverfax: so before thou art in the saddle, where shall I be? Yea," (for the Knight was handling his anlace) "thou mayst cast it, and peradventure mayst hit Silverfax and not me, and peradventure not; and I deem that it is my body alive that thou wouldest have back with thee. So now, wilt thou hearken?"

"Yea," quoth the knight, though for wrath he could scarce bring the word from his mouth.

"Hearken," she said, "this is the bargain to be struck between us: even now thou wouldst not refrain from slaying this young man, unless perchance he should swear to depart from us; and as for me, I would not go back with thee to Sunhome, where erst thou shamedst me. Now will I buy thy nay-say with mine, and if thou give the youngling his life, and suffer him to come his ways with us, then will I go home with thee and will ride with thee in all the love and duty that I owe thee; or if thou like this fashion of words better, I will give thee my body for his life. But if thou likest not the

120

bargain, there is not another piece of goods for thee in the market, for then I will ride my ways to the Dry Tree, and thou shalt slay the poor youth, or make of him thy sworn friend, like as was Walter—which thou wilt."

So she spake, and Ralph yet lay on the grass and heard nought. But the Knight's face was dark and swollen with anger as he answered: "My sworn friend! yea, I understand thy gibe. I need not thy words to bring to my mind how I have slain one sworn friend for thy sake."

"Nay," she said, "not for my sake, for thine own folly's sake." He heeded her not, but went on: "And as for this one, I say again of him, if he be not thy devil, then thou meanest him for thy lover. And now I deem that I will verily slay him, ere he wake again; belike it were his better luck."

She said: "I wot not why thou hagglest over the price of that thou wouldest have. If thou have him along with thee, shall he not be in thy power—as I shall be? and thou mayst slay him—or me—when thou wilt."

"Yea," he said, grimly, "when thou art weary of him. O art thou not shameless amongst women! Yet must I needs pay thy price, though my honour and the welfare of my life go with it. Yet how if he have no will to fare with us?" She laughed and said: "Then shalt thou have him with thee as thy captive and thrall. Hast thou not conquered him in battle?" He stood silent a moment and then he said: "Thou sayest it; he shall come with me, will he, nill he, unarmed, and as a prisoner, and the spoil of my valiancy." And he laughed, not altogether in bitterness, but as if some joy were rising in his heart. "Now, my Queen," said he, "the bargain is struck betwixt us, and thou mayest light down off Silverfax; as for me, I will go fetch water from the lake, that we may wake up this valiant and mighty youth, this newfound jewel, and bring him to his wits again."

She answered nought, but rode her horse close to him and lighted down nimbly, while his greedy eyes devoured her beauty. Then he took her hand and drew her to him, and kissed her cheek, and she suffered it, but kissed him not again. Then he took off his helm, and went down to the lake to fetch up water therein.

CHAPTER 23

The Leechcraft of the Lady

Meanwhile she went to Ralph and stood by him, who now began to stir again; and she knelt down by him and kissed his face gently, and rose up hastily and stood a little aloof again.

Now Ralph sat up and looked about him, and when he saw the Lady he first blushed red, and then turned very pale; for the full life was in him again, and he knew her, and love drew strongly at his heart-strings. But she looked on him kindly and said to him: "How fares it with thee? I am sorry of thy hurt which thou hast had for me." He said: "Forsooth, Lady, a chance knock or two is no great matter for a lad of Upmeads. But oh! I have seen thee before." "Yea," she said, "twice before, fair knight." "How is that?" he said; "once I saw thee, the fairest thing in the world, and evil men would have led thee to slaughter; but not twice."

She smiled on him still more kindly, as if he were a dear friend, and said simply: "I was that lad in the cloak that ye saw in the Flower de Luce; and afterwards when ye, thou and Roger, fled away from the Burg of the Four Friths. I had come into the Burg with my captain of war at the peril of our lives to deliver four faithful friends of mine who were else doomed to an evil death."

He said nought, but gazed at her face, wondering at her valiancy and goodness. She took him by the hand now, and held it without speaking for a little while, and he sat there still looking up into her face, wondering at her sweetness and his happiness. Then she said, as she drew her hand away and spake in such a voice, and so looking at him, that every word was as a caress to him: "Thy soul is coming back to thee, my friend, and thou art well at ease: is it not so?"

"O yea," he said, "and I woke up happily e'en now; for

me-dreamed that my gossip came to me and kissed me kindly; and she is a fair woman, but not a young woman."

As he spoke the knight, who had come nearly noiselessly over the grass, stood by them, holding his helm full of water, and looking grimly upon them; but the Lady looked up at him with wide eyes wonderingly, and Ralph, beholding her, deemed that all he had heard of her goodness was but the very sooth. But the knight spake: "Young man, thou hast fought with me, thou knowest not wherefore, and grim was my mood when thou madest thine onset, and still is, so that never but once wilt thou be nigher thy death than thou hast been this hour. But now I have given thee life because of the asking of this lady; and therewith I give thee leave to come thy ways with us: nay, rather I command thee to come, for thou art my prisoner, to be kept or ransomed, or set free as I will. But my will is that thou shalt not have thine armour and weapons; and there is a cause for this, which mayhappen I will tell thee hereafter. But now I bid thee drink of this water, and then do off thine helm and hauberk and give me thy sword and dagger, and go with us peaceably; and be not overmuch ashamed, for I have overcome men who boasted themselves to be great warriors.

So Ralph drank of the water, and did off his helm, and cast water on his face, and arose, and said smiling: "Nay, my master, I am nought ashamed of my mishaps: and as to my going with thee and the Lady, thou hast heard me say under thy dagger that I would not forbear to follow her; so I scarce need thy command thereto." The knight scowled on him and said: "Hold thy peace, fool! Thou wert best not stir my wrath again." "Nay," said Ralph, "thou hast my sword, and mayst slay me if thou wilt; therefore be not word-valiant with me."

Said the Knight of the Sun: "Well, well, thou hast the right of it there. Only beware lest thou try me overmuch. But now must we set forth on our road; and here is work for thee to do: a hundred yards within the thick wood in a straight line from the oak-tree thou shalt find two horses, mine and the knight's who fell before me; go thou and bring them hither; for I will not leave thee with my lady, lest I have to slay thee in the end, and maybe her also."

Ralph nodded cheerfully, and set off on his task, and was the readier therein because the Lady looked on him kindly and compassionately as he went by her. He found the horses speedily, a black horse that was of the Black Knight, and a bay of the Knight of the Sun, and he came back with them lightly.

But when he came to the oak-tree again, lo, the knight and the Lady both kneeling over the body of the Black Knight, and Ralph saw that the Knight of the Sun was sobbing and weeping sorely, so that he deemed that he was taking leave of his friend that lay dead there: but when Ralph had tied up those other two steeds by Silverfax and drawn near to those twain, the Knight of the Sun looked up at him, and spake in a cheerful voice: "Thou seemest to be no ill man, though thou hast come across my lady; so now I bid thee rejoice that there is a good knight more in the world than we deemed e'en now; for this my friend Walter the Black is alive still." "Yea," said the Lady, "and belike he shall live a long while yet."

So Ralph looked, and saw that they had stripped the knight of his hauberk and helm, and bared his body, and that the Lady was dressing a great and sore wound in his side; neither was he come to himself again: he was a young man, and very goodly to look on, dark haired and straight of feature, fair of face; and Ralph felt a grief at his heart as he beheld the Lady's hands dealing with his bare flesh, though nought the man knew of it belike.

As for the Knight of the Sun, he was no more grim and moody, but smiling and joyous, and he spake and said: "Young man, this shall stand thee in good stead that I have not slain my friend this bout. Sooth to say, it might else have gone hard with thee on the way to my house, or still more in my house. But now be of good heart, for unless of thine own folly thou run on the sword's point, thou mayst yet live and do well." Then he turned to the Lady and said: "Dame, for as good a leech as ye be, ye may not heal this man so that he may sit in his saddle within these ten days; and now what is to do in this matter?"

She looked on him with smiling lips and a strange light in her eyes, and said: "Yea, forsooth, what wilt thou do? Wilt thou abide here by Walter thyself alone, and let me bring the imp of Upmeads home to our house? Or wilt thou ride home and send folk with a litter to us? Or shall this youngling ride at all adventure, and seek to Sunway through the blind woodland? Which shall it be?"

The knight laughed outright, and said: "Yea, fair one, this is much like to the tale of the carle at the ferry with the fox, and the goat, and the cabbage."

There was scarce a smile on her face as she said gently: "One thing is to be thought of, that Walter's soul is not yet so fast in his body that either thou or some rough-handed leech may be sure of healing him; it must be this hand, and the learning which it hath learned which must deal with him for a while. And she stretched out her arm over the wounded man, with the fingers pointing down the water, and reddened withal, as if she felt the hearts' greediness of the two men who were looking on her beauty.

The big knight sighed, and said: "Well, unless I am to kill him over again, there is nothing for it but our abiding with him for the next few hours at least. To-morrow is a new day, and fair is the woodland-hall of summer-tide; neither shall water fail us. But as to victual, I wot not save that we have none."

The Lady laughed, and said to Ralph; "Who knoweth what thou mayst find if thou go to the black horse and look into the saddle-bags which I saw upon him awhile agone? For indeed we need somewhat, if it were but to keep the life in the body of this wounded man."

Ralph sprang up and turned to the horse, and found the saddle-bags on him, and took from them bread and flesh, and a flask of good wine, and brought them to the Lady, who laughed and said: "Thou art a good seeker and no ill finder." Then she gave the wounded man to drink of the wine, so that he stirred somewhat, and the colour came into his face a little. Then she bade gather store of bracken for a bed for the Black Knight, and Ralph bestirred himself therein, but the Knight of the Sun sat looking at the Lady as she busied herself with his friend, and gloom seemed gathering on him again.

But when the bracken was enough, the Lady made a bed

deftly and speedily; and between the three they laid the wounded man thereon, who seemed coming to himself somewhat, and spake a few words, but those nothing to the point. Then the Lady took her gay embroidered cloak, which lay at the foot of the oak tree, and cast it over him and, as Ralph deemed, eyed him lovingly, and belike the Knight of the Sun thought in likewise, for he scowled upon her; and for awhile but little was the joyance by the ancient oak, unless it were with the Lady.

CHAPTER 24

Supper and Slumber in the Woodland Hall

But when all was done to make the wounded knight as easy as might be, the Lady turned to the other twain, and said kindly: "Now, lords, it were good to get to table, since here is wherewithal." And she looked on them both full kindly as she spake the words, but nowise wantonly; even as the lady of a fair house might do by honoured guests. So the hearts of both were cheered, and nothing loth they sat down by her on the grass and fell to meat. Yet was the Knight of the Sun a little moody for a while, but when he had eaten and drunken somewhat, he said: "It were well if someone might come hereby, some hermit or holy man, to whom we might give the care of Walter: then might we home to Sunway, and send folk with a litter to fetch him home softly when the due time were."

"Yea," said the Lady, "that might happen forsooth, and perchance it will; and if it were before nightfall it were better."

Ralph saw that as she spake she took hold of the two fingers of her left hand with her right forefinger, and let the thumb meet it, so that it made a circle about them, and she spake something therewith in a low voice, but he heeded it little, save as he did all ways that her body moved. As for the Knight of the Sun, he was looking down on the grass as one pondering matters, and noted this not. But he said presently: "What hast thou to say of Walter now? Shall he live?" "Yea," she said, "maybe as long as either of you twain." The knight looked hard at Ralph, but said nothing, and Ralph heeded not his looks, for his eyes were busy devouring the Lady.

So they abode a little, and the more part of what talk there was came from the Lady, and she was chiefly asking Ralph of his home in Upmeads, and his brethren and kindred, and he told her all openly, and hid naught, while her voice ravished his very soul from him, and it seemed strange to him, that such an one should hold him in talk concerning these simple matters and familiar haps, and look on him so kindly and simply. Ever and anon would she go and look to the welfare of the wounded man, and come back from him (for they sat a little way aloof), and tell them how he did. And still the Knight of the Sun took little heed, and once again gloom settled down on him.

Amidst all this the sun was set, and the long water lay beneath the heavens like a sheet of bright, fairhued metal, and naught stirred it: till at last the Lady leaned forward to Ralph, and touched his shoulder (for he was sitting over against her, with his back to the water), and she said: "Sir Knight, Sir Knight, his wish is coming about, I believe verily." He turned his head to look over his shoulder, and, as if by chance-hap, his cheek met the outstretched hand she was pointing with: she drew it not away very speedily, and as sweet to him was the touch of it as if his face had been brushed past by a summer lily.

"Nay, look! something cometh," she cried; and he looked and saw a little boat making down the water toward the end anigh them. Then the Knight of the Sun seemed to awake at her word, and he leapt to his feet, and stood looking at the new comer.

It was but a little while ere the boat touched the shore, and a man stepped out of it on to the grass and made it fast to the bank, and then stood and looked about him as if seeking something; and lo, it was a holy man, a hermit in the habit of the Blackfriars.

Then the Knight of the Sun hastened down to the strand to meet him, and when Ralph was thus left alone with the Lady, though it were but for a little, his heart beat and he longed sore to touch her with his hand, but durst not, and did but hope that her hand would stray his way as it had e'en now. But she arose and stood a little way from him, and spake to him sweetly of the fairness of the evening, and the wounded man, and the good hap of the friar's coming before nightfall; and his heart was wrung sore with the love of her.

So came the knight up from the strand, and the holy man with him, who greeted Ralph and the Lady and blessed them, and said: "Now, daughter, show me thy sick man; for I am somewhat of a leech, and this thy baron would have me heal him, and I have a right good will thereto."

So he went to the Black Knight, and when he had looked to his hurts, he turned to them and said: "Have ye perchance any meat in the wilderness?" "Yea," quoth the Knight of the Sun; "there is enough for a day or more, and if we must needs abide here longer, I or this young man may well make shift to slay some deer, great or little, for our sustenance and the healing of my friend."

"It is well," said the Friar; "my hermitage is no great way hence, in the thicket at the end of this water. But now is the fever on this knight, and we may not move him ere morning at soonest; but to-morrow we may make a shift to bear him hence by boat: or, if not, then may I go and fetch from my cell bread and other meat, and milk of my goats; and thus shall we do well till we may bring him to my cell, and then shall ye leave him there; and afterwards I will lead him home to Sunway where thou dwellest, baron, when he is well enough healed; or, if he will not go thither, let him go his ways, and I myself will come to Sunway and let thee wot of his welfare."

The knight yeasaid all this, and thereafter the Friar and the Lady together tended the wounded knight, and gave him water to drink, and wine. And meanwhile Ralph and the Knight of the Sun lay down on the grass and watched the eve darkening, and Ralph marvelled at his happiness, and wondered what the morrow would bring forth.

But amidst his happy thoughts the Knight of the Sun spake to him and said: "Young knight, I have struck a bargain with her that thou shalt follow us home, if thou wilt: but to say sooth, I think when the bargain was struck I was minded when I had thee at Sunway to cast thee into my prison. But now I will do otherwise, and if thou must needs follow after thine own perdition, as I have, thou shalt do so freely; therefore take again thine armour and weapons, and do what thou wilt with them. But if thou wilt do after my rede, get thee away to-morrow, or better, to-night, and desire our fellowship no more."

Ralph heard him, and the heart within him was divided. It was in his mind to speak debonairely to the knight; but again he felt as if he hated him, and the blythe words would not come, and he answered doggedly: "I will not leave my Lady since she biddeth me go with her. If thou wilt then, make the most of it that thou art stronger than I, and a warrior more proven; set me before thy sword, and fight with me and slay me."

Then rose the wrath to the knight's lips, and he brake forth: "Then is there one other thing for thee to do, and that is that thou take thy sword, which I have just given back to thee, and thrust her through therewith. That were better for thee and for me, and for him who lieth yonder."

Therewith he arose and strode up and down in the dusk, and Ralph wondered at him, yet hated him now not so much, since he deemed that the Lady would not love him, and that he was angered thereby. Yet about Ralph's heart there hung a certain fear of what should be.

But presently the knight came and sat down by him again, and again fell to speech with him, and said: "Thou knowest that I may not slay thee, and yet thou sayest, fight with me; is this well done?" "Is it ill done?" said Ralph, "I wot not why."

The knight was silent awhile, and then he said: "With what words shall I beseech thee to depart while it is yet time? It may well be that in days to come I shall be good to thee, and help thee."

129

But Ralph said never a word. Then said the knight, and sighed withal: "I now see this of thee, that thou mayst not depart; well, so let it be!" and he sighed heavily again. Then Ralph strove with himself, and said courteously: "Sir, I am sorry that I am a burden irksome to thee; and that, why I know not, thou mayst not rid thyself of me by the strong hand, and that otherwise thou mayst not be rid of me. What then is this woman to thee, that thou wouldst have me slay her, and yet art so fierce in thy love for her?" The Knight of the Sun laughed wrathfully thereat, and was on the point of answering him, when up came those two from the wounded man, and the Friar said: "The knight shall do well; but well it is for him that the Lady of Abundance was here for his helping; for from her hands goeth all healing, as it was with the holy men of old time. May the saints keep her from all harm; for meek and holy indeed she is, as oft we have heard it."

The Lady put her hand on his shoulder, as if to bid him silence, and then set herself down on the grass beside the Knight of the Sun, and fell to talking sweetly and blithely to the three men. The Friar answered her with many words, and told her of the deer and fowl of the wood and the water that he was wont to see nigh to his hermitage; for of such things she asked him, and at last he said: "Good sooth, I should be shy to say in all places and before all men of all my dealings with God's creatures which live about me there. Wot ye what? E'en now I had no thought of coming hitherward; but I was sitting amongst the trees pondering many things, when I began to drowse, and drowsing I heard the thornbushes speaking to me like men, and they bade me take my boat and go up the water to help a man who was in need; and that is how I came hither; benedicite."

So he spake; but the Knight of the Sun did but put in a word here and there, and that most often a sour and snappish word. As for Ralph, he also spake but little, and strayed somewhat in his answers; for he could not but deem that she spake softlier and kinder to him than to the others; and he was dreamy with love and desire, and scarce knew what he was saying.

Thus they wore away some two hours, the Friar or the

Lady turning away at whiles to heed the wounded man, who was now talking wildly in his fever.

But at last the night was grown as dark as it would be, since cloud and storm came not, for the moon had sunk down: so the Lady said: "Now, lords, our candle hath gone out, and I for my part will to bed; so let us each find a meet chamber in the woodland hall; and I will lie near to thee, father, and the wounded friend, lest I be needed to help thee in the night; and thou, Baron of Sunway, lie thou betwixt me and the wood, to ward me from the wild deer and the wood-wights. But thou, Swain of Upmeads, wilt thou deem it hard to lie anear the horses, to watch them if they be scared by aught?"

"Yea," said the Knight of the Sun, "thou art Lady here forsooth; even as men say of thee, that thou swayest man and beast in the wildwood. But this time at least it is not so ill-marshalled of thee: I myself would have shown folk to chamber here in likewise."

Therewith he rose up, and walked to and fro for a little, and then went, and sat down on a root of the oak-tree, clasping his knees with his hands, but lay not down awhile. But the Lady made herself a bed of the bracken which was over from those that Ralph had gathered for the bed of the wounded Knight; and the Friar lay down on the grass nigh to her, and both were presently asleep.

Then Ralph got up quietly; and, shamefacedly for very love, passed close beside the sleeping woman as he went to his place by the horses, taking his weapons and wargear with him: and he said to himself as he laid him down, that it was good for him to be quite alone, that he might lie awake and think at his ease of all the loveliness and kindness of his Lady. Howbeit, he was a young man, and a sturdy, used to lying abroad in the fields or the woods, and it was his custom to sleep at once and sweetly when he lay down after the day's work had wearied him, and even so he did now, and was troubled by no dreams of what was past or to come.

131

BOOK TWO
The Road Unto Trouble

CHAPTER 1

Ralph Meets With Love in the Wilderness

He woke up while it was yet night, and knew that he had been awakened by a touch; but, like a good hunter and warrior, he forebore to start up or cry out till sleep had so much run off him that he could tell somewhat of what was toward. So now he saw the Lady bending over him, and she said in a kind and very low voice: "Rise up, young man, rise up, Ralph, and say no word, but come with me a little way into the wood ere dawn come, for I have a word for thee."

So he stood up and was ready to go with her, his heart beating hard for joy and wonder. "Nay," she whispered, "take thy sword and war-gear lest ill befall: do on thine hauberk; I will be thy squire." And she held his war-coat out for him to do on. "Now," she said, still softly, "hide thy curly hair with the helm, gird thy sword to thee, and come without a word."

Even so he did, and therewithal felt her hand take his (for it was dark as they stepped amidst the trees), and she led him into the Seventh Heaven, for he heard her voice, though it were but a whisper, as it were a caress and a laugh of joy in each word.

She led him along swiftly, fumbling nought with the paths betwixt the pine-tree boles, where it was as dark as dark might be. Every minute he looked to hear her say a word of why she had brought him thither, and that then she would depart from him; so he prayed that the silence and the holding of his hand might last a long while—for he might think of naught save her—and long it lasted forsooth, and still she spake no word, though whiles a little sweet chuckle, as of the garden warbler at his softest, came from her lips, and the ripple of her raiment as her swift feet drave it, sounded loud to his eager ears in the dark, windless wood.

At last, and it was more than half-an-hour of their walking thus, it grew lighter, and he could see the shape of her alongside of him; and still she held his hand and glided on swifter and swifter, as he thought; and soon he knew that outside the wood dawn was giving place to day, and even there, in the wood, it was scarce darker than twilight.

Yet a little further, and it grew lighter still, and he heard the throstles singing a little way off, and knew that they were on the edge of the pine-wood, and still her swift feet sped on till they came to a little grassy wood-lawn, with nought anear it on the side away from the wood save maples and thorn-bushes: it was broad daylight there, though the sun had not yet arisen.

There she let fall his hand and turned about to him and faced him flushed and eager, with her eyes exceeding bright and her lips half open and quivering. He stood beholding her, trembling, what for eagerness, what for fear of her words when he had told her of his desire. For he had now made up his mind to do no less. He put his helm from off his head and laid it down on the grass, and he noted therewith that she had come in her green gown only, and had left mantle and cote hardie behind.

Now he stood up again and was just going to speak, when lo! she put both her palms to her face, and her bosom heaved, and her shoulders were shaken with sobs, and she burst out a weeping, so that the tears ran through her fingers. Then he cast himself on the ground before her, and kissed her feet, and clasped her about the knees, and laid his cheek to her raiment, and fawned upon her, and cried out many an idle word of love, and still she wept a while and spake not. At last she reached her hand down to his face and fondled it, and he let his lips lie on the hand, and she suffered it a while, and then took him by the arm and raised him up and led him on swiftly as before; and he knew not what to do or say, and durst by no means stay her, and could frame no word to ask her wherefore.

So they sped across a waste not much beset with trees, he silent, she never wearying or slacking her pace or faltering as to the way, till they came into the thick wood again, and ever when he would have spoken she hushed him, with "Not yet! Not yet!" Until at last when the sun had been up for some three hours, she led him through a hazel copse, like a deep hedge, into a cleared grassy place where were great grey stones lying about, as if it had been the broken doom-ring of a forgotten folk. There she threw herself down on the grass and buried her face amidst the flowers, and was weeping and sobbing again and he bending over her, till she turned to him and drew him down to her and put her hands to his face, and laid her cheeks all wet with tears to his, and fell to kissing him long and sweetly, so that in his turn he was like to weep for the very sweetness of love.

Then at last she spake: "This is the first word, that now I have brought thee away from death; and so sweet it is to me that I can scarce bear it."

"Oh, sweet to me," he said, "for I have waited for thee many days." And he fell to kissing and clipping her, as one who might not be satisfied. At last she drew herself from him a little, and, turning on him a face smiling with love, she said: "Forbear it a little, till we talk together." "Yea," quoth he, "but may I hold thine hand awhile?" "No harm in that," she said, laughing, and she gave him her hand and spake:

"I spake it that I have brought thee from death, and thou hast asked me no word concerning what and how." "I will ask it now, then," said he, "since thou wilt have it so." She said: "Dost thou think that he would have let thee live?"

"Who," said he, "since thou lettest me live?"

"He, thy foeman, the Knight of the Sun," she said. "Why

didst thou not flee from him before? For he did not so much desire to slay thee, but that he would have had thee depart; but if thou wert once at his house, he would thrust a sword through thee, or at the least cast thee into his prison and let thee lie there till thy youth be gone—or so it seemed to me," she said, faltering as she looked on him.

Said Ralph: "How could I depart when thou wert with him? Didst thou not see me there? I was deeming that thou wouldst have me abide."

She looked upon him with such tender love that he made as if he would cast himself upon her; but she refrained him, and smiled and said: "Ah, yes, I saw thee, and thought not that thou wouldst sunder thyself from me; therefore had I care of thee." And she touched his cheek with her other hand; and he sighed and knit his brows somewhat, and said: "But who is this man that he should slay me? And why is he thy tyrant, that thou must flee from him?"

She laughed and said: "Fair creature, he is my husband."

Then Ralph flushed red, and his visage clouded, and he opened his mouth to speak; but she stayed him and said: "Yet is he not so much my husband but that or ever we were bedded he must needs curse me and drive me away from his house." And she smiled, but her face reddened so deeply that her grey eyes looked strange and light therein.

But Ralph leapt up, and half drew his sword, and cried out loud: "Would God I had slain him! Wherefore could I not slay him?" And he strode up and down the sward before her in his wrath. But she leaned forward to him and laughed and said: "Yet, O Champion, we will not go back to him, for he is stronger than thou, and hath vanquished thee. This is a desert place, but thou art loud, and maybe over loud. Come rest by me."

So he came and sat down by her, and took her hand again and kissed the wrist therof and fondled it and said: "Yea, but he desireth thee sorely; that was easy to see. It was my ill-luck that I slew him not."

She stroked his face again and said: "Long were the tale if I told thee all. After he had driven me out, and I had fled from him, he fell in with me again divers times, as was like to be; for his brother is the Captain of the Dry Tree; the tall man whom thou hast seen with me: and every time this baron hath come on me he has prayed my love, as one who would die despaired if I granted it not, but O my love with the bright sword" (and she kissed his cheek therewith, and fondled his hand with both her hands), "each time I said him nay, I said him nay." And again her face burned with blushes.

"And his brother," said Ralph, "the big captain that I have come across these four times, doth he desire thee also?" She laughed and said: "But as others have, no more: he will not slay any man for my sake."

Said Ralph: "Didst thou wot that I was abiding thy coming at the Castle of Abundance?" "Yea," she said, "have I not told thee that I bade Roger lead thee thither?" Then she said softly: "That was after that first time we met; after I had ridden away on the horse of that butcher whom thou slayedst."

"But why camest thou so late?" said he; "Wouldst thou have come if I had abided there yet?" She said: "What else did I desire but to be with thee? But I set out alone looking not for any peril, since our riders had gone to the north against them of the Burg: but as I drew near to the Water of the Oak, I fell in with my husband and that other man; and this time all my naysays were of no avail, and whatsoever I might say he constrained me to go with them; but straightway they fell out together, and fought, even as thou sawest." And she looked at him sweetly, and as frankly as if he had been naught but her dearest brother.

But he said: "It was concerning thee that they fought: hast thou known the Black Knight for long?"

"Yea," she said, "I may not hide that he hath loved me: but he hath also betrayed me. It was through him that the Knight of the Sun drave me from him. Hearken, for this concerneth thee: he made a tale of me of true and false mingled, that I was a wise-wife and an enchantress, and my lord trowed in him, so that I was put to shame before all the house, and driven forth wrung with anguish, barefoot and bleeding."

He looked and saw pain and grief in her face, as it had been the shadow of that past time, and the fierceness of love in him so changed his face, that she arose and drew a little way from him, and stood there gazing at him. But he also rose and knelt before her, and reached up for her hands and took them in his and said: "Tell me truly, and beguile me not; for I am a young man, and without guile, and I love thee, and would have thee for my speech-friend, what woman soever may be in the world. Whatever thou hast been, what art thou now? Art thou good or evil? Wilt thou bless me or ban me? For it is the truth that I have heard tales and tales of thee: many were good, though it maybe strange; but some, they seemed to warn me of evil in thee. O look at me, and see if I love thee or not! and I may not help it. Say once for all, shall that be for my ruin or my bliss? If thou hast been evil, then be good this one time and tell me."

She neither reddened now, nor paled at his words, but her eyes filled with tears, and ran over, and she looked down on him as a woman looks on a man that she loves from the heart's root, and she said: "O my lord and love, may it be that thou shalt find me no worse to thee than the best of all those tales. Forsooth how shall I tell thee of myself, when, whatever I say, thou shalt believe every word I tell thee? But O my heart, how shouldest thou, so sweet and fair and good, be taken with the love of an evil thing? At the least I will say this, that whatsoever I have been, I am good to thee—I am good to thee, and will be true to thee."

He drew her down to him as he knelt there, and took his arms about her, and though she yet shrank from him a little and the eager flame of his love, he might not be gainsayed, and she gave herself to him and let her body glide into his arms, and loved him no less than he loved her. And there between them in the wilderness was all the joy of love that might be.

CHAPTER 2

They Break Their Fast
in the Wildwood

Now when it was hard on noon, and they had lain long in that grassy place, Ralph rose up and stood upon his feet, and made as one listening. But the Lady looked on him and said: "It is naught save a hart and his hind running in the wood; yet mayhappen we were best on the road, for it is yet long." "Yea," said Ralph, "and it may be that my master will gather folk and pursue us." "Nay, nay," she said, "that were to wrong him, to deem that he would gather folk to follow one man; if he come, he will be by himself alone. When he found us gone he doubtless cast himself on Silverfax, my horse, in trust of the beast following after my feet."

"Well," said Ralph, "and if he come alone, there is yet a sword betwixt him and thee."

She was standing up by him now with her hand on his shoulder, "Hear now the darling, the champion! how he trusteth well in his heart and his right hand. But nay, I have cared for thee well. Hearken, if thou wilt not take it amiss that I tell thee all I do, good or evil. I said a word in the ear of Silverfax or ever I departed, and now the good beast knows my mind, and will lead the fierce lord a little astray, but not too much, lest he follow us with his eager heart and be led by his own keen woodcraft. Indeed, I left the horse behind to that end, else hadst thou ridden the woodland ways with me, instead of my wearying thee by our going afoot; and thou with thy weapons and wargear."

He looked upon her tenderly, and said smiling: "And thou, my dear, art thou not a little wearied by what should weary a knight and one bred afield?" "Nay," she said, "seest thou not how I walk lightly clad, whereas I have left behind my mantle and cote-hardie?" Thereat she gathered up her gown into her girdle ready for the way, and smiled as she saw his eyes embrace the loveliness of her feet; and she spake as she moved them daintily on the flowery grass: "Sooth to say, Knight, I am no weakling dame, who cannot move her limbs save in the dance, or to back the white palfrey and ride the meadows, goshawk on wrist; I am both well-knit and light-foot as the Wood-wife and Goddess of yore agone. Many a toil hath gone to that, whereof I may tell thee presently; but now we were best on our way. Yet before we go, I will at least tell thee this, that in my knowing of these woods, there is no sorcery at all; for in the woods, though not in these woods, was I bred; and here also I am at home, as I may say."

Hand in hand then they went lightly through the hazel copse, and soon was the wood thick about them, but, as before, the Lady led unfalteringly through the thicket paths. Now Ralph spake and said: "It is good that thou lead me whither thou wilt; but this I may say, that it is clear to me that we are not on the way to the Castle of Abundance." "Even so," said she; "indeed had I come to thee there, as I was minded, I should presently have brought thee on the way which we are wending now, or one nigh to it; and that is that which leadeth to Hampton under Scaur, and the Fellowship of Champions who dwell on the rock."

Said Ralph: "It is well; yet will I tell thee the truth, that a little sojourn in that fair house had liked me better. Fain had I been to see thee sitting in thine ivory chair in thy chamber of dais with the walls hung round with thee woven in pictures—wilt thou not tell me in words the story of those pictures? and also concerning the book which I read, which was also of thee?"

"Ah," she said, "thou hast read in the book—well, I will tell thee the story very soon, and that the more since there are matters written wrong in the book." Therewith she hurried him on, and her feet seemed never tired, though now, to say sooth, he began to go somewhat heavily.

Then she stayed him, and laughed sweetly in his face, and said: "It is a long while now since the beginning of the June day, and meseems I know thy lack, and the slaking of it lieth somewhat nearer than Hampton under Scaur, which we shall not reach these two days if we go afoot all the way."

"My lack?" said he; "I lack nought now, that I may not have when I will." And he put his arms about her shoulders and strained her to his bosom. But she strove with him, and freed herself and laughed outright, and said: "Thou art a bold man, and rash, my knight, even unto me. Yet must I see to it that thou die not of hunger." He said merrily: "Yea, by St. Nicholas, true it is: a while ago I felt no hunger, and had forgotten that men eat; for I was troubled with much longing, and in doubt concerning my life; but now am I free and happy, and hungry therewithal."

"Look," she said, pointing up to the heavens, "it is now past two hours after noon; that is nigh two hours since we left the lawn amidst the hazels, and thou longest to eat, as is but right, so lovely as thou art and young; and I withal long to tell thee something of that whereof thou hast asked me; and lastly, it is the hottest of the day, yea, so hot, that even Diana, the Wood-wife of yore agone, might have fainted somewhat, if she had been going afoot as we twain have been, and little is the risk of our resting awhile. And hereby is a place where rest is good as regards the place, whatever the resters may be; it is a little aside the straightest way, but meseems we may borrow an hour or so of our journey, and hope to pay it back ere nightfall. Come, champion!"

Therewith she led north through a thicket of mingled trees till Ralph heard water running, and anon they came to a little space about a brook, grassy and clear of trees save a few big thorn-bushes, with a green ridge or bank on the other side. There she stayed him and said: "Do off thy war-gear, knight. There is naught to fear here, less than there was amidst the hazels." So did he, and she kneeled down and drank of the clear water, and washed her face and hands therein, and then came and kissed him and said: "Lovely imp of Upmeads, I have some bread of last night's meal in my scrip here, and under the bank I shall find some woodland meat withal; abide a little and the tale and the food shall come back to thee together." Therewith she stepped lightly into the stream, and stood therein a minute to let her naked feet feel the cold ripple (for she had stripped off her foot-gear as she first came to the water), and then went hither and thither gathering strawberries about the bank, while he watched her, blessing her, till he well nigh wept at the thought of his happiness.

Back she came in a little while with good store of strawberries in the lap of her gown, and they sat down on the green lip of the brook, and she drew the bread from her scrip and they ate together, and she made him drink from the hollow of her hands, and kissed him and wept over him for joy, and the eagerness of her love. So at last she sat down quietly beside him, and fell to speaking to him, as a tale is told in the ingle nook on an even of Yule-tide.

CHAPTER 3

The Lady Telleth Ralph of the Past Days of Her Life

"Now shalt thou hear of me somewhat more than the arras and the book could tell thee; and yet not all , for time would fail us therefor—and moreover my heart would fail me. I cannot tell where I was born nor of what lineage, nor of who were my father and mother; for this I have known not of myself, nor has any told me. But when I first remember anything, I was playing about a garden, wherein was a little house built of timber and thatched with reed, and the great trees of the forest were all about the garden save for a little croft which was grown over with high grass and another somewhat bigger, wherein were goats. There was a woman at the door of the house and she spinning, yet clad in glittering raiment, and with jewels on her neck and fingers; this was the first thing that I remember, but all as it were a matter of every day, and use and wont, as it goes with the memories of children. Of such matters I will not tell thee at large, for thou knowest how it will be. Now the woman, who as I came to know was neither old nor young in those days, but of middle age, I called mother; but now I know that she was not my mother. She was hard and stern with me, but never beat me in those days, save to make me do what I would not have done unbeaten; and as to meat I ate and drank what I could get, as she did, and indeed was well-fed with simple meats as thou mayest suppose from the aspect of me to-day. But as she was not fierce but rather sour to me in her daily wont in my youngest days so also she was never tender, or ever kissed me or caressed me, for as little as I was. And I loved her naught, nor did it ever come into my mind that I should love her, though I loved a white goat of ours and deemed it dear and lovely; and afterwards other things also that came to me from time to time, as a squirrel that I saved from a weasel, and a jackdaw that fell from a tall ash-tree nigh our house before he had learned how to fly, and a house-mouse that would run up and down my hand and arm, and other such-like things; and shortly I may say that the wild things, even to the conies and fawns loved me, and had but little fear of me, and made me happy, and I loved them.

"Further, as I grew up, the woman set me to do such work as I had strength for as needs was; for there was no man dwelt anigh us and seldom did I ever see man or woman there, and held no converse with any, save as I shall tell thee presently: though now and again a man or a woman passed by; what they were I knew not, nor their whence and whither, but by seeing them I came to know that there were other folk in the world besides us two. Nought else I knew save how to spin, and to tend our goats and milk them, and to set snares for birds and small deer: though when I had caught them, it irked me sore to kill them, and I had let them go again had I not feared the carline. Every day early I was put forth from the house and garth, and forbidden to go back thither till dusk. While the days were long and the grass was growing, I had to lead our goats to pasture in the wood-lawns, and must take with me rock and spindle, and spin so much of flax or hair as the woman gave me, or be beaten. But when the winter came and the snow was on the ground, then that watching and snaring of wild things was my business.

"At last one day of late summer when I, now of some fifteen summers, was pasturing the goats not far from the house, the sky darkened, and there came up so great a storm of thunder and lightning, and huge drift of rain, that I was afraid, and being so near to the house, I hastened thither, driving the goats, and when I had tethered them in the shed of the croft, I crept trembling up to the house, and when I was at the door, heard the clack of the loom in the weaving-chamber, and deemed that the woman was weaving there, but when I looked, behold there was no one on the bench, though the shuttle was flying from side to side, and the shed opening and changing, and the sley coming home in due order. Therewithal I heard a sound as of one singing a song in a low voice, but the words I could not understand: then terror seized on my heart, but I stepped over the threshold, and as the door of the chamber was open, I looked aside and saw therein the woman sitting stark naked on the floor with a great open book before her, and it was from her mouth that the song was coming: grim she looked, and awful, for she was a big woman, black-haired and stern of aspect in her daily wont, speaking to me as few words as might be, and those harsh enough, yea harsher than when I was but little. I stood for one moment afraid beyond measure, though the woman did not look at me, and I hoped she had not seen me; then I ran back into the storm, though it was now wilder than ever, and ran and hid myself in the thicket of the wood, half-dead with fear, and wondering what would become of me. But finding that no one followed after me, I grew calmer, and the storm also drew off, and the sun shone out a little before his setting: so I sat and spun, with fear in my heart, till I had finished my tale of thread, and when dusk came, stole back again to the house, though my legs would scarce bear me over the threshold into the chamber.

"There sat the woman in her rich attire no otherwise than her wont, nor did she say aught to me; but looked at the yarn that I had spun, to see that I had done my task, and nodded sternly to me as her wont was, and I went to bed amongst my goats as I was used to do, but slept not till towards morning, and then images of dreadful things, and of miseries that I may not tell thee of, mingled with my sleep for long.

"So I awoke and ate my meat and drank of the goats' milk

with a heavy heart, and then went into the house; and when I came into the chamber the woman looked at me, and contrary to her wont spoke to me, and I shook with terror at her voice; though she said naught but this: 'Go fetch thy white goat and come back to me therewith.' I did so, and followed after her, sick with fear; and she led me through the wood into a lawn which I knew well, round which was a wall, as it were, of great yew trees, and amidst, a table of stone, made of four uprights and a great stone plank on the top of them; and this was the only thing in all the wood wherein I was used to wander which was of man's handiwork, save and except our house, and the sheds and fences about it.

"The woman stayed and leaned against this stonework and said to me: 'Go about now and gather dry sticks for a fire.' I durst do naught else, and said to myself that I should be whipped if I were tardy, though, forsooth, I thought she was going to kill me; and I brought her a bundle, and she said, 'Fetch more.' And when I had brought her seven bundles, she said: 'It is enough: stand over against me and hearken.' So I stood there quaking; for my fear, which had somewhat abated while I went to and fro after the wood, now came back upon me tenfold.

"She said: 'It were thy due that I should slay thee here and now, as thou slayest the partridges which thou takest in thy springes: but for certain causes I will not slay thee. Again, it were no more than thy earnings were I to torment thee till thou shouldst cry out for death to deliver thee from the anguish; and if thou wert a woman grown, even so would I deal with thee. But thou art yet but a child, therefore I will keep thee to see what shall befall betwixt us. Yet must I do somewhat to grieve thee, and moreover something must be slain and offered up here on this altar, lest all come to naught, both thou and I, and that which we have to do. Hold thy white goat now, which thou lovest more than aught else, that I may redden thee and me and this altar with the blood thereof.'

"I durst do naught but obey her, and I held the poor beast, that licked my hands and bleated for love of me: and now since my terror and the fear of death was lessened at her words, I wept sore for my dear friend.

145

"But the woman drew a strong sharp knife from her girdle and cut the beast's throat, and dipped her fingers in the blood and reddened both herself and me on the breast, and the hands, and the feet; and then she turned to the altar and smote blood upon the uprights, and the face of the stone plank. Then she bade me help her, and we laid the seven faggots on the alter, and laid the carcase of the goat upon them: and she made fire, but I saw not how, and set it to the wood, and when it began to blaze she stood before it with her arms outspread, and sang loud and hoarse to a strange tune; and though I knew not the words of her song, it filled me with dread, so that I cast myself down on the ground and hid my face in the grass.

"So she went on till the beast was all burned up and the fire became naught but red embers, and then she ceased her song and sank down upon the grass, and laid her head back and so fell asleep; but I durst not move from the place, but cowered in the grass there, I know not how long, till she arose and came to me, and smote me with her foot and cried: 'Rise up, fool! what harm hast thou? Go milk thy goats and lead them to pasture.' And therewith she strode away home, not heeding me.

"As for me, I arose and dealt with my goats as she bade me; and presently I was glad that I had not been slain, yet thenceforth was the joy of my life that I had had amongst my goats marred with fear, and the sounds of the woodland came to me mingled with terror; and I was sore afraid when I entered the house in the morning and the evening, and when I looked on the face of the woman; though she was no harder to me than heretofore, but maybe somewhat softer.

"So wore the autumn, and winter came, and I fared as I was wont, setting springes for fowl and small-deer. And for all the roughness of the season, at that time it pleased me better than the leafy days, because I had less memory then of the sharpness of my fear on that day of the altar. Now one day as I went under the snow-laden trees, I saw something bright and big lying on the ground, and drawing nearer I saw that it was some child of man: so I stopped and cried out, 'Awake and arise, lest death come on thee in this bitter cold,' But it stirred not; so I plucked up heart and came up to it,

146

and lo! a woman clad in fair raiment of scarlet and fur, and I knelt down by her to see if I might help her; but when I touched her I found her cold and stiff, and dead, though she had not been dead long, for no snow had fallen on her. It still wanted more than an hour of twilight, and I by no means durst go home till nightfall; so I sat on there and watched her, and put the hood from her face and the gloves from her hands, and I deemed her a goodly and lovely thing, and was sorry that she was not alive, and I wept for her, and for myself also, that I had lost her fellowship. So when I came back to the house at dark with the venison, I knew not whether to tell my mistress and tyrant concerning this matter; but she looked on me and said at once: 'Wert thou going to tell me of something that thou hast seen?' So I told her all, even as it was, and she said to me: 'Hast thou taken aught from the corpse?' 'Nay,' said I. 'Then must I hasten,' she said, 'and be before the wolves.' Therewith she took a brand from the fire, and bade me bear one also and lead her: so did I easily enough, for the moon was up, and what with moon and snow, it was well nigh as bright as the day. So when we came to the dead woman, my mistress kneeled down by her and undid the collar of her cloak, which I had not touched, and took something from her neck swiftly, and yet I, who was holding the torch, saw that it was a necklace of blue stones and green, with gold between—Yea, dear Champion, like unto thine as one peascod is to another," quoth she.

And therewith the distressfulness of her face which had worn Ralph's heart while she had been telling her tale changed, and she came, as it were, into her new life and the love of him again, and she kissed him and laid her cheek to his and he kissed her mouth. And then she fetched a sigh, and began with her story again.

"My mistress took the necklace and put it in her pouch, and said as to herself: 'Here, then, is another seeker who hath not found, unless one should dig a pit for her here when the thaw comes, and call it the Well at the World's End: belike it will be for her as helpful as the real one.' Then she turned to me and said: 'Do thou with the rest what thou wilt,' and therewith she went back hastily to the house. But as for me, I went back also, and found a pick and a mattock in the goat-house, and came back in the moonlight and scraped the snow away, and dug a pit, and buried the poor damsel there with all her gear.

"Wore the winter thence with naught that I need tell of, only I thought much of the words that my mistress had spoken. Spring came and went, and summer also, well nigh tidingless. But one day as I drave the goats from our house there came from the wood four men, a-horseback and weaponed, but so covered with their armour that I might see little of their faces. They rode past me to our house, and spake not to me, though they looked hard at me; but as they went past I heard one say: 'If she might but be our guide to the Well at the World's End!' I durst not tarry to speak with them, but as I looked over my shoulder I saw them talking to my mistress in the door; but meseemed she was clad but in poor homespun cloth instead of her rich apparel, and I am far-sighted and clear-sighted. After this the autumn and winter that followed it passed away tidingless.

CHAPTER 4

The Lady Tells of Her Deliverance

"Now I had outgrown my old fear, and not much befell to quicken it: and ever I was as much out of the house as I could be. But about this time my mistress, from being kinder to me than before, began to grow harder, and ofttimes used me cruelly: but of her deeds to me, my friend, thou shalt ask me no more than I tell thee. On a day of May-tide I fared abroad with my goats, and went far with them, further from the house than I had been as yet. The day was the fairest of the year, and I rejoiced in it, and felt as if some exceeding great good were about to befall me; and the burden of fears seemed to have fallen from me. So I went till I came to a little flowery dell, beset with blossoming whitethorns and with a fair stream running through it; a place somewhat like to this, save that the stream there was bigger. And the sun was hot about noontide, so I did off my raiment, which was rough and poor, and more meet for winter than May-tide, and I entered a pool of the clear water, and bathed me and sported therein, smelling the sweet scent of the whitethorns and hearkening to the song of the many birds; and when I came forth from the water, the air was so soft and sweet to me, and the flowery grass so kind to my feet, and the May-blooms fell upon my shoulders, that I was loth to do on my rough raiment hastily, and withal I looked to see no child of man in that wilderness: so I sported myself there a long while, and milked a goat and drank of the milk, and crowned myself with white-thorn and hare-bells; and held the blossoms in my hand, and felt that I also had some might in me, and that I should not be a thrall of that sorceress for ever. And that day, my friend, belike was the spring-tide of the life and the love that thou holdest in thy kind arms.

"But as I abode thus in that fair place, and had just taken my rock and spindle in hand that I might go on with my task and give as little occasion as I might for my mistress to chastise me, I looked up and saw a child of man coming down the side of the little dale towards me, so I sprang up, and ran to my raiment and cast them on me hastily, for I was ashamed; and when I saw that it was a woman, I thought at first that it was my mistress coming to seek me; and I thought within myself that if she smote me I would bear it no more, but let it be seen which of the twain was the mightier. But I looked again and saw that it was not she but a woman smaller and older. So I stood where I was and abode her coming, smiling and unafraid, and half-clad.

"She drew near and I saw that it was an old woman grey haired, uncomely of raiment, but with shining bright eyes in her wrinkled face. And she made an obeisance to me and said: 'I was passing through this lonely wilderness and I looked down into the little valley and saw these goats there and the lovely lady lying naked amongst them, and I said I am too old to be afraid of aught; for if she be a goddess come back again from yore agone, she can but make an end of a poor old carline, a gangrel body, who hath no joy of her life now. And if she be of the daughters of men, she will belike methink her of her mother, and be kind to me for her sake, and give me a piece of bread and a draught of her goats' milk.'

"I spake hastily, for I was ashamed of her words, though I only half understood them: 'I hear thee and deem that thou mockest me: I have never known a mother; I am but a poor thrall, a goatherd dwelling with a mistress in a nook of this wildwood: I have never a piece of bread; but as to the goats' milk, that thou shalt have at once.' So I called one of my goats to me, for I knew them all, and milked her into a wooden bowl that I carried slung about me, and gave the old woman to drink: and she kissed my hand and drank and spake again, but no longer in a whining voice, like a beggar bidding alms in the street, but frank and free.

" 'Damsel,' she said, 'now I see that thy soul goes with thy body, and that thou art kind and proud at once. And whatever thou art, it is no mock to say of thee, that thou art as fair as the fairest; and I think that this will follow thee, that henceforth no man who seeth thee once will forget thee ever, or cease to long for thee: of a surety this is thy weird. Not I see that thou knowest no more of the world and its ways than one of the hinds that run in these woods. So if thou wilt, I will sit down by thee and tell thee much that shall avail thee; and thou in thy turn shalt tell me all the tale concerning thy dwelling and thy service, and the like.'

"I said, I may not, I durst not; I serve a mighty mistress, and she would slay me if she knew that I had spoken to thee; and woe's me! I fear that even now she will not fail to know it. Depart in peace."

" 'Nay,' she said, 'thou needest not tell me, for I have an inkling of her and her ways: but I will give thee wisdom, and not sell it thee at a price. Sit down then, fair child, on this flowery grass, and I will sit beside thee and tell thee of many things worth thine heeding.' So there we sat awhile, and in good sooth she told me much of the world which I had not yet seen, of its fairness and its foulness; of life and death, and desire and disappointment, and despair; so that when she had done, if I were wiser than erst, I was perchance little more joyous; and yet I said to myself that come what would I would be a part of all that.

"But at last she said: 'Lo the day is waning, and thou hast two things to do; either to go home to thy mistress at once, or flee away from her by the way that I shall show thee; and if thou wilt be ruled by me, and canst bear thy thralldom yet a little while thou wilt not flee at once, but abide till thou hast seen me again. And since it is here that thou hast met me, here mayst thou meet me again; for the days are long now, and thou mayst easily win thy way hither before noon on any day.'

"So I tied my goatskin shoes to my feet, and drave my goats together, and we went up together out of the dale, and were in the wide-spreading plain of the waste; and the carline said: 'Dost thou know the quarters of the heaven by the sun?' 'Yea,' said I. 'Then,' quoth she, 'whenso thou desirest to depart and come into the world of folk that I have told thee of, set thy face a little north of west, and thou shalt fall in with something or somebody before long; but be speedy on that day as thou art light-footed, and make all the way thou canst before thy mistress comes to know of thy departure; for not lightly will any one let loose such a thrall as thou.'

"I thanked her, and she went her ways over the waste, I wotted not whither, and I drave my goats home as speedily as I might; the mistress meddled not with me by word or deed, though I was short of my due tale of yarn. The next day I longed sore to go to the dale and meet the carline but durst not, and the next day I fared in likeways; but the third day I longed so to go, that my feet must needs take me there, whatsoever might befall. And when I had been in the dale a little, thither came the carline, and sat down by me and fell to teaching me wisdom, and showed me letters and told me what they were, and I learned like a little lad in the chorister's school.

"Thereafter I mastered my fear of my mistress and went to that dale day by day, and learned of the carline; though at whiles I wondered when my mistress would let loose her fury upon me; for I called to mind the threat she had made to me on the day when she offered up my white goat. And I made up my mind to this, that if she fell upon me with deadly intent

151

I would do my best to slay her before she should slay me. But so it was, that now again she held her hand from my body, and scarce cast a word at me ever, but gloomed at me, and fared as if hatred of me had grown great in her heart.

"So the days went by, and my feet had worn a path through the wilderness to the Dale of Lore, and May had melted into June, and the latter days of June were come. And on Midsummer Day I went my ways to the dale according to my wont, when, as I as driving on my goats hastily I saw a bright thing coming over the heath toward me, and I went on my way to meet it, for I had no fear now, except what fear of my mistress lingered in my heart; nay, I looked that everything I saw of new should add some joy to my heart. So presently I saw that it was a weaponed man riding a white horse, and anon he had come up to me and drawn rein before me. I wondered exceedingly at beholding him and the heart leaped within me at his beauty; for though the carline had told me of the loveliness of the sons of men, that was but words and I knew not what they meant; and the others that I had seen were not young men or goodly, and those last, as I told thee, I could scarce see their faces.

"And this one was even fairer than the dead woman that I had buried, whose face was worn with toil and trouble, as now I called to mind. He was clad in bright shining armour with a gay surcoat of green, embroidered with flowers over it; he had a light sallet on his head, and the yellow locks of his hair flowed down from under, and fell on his shoulders: his face was as beardless as thine, dear friend, but not clear brown like to thine but white and red like a blossom."

Ralph spake and said: "Belike it was a woman;" and his voice sounded loud in the quiet place. She smiled on him and kissed his cheek, and said: "Nay, nay, dear Champion, it is not so. God rest his soul! many a year he has been dead."

Said Ralph: "Many a year! what meanest thou?" "Ah!" she said, "fear not! as I am now, so shall I be for thee many a year. Was not thy fear that I should vanish away or change into something unsightly and gruesome? Fear not, I say; am I not a woman, and thine own?" And again she flushed bright red, and her grey eyes lightened, and she looked at him all confused and shamefaced.

He took her face between his hands and kissed her over and over; then he let her go, and said: "I have no fear: go on with thy tale, for the words thereof are as thy kisses to me, and the embracing of thine hands and thy body: tell on, I pray thee." She took his hand in hers and spake, telling her tale as before.

"Friend, well-beloved for ever! This fair young knight looked on me, and as he looked, his face flushed as red as mine did even now. And I tell thee that my heart danced with joy as I looked on him, and he spake not for a little while, and then he said: 'Fair maiden, canst thou tell me of any who will tell me a word of the way to the Well at the World's End?' I said to him, 'Nay, I have heard the word once and no more, I know not the way: and I am sorry that I cannot do for thee that which thou wouldest.' And then I spake again, and told him that he should by no means stop at our house, and I told him what it was like, so that he might give it the go by. I said, 'Even if thou hast to turn back again, and fail to find the thing thou seekest, yet I beseech thee ride not into that trap.'

"He sat still on his saddle a while, staring at me and I at him; and then he thanked me, but with so bad a grace, that I wondered of him if he were angry; and then he shook his rein, and rode off briskly, and I looked after him a while, and then went on my way; but I had gone but a short while, when I heard horse-hoofs behind me, and I turned and looked, and lo! it was the knight coming back again. So I stayed and abided him; and when he came up to me, he leapt from his horse and stood before me and said: 'I must needs see thee once again.'

"I stood and trembled before him, and longed to touch him. And again he spake, breathlessly, as one who has been running: 'I must depart, for I have a thing to do that I must do; but I long sorely to touch thee, and kiss thee; yet unless thou freely willest it, I will refrain me.' Then I looked at him and said, 'I will it freely.' Then he came close up to me, and put his hand on my shoulder and kissed my cheek; but I kissed his lips, and then he took me in his arms, and kissed me and embraced me; and there in that place, and in a little while, we loved each other sorely.

153

"But in a while he said to me: 'I must depart, for I am as one whom the Avenger of Blood followeth; and now I will give thee this, not so much as a gift, but as a token that we have met in the wilderness, thou and I.' Therewith he put his hand to his neck, and took from it this necklace which thou seest here, and I saw that it was like that which my mistress took from the neck of the dead woman. And no less is it like to the one that thou wearest, Ralph.

"I took it in my hand and wept that I might not help him. And he said: 'It is little likely that we shall meet again; but by the token of this collar thou mayest wot that I ever long for thee till I die: for though I am a king's son, this is the dearest of my possessions.' I said: 'Thou art young, and I am young; mayhappen we shall meet again: but thou shalt know that I am but a thrall, a goatherd.' For I knew by what the old woman told me of somewhat of the mightiness of the kings of the world. 'Yea,' he said, and smiled most sweetly, 'that is easy to be seen: yet if I live, as I think not to do, thou shalt sit where great men shall kneel to thee; not as I kneel now for love, and that I may kiss thy knees and thy feet, but because they needs must worship thee.'

"Therewith he arose to his feet and leapt on his horse, and rode his ways speedily: and I went upon my way with my goats, and came down into the Dale of Lore, and found the old woman abiding me; and she came to me, and took me by the hands, and touched the collar (for I had done it about my neck), and said:

"'Dear child, thou needest not to tell me thy tale, for I have seen him. But if thou must needs wear this necklace, I must give thee a gift to go with it. But first sit down by the old carline awhile and talk with her; for meseemeth it will be but a few days ere thou shalt depart from this uttermost wilderness, and the woods before the mountains.

"So I sat down by her, and in spite of her word I told her all that had befallen betwixt me and the king's son: for my heart was too full that I might refrain me. She nodded her head from time to time, but said naught, till I had made an end: and then fell to telling me of many matters for my avail; but yet arose earlier than her wont was; and when we were about sundering on the path which I had trodden above the Dale, she said: 'Now must I give thee that gift to go along with the gift of the lover, the King's son; and I think thou wilt find it of avail before many days are gone by.' Therewith she took from her pouch a strong sharp knife, and drew it from the sheath, and flashed it in the afternoon sun, and gave it to me; and I took it and laid it in my bosom and thanked her; for I thought that I understood her meaning, and how it would avail me. Then I went driving my goats home speedily, so that the sun was barely set when I came to the garth; and a great horror rather than a fear of my mistress was on me; and lo! she stood in the door of the house gazing down the garth and the woodland beyond, as though she were looking for my coming: and when her eyes lighted on me, she scowled, and drew her lips back from her teeth and clenched her hands with fury, though there was nought in them; and she was a tall and strong woman, though now growing somewhat old: but as for me, I had unsheathed the carline's gift before I came to the garth, and now I held it behind my back in my left hand.

"I had stayed my feet some six paces from the threshold, and my heart beat quick, but the sick fear and cowering had left me, though the horror of her grew in my heart. My goats had all gone off quietly to their house, and there was nothing betwixt me and her. In clearing from my sleeve the arm of me which held the knife, the rough clasp which fastened my raiment together at the shoulder had given way, and the cloth had fallen and left my bosom bare, so that I knew that the collar was clearly to be seen. So we stood a moment, and I had no words, but she spake at last in a hard, snarling voice, such as she oftenest used to me, but worse.

" 'Now at last the time has come when thou art of no more use to me; for I can see thee what thou hast got for thyself. But know now that thou hast not yet drunk of the Well at the World's End, and that it will not avail thee to flee out of this wood; for as long as I live thou wilt not be able to get out of reach of my hand; and I shall live long: I shall live long. Come, then, and give thyself up to me, that I may deal with thee as I threatened when I slew thy friend the white goat; for, indeed, I knew then that it would come to this.'

"She had but twice or thrice spoken to me so many words

together as this; but I answered never a word, but stood watching her warily. And of a sudden she gave forth a dreadful screaming roar, wherewith all the wood rang again, and rushed at me; but my hand came from behind my back, and how it was I know not, but she touched me not till the blade had sunk into her breast, and she fell across my feet, her right hand clutching my raiment. So I loosed her fingers from the cloth, shuddering with horror the while, and drew myself away from her and stood a little aloof, wondering what should happen next. And indeed I scarce believed but she would presently rise up from the ground and clutch me in her hands, and begin the tormenting of me. But she moved no more, and the grass all about her was reddened with her blood; and at last I gathered heart to kneel down beside her, and found that she no more breathed than one of those conies or partridges which I had been used to slay for her.

"Then I stood and considered what I should do, and indeed I had been pondering this all the way from the Dale thereto, in case I should escape my mistress. So I soon made up my mind that I would not dwell in that house even for one night; lest my mistress should come to me though dead, and torment me. I went into the house while it was yet light, and looked about the chamber, and saw three great books there laid on the lectern, but durst not have taken them even had I been able to carry them; nor durst I even to look into them, for fear that some spell might get to work in them if they were opened; but I found a rye loaf whereof I had eaten somewhat in the morning, and another untouched, and hanging to a horn of the lectern I found the necklace which my mistress had taken from the dead woman. These I put into my scrip, and as to the necklace, I will tell thee how I bestowed it later on. Then I stepped out into the twilight which was fair and golden, and full fain I was of it. Then I drove the goats out of their house and went my way towards the Dale of Lore, and said to myself that the carline would teach me what further to do, and I came there before the summer dark had quite prevailed, and slept sweetly and softly amongst my goats after I had tethered them in the best of the pasture.

CHAPTER 5

Yet More of the Lady's Story

"Lo thou, beloved," she said, "thou hast seen me in the wildwood with little good quickened in me: doth not thine heart sink at the thought of thy love and thy life given over to the keeping of such an one?" He smiled in her face, and said: "Belike thou hast done worse than all thou hast told me: and these days past I have wondered often what there was in the stories which they of the Burg had against thee: yet sooth to say, they told little of what thou hast done: no more belike than being their foe." She sighed and said: "Well, hearken; yet shall I not tell thee every deed that I have been partaker in.

"I sat in the Dale that next day and was happy, though I longed to see that fair man again: sooth to say, since my mistress was dead, everything seemed fairer to me, yea even mine own face, as I saw it in the pools of the stream, though whiles I wondered when I should have another mistress, and how she would deal with me; and ever I said I would ask the carline when she came again to me. But all that day she came not: nor did I marvel thereat. But when seven days passed and still she came not, I fell to wondering what I should do: for my bread was all gone, and I durst not go back to the house to fetch meal; though there was store of it there. Howbeit, I drank of the milk of the goats, and made curds thereof with the woodland roots, and ate of the woodberries like as thou hast done, friend, e'en now. And it was easier for me to find a livelihood in the woods than it had been for most folk, so well as I knew them. So wore the days, and she came not, and I began to think that I should see the wise carline no more, as indeed fell out at that time; and the days began to hang heavy on my hands, and I fell to thinking of that way to the west and the peopled parts, whereof the carline had told me; and whiles I went out of the Dale and went away hither and thither through the woods, and so far, that thrice I slept away out of the Dale: but I knew that the peopled parts would be strange to me and I feared to face them all alone.

"Thus wore the days till July was on the wane, and on a morning early I awoke with unwonted sounds in mine ears; and when my eyes were fairly open I saw a man standing over me and a white horse cropping the grass hard by. And my heart was full and fain, and I sprang to my feet and showed him a smiling happy face, for I saw at once that it was that fair man come back again. But lo! his face was pale and worn, though he looked kindly on me, and he said: 'O my beloved, I have found thee, but I am faint with hunger and can speak but little.' And even therewith he sank down on the grass. But I bestirred myself, and gave him milk of my goats, and curds and berries, and the life came into him again, and I sat down by him and laid his head in my lap, and he slept a long while; and when he awoke (and it was towards sunset) he kissed my hands and my arms, and said to me: 'Fair child, perhaps thou wilt come with me now; and even if thou art a thrall thou mayest flee with me; for my horse is strong and fat, though I am weak, for he can make his dinner on the grass.'

"Then he laughed and I no less; but I fed him with my poor victual again, and as he ate I said: 'I am no mistress's thrall now; for the evening of the day whereon I saw thee I slew her, else had she slain me.' 'The saints be praised,' said he: 'Thou wilt come with me, then?' 'O yea,' said I. Then I felt shamefaced and I reddened; but I said: 'I have abided here many days for a wise woman who hath taught me many things; but withal I hoped that thou wouldst come also.'

"Then he put his arms about my shoulders and loved me much; but at last he said: "Yet is it now another thing than that which I looked for, when I talked of setting thee by me on the golden throne. For now am I a beaten man; I have failed of that I sought, and suffered shame and hunger and many ills. Yet ever I thought that I might find thee here or hereby.' Then a thought came into my mind, and I said:

'Else maybe thou hadst found what thou soughtest, and overcome the evil things.' 'Maybe,' he said; 'it is now but a little matter.' "

"As for me, I could have no guess at what were the better things he had meant for me, and my heart was full of joy, and all seemed better than well. And we talked together long till the day was gone. Then we kissed and embraced each other in the Dale of Lore, and the darkness of summer seemed but short for our delight."

CHAPTER 6

The Lady Tells Somewhat of Her Doings After She Left the Wilderness

Ralph stayed her speech now, and said: "When I asked of thee in the Land of Abundance, there were some who seemed to say that thou hast let more men love thee than one: and it was a torment to me to think that even so it might be. But now when thine own mouth telleth me of one of them it irks me little. Dost thou think it little-hearted in me?"

"O friend," she said, "I see that so it is with thee that thou wouldst find due cause for loving me, whatever thou foundest true of me. Or dost thou deem that I was another woman in those days? Nay, I was not: I can see myself still myself all along the way I have gone." She was silent a little, and then she said: "Fear not, I will give thee much cause to love me. But now I know thy mind the better, I shall tell thee less of what befell me after I left the wilderness; for whatever I did and whatever I endured, still it was always I myself that was there, and it is me that thou lovest. Moreover, my life in the wilderness is a stranger thing to tell thee of than my dealings with the folk, and with Kings and Barons and Knights. But hereafter thou shalt hear of me what tales thou wilt of these matters, as the days and the years pass over our heads.

"Now on the morrow we would not depart at once, because there we had some victual, and the king's son was not yet so well fed as he should be; so we abode in that fair place another day, and then we went our ways westward, according to the rede of the carline; and it was many days before we gat us out of the wilderness, and we were often hard put to it for victual; whiles I sat behind my knight a-horseback, whiles he led the beast while I rode alone, and not seldom I went afoot, and that nowise slowly, while he rode the white horse, for I was as light-foot then as now.

"And of the way we went I will tell thee nought as now, because sure it is that if we both live, thou and I shall tread that road together, but with our faces turned the other way; for it is the road from the Well at the World's End, where I myself have been, or else never had thine eyes fallen on me."

Ralph said, "Even so much I deemed by reading in the book; yet it was not told clearly that thou hadst been there." "Yea," she said, because the said book was made not by my friends but my foes, and they would have men deem that my length of days and the endurance of my beauty and never-dying youth of my heart came from evil and devilish sources; and if thou wilt trust my word it is not so, for in the Well at the World's End is no evil, but only the Quenching of Sorrow, and Clearing of the Eyes that they may behold. And how good it is that they look on thee now. And moreover, the history of that book is partly false of intention and ill-will, and partly a confused medley of true and false, which has come of mere chance-hap.

"Hearken now," she said, "till I tell thee in few word what befell me before I came to drink the Water of the Well. After we had passed long deserts of wood and heath, and gone through lands exceeding evil and perilous, and despaired of life for the horror of those places, and seen no men, we came at last amongst a simple folk who dealt kindly with us, yea, and more. These folk seemed to me happy and of good wealth, though to my lord they seemed poor and lacking of the goods of the world. Forsooth, by that time we lacked more than they, for we were worn with cold and hunger, and hard life: though for me, indeed, happy had been the days of my wayfaring, but my lord remembered the days of his riches and the kingdom of his father, and the worship of mighty men, and all that he had promised me on the happy day when I first beheld him: so belike he was scarce so happy as I was.

"It was springtime when we came to that folk; for we had worn through the autumn and winter in getting clear of the wilderness. Not that the way was long, as I found out afterwards, but that we went astray in the woodland, and at last came out of it into a dreadful stony waste which we strove to cross thrice, and thrice were driven back into the greenwood by thirst and hunger; but the fourth time, having gotten us store of victual by my woodcraft, we overpassed it and reached the peopled country.

"Yea, spring was on the earth, as we, my lord and I, came down from the desolate stony heaths, and went hand and hand across the plain, where men and women of that folk were feasting round about the simple roofs and woodland halls which they had raised there. Then they left their games and sports and ran to us, and we walked on quietly, though we knew not whether the meeting was to be for death or life. But that kind folk gathered round us, and asked us no story till they had fed us, and bathed us, and clad us after their fashion. And then, despite the nakedness and poverty wherein they had first seen us, they would have it that we were gods sent down to them from the world beyond the mountains by their fathers of old time; for of Holy Church, and the Blessed Trinity, and the Mother of God they knew no more than did I at that time, but were heathen, as the Gentiles of yore agone. And even when we put all that Godhood from us, and told them as we might and could what we were (for we had no heart to lie to such simple folk), their kindness abated nothing, and they bade us abide there, and were our loving friends and brethren.

"There in sooth had I been content to abide till eld came upon me, but my lord would not have it so, but longed for greater things for me. Though in sooth to me it seemed as if his promise of worship of me by the folk had been already fulfilled; for when we had abided there some while, and our

161

beauty, which had been marred by the travail of our wayfaring, had come back to us in full, or it maybe increased somewhat, they did indeed deal with us with more love than would most men with the saints, were they to come back on the earth again; and their children would gather round about me and make me a partaker of their sports, and be loth to leave me; and the faces of their old folk would quicken and gladden when I drew nigh: and as for their young men, it seemed of them that they loved the very ground that my feet trod on, though it grieved me that I could not pleasure some of them in such wise as they desired. And all this was soft and full of delight for my soul: and I, whose body a little while ago had been driven to daily toil with evil words and stripes, and who had known not what words of thanks and praise might mean!

"But so it must be that we should depart, and the kind folk showed us how sore their hearts were of our departure, but they gainsaid us in nowise, but rather furthered us all they might, and we went our ways from them riding on horned neat (for they knew not of horses), and driving one for a sumpter beast before us; and they had given us bows and arrows for our defence, and that we might get us venison.

"It is not to be said that we did not encounter perils; but thereof I will tell thee naught as now. We came to other peoples, richer and mightier than these, and I saw castles, and abbies, and churches, and walled towns, and wondered at them exceedingly. And in these places folk knew of the kingdom of my lord and his father, and whereas they were not of his foes (who lay for the more part on the other side of his land), and my lord could give sure tokens of what he was, we were treated with honour and worship, and my lord began to be himself again, and to bear him as a mighty man. And here to me was some gain in that poverty and nakedness wherewith we came out of the mountains and the raiment of the simple folk; for had I been clad in my poor cloth and goat-skins of the House of the Sorcerer, and he in his brave attire and bright armour, they would have said, it is a thrall that he is assotted of, and would have made some story and pretence of taking me from him; but they deemed me a great lady indeed, and a king's daughter, according to the tale that he told them. Forsooth many men that saw me desired me beyond measure, and assuredly some great proud man or other would have taken me from my lord, but that they feared the wrath of his father, who was a mighty man indeed.

"Yea, one while as we sojourned by a certain town but a little outside the walls, a certain young man, a great champion and exceeding masterful, came upon me with his squires as I was walking in the meadows, and bore me off, and would have taken me to his castle, but that my lord followed with a few of the burghers, and there was a battle fought, wherein my lord was hurt; but the young champion he slew; and I cannot say but I was sorry of his death, though glad of my deliverance.

"Again, on a time we guested in a great baron's house, who dealt so foully by us that he gave my lord a sleeping potion in his good-night cup, and came to me in the dead night and required me of my love; and I would not, and he threatened me sorely, and called me a thrall and a castaway that my lord had picked up off the road: but I gat a knife in my hand and was for warding myself when I saw that my lord might not wake: so the felon went away for that time. But on the morrow came two evil men into the hall whom he had suborned, and bore false witness that I was a thrall and a runaway. So that the baron would have held me there (being a mighty man) despite my lord and his wrath and his grief, had not a young knight of his house been, who swore that he would slay him unless he let us go; and whereas there were other knights and squires there present who murmured, the baron was in a way compelled. So we departed, and divers of the said knights and squires went with us to see us safe on the way.

"But this was nigh to the kingdom of my lord's father, and that felon baron I came across again, and he was ever after one of my worst foes.

"Moreover, that young champion who had first stood up in the hall rode with us still, when the others had turned back; and I soon saw of him that he found it hard to keep his eyes off me; and that also saw my lord, and it was a near thing that they did not draw sword thereover: yet was that knight

163

no evil man, but good and true, and I was exceedingly sorry for him; but I could not help him in the only way he would take help of me.

"Lo you, my friend, the beginnings of evil in those long past days, and the seeds of ill-hap sown in the field of my new life even before the furrow was turned.

"Well, we came soon into my lord's country, and fair and rich and lovely was it in those days; free from trouble and unpeace, a happy abode for the tillers of the soil, and the fashioners of wares. The tidings had gone to the king that my lord was come back, and he came to meet him with a great company of knights and barons, arrayed in the noblest fashion that such folk use; so that I was bewildered with their glory, and besought my lord to let me fall back out of the way, and perchance he might find me again. But he bade me ride on his right hand, for that I was the half of his life and his soul, and that my friends were his friends and my foes his foes.

"Then there came to me an inkling of the things that should befall, and I saw that the sweet and clean happiness of my new days was marred, and had grown into something else, and I began to know the pain of strife and the grief of confusion: but whereas I had not been bred delicately, but had endured woes and griefs from my youngest days, I was not abashed, but hardened my heart to face all things, even as my lord strove to harden his heart: for, indeed, I said to myself that if I was to him as the half of his life, he was to me little less than the whole of my life.

"It is as if it had befallen yesterday, my friend, that I call to mind how we stood beside our horses in the midst of the ring of great men clad in gold and gleaming with steel, in the meadow without the gates, the peace and lowly goodliness whereof with its flocks and herds feeding, and husbandmen tending the earth and its increase, that great and noble array had changed so utterly. There we stood, and I knew that the eyes of all those lords and warriors were set upon me wondering. But the love of my lord and the late-learned knowledge of my beauty sustained me. Then the ring of men opened, and the king came forth towards us; a tall man and big, of fifty-five winters, goodly of body and like to my lord to

164

look upon. He cast his arms about my lord, and kissed him and embraced him, and then stood a little aloof from him and said: 'Well, son, hast thou found it, the Well at the World's End?'

" 'Yea,' said my lord, and therewith lifted my hand to his lips and kissed it, and I looked the king in his face, and his eyes were turned to me, but it was as if he were looking through me at something behind me.

"Then he said: 'It is good, son: come home now to thy mother and thy kindred.' Then my lord turned to me while the king took no heed, and no man in the ring of knights moved from his place, and he set me in the saddle, and turned about to mount, and there came a lord from the ring of men gloriously bedight, and he bowed lowly before my lord, and held his stirrup for him: but lightly he leapt up into the saddle, and took my reins and led me along with him, so that he and the king and I went on together, and all the baronage and their folk shouted and tossed sword and spear aloft and followed after us. And we left the meadow quiet and simple again, and rode through the gate of the king's chief city, wherein was his high house and his castle, the dwelling-place of his kindred from of old.

CHAPTER 7

The Lady Tells of the Strife and Trouble That Befell After Her Coming to the Country of the King's Son

"When we came to the King's House, my lord followed his father into the hall, where sat his mother amongst her damsels: she was a fair woman, and looked rather meek than high-hearted; my lord led me up to her, and she embraced and kissed him and caressed him long; then she turned about to me and would have spoken to me, but the king, who stood behind us, scowled on her, and she forebore; but she looked me on somewhat kindly, and yet as one who is afeard.

"Thus it went for the rest of the day, and my lord had me to sit beside him in the great hall when the banquet was holden, and I ate and drank with him and beheld all the pageants by his side, and none meddled with me either to help or to hinder, because they feared the king. Yet many eyes I saw that desired my beauty. And so when night came, he took me to his chamber and his bed, as if I were his bride new wedded, even as it had been with us on the grass of the wilderness and the bracken of the wildwood. And then, at last, he spake to me of our case, and bade me fear not, for that a band of his friends, all-armed, was keeping watch and ward in the cloister without. And when I left the chamber on the morrow's morn, there were they yet, all in bright armour, and amongst them the young knight who had delivered me from the felon baron, and he looked mournfully at me, so that I was sorry for his sorrow.

"And I knew now that the king was minded to slay me, else had he bidden thrust me from my lord's side.

"So wore certain days; and on the seventh night, when we were come into our chamber, which was a fair as any house outside of heaven, my lord spake to me in a soft voice, and bade me not do off my raiment. 'For,' said he, 'this night we must flee the town, or we shall be taken and cast into prison to-morrow; for thus hath my father determined.' I kissed him and clung to him, and he no less was good to me. And when it was the dead of night we escaped out of our window by a knotted rope which he had made ready, and beneath was the city wall; and that company of knights, amongst whom was the young knight abovesaid, had taken a postern thereby, and were abiding us armed and with good horses. So we came into the open country, and rode our ways with the mind to reach a hill-castle of one of those young barons, and to hold ourselves there in despite of the king. But the king had been as wary as we were privy, and no less speedy than we; and he was a mighty and deft warrior, and he himself followed us on the spur with certain of his best men-at-arms. And they came upon us as we rested in a woodside not far from our house of refuge: and the king stood by to see the battle with his sword in his sheath, but soon was it at an end, for though our friends fought valiantly, they were everyone slain or hurt, and but few escaped with bare life; but that young man who loved me so sorely crept up to me grievously hurt, and I did not forbear to kiss him once on the face, for I deemed I should soon die also, and his blood stained my sleeve and my wrist, but he died not as then, but lived to be a dear friend to me for long.

"So we, my lord and I, were led back to the city, and he was held in ward and I was cast into prison with chains and hunger and stripes. And the king would have had me lie there till I perished, that I might be forgotten utterly; but there were many of the king's knights who murmured at this, and would not forget me; so the king being constrained, had me brought forth to be judged by his bishops of sorcery for the beguiling of my lord. Long was the tale to me then, but I will not make it long for thee; as was like to be, I was brought in guilty of sorcery, and doomed to be burned in the Great Square in three days time.

"Nay, my friend, thou hast no need to look so troubled; for thou seest that I was not burned. This is the selfsame body that was tied to the stake in the market place of the king's city many a year ago.

"For the friends of my lord, young men for the most part, and many who had been fain to be my friends also, put on their armour, and took my lord out of the courteous prison wherein he was, and came to the Great Square whenas I stood naked in my smock bound amid the faggots; and I saw the sheriffs' men give back, and great noise and rumour rise up around me: and then all about me was a clear space for a moment and I heard the tramp of the many horse-hoofs, and the space was full of weaponed men shouting, and crying out, 'Life for our Lord's Lady!' Then a minute, and I was loose and in my lord's arms, and they brought me a horse and I mounted, lest the worst should come and we might have to flee. So I could see much of what went on; and I saw that all the unarmed folk and lookers-on were gone, but at our backs was a great crowd of folk with staves and bows who cried out, 'Life for the Lady!' But before us was naught but the sheriffs' sergeants and a company of knights and men-at-arms, about as many as we were, and the king in front of them, fully armed, his face hidden by his helm, and a royal surcoat over his hauberk beaten with his bearing, to wit, a silver tower on a blue sky bestarred with gold.

"And now I could see that despite the bills and bows behind us the king was going to fall on with his folk; and to say sooth I feared but little and my heart rose high within me, and I wished I had a sword in my hand to strike once for life and love. But lo! just as the king was raising his sword, and his trumpet was lifting the brass to his lips, came a sound of singing, and there was come the Bishop and the Abbot of St. Peter's and his monks with him, and cross bearers and readers and others of the religious: and the Bishop bore in his hand the Blessed Host (as now I know it was) under a golden canopy, and he stood between the two companies and faced the king, while his folk sang loud and sweet about him.

"Then the spears went up and from the rest, and swords were sheathed, and there went forth three ancient knights from out of the king's host and came up to him and spake with him. Then he gat him away unto his High House; and the three old knights came to our folk, and spake with the chiefs; but not with my lord, and I heard not what they said. But my lord came to me in all loving-kindness and brought me into the house of one of the Lineage, and into a fair chamber there, and kissed me, and made much of me; and brought me fair raiment and did it on me with his own hands, even as his wont was to be for my tire-maiden.

"Then in a little while came those chiefs of ours and said that truce had been hanselled them for this time, but on these terms, that my lord and I and all those who had been in arms, and whosoever would, that feared the king's wrath, should have leave to depart from his city so that they went and abode no nearer than fifty miles thereof till they should know his further pleasure. Albeit that whosoever would go home peaceably might abide in the city still and need not fear the king's wrath if he stirred no further: but that in any case the Sorceress should get her gone from those walls.

"So we rode out of the gates that very day before sunset; for it was now midsummer again, and it was three hours before noon that I was to have been burned; and we were a gallant company of men-at-arms and knights; yet did I bethink me of those who were slain on that other day when we were taken, and fain had I been that they were riding with us; but at least that fair young man was in our company, though still weak with his hurts: for the prison and the process had worn away wellnigh two months. True it is that I rejoiced to see him, for I had deemed him dead.

"Dear friend, I pray thy pardon if I weary thee with making so long a tale of my friends of the past days; but needs must I tell thee somewhat of them, lest thou love that which is not. Since truly it is myself that I would have thee to love, and none other.

"Many folk gathered to us as we rode our ways to a town which was my lord's own, and where all men were his friends, so that we came there with a great host and sat down there in no fear of what the king might do against us. There was I duly wedded to my lord by a Bishop of Holy Church, and made his Lady and Queen; for even so he would have it.

"And now began the sore troubles of that land, which had been once so peaceful and happy; the tale whereof I may one day tell thee; or rather many tales of what befell me therein; but not now; for the day weareth; and I still have certain things that I must needs tell thee.

"We waged war against each other, my lord and the king, and whiles one, and whiles the other overcame. Either side belike deemed that one battle or two would end the strife; but so it was not, but it endured year after year, till fighting became the chief business of all in the land.

"As for me, I had many tribulations. Thrice I fled from the stricken field with my lord to hide in some stronghold of the mountains. Once was I taken of the foemen in the town where I abode when my lord was away from me, and a huge slaughter of innocent folk was made, and I was cast into prison and chains, after I had seen my son that I had borne to my lord slain before mine eyes. At last we were driven clean out of the Kingdom of the Tower, and abode a long while, some two years, in the wilderness, living like outlaws and wolves' heads, and lifting the spoil for our livelihood.

Forsooth of all the years that I abode about the Land of Tower those were the happiest. For we robbed no poor folk and needy, but rewarded them rather, and drave the spoil from rich men and lords, and hard-hearted chapmen-folk: we ravished no maid of the tillers, we burned no cot, and taxed no husbandman's croft or acre, but defended them from their tyrants. Nevertheless we gat an ill name wide about through the kingdoms and cities; and were devils and witches to the boot of thieves and robbers in the mouths of these men; for when the rich man is hurt his wail goeth heavens high, and none may say he heareth not.

"Now it was at this time that I first fell in with the Champions of the Dry Tree; for they became our fellows and brothers in arms in the wildwood: for they had not as yet builded their stronghold of the Scaur, whereas thou and I shall be in two days time. Many a wild deed did our folk in their company, and many that had been better undone. Whiles indeed they went on journeys wherein we were not partakers, as when they went to the North and harried the lands of the Abbot of Higham, and rode as far even as over the Downs to Bear Castle and fought a battle there with the Captain of Higham: whereas we went never out of the Wood Perilous to the northward; and lifted little save in the lands of our own proper foemen, the friends of the king.

"Now I say not of the men of the Dry Tree that they were good and peaceable men, nor would mercy hold their hands every while that they were hard bestead and thrust into a corner. Yet I say now and once for all that their fierceness was and is but kindness and pity when set against the cruelty of the Burg of the Four Friths; men who have no friend to love, no broken foe to forgive, and can scarce be kind even to themselves: though forsooth they be wise men and cautelous and well living before the world, and wealthy and holy."

She stayed her speech a while, and her eyes glittered in her flushed face and she set her teeth; and she was as one beside herself till Ralph kissed her feet, and caressed her, and she went on again.

"Dear friend, when thou knowest what these men are and have been thou wilt bless thy friend Roger for leading thee forth from the Burg by night and cloud, whatever else may happen to thee.

"Well, we abode in the wildwood, friends and good fellows from the first; and that young man, though he loved me ever, was somewhat healed of the fever of love, and was my faithful friend, in such wise that neither I nor my lord had aught to find fault with in him. Meanwhile we began to grow strong, for many joined us therein who had fled from their tyrants of the good towns and the manors of the baronage, and at last in the third year naught would please my lord but we must enter into the Kingdom of the Tower, and raise his banner in the wealthy land, and the fair cities.

"Moreover, his father, the King of the Tower, died in his bed in these days, and no word of love or peace had passed between them since that morning when I was led out to be burned in the Great Square.

"So we came forth from the forest, we, and the Champions of the Dry Tree; and made the tale a short one. For the king, the mighty warrior and wise man, was dead: and his captains of war, some of them were dead, and some weary of strife; and those who had been eager in debate were falling to ask themselves wherefore they had fought and what was to do that they should still be fighting; and lo! when it came to be looked into, it was all a matter of the life and death of one woman, to wit me myself, and why should she not live, why should she not sit upon the throne with the man who loved her?

"Therefore when at last we came out from the twilight of the woods into the sunny fields of the Land of the Tower, there was no man to naysay us; nay, the gates of the strong places flew open before the wind of our banners, and the glittering of our spears drew the folk together toward the places of rejoicing. We entered the master City in triumph, with the houses hung with green boughs and the maidens casting flowers before our feet, and I sat a crowned Queen upon the throne high raised on the very place where erst I stood awaiting the coming of the torch to the faggots which were to consume me.

"There then began the reign of the Woman of the Waste; for so it was, that my lord left to my hands the real ruling of

171

the kingdom, though he wore the crown and set the seal to parchments. As to them of the Dry Tree, though some few of them abode in the kingdom, and became great there, the more part of them went back to the wildwood and lived the old life of the Wood, as we had found them living it aforetime. But or ever they went, the leaders of them came before me, and kissed my feet, and with tears and prayers besought me, and bade me that if aught fell amiss to me there, I should come back to them and be their Lady and Queen; and whereas these wild men loved me well, and I deemed that I owed much to their love and their helping, I promised them and swore to them by the Water of the Well at the World's End that I would do no less than they prayed me: albeit I set no term or year for the day that I would come to them.

"And now my lord and I, we set ourselves to heal the wounds which war had made in the land: and hard was the work, and late the harvest; so used had men become to turmoil and trouble. Moreover, there were many, and chiefly the women who had lost husband, lover, son or brother, who laid all their griefs on my back; though forsooth how was I guilty of the old king's wrath against me, which was the cause of all? About this time my lord had the Castle of Abundance built up very fairly for me and him to dwell in at whiles; and indeed we had before that dwelt at a little manor house that was there, when we durst withdraw a little from the strife; but now he had it done as fair as ye saw it, and had those arras cloths made with the story of my sojourn in the wilderness, even as ye saw them. But the days and the years wore, and wealth came back to the mighty of the land, and fields flourished and the acres bore increase, and fair houses were builded in the towns; and the land was called happy again.

"But for me I was not so happy: and I looked back fondly to the days of the greenwood and the fellowship of the Dry Tree, and the days before that, of my flight with my lord. And moreover with the wearing of the years those murmurs against me and the blind causeless hatred began to grow again, and chiefly methinks because I was the king, and my lord the king's cloak: but therewith tales concerning me began to spring up, how that I was not only a sorceress, but even one foredoomed from of old and sent by the lords of hell to wreck that fair Land of the Tower and make it unhappy and desolate. And the tale grew and gathered form, till now, when the bloom of my beauty was gone, I heard hard and fierce words cried after me in the streets when I fared abroad, and that still chiefly by the women: for yet most men looked on me with pleasure. Also my counsellors and lords warned me often that I must be wary and of great forbearance if trouble were to be kept back.

"Now amidst these things as I was walking pensively in my garden one summer day, it was told me that a woman desired to see me, so I bade them bring her. And when she came I looked on her, and deemed that I had seen her aforetime: she was not old, but of middle age, of dark red hair, and brown eyes somewhat small: not a big woman, but well fashioned of body, and looking as if she had once been exceeding dainty and trim. She spake, and again I seemed to have heard her voice before: 'Hail, Queen,' she said, 'it does my heart good to see thee thus in thy glorious estate.' So I took her greeting; but those tales of my being but a sending of the Devil for the ruin of that land came into my mind, and I sent away the folk who were thereby before I said more to her. Then she spake again: 'Even so I guessed it would be that thou wouldst grow great amongst women.'

"But I said, 'What is this? and when have I known thee before-time?' She smiled and said naught; and my mind went back to those old days, and I trembled, and the flesh crept upon my bones, lest this should be the coming back in a new shape of my mistress whom I had slain. But the woman laughed, and said, as if she knew my thoughts: 'Nay, it is not so: the dead are dead; fear not: but hast thou forgotten the Dale of Lore?'

" 'Nay,' said I, 'never; and art thou then the carline that learned me lore? But if the dead come not back, how do the old grow young again? for 'tis a score of years since we two sat in the Dale, and I longed for many things.'

"Said the woman: 'The dead may not drink of the Well at the World's End; yet the living may, even if they be old; and that blessed water giveth them new might and changeth their

173

blood, and they are as young folk for a long while again after they have drunken.' 'And hast thou drunken?' said I.

" 'Yea,' she said; 'but I am minded for another draught.' I said: 'And wherefore hast thou come to me, and what shall I give to thee?' She said, 'I will take no gift of thee as now, for I need it not, though hereafter I may ask a gift of thee. But I am to ask this of thee, if thou wilt be my fellow-farer on the road thither?' 'Yea?' said I, 'and leave my love and my lord, and my kingship which he hath given me? for this I will tell thee, that all that here is done, is done by me.'

" 'Great is thy Kingship, Lady,' said the woman, and smiled withal. Then she sat silent a little, and said: 'When six months are worn, it will be springtide; I will come to thee in the spring days, and know what thy mind is then. But now I must depart.' Quoth I: 'Glad shall I be to talk with thee again; for though thou hast learned me much of wisdom, yet much more I need; yea, as much as the folk here deem I have already.' 'Thou shalt have no less,' said the woman. Then she kissed my hands and went her ways, and I sat musing still for a long while: because for all my gains, and my love that I had been loved withal, and the greatness that I had gotten, there was as it were a veil of unhappiness wrapped round about my heart.

"So wore the months, and ere the winter had come befell an evil thing, for my lord, who had loved me so, and taken me out of the wilderness, died, and was gathered to the fathers, and there was I left alone; for there was no fruit of my womb by him alive. My first-born had been slain by those wretches, and a second son that I bore had died of a pestilence that war and famine had brought upon the land. I will not wear thy soul with words about my grief and sorrow: but it is to be told that I sat now in a perilous place, and yet I might not step down from it and abide in that land, for then it was a sure thing, that some of my foes would have laid hand on me and brought me to judgment for being but myself, and I should have ended miserably. So I gat to me all the strength that I might, and whereas there were many who loved me still, some for my own sake, and some for the sake of my lord that was, I endured in good hope that all my days were not done. Yet I longed for the coming of the Teacher

174

of Lore; for now I made up my mind that I would go with her, and seek to the Well at the World's End for weal and woe.

"She came while April was yet young: and I need make no long tale of how we gat us away: for whereas she was wise in hidden lore, it was no hard matter for her to give me another semblance than mine own, so that I might have walked about the streets of our city from end to end, and none had known me. So I vanished away from my throne and my kingdom, and that name and fame of a witch-wife clove to me once and for all, and spread wide about the cities of folk and the kingdoms, and many are the tales that have arisen concerning me, and belike some of these thou hast heard told."

Ralph reddened and said: "My soul has been vexed by some inkling of them; but now it is at rest from them for ever."

"May it be so!" she said: "and now my tale is wearing thin for the present time.

"Back again went my feet over the ways they had trodden before, though the Teacher shortened the road much for us by her wisdom. Once again what need to tell thee of these ways when thine own eyes shall behold them as thou wendest them beside me? Be it enough to say that once again I came to that little house in the uttermost wilderness, and there once more was the garth and the goat-house, and the trees of the forest beyond it, and the wood-lawns and the streams and all the places and things that erst I deemed I must dwell amongst for ever."

Said Ralph: "And did the carline keep troth with thee? Was she not but luring thee thither to be her thrall? Or did the book that I read in the Castle of Abundance but lie concerning thee?"

"She held her troth to me in all wise," said the Lady, "and I was no thrall of hers, but as a sister, or it may be even as a daughter; for ever to my eyes was she the old carline who learned me lore in the Dale of the wildwood.

"But now a long while, years long, we abode in that House of the Sorceress ere we durst seek further to the Well at the World's End. And yet meseems though the years wore, they

175

wore me no older; nay, in the first days at least I waxed stronger of body and fairer than I had been in the King's Palace in the Land of the Tower, as though some foretaste of the Well was there for us in the loneliness of the desert; although forsooth the abiding there amidst the scantiness of livelihood, and the nakedness, and the toil, and the torment of wind and weather were as a penance for the days and deeds of our past lives. What more is to say concerning our lives here, saving this, that in those days I learned yet more wisdom of the Teacher of Lore, and amidst that wisdom was much of that which ye call sorcery: as the foreseeing of things to come, and the sending of dreams or visions, and certain other matters. And I may tell thee that the holy man who came to us last even, I sent him the dream which came to him drowsing, and bade him come to the helping of Walter the Black: for I knew that I should take thy hand and flee with thee this morning e'en as I have done: and I would fain have a good leech to Walter lest he should die, although I owe him hatred rather than love. Now, my friend, tell me, is this an evil deed, and dost thou shrink from the Sorceress?"

He strained her to his bosom and kissed her mouth, and then he said: "Yet thou hast never sent a dream to me." She laughed and said: "What! hast thou never dreamed of me since we met at the want-way of the Wood Perilous?" "Never," said he. She stroked his cheek fondly, and said: "Young art thou, sweet friend, and sleepest well a-nights. It was enough that thou thoughtest of me in thy waking hours." Then she went on with her tale.

CHAPTER 8

The Lady Maketh an End
of Her Tale

"Well, my friend, after we had lived thus a long time, we set out one day to seek to the Well at the World's End, each of us signed and marked out for the quest by bearing such-like beads as thou and I both bear upon our necks today. Once again of all that befell us on that quest I will tell thee naught as now: because to that Well have I to bring thee: though myself, belike, I need not its waters again."

Quoth Ralph: "And must thou lead me thy very self, mayest thou not abide in some safe place my going and returning? So many and sore as the toils and perils of the way may be." "What!" she said, "and how shall I be sundered from thee now I have found thee? Yea, and who shall lead thee, thou lovely boy? Shall it be a man to bewray thee, or a woman to bewray me? Yet need we not go tomorrow, my beloved, nor for many days: so sweet as we are to each other.

"But in those past days it was needs must we begin our quest before the burden of years was over heavy upon us. Shortly to say it, we found the Well, and drank of its waters after abundant toil and peril, as thou mayst well deem. Then the life and the soul came back to us, and the past years were as naught to us, and my youth was renewed in me, and I became as thou seest me to-day. But my fellow was as a woman of forty summers again, strong and fair as I had seen her when she came into the garden in the days of my Queen-hood, and thus we returned to the House of the Sorceress, and rested there for a little from our travel and our joy.

"At last, and that was but some five years ago, the Teacher said to me: 'Sister, I have learned thee all that thine heart can take of me, and thou art strong in wisdom, and more-

177

over again shall it be with thee, as I told of thee long ago, that no man shall look on thee that shall not love thee. Now I will not seek to see thy life that is coming, nor what thine end shall be, for that should belike be grievous to both of us; but this I see of thee, that thou wilt now guide thy life not as I will, but as thou wilt; and since my way is not thy way, and that I see thou shalt not long abide alone, now shall we sunder; for I am minded to go to the most ancient parts of the world, and seek all the innermost of wisdom whiles I yet live; but with kings and champions and the cities of folk will I have no more to do: while thou shalt not be able to refrain from these. So now I bid thee farewell.'

"I wept at her words, but gainsaid them naught, for I wotted that she spake but the truth; so I kissed her, and we parted; she went her ways through the wildwood, and I abode at the House of the Sorceress, and waited on the wearing of the days.

"But scarce a month after her departure, as I stood by the threshold one morning amidst of the goats, I saw men come riding from out the wood; so I abode them, and they came to the gate of the garth and there lighted down from their horses, and they were three in company; and no one of them was young, and one was old, with white locks flowing down from under his helm: for they were all armed in knightly fashion, but they had naught but white gaberdines over their hauberks, with no coat-armour or token upon them. So they came through the garth-gate and I greeted them and asked them what they would; then the old man knelt down on the grass before me and said: 'If I were as young as I am old my heart would fail me in beholding thy beauty: but now I will ask thee somewhat: far away beyond the forest we heard rumours of a woman dwelling in the uttermost desert, who had drunk of the Well at the World's End, and was wise beyond measure. Now we have set ourselves to seek that woman, and if thou be she, we would ask a question of thy wisdom.'

"I answered that I was even such as they had heard of, and bade them ask.

"Said the old man:

"'Fifty years ago, when I was yet but a young man, there

178

was a fair woman who was Queen of the Land of the Tower and whom we loved sorely because we had dwelt together with her amidst tribulation in the desert and the wildwood: and we are not of her people, but a fellowship of free men and champions hight the Men of the Dry Tree: and we hoped that she would one day come back and dwell with us and be our Lady and Queen: and indeed trouble seemed drawing anigh her, so that we might help her and she might become our fellow again, when lo! she vanished away from the folk and none knew where she was gone. Therefore a band of us of the Dry Tree swore an oath together to seek her till we found her, that we might live and die together: but of that band of one score and one, am I the last one left that seeketh; for the rest are dead, or sick, or departed: and indeed I was the youngest of them. But for these two men, they are my sons whom I have bred in the knowledge of these things and in the hope of finding tidings of our Lady and Queen, if it were but the place where her body lieth. Thou art wise: knowest thou the resting place of her bones?"

"When I had heard the tale of the old man I was moved to my inmost heart, and I scarce knew what to say. But now this long while fear was dead in me, so I thought I would tell the very sooth: but I said first: 'Sir, what I will tell, I will tell without beseeching, so I pray thee stand up.' So did he, and I said: 'Geoffrey, what became of the white hind after the banners had left the wildwood'? He stared wild at me, and I deemed that tears began to come into his eyes; but I said again: 'What betid to dame Joyce's youngest born, the fair little maiden that we left sick of a fever when we rode to Up-castle?' Still he said naught but looked at me wondering: and said: 'Hast thou ever again seen that great old oak nigh the clearing by the water, the half of which fell away in the summer-storm of that last July?'

"Then verily the tears gushed out of his eyes, and he wept, for as old as he was; and when he could master himself he said: 'Who art thou? Who art thou? Art thou the daughter of my Lady, even as these are my sons?' But I said: 'Now will I answer thy first question, and tell thee that the Lady thou seekest is verily alive; and she has thriven, for she has drunk of the Well at the World's End, and has put from her the burden of the years. O Geoffrey, and dost thou not know me?' And I held out my hand to him, and I also was weeping, because of my thought of the years gone by; for this old man had been that swain who had nigh died for me when I fled with my husband from the old king; and he became one of the Dry Tree, and had followed me with kind service about the woods in the days when I was at my happiest.

"But now he fell on his knees before me not like a vassal but like a lover, and kissed my feet, and was beside himself for joy. And his sons, who were men of some forty summers, tall and warrior-like, kissed my hands and made obeisance before me.

"Now when we had come to ourselves again, old Geoffrey, who was now naught but glad, spake and said: 'It is told amongst us that when our host departed from the Land of the Tower, after thou hadst taken thy due seat upon the throne, that thou didst promise our chieftains how thou wouldst one day come back to the fellowship of the Dry Tree and dwell amongst us. Wilt thou now hold to thy promise?' I said: 'O Geoffrey, if thou art the last of those seekers, and thou wert but a boy when I dwelt with you of old, who of the Dry Tree is left to remember me?' He hung his head awhile then, and spake: 'Old are we grown, yet art thou fittest to be amongst young folk: unless mine eyes are beguiled by some semblance which will pass away presently.' 'Nay,' quoth I, 'it is not so; as I am now, so shall I be for many and many a day.' 'Well,' said Geoffrey, 'wherever thou mayst be, thou shalt be Queen of men.'

" 'I list not to be Queen again,' said I. He laughed and said: 'I wot not how thou mayst help it.'

"I said: 'Tell me of the Dry Tree, how the champions have sped, and have they grown greater or less.' Said he: 'They are warriors and champions from father to son; therefore have they thriven not over well; yet they have left the thick of the wood, and built them a great castle above the little town hight Hampton; so that is now called Hampton under Scaur, for upon the height of the said Scaur is our castle builded: and there we hold us against the Burg of the Four

Friths which hath thriven greatly; there is none so great as the Burg in all the lands about.'

"I said: 'And the Land of the Tower, thriveth the folk thereof at all?' 'Nay,' he said, 'they have been rent to pieces by folly and war and greediness: in the Great City are but few people, grass grows in its streets; the merchants wend not the ways that lead thither. Naught thriveth there since thou stolest thyself away from them.'

" 'Nay,' I said, 'I fled from their malice, lest I should have been brought out to be burned once more; and there would have been none to rescue then.' 'Was it so?' said old Geoffrey; 'well it is all one now; their day is done.'

" 'Well,' I said, 'come into my house, and eat and drink therein and sleep here to-night, and to-morrow I shall tell thee what I will do.'

"Even so they did; and on the morrow early I spake to Geoffrey and said: 'What hath befallen the Land of Abundance, and the castle my lord built for me there; which we held as our refuge all through the War of the Tower, both before we joined us to you in the wildwood, and afterwards?' He said: 'It is at peace still; no one hath laid hand on it; there is a simple folk dwelling there in the clearing of the wood, which forgetteth thee not; though forsooth strange tales are told of thee there; and the old men deem that it is but a little since thou hast ceased to come and go there; and they are ready to worship thee as somewhat more than the Blessed Saints, were it not for the Fathers of the Thorn who are their masters.'

"I pondered this a while, and then said: 'Geoffrey, ye shall bring me hence away to the peopled parts, and on the way, or when we are come amongst the cities and the kingdoms, we will settle it whither I shall go. See thou! I were fain to be of the brotherhood of the Dry Tree; yet I deem it will scarce be that I shall go and dwell there straightway.'

"Therewith the old man seemed content; and indeed now that the first joy of our meeting, when his youth sprang up in him once more, was over, he found it hard to talk freely with me, and was downcast and shy before me, as if something had come betwixt us, which had made our lives cold to each other.

181

"So that day we left the House of the Sorceress, which I shall not see again, till I come there hand in hand with thee, beloved. When we came to the peopled parts, Geoffrey and his sons brought me to the Land of Abundance, and I found it all as he had said to me: and I took up my dwelling in the castle, and despised not those few folk of the land, but was kind to them: but though they praised my gifts, and honoured me as the saints are honoured, and though they loved me, yet it was with fear, so that I had little part with them. There I dwelt then; and the book which thou didst read there, part true and part false, and altogether of malice against me, I bought of a monk who came our way, and who at first was sore afeared when he found that he had come to my castle. As to the halling of the Chamber of Dais, I have told thee before how my lord, the King's Son, did do make it in memory of the wilderness wherein he found me, and the life of thralldom from which he brought me. There I dwelt till nigh upon these days in peace and quiet: not did I go to the Dry Tree for a long while, though many of them sought to me there at the Castle of Abundance; and, woe worth the while! there was oftenest but one end to their guesting, that of all gifts, they besought me but of one, which, alack! I might not give them: and that is the love that I have given to thee, beloved.—And, oh! my fear, that it will weigh too light with thee, to win me pardon of thee for all that thou must needs pardon me, ere thou canst give me all thy love, that I long for so sorely."

CHAPTER 9

They Go On Their Way
Once More

"Look now," she said, "I have held thee so long in talk, that the afternoon is waning; now is it time for us to be on the way again; not because I misdoubt me of thy foeman, but because I would take thee to a fairer dwelling of the desert, and one where I have erst abided; and moreover, there thou shalt not altogether die of hunger. See, is it not as if I had thought to meet thee here?"

"Yea, in good sooth," said he, "I wot that thou canst see the story of things before they fall."

She laughed and said: "But all this that hath befallen since I set out to meet thee at the Castle of Abundance I foresaw not, any more than I can foresee to-morrow. Only I knew that we must needs pass by the place whereto I shall now lead thee, and I made provision there. Lo! now the marvel slain: and in such wise shall perish other marvels which have been told of me; yet not all. Come now, let us to the way."

So they joined hands and left the pleasant place, and were again going speedily amidst the close pine woods awhile, where it was smooth underfoot and silent of noises withal.

Now Ralph said: "Beloved, thou hast told me of many things, but naught concerning how thou camest to be wedded to the Knight of the Sun, and of thy dealings with him."

Said she, reddening withal: "I will tell thee no more than this, unless thou compel me: that he would have me wed him, as it were against my will, till I ceased striving against him, and I went with him to Sunway, which is no great way from the Castle of Abundance, and there befell that treason of Walter the Black, who loved me and prayed for my love, and when I gainsaid him, swore by all that was holy, before my lord, that it was I who sought his love, and how I had told and taught him ways of witchcraft, whereby we might fulfill our love, so that the Baron should keep a wife for another man. And the Knight of the Sun, whose heart had been filled with many tales of my wisdom, true and false, believed his friend whom he loved, and still believeth him, though he burneth for the love of me now; whereas in those first days of the treason, he burned with love turned to hatred. So of this came that shaming and casting-forth of me. Whereof I will tell thee but this, that the brother of my lord, even the tall champion whom thou hast seen, came upon me presently, when I was cast forth; because he was coming to see the Knight of the Sun at his home; and he loved me, but not after the fashion of his brother, but was

183

kind and mild with me. So then I went with him to Hampton and the Dry Tree, and great joy made the folk thereof of my coming, whereas they remembered their asking of aforetime that I would come to be a Queen over them, and there have I dwelt ever since betwixt Hampton and the Castle of Abundance; and that tall champion has been ever as a brother unto me."

Said Ralph, "And thou art their Queen there?" "Yea," she said, "in a fashion; yet have they another who is mightier than I, and might, if she durst, hang me over the battlements of the Scaur, for she is a fierce and hard woman, and now no longer young in years."

"Is it not so then," said Ralph, "that some of the ill deeds that are told of thee are of her doing?

"It is even so," she said, "and whiles when she has spoken the word I may not be against her openly, therefore I use my wisdom which I have learned, to set free luckless wights from her anger and malice. More by token the last time I did thus was the very night of the day we parted, after thou hadst escaped from the Burg."

"In what wise was that?" said Ralph. She said: "When I rode away from thee on that happy day of my deliverance by thee, my heart laughed for joy of the life thou hadst given me, and of thee the giver, and I swore to myself that I would set free the first captive or death-doomed creature that I came across, in honour of my pleasure and delight: now speedily I came to Hampton and the Scaur; for it is not very far from the want-ways of the wood: and there I heard how four of our folk had been led away by the men of the Burg, therefore it was clear to me that I must set these men free if I could; besides, it pleased me to think that I could walk about the streets of the foemen safely, who had been but just led thitherward to the slaughter. Thou knowest how I sped therein. But when I came back again to our people, after thou hadst ridden away from us with Roger, I heard these tidings, that there was one new-come into our prison, a woman to wit, who had been haled before our old Queen for a spy and doomed by her, and should be taken forth and slain, belike, in a day or two. So I said to myself that I was not free of my vow as yet, because those friends of mine, I should in any case have done my best to deliver them: therefore I deemed my oath bound me to set that woman free. So in the night-tide when all was quiet I went to the prison and brought her forth, and led her past all the gates and wards, which was an easy thing to me, so much as I had learned, and came with her into the fields betwixt the thorp of Hampton and the wood, when it was more daylight than dawn, so that I could see her clearly, and no word as yet had we spoken to each other. But then she said to me: 'Am I to be slain here or led to a crueller prison?' And I said: 'Neither one thing nor the other: for lo! I have set thee free, and I shall look to it that there shall be no pursuit of thee till thou hast had time to get clear away.' But she said: 'What thanks wilt thou have for this? Wherefore hast thou done it?' And I said, 'It is because of the gladness I have gotten.' Said she, 'And would that I might get gladness!' So I asked her what was amiss now that she was free. She said: 'I have lost one thing that I loved, and found another and lost it also.' So I said: 'Mightest thou not seek for the lost?' She said, 'It is in this wood, but when I shall find it I shall not have it.' 'It is love that thou art seeking,' said I. 'In what semblance is he?'

"What wilt thou, my friend? Straightway she fell to making a picture of thee in words; so that I knew that she had met thee, and belike after I had departed from thee, and my heart was sore thereat; for now I will tell thee the very truth, that she was a young woman and exceeding fair, as if she were of pearl all over, and as sweet as eglantine; and I feared her lest she should meet thee again in these wildwoods. And so I asked her what would she, and she said that she had a mind to seek to the Well at the World's End, which quencheth all sorrow; and I rejoiced thereat, thinking that she would be far away from thee, not thinking that thou and I must even meet to seek to it also. So I gave her the chaplet which my witch-mistress took from the dead woman's neck; and went with her into the wildwood, and taught her wisdom of the way and what she was to do. And again I say to thee that she was so sweet and yet with a kind of pity in her both of soul and body, and wise withal and quiet, that I feared her, though I loved her; yea and still do: for I deem her better than me, and meeter for thee and thy love than I be.—Dost thou know her?"

"Yea," said Ralph, "and fair and lovely she is in sooth. Yet hast thou naught to do to fear her. And true it is that I saw her and spake with her after thou hadst ridden away. For she came by the want-ways of the Wood Perilous in the dawn of the day after I had delivered thee; and in sooth she told me that she looked either for Death, or the Water of the Well to end her sorrow."

Then he smiled and said; "As for that which thou sayest, that she had been meeter for me than thou, I know not this word. For look you, beloved, she came, and passed, and is gone, but thou art there and shalt endure."

She stayed, and turned and faced him at that word; and love so consumed her, that all sportive words failed her; yea and it was as if mirth and light-heartedness were swallowed up in the fire of her love; and all thought of other folk departed from him as he felt her tears of love and joy upon his face, and she kissed and embraced him there in the wilderness.

CHAPTER 10

Of the Desert-House and the Chamber of Love in the Wilderness

Then in a while they grew sober and went on their ways, and the sun was westering behind them, and casting long shadows. And in a little while they were come out of the thick woods and were in a country of steep little valleys, grassy, besprinkled with trees and bushes, with hills of sandstone going up from them, which were often broken into cliffs rising sheer from the tree-beset bottoms: and they saw plenteous deer both great and small, and the wild things seemed to fear them but little. To Ralph it seemed an exceeding fair land, and he was as joyous as it was fair; but the Lady was pensive, and at last she said: "Thou deemest it fair, and so it is; yet is it the lonesomest of deserts. I deem indeed that it was once one of the fairest of lands, with castles and cots and homesteads all about, and fair people no few, busy with many matters amongst them. But now it is all passed away, and there is no token of a dwelling of man, save it might be that those mounds we see, as yonder, and yonder again, are tofts of house-walls long ago sunken into the earth of the valley. And now few even are the hunters or way-farers that wend through it."

Quoth Ralph: "Thou speakest as if there had been once histories and tales of this pleasant wilderness: tell me, has it anything to do with that land about the wide river which we went through, Roger and I, as we rode to the Castle of Abundance the other day? For he spoke of tales of deeds and mishaps concerning it." "Yea," she said, "so it is, and the little stream that runs yonder beneath those cliffs, is making its way towards that big river aforesaid, which is called the Swelling Flood. Now true it is also that there are many tales about of the wars and miseries that turned this land into a desert, and these may be true enough, and belike are true. But these said tales have become blended with the story of those aforesaid wars of the Land of the Tower; of which indeed this desert is verily a part, but was desert still in the days when I was Queen of the Land; so thou mayst well think that they who hold me to be the cause of all this loneliness (and belike Roger thought it was so) have scarce got hold of the very sooth of the matter."

"Even so I deemed," said Ralph: "and to-morrow we shall cross the big river, thou and I. Is there a ferry or a ford there whereas we shall come, or how shall we win over it?"

She was growing merrier again now, and laughed at this and said: "O fair boy! the crossing will be to-morrow and not to-day; let to-morrow cross its own rivers; for surely to-day is fair enough, and fairer shall it be when thou hast been fed and art sitting by me in rest and peace till to-morrow morning. So now hasten yet a little more; and we will keep the said little stream in sight as well as we may for the bushes."

So they sped on, till Ralph said: "Will thy feet never tire, beloved?" "O child," she said, "thou hast heard my story, and mayst well deem that they have wrought many a harder day's work than this day's. And moreover they shall soon rest; for look! yonder is our house for this even, and till to-morrow's sun is high: the house for me and thee and none else with us." And therewith she pointed to a place where the stream ran in a chain of pools and stickles, and a sheer cliff rose up some fifty paces beyond it, but betwixt the stream and the cliff was a smooth table of greensward, with three fair thorn bushes thereon, and it went down at each end to the level of the river's lip by a green slope, but amidmost, the little green plain was some ten feet above the stream, and was broken by a little undercliff, which went down sheer into the water. And Ralph saw in the face of the high cliff the mouth of a cave, however deep it might be.

"Come," said the Lady, "tarry not, for I know that hunger hath hold of thee, and look, how low the sun is growing!" Then she caught him by the hand, and fell to running with him to the edge of the stream, where at the end of the further slope it ran wide and shallow before it entered into a deep pool overhung with boughs of alder and thorn. She stepped daintily over a row of big stones laid in the rippling shallow; and staying herself in mid-stream on the biggest of them, and gathering up her gown, looked up stream with a happy face, and then looked over her shoulder to Ralph and said: "The year has been good to me these seasons, so that when I stayed here on my way to the Castle of Abundance, I found but few stones washed away, and crossed wellnigh dry-shod, but this stone my feet are standing on now, I brought down from under the cliff, and set it amid-most, and I said that when I brought thee hither I would stay thereon and talk with thee while I stood above the freshness of the water, as I am doing now."

Ralph looked on her and strove to answer her, but no words would come to his lips, because of the greatness of his longing; she looked on him fondly, and then stooped to look at the ripples that bubbled up about her shoes, and touched them at whiles; then she said: "See how they long for the water, these feet that have worn the waste so long, and know how kind it will run over them and lap about them: but ye must abide a little, waste-wearers, till we have done a thing or two. Come, love!" And she reached her hand out behind her to Ralph, not looking back, but when she felt his hand touch it, she stepped lightly over the other stones, and on to the grass with him, and led him quietly up the slope that went up to the table of greensward before the cave. But when they came on to the level grass she kissed him, and then turned toward the valley and spake solemnly: "May all blessings light on this House of the wilderness and this Hall of the Summer-tide, and the Chamber of Love that here is!"

Then was she silent a while, and Ralph brake not the silence. Then she turned to him with a face grown merry and smiling, and said: "Lo! how the poor lad yearneth for meat, as well he may, so long as the day hath been. Ah, beloved, thou must be patient a little. For belike our servants have not yet heard of the wedding of us. So we twain must feed each the other. Is that so much amiss?"

He laughed in her face for love, and took her by the wrist, but she drew her hand away and went into the cave, and came forth anon holding a copper kettle with an iron bow, and a bag of meal, which she laid at his feet; then she went into the cave again, and brought forth a flask of wine and a beaker; then she caught up the little cauldron, which was well-beaten, and thin and light, and ran down to the stream therewith, and came up thence presently, bearing it full of water on her head, going as straight and stately as the spear is seen on a day of tourney, moving over the barriers that hide the knight, before he lays it in the rest. She came up to him and set the water-kettle before him, and put her hands on his shoulders, and kissed his cheek, and then stepped back from him and smote her palms together, and said: "Yea, it is well! But there are yet more things to do before we rest. There is the dighting of the chamber, and the gathering of wood for the fire, and the mixing of the meal, and the kneading and the baking of cakes; and all that is my work, and there is the bringing of the quarry for the roast, and that is thine."

Then she ran into the cave and brought forth a bow and a quiver of arrows, and said: "Art thou somewhat of an archer?" Quoth he: "I shoot not ill." "And I," she said, "shoot well, all woodcraft comes handy to me. But this eve I must trust to thy skill for my supper. Go swiftly and come back speedily. Do off thine hauberk, and beat the bushes down in the valley, and bring me some small deer, as roe or hare or coney. And wash thee in the pool below the stepping-stones, as I shall do whiles thou art away, and by then thou comest back, all shall be ready, save the roasting of the venison."

So he did off his wargear, but thereafter tarried a little, looking at her, and she said: "What aileth thee not to go? the hunt's up." He said: "I would first go see the rock-hall that is for our chamber to-night; wilt thou not bring me in thither?" "Nay," she said, "for I must be busy about many matters; but thou mayst go by thyself, if thou wilt."

So he went and stooped down and entered the cave, and found it high and wide within, and clean and fresh and well-smelling, and the floor of fine white sand without a stain.

So he knelt down and kissed the floor, and said aloud: "God bless this floor of the rock-hall whereon my love shall lie to-night!" Then he arose and went out of the cave, and found the Lady at the entry stooping down to see what he would do; and she looked on him fondly and anxiously; but he turned a merry face to her, and caught her round the middle and strained her to his bosom, and then took the bow and arrows and ran down the slope and over the stream, into the thicket of the valley.

He went further than he had looked for, ere he found a prey to his mind, and then he smote a roe with a shaft and slew her, and broke up the carcase and dight it duly, and so went his ways back. When he came to the stream he looked up and saw a little fire glittering not far from the cave, but had no clear sight of the Lady, though he thought he saw her gown fluttering nigh one of the thorn-bushes. Then he did off his raiment and entered that pool of the stream, and was glad to bathe him in the same place where her body had been but of late; for he had noted that the stones of the little shore were still wet with her feet where she had gone up from the water.

But now, as he swam and sported in the sun-warmed pool

he deemed he heard the whinnying of a horse, but was not sure, so he held himself still to listen, and heard no more. Then he laughed and bethought him of Falcon his own steed, and dived down under the water; but as he came up, laughing still and gasping, he heard a noise of the clatter of horse hoofs, as if some one were riding swiftly up the further side of the grassy table, where it was stony, as he had noted when they passed by.

A deadly fear fell upon his heart as he thought of his love left all alone; so he gat him at once out of the water and cast his shirt over his head; but while his arms were yet entangled in the sleeves thereof, came to his ears a great and awful sound of a man's voice roaring out, though there were no shapen words in the roar. Then were his arms free through the sleeves, and he took up the bow and fell to bending it, and even therewith he heard a great wailing of a woman's voice, and she cried out, piteously: "Help me, O help, lovely creature of God!"

Yet must he needs finish bending the bow howsoever his heart died within him; or what help would there be of a naked and unarmed man? At last it was bent and an arrow nocked on the string, as he leapt over the river and up the slope.

But even as he came up to that pleasant place he saw all in a moment of time; that there stood Silverfax anigh the Cave's mouth, and the Lady lying on the earth anigh the horse; and betwixt her and him the Knight of the Sun stood up stark, his shining helm on his head, the last rays of the setting sun flashing in the broidered image of his armouries.

He turned at once upon Ralph, shaking his sword in the air (and there was blood upon the blade) and he cried out in terrible voice: "The witch is dead, the whore is dead! And thou, thief, who hast stolen her from me, and lain by her in the wilderness, now shalt thou die, thou!"

Scarce had he spoken than Ralph drew his bow to the arrow-head and loosed; there was but some twenty paces betwixt them, and the shaft, sped by that fell archer, smote the huge man through the eye into the brain, and he fell down along clattering, dead without a word more.

But Ralph gave forth a great wail of woe, and ran forward

191

and knelt by the Lady, who lay all huddled up face down upon the grass, and he lifted her up and laid her gently on her back. The blood was flowing fast from a great wound in her breast, and he tore off a piece of his shirt to staunch it, but she without knowledge of him breathed forth her last breath ere he could touch the hurt, and he still knelt by her, staring on her as if he knew not what was toward.

She had dight her what she could to welcome his return from the hunting, and had set a wreath of meadow-sweet on her red hair, and a garland of eglantine about her girdle-stead, and left her feet naked after the pool of the stream, and had turned the bezels of her finger-rings outward, for joy of that meeting.

After a while he rose up with a most bitter cry, and ran down the green slope and over the water, and hither and thither amongst the bushes like one mad, till he became so weary that he might scarce go or stand for weariness. Then he crept back again to that Chamber of Love, and sat down beside his new-won mate, calling to mind all the wasted words of the day gone by; for the summer night was come now, most fair and fragrant. But he withheld the sobbing passion of his heart and put forth his hand, and touched her, and she was still, and his hand felt her flesh that it was cold as marble. And he cried out aloud in the night and the wilderness, where there was none to hear him, and arose and went away from her, passing by Silverfax who was standing nearby, stretching out his head, and whinnying at whiles. And he sat on the edge of the green table, and there came into his mind despite himself thoughts of the pleasant fields of Upmeads, and his sports and pleasures there, and the even-song of the High House, and the folk of his fellowship and his love. And therewith his breast arose and his face was wryed, and he wept loud and long, and as if he should never make an end of it. But so weary was he, that at last he lay back and fell asleep, and woke not till the sun was high in the heavens. And so it was, that his slumber had been so heavy, that he knew not at first what had befallen; and one moment he felt glad, and the next as if he should never be glad again, though why he wotted not. Then he turned about and saw Silverfax cropping the grass nearby, and the Lady lying there like an image that could move no whit, though the world awoke about her. Then he remembered, yet scarce all, so that wild hopes swelled his heart, and he rose to his knees and turned to her, and called to mind that he should never see her alive again, and sobbing and wailing broke out from him, for he was young and strong, and sorrow dealt hardly with him.

But presently he arose to his feet and went hither and thither, and came upon the quenched coals of the cooking-fire: she had baked cakes for his eating, and he saw them lying thereby, and hunger constrained him, so he took and ate of them while the tears ran down his face and mingled with the bread he ate. And when he had eaten, he felt stronger and therefore was life more grievous to him, and when he thought what he should do, still one thing seemed more irksome than the other.

He went down to the water to drink, and passed by the body of the Knight of the Sun, and wrath was fierce in his heart against him who had overthrown his happiness. But when he had drunk and washed hands and face he came back again, and hardened his heart to do what he must needs do. He took up the body of the Lady and with grief that may not be told of, he drew it into the cave, and cut boughs of trees and laid them over her face and all her body, and then took great stones from the scree at that other end of the little plain, and heaped them upon her till she was utterly hidden by them. Then he came out on to the green place and looked on the body of his foe, and said to himself that all must be decent and in order about the place whereas lay his love. And he came and stood over the body and said: "I have naught to do to hate him now: if he hated me, it was but for a little while, and he knew naught of me. So let his bones be covered up from the wolf and the kite. Yet shall they not lie alongside of her. I will raise a cairn above him here on this fair little plain which he spoilt of all joy." Therewith he fell to, and straightened his body, and laid his huge limbs together and closed his eyes and folded his arms over his breast; and then he piled the stones above him, and went on casting them on the heap a long while after there was need thereof.

Ralph had taken his raiment from the stream-side and

done them on before this, and now he did on helm and hauberk, and girt his sword to his side. Then as he was about leaving the sorrowful place, he looked on Silverfax, who had not strayed from the little plain, and came up to him and did off saddle and bridle, and laid them within the cave, and bade the beast go whither he would. He yet lingered about the place, and looked all around him and found naught to help him, and could frame in his mind no intent of a deed then, nor any tale of a deed he should do thereafter. Yet belike in his mind were two thoughts, and though neither softened his grief save a little, he did not shrink from them as he did from all others; and these two were of his home at Upmeads, which was so familiar to him, and of the Well at the World's End, which was but a word.

CHAPTER 11

Ralph Cometh Out of the Wilderness

Long he stood letting these thoughts run through his mind, but at last when it was now midmorning, he stirred and gat him slowly down the green slope, and for very pity of himself the tears brake out from him as he crossed the stream and came into the bushy valley. There he stayed his feet a little, and said to himself: "And whither then am I going?" He thought of the Castle of Abundance and the Champions of the Dry Tree, of Higham, and the noble warriors who sat at the Lord Abbot's board, and of Upmeads and his own folk: but all seemed naught to him, and he thought: "And how can I go back and bear folk asking me curiously of my wayfarings, and whether I will do this, that, or the other thing." Withal he thought of that fair damsel and her sweet mouth in the hostelry at Bourton Abbas, and groaned when he thought of love and its ending, and he said within himself: "and now she is a wanderer about the earth as I am;" and he thought of her quest, and the chaplet of dame Katherine, his gossip, which he yet bore on his neck, and he deemed that he had naught to choose but to go forward and seek that he was doomed to; and now it seemed to him that there was that one thing to do and no other. And though this also seemed to him but weariness and grief, yet whereas he had ever lightly turned him to doing what work lay ready to hand; so now he knew that he must first of all get him out of that wilderness, that he might hear the talk of folk concerning the Well at the World's End, which he doubted not to hear again when he came into the parts inhabited.

So now, with his will or without it, his feet bore him on, and he followed up the stream which the Lady had said ran into the broad river called the Swelling Flood; "for," thought he, "when I come thereabout I shall presently find some castle or good town, and it is like that either I shall have some tidings of the folk thereof, or else they will compel me to do something, and that will irk me less than doing deeds of mine own will."

He went his ways till he came to where the wood and the trees ended, and the hills were lower and longer, well grassed with short grass, a down country fit for the feeding of sheep; and indeed some sheep he saw, and a shepherd or two, but far off. At last, after he had left the stream awhile, because it seemed to him to turn and wind round over much to the northward, he came upon a road running athwart the down country, so that he deemed that it must lead one way down to the Swelling Flood; so he followed it up, and after a while began to fall in with folk; and first two Companions armed and bearing long swords over their shoulders: he stopped as they met, and stared at them in the face, but answered not their greeting; and they had no will to meddle with him, seeing his inches and that he was well armed, and looked no craven: so they went on.

Next he came on two women who had with them an ass between two panniers, laden with country stuff; and they were sitting by the wayside, one old and the other young. He made no stay for them, and though he turned his face their way, took no heed of them more than if they were trees; though the damsel, who was well-liking and somewhat gaily

195

clad, stood up when she saw his face anigh, and drew her gown skirt about her and moved daintily, and sighed and looked after him as he went on, for she longed for him.

Yet again came two men a-horseback, merchants clad goodly, with three carles, their servants, riding behind them; and all these had weapons and gave little more heed to him than he to them. But a little after they were gone, he stopped and said within himself: "Maybe I had better have gone their way, and this road doubtless leadeth to some place of resort."

But even therewith he heard horsehoofs behind him, and anon came up a man a-horseback, armed with jack and sallet, a long spear in his hand, and budgets at his saddle-bow, who looked like some lord's man going a message. He nodded to Ralph, who gave him good-day; for seeing these folk and their ways had by now somewhat amended his mind; and now he turned not, but went on as before.

At last the way clomb a hill longer and higher than any he had yet crossed, and when he had come to the brow and looked down, he saw the big river close below running through the wide valley which he had crossed with Roger on that other day. Then he sat down on the green bank above the way, so heavy of heart that not one of the things he saw gave him any joy, and the world was naught to him. But within a while he came somewhat to himself, and, looking down toward the river, he saw that where the road met it, it was very wide, and shallow withal, for the waves rippled merrily and glittered in the afternoon sun, though there was no wind; moreover the road went up white from the water on the other side, so he saw clearly that this was the ford of a highway. The valley was peopled withal: on the other side of the river was a little thorp, and there were carts and sheds scattered about the hither side, and sheep and neat feeding in the meadows, and in short it was another world from the desert.

CHAPTER 12

Ralph Falleth in With Friends and Rideth to Whitwall

Ralph looks on to the ford and sees folk riding through the thorp aforesaid and down to the river, and they take the water and are many in company, some two score by his deeming, and he sees the sun glittering on their weapons.

Now he thought that he would abide their coming and see if he might join their company, since if he crossed the water he would be on the backward way: and it was but a little while ere the head of them came up over the hill, and were presently going past Ralph, who rose up to look on them, and be seen of them, but they took little heed of him. So he sees that though they all bore weapons, they were not all men-at-arms, nay, not more than a half score, but those proper men enough. Of the others, some half-dozen seemed by their attire to be merchants, and the rest their lads; and withal they had many sumpter horses and mules with them. They greeted him not, nor he them, nor did he heed them much till they were all gone by save three, and then he leapt into the road with a cry, for who should be riding there but Blaise, his eldest brother, and Richard the Red with him, both in good case by seeming; for Blaise was clad in a black coat welted with gold, and rode a good grey palfrey, and Richard was armed well and knightly.

They knew him at once, and drew rein, and Blaise lighted down from his horse and cast his arms about Ralph, and said: "O happy day! when two of the Upmeads kindred meet thus in an alien land! But what maketh thee here, Ralph? I thought of thee as merry and safe in Upmeads?"

Ralph said smiling, for his heart leapt up at the sight of his kindred: "Nay, must I not seek adventures like the rest? So I stole myself away from father and mother." "Ill done, little lord!" said Blaise, stroking Ralph's cheek.

Then up came Richard, and if Blaise were glad, Richard was twice glad, and quoth he: "Said I not, Lord Blaise, that this chick would be the hardest of all to keep under the coop? Welcome to the Highways, Lord Ralph! But where is thine horse? and whence and whither is it now? Hast thou met with some foil and been held to ransom?"

Ralph found it hard and grievous and dull work to answer; for now again his sorrow had taken hold of him: so he said: "Yea, Richard, I have had adventures, and have lost rather than won; but at least I am a free man, and have spent but little gold on my loss."

"That is well," said Richard, "but whence gat ye any gold for spending?" Ralph smiled, but sadly, for he called to mind the glad setting forth and the kind face of dame Katherine his gossip, and he said: "Clement Chapman deemed it not unmeet to stake somewhat on my luck, therefore I am no pauper."

"Well," said Blaise, "if thou hast no great errand elsewhere, thou mightest ride with us, brother. I have had good hap in these days, though scarce kingly or knightly, for I have been buying and selling: what matter? few know Upmeads and its kings to wite me with fouling a fair name. Richard, go fetch a horse hither for Lord Ralph's riding, and we will tarry no longer." So Richard trotted on, and while they abode him, Ralph asked after his brethren, and Blaise told him that he had seen or heard naught of them. Then Ralph asked of whither away, and Blaise told him to Whitwall, where was much recourse of merchants from many lands, and a noble market.

Back then cometh Richard leading a good horse while Ralph was pondering his matter, and thinking that at such a town he might well hear tidings concerning the Well at the World's End.

Now Ralph mounts, and they all ride away together. On the way, partly for brotherhood's sake, partly that he might not be questioned overmuch himself, Ralph asked Blaise to tell him more of his farings; and Blaise said, that when he had left Upmeads he had ridden with Richard up and down and round about, till he came to a rich town which had just been taken in war, and that the Companions who had conquered it were looking for chapmen to cheapen their booty, and that he was the first or nearly the first to come who had will and money to buy, and the Companions, who were eager to depart, had sold him thieves' penny-worths, so that his share of the Upmeads' treasure had gone far; and thence he had gone to another good town where he had the best of markets for his newly cheapened wares, and had brought more there, such as he deemed handy to sell, and so had gone on from town to town, and had ever thriven, and had got much wealth: and so at last having heard tell of Whitwall as better for chaffer than all he had yet seen, he and other chapmen had armed them, and waged men-at-arms to defend them, and so tried the adventure of the wildwoods, and come safe through.

Then at last came the question to Ralph concerning his adventures, and he enforced himself to speak, and told all as truly as he might, without telling of the Lady and her woeful ending.

Thus they gave and took in talk, and Ralph did what he might to seem like other folk, that he might nurse his grief in his own heart as far asunder from other men as might be.

So they rode on till it was even, and came to Whitwall before the shutting of the gates and rode into the street, and found it a fair and great town, well defensible, with high and new walls, and men-at-arms good store to garnish them.

Ralph rode with his brother to the hostel of the chapmen, and there they were well lodged.

CHAPTER 13

Richard Talketh With Ralph Concerning the Well at the World's End. Concerning Swevenham

On the morrow Blaise went to his chaffer and to visit the men of the Port at the Guildhall: he bade Ralph come with him, but he would not, but abode in the hall of the hostel and sat pondering sadly while men came and went; but he heard no word spoken of the Well at the World's End. In like wise passed the next day and the next, save that Richard was among those who came into the hall, and he talked long with Ralph at whiles; that is to say that he spake, and Ralph made semblance of listening.

Now as is aforesaid Richard was old and wise, and he loved Ralph much, more belike than Lord Blaise his proper master, whereas he had no mind for chaffer, or aught pertaining to it: so he took heed of Ralph and saw that he was sad and weary-hearted; so on the sixth day of their abiding at Whitwall, in the morning when all the chapmen were gone about their business, and he and Ralph were left alone in the Hall, he spake to Ralph and said: "This is no prison, lord." "Even so," quoth Ralph. "Nay, if thou doubtest it," said Richard, "let us go to the door and try if they have turned the key and shot the bolt on us." Ralph smiled faintly and stood up, and said: "I will go with thee if thou willest it, but sooth to say I shall be but a dull fellow of thine to-day." Said Richard: "Wouldst thou have been better yesterday, lord, or the day before?" "Nay," said Ralph. "Wilt thou be better to-morrow?" said Richard. Ralph shook his head. Said Richard: "Yea, but thou wilt be, or thou mayst call me a fool else." "Thou art kind, Richard," said Ralph; "and I will come with thee, and do what thou biddest me; but I must needs tell thee that my heart is sick." "Yea," quoth Richard, "and thou needest not tell me so much, dear youngling; he who runs might read that in thee. But come forth."

So into the street they went, and Richard brought Ralph into the market-place, and showed him where was Blaise's booth (for he was thriving greatly) but Ralph would not go anigh it lest his brother should entangle him in talk; and they went into the Guildhall which was both great and fair, and the smell of the new-shaven oak (for the roof was not yet painted) brought back to Ralph's mind the days of his childhood when he was hanging about the building of the water-reeve's new house at Upmeads. Then they went into the Great Church and heard a Mass at the altar of St. Nicholas, Ralph's very friend; and the said church was great to the letter, and very goodly, and somewhat new also, since the blossom-tide of Whitwall was not many years old: and the altars of its chapels were beyond any thing for fairness that Ralph had seen save at Higham on the Way.

But when they came forth from the church, Ralph looked on Richard with a face that was both blank and weary, as who should say: "What is to do now?" And forsooth so woe-begone he looked, that Richard, despite his sorrow and trouble for him, could scarce withhold his laughter. But he said: "Well, foster son (for thou art pretty much that to me), since the good town pleasureth thee little, go we further afield."

So he led him out of the market-place, and brought him to the east gate of the town which hight Petergate Bar, and forth they went and out into the meadows under the walls, and stayed him at a little bridge over one of the streams, for it was a land of many waters; there they sat down in a nook, and spake Richard to Ralph, saying:

"Lord Ralph, ill it were if the Upmeads kindred came to naught, or even to little. Now as for my own master Blaise, he hath, so please you, the makings of a noble chapman, but not of a noble knight; though he sayeth that when he is right rich he will cast aside all chaffer; naught of which he will do. As for the others, my lord Gregory is no better, or indeed worse, save that he shall not be rich ever, having no mastery over himself; while lord Hugh is like to be slain in some empty brawl, unless he come back speedily to Upmeads."

"Yea, yea," said Ralph, "what then? I came not hither to hear thee missay my mother's sons." But Richard went on: "As for thee, lord Ralph, of thee I looked for something; but now I cannot tell; for the heart in thee seemeth to be dead; and thou must look to it lest the body die also." "So be it!" said Ralph.

Said Richard: "I am old now, but I have been young, and many things have I seen and suffered, ere I came to Upmeads. Old am I, and I cannot feel certain hopes and griefs as a young man can; yet have I bought the knowledge of them dear enough, and have not forgotten. Whereby I wot well that thy drearihead is concerning a woman. Is it not so?" "Yea," quoth Ralph. Said Richard: "Now shalt thou tell me thereof, and so lighten thine heart a little." "I will not tell thee," said Ralph; "or, rather, to speak more truly, I cannot." "Yea," said Richard, "and though it were now an easier thing for me to tell thee of the griefs of my life than for thee to hearken to the tale, yet I believe thee. But mayhappen thou mayst tell me of one thing that thou desirest more than another." Said Ralph: "I desire to die." And the tears started in his eyes therewith. But Richard spake, smiling on him kindly: "That way is open for thee on any day of the week. Why hast thou not taken it already?" But Ralph answered naught. Richard said: "Is it not because thou hopest to desire something; if not to-day, then to-morrow, or the next day or the next?" Still Ralph spake no word; but he wept. Quoth Richard: "Maybe I may help thee to a hope, though thou mayest think my words wild. In the land and the thorp where I was born and bred there was talk now and again of a thing to be sought, which should cure sorrow, and make life blossom in the old, and uphold life in the young." "Yea," said Ralph, looking up from his tears, "and what was that? and why hast thou never told me thereof before?" "Nay," said Richard, "and why should I tell it to the merry lad I knew in Upmeads? but now thou art a man, and hast seen the face of sorrow, it is meet that thou shouldest hear of THE WELL AT THE WORLD'S END."

Ralph sprang to his feet as he said the word, and cried out

202

eagerly: "Old friend, and where then wert thou bred and born?" Richard laughed and said: "See, then, there is yet a deed and a day betwixt thee and death! But turn about and look straight over the meadows in a line with yonder willow-tree, and tell me what thou seest." Said Ralph: "The fair plain spreading wide, and a river running through it, and little hills beyond the water, and blue mountains beyond them, and snow yet lying on the tops of them, though the year is in young July." "Yea," quoth Richard; "and seest thou on the first of the little hills beyond the river, a great grey tower rising up and houses anigh it?" "Yea," said Ralph, "the tower I see, and the houses, for I am far-sighted; but the houses are small." "So it is," said Richard; "now yonder tower is of the Church of Swevenham, which is under the invocation of the Seven Sleepers of Ephesus; and the houses are the houses of the little town. And what has that to do with me? sayest thou: why this, that I was born and bred at Swevenham. And indeed I it was who brought my lord Blaise here to Whitwall, with tales of how good a place it was for chaffer, that I might see the little town and the great grey tower once more. Forsooth I lied not, for thy brother is happy here, whereas he is piling up the coins one upon the other. Forsooth thou shouldest go into his booth, fair lord; it is a goodly sight."

But Ralph was walking to and fro hastily, and he turned to Richard and said: "Well, well! but why dost thou not tell me more of the Well at the World's End?"

Said Richard: "I was going to tell thee somewhat which might be worth thy noting; or might not be worth it: hearken! When I dwelt at Swevenham over yonder, and was but of eighteen winters, who am now of three score and eight, three folk of our township, two young men and one young woman, set out thence to seek the said Well: and much lore they had concerning it, which they had learned of an old man, a nigh kinsman of one of them. This ancient carle I had never seen, for he dwelt in the mountains a way off, and these men were some five years older than I, so that I was a boy when they were men grown; and such things I heeded not, but rather sport and play; and above all, I longed for the play of war and battle. God wot I have had my bellyful of it since those days! Howbeit I mind me the setting forth of these three. They had a sumpter-ass with them for their livelihood on the waste; but they went afoot crowned with flowers, and the pipe and tabour playing before them, and much people brought them on the way. By St. Christopher! I can see it all as if it were yesterday. I was sorry of the departure of the damsel; for though I was a boy I had loved her, and she had suffered me to kiss her and toy with her; but it was soon over. Now I call to mind that they had prayed our priest, Sir Cyprian, to bless them on their departure, but he naysaid them; for he held that such a quest came of the inspiration of the devils, and was but a memory of the customs of the ancient gentiles and heathen. But as to me, I deemed it naught, and was sorry that my white-bosomed, sweet-breathed friend should walk away from me thus into the clouds."

"What came of it?" said Ralph, "did they come back, or any of them?" "I wot not," said Richard, "for I was weary of Swevenham after that, so I girt myself to a sword and laid a spear upon my shoulder and went my ways to the Castle of the Waste March, sixty miles from Swevenham town, and the Baron took me in and made me his man: and almost as little profit were in my telling thee again of my deeds there, as there was in my doing them: but the grey tower of Sweven- ham I have never seen again till this hour."

Said Ralph: "Now then it behoveth me to go to Sweven- ham straightway: wilt thou come with me? it seemeth to be but some four miles hence."

Richard held his peace and knit his brows as if pondering the matter, and Ralph abided till he spake: so he said: "Foster-son, so to call thee, thou knowest the manner of up-country carles, that tales flow forth from them the better if they come without over much digging and hoeing of the ground; that is, without questioning; so meseems better it will be if I go to Swevenham alone, and better if I be asked to go, than if I go of myself. Now to-morrow is Saturday, and high market in Whitwall; and I am not so old but that it is likeliest that there will be some of my fellows alive and on their legs in Swevenham: and if such there be, there will be one at the least in the market to-morrow, and I will be there to find him out: and then it will go hard if he bring me not to Swevenham as a well-beloved guest; and when I am there, and telling my tidings, and asking them of theirs, if there be any tales concerning the Well at the World's End working in their bellies, then shall I be the midwife to bring them to birth. Ha? Will it do?"

"Yea," said Ralph, "but how long wilt thou be?" Said Richard: "I shall come back speedily if I find the land barren; but if the field be in ear I shall tarry to harvest it. So keep thou thy soul in patience." "And what shall I do now?" said Ralph. "Wear away the hours," said Richard. And to begin with, come back within the gates with me and let us go look at thy brother's booth in the market-place: it is the nethermost of a goodly house which he is minded to dwell in; and he will marry a wife and sit down in Whitwall, so well he seemeth like to thrive; for they have already bidden him to the freedom of the city, and to a brother of the Faring-Knights, whereas he is not only a stirring man, but of good lineage also: for now he hideth not that he is of the Upmeads kindred."

CHAPTER 14

Ralph Falleth in With Another Old Friend

Ralph went with Richard now without more words, and they came into the market-place and unto Blaise's booth and house, which was no worse than the best in the place; and the painters and stainers were at work on the upper part of it to make it as bright and goodly as might be with red and blue and green and gold, and all fair colours, and already was there a sign hung out of the fruitful tree by the water-side. As for the booth, it was full within of many wares and far-fetched and dear-bought things; as pieces of good and fine cloth plumbed with the seal of the greatest of the cities;

and silk of Babylon, and spices of the hot burning islands, and wonders of the silversmith's and the goldsmith's fashioning, and fair-wrought weapons and armour of the best, and every thing that a rich chapman may deal in. And amidst of it all stood Blaise clad in fine black cloth welted with needle work, and a gold chain about his neck. He was talking with three honourable men of the Port, and they were doing him honour with kind words and the bidding of help. When he saw Ralph and Richard come in, he nodded to them, as to men whom he loved, but were beneath him in dignity, and left not talking with the great men. Richard grinned a little thereat, as also did Ralph in his heart; for he thought: "Here then is one of the Upmeads kin provided for, so that soon he may buy with his money two domains as big as Upmeads and call them his manors."

Now Ralph looks about him, and presently he sees a man come forward to meet him from the innermost of the booth, and lo! there was come Clement Chapman. His heart rose at the sight of him, and he thought of his kind gossip till he could scarce withhold his tears. But Clement came to him and cast his arms about him, and kissed him, and said: "Thou shalt pardon me for this, lord, for it is the kiss of the gossip which she bade me give thee, if I fell in with thee, as now I have, praised be the Saints! Yet it irks me that I shall see little more of thee at this time, for to-morrow early I must needs join myself to my company; for we are going south awhile to a good town some fifty miles hence. Nevertheless, if thou dwellest here some eight days I shall see thee again belike, since thereafter I get me eastward on a hard and long journey not without peril. How sayest thou?"

"I wot not," quoth Ralph looking at Richard. Said Richard: "Thou mayst wot well, master Clement, that my lord is anhungered of the praise of the folks, and is not like to abide in a mere merchant-town till the mould grow on his back." "Well, well," said Clement, "however that may be, I have now done my matters with this cloth-lord, Blaise, and he has my florins in his pouch: so will not ye twain come with me and drink a cup till he hath done his talk with these magnates?"

Ralph was nothing loth, for besides that he loved master

Clement, and that his being in company was like having a piece of his home anigh him, he hoped to hear some tidings concerning the Well at the World's End.

So he and Richard went with master Clement to the Christopher, a fair ale-house over against the Great Church, and sat down to good wine; and Ralph asked of Clement many things concerning dame Katherine his gossip, and Clement told him all, and that she was well, and had been to Upmeads, and had seen King Peter and the mother of Ralph; and how she had assuaged his mother's grief at his departure by forecasting fair days for her son. All this Ralph heard gladly, though he was somewhat shamefaced withal, and sat silent and thinking of many matters. But Richard took up the word and said: "Which way camest thou from Wulstead, master Clement?" "The nighest way I came," said Clement, "through the Woods Perilous." Said Richard: "And they of the Dry Tree, heardest thou aught of them?" "Yea, certes," quoth Clement, "for I fell in with their Bailiff, and paid him due scot for the passage of the Wood; he knoweth me withal, and we talked together." "And had he any tidings to tell thee of the champions?" said Richard. Said Clement, "Great tidings maybe, how that there was a rumour that they had lost their young Queen and Lady; and if that be true, it will go nigh to break their hearts, so sore as they loved her. And that will make them bitter and fierce, till their grief has been slaked by the blood of men. And that the more as their old Queen abideth still, and she herself is ever of that mind."

Ralph hearkened, and his heart was wounded that other men should speak of his beloved: but he heard how Richard said: "Hast thou ever known why that company of champions took the name of the Dry Tree?" "Why, who should know that, if thou knowest it not, Richard of Swevenham?" said Clement: "Is it not by the token of the Dry Tree that standeth in the lands on the hither side of the Wall of the World?" Richard nodded his head; but Ralph cried out: "O Master Clement, and hast thou seen it, the Wall of the World?" "Yea, afar off, my son," said he; "or what the folk with me called so; as to the Dry Tree, I have told thee at Wulstead that I have seen it not, though I have known men who have told me that they have seen it." "And must they

207

who find the Well at the World's End come by the Dry Tree?" "Yea, surely," said Clement. Quoth Richard: "And thus have some heard, who have gone on that quest, and they have heard of the Champions of Hampton, and have gone thither, being deceived by that name of the Dry Tree, and whiles have been slain by the champions, whiles have entered their company." "Yea," said Clement, "so it is that their first error hath ended their quest. But now, lord Ralph, I will tell thee one thing; to wit, that when I return hither after eight days wearing, I shall be wending east, as I said e'en now, and what will that mean save going somewhat nigher to the Wall of the World; for my way lieth beyond the mountains that ye see from hence, and beyond the mountains that lie the other side of those; and I bid thee come with us, and I will be thy warrant that so far thou shalt have no harm: but when thou hast come so far, and hast seen three very fair cities, besides towns and castles and thorps and strange men, and fair merchandize, God forbid that thou shouldest wend further, and so cast away thy young life for a gay-coloured cloud. Then will be the time to come back with me, that I may bring thee through the perils of the way to Wulstead, and Upmeads at the last, and the folk that love thee."

Richard held his peace at this word, but Ralph said: "I thank thee, Master Clement, for thy love and thy helping hand; and will promise thee to abide thee here eight days at the least; and meanwhile I will ponder the matter well."

CHAPTER 15

Ralph Dreams a Dream Or Sees a Vision

Therewithall they parted after more talk concerning small matters, and Ralph wore through the day, but Richard again did him to wit, that on the morrow he would find his old friends of Swevenham in the Market. And Ralph was come to life again more than he had been since that evil hour in the desert; though hard and hard he deemed it that he should never see his love again.

Now as befalleth young men, he was a good sleeper, and dreamed but seldom, save such light and empty dreams as he might laugh at, if perchance he remembered them by then his raiment was on him in the morning. But that night himseemed that he awoke in his chamber at Whitwall, and was lying on his bed, as he verily was, and the door of the chamber opened, and there entered quietly the Lady of the Woodland, dight even as he had seen her as she lay dead beside their cooking fire on that table of greensward in the wilderness, barefoot and garlanded about her brow and her girdlestead, but fair and fresh coloured as she was before the sword had pierced her side; and he thought that he rejoiced to see her, but no wild hope rose in his heart, and no sobbing passion blinded his eyes, nor did he stretch out hand to touch her, because he remembered that she was dead. But he thought she spake to him and said: "I know that thou wouldst have me speak, therefore I say that I am come to bid thee farewell, since there was no farewell between us in the wilderness, and I know that thou are about going on a long and hard and perilous journey: and I would that I could kiss thee and embrace thee, but I may not, for this is but the image of me as thou hast known me. Furthermore, as I loved thee when I saw thee first, for thy youth, and thy fairness, and thy kindness and thy valiancy, so now I rejoice that all this shall endure so long in thee, as it surely shall."

Then the voice ceased, but still the image stood before him awhile, and he wondered if she would speak again, and tell him aught of the way to the Well at the World's End; and she spake again: "Nay," she said, "I cannot, since we may not tread the way together hand in hand; and this is part of the loss that thou hast had of me; and oh! but it is hard and hard." And her face became sad and distressful, and she turned and departed as she had come.

Then he knew not if he awoke, or if it were a change in his dream; but the chamber became dark about him, and he lay there thinking of her, till, as it seemed, day began to dawn, and there was some little stir in the world without, and the new wind moved the casement. And again the door opened, and someone entered as before; and this also was a woman: green-clad she was and barefoot, yet he knew at once that it was not his love that was dead, but the damsel of the ale-house of Bourton, whom he had last seen by the wantways of the Wood Perilous, and he thought her wondrous fair, fairer than he had deemed. And the word came from her: "I am a sending of the woman whom thou hast loved, and I should not have been here save she had sent me." Then the words ended, while he looked at her and wondered if she also had died on the way to the Well at the World's End. And it came into his mind that he had never known her name upon the earth. Then again came the word: "So it is that I am not dead but alive in the world, though I am far away from this land; and it is good that thou shouldst go seek the Well at the World's End not all alone: and the seeker may find me: and whereas thou wouldst know my name, I hight Dorothea."

So fell the words again: and this image stood awhile as the other had done, and as the other had done, departed, and once more the chamber became dark, so that Ralph could not so much as see where was the window, and he knew no more till he woke in the early morn, and there was stir in the street and the voice of men, and the scent of fresh herbs and worts, and fruits; for it was market-day, and the country folk were early afoot, that they might array their wares timely in the market-place.

CHAPTER 16

Of the Tales of Swevenham

Old Richard was no worse than his word, and failed not to find old acquaintance of Swevenham in the Saturday's market: and Ralph saw naught of him till midweek afterwards.

And he was sitting in the chamber of the hostel when Richard came in to him. Forsooth Blaise had bidden him come dwell in his fair house, but Ralph would not, deeming that he might be hindered in his quest and be less free to go whereso he would, if he were dwelling with one who was so great with the magnates as was Blaise.

Now Ralph was reading in a book when Richard came in, but he stood up and greeted him; and Richard said smiling: "What have ye found in the book, lord?" Said Ralph: "It telleth of the deeds of Alexander." "Is there aught concerning the Well at the World's End therein?" said Richard. "I have not found aught thereof as yet," said Ralph; "but the book tells concerning the Dry Tree, and of kings sitting in their chairs in the mountains nearby."

"Well then," said Richard, "maybe thou wilt think me the better tale-teller." "Tell on then," quoth Richard. So they went and sat them down in a window, and Richard said:

"When I came to Swevenham with two old men that I had known young, the folk made much of me, and made me good cheer, whereof were over long to tell thee; but to speak shortly, I drew the talk round to the matter that we would wot of: for we spake of the Men of the Dry Tree, and an old man began to say, as master Clement the other day, that this name of theirs was but a token and an armoury which those champions have taken from the Tree itself, which Alexander the Champion saw in his wayfarings; and he said that this tree was on the hither side of the mountains called the Wall of the World, and no great way from the last of the towns whereto Clement will wend; for Clement told me the name thereof, to wit, Goldburg. Then another and an older man, one that I remember a stout carle ere I left Swevenham, said that this was not so, but that the Tree was on the further side of the Wall of the World, and that he who could lay his hand on the bole thereof was like enough to drink of the Well at the World's End. Thereafter another spake, and told a tale of how the champions at Hampton first took the Dry Tree for a token; and he said that the rumour ran, that a woman had brought the tidings thereof to those valiant men, and had fixed the name upon them, though wherefore none knew. So the talk went on.

211

"But there was a carline sitting in the ingle, and she knew me and I her. And indeed in days past, when I was restless and longing to depart, she might have held me at Swevenham, for she was one of the friends that I loved there: a word and a kiss had done it, or maybe the kiss without the word: but if I had the word, I had not the kiss of her. Well, when the talk began to fall, she spake and said to me:

" 'Now it is somewhat strange that the talk must needs fall on this seeking of that which shall not be found, whereas it was but the month before thou wert last at Swevenham, that Wat Miller and Simon Bowyer set off to seek the Well at the World's End, and took with them Alice of Queenhough, whom Simon loved as well as might be, and Wat somewhat more than well. Mindest thou not? There are more than I alive that remember it.'

" 'Yea,' said I, 'I remember it well.'

"For indeed, foster-son, these were the very three of whom I told thee, though I told thee not their names.

" 'Well,' said I; 'how sped they? Came they back, or any of them?' 'Nay,' she said, 'that were scarce to be looked for.' Said I: 'Have any other to thy knowledge gone on this said quest?'

" 'Yea,' she said, 'I will tell thee all about it, and then there will be an end of the story, for none knoweth better thereof than I. First there was that old man, the wizard, to whom folk from Swevenham and other places about were used to seek for his lore in hidden matters; and some months after those three had departed, folk who went to his abode amongst the mountains found him not; and soon the word was about that he also, for as feeble as he was, had gone to seek the Well at the World's End; though may-happen it was not so. Then the next spring after thy departure, Richard, comes home Arnold Wright from the wars, and asks after Alice; and when he heard what had befallen, he takes a scrip with a little meat for the road, lays his spear on his shoulder, and is gone seeking the lost, and the thing which they found not—that, I deem, was the end of him. Again the year after that, as I deem, three of our carles fell in with two knights riding east from Whitwall, and were questioned of them concerning the road to the said Well, and doubted not but that they were

212

on that quest. Furthermore (and some of you wot this well enough, and more belike know it not) two of our young men were faring by night and cloud on some errand, good or bad, it matters not, on the highway thirty miles east of Whitwall: it was after harvest, and the stubble-fields lay on either side of the way, and the moon was behind thin clouds, so that it was light on the way, as they told me; and they saw a woman wending before them afoot, and as they came up with her, the moon ran out, and they saw that the woman was fair, and that about her neck was a chaplet of gems that shone in the moon, and they had a longing both for the jewel and the woman: but before they laid hand on her they asked her of whence and whither, and she said: From ruin and wrack to the Well at the World's End, and therewith turned on them with a naked sword in her hand; so that they shrank from before her.

" 'Hearken once more: the next year came a knight to Swevenham, and guested in this same house, and he sat just where sitteth now yon yellow-headed swain, and the talk went on the same road as it hath gone to-night; and I told him all the tale as I have said it e'en now; and he asked many questions, but most of the Lady with the pair of beads. And on the morrow he departed and we saw him not again.

"Then she was silent, but the young man at whom she had pointed flushed red and stared at her wide-eyed, but said no word. But I spake: 'Well dame, but have none else gone from Swevenham, or what hath befallen them?'

"She said: 'Hearken yet! Twenty years agone a great sickness lay heavy upon us and the folk of Whitwall, and when it was at its worst, five of our young men, calling to mind all the tales concerning the Well at the World's End, went their ways to seek it, and swore that back would they never, save they found it and could bear its water to the folk of Swevenham; and I suppose they kept their oath; for we saw naught either of the water or of them. Well, I deem that this is the last that I have to tell thee, Richard, concerning this matter: and now is come the time for thee to tell tales of thyself.'

"Thus for that time dropped the talk of the Well at the World's End, Lord Ralph, and of the way thither. But I hung about the township yet a while, and yesterday as I stood on their stone bridge, and looked on the water, up comes that long lad with the yellow hair that the dame had pointed at, and says to me: 'Master Richard, saving thine age and thy dignity and mastery, I can join an end to the tale which the carline began on Sunday night.' 'Yea, forsooth?' said I, and how, my lad?' Said he: 'Thou hast a goodly knife there in thy girdle, give it to me, and I will tell thee.' 'Yea,' quoth I, 'if thy tale be knife-worthy.'

"Well, the end of it was that he told me thus: That by night and moon he came on one riding the highway, just about where the other woman had been seen, whose tale he had heard of. He deemed at first this rider to be a man, or a lad rather for smallness and slenderness, but coming close up he found it was a woman, and saw on her neck a chaplet of gems, and deemed it no great feat to take it of her: but he asked her of whence and whither, and she answered:

" 'From unrest to the Well at the World's End.'

"Then when he put out his hand to her, he saw a great anlace gleaming in her hand, wherefore he forbore her; and this was but five days ago.

"So I gave the lad my knife, and deemed there would be little else to hear in Swevenham for this bout; and at least I heard no more tales to tell till I came away this morning; so there is my poke turned inside out for thee. But this word further would I say to thee, that I have seen on thy neck also a pair of beads exceeding goodly. Tell me now whence came they."

"From my gossip, dame Katherine," said Ralph; "and it seems to me now, though at the time I heeded the gift little save for its kindness, that she thought something great might go with it; and there was a monk at Higham on the Way, who sorely longed to have it of me." "Well," said Richard, "that may well come to pass, that it shall lead thee to the Well at the World's End. But as to the tales of Swevenham, what deemest thou of them?" Said Ralph: "What are they, save a token that folk believe that there is such a thing on earth as the Well? Yet I have made up my mind already that I would so do as if I trowed in it. So I am no nearer to it than erst. Now is there naught for it save to abide Master

214

Clement's coming; and when he hath brought me to Gold-burg, then shall I see how the quest looks by the daylight of that same city." He spake so cheerfully that Richard looked at him askance, wondering what was toward with him, and if mayhappen anything lay underneath those words of his.

But in his heart Ralph was thinking of that last tale of the woman whom the young man had met such a little while ago; and it seemed to him that she must have been in Whitwall when he first came there; and he scarce knew whether he were sorry or not that he had missed her: for though it seemed to him that it would be little more than mere grief and pain, nay, that it would be wicked and evil to be led to the Well at the World's End by any other than her who was to have brought him there; yet he longed, or thought he longed to speak with her concerning that love of his heart, so early rewarded, so speedily beggared. For indeed he doubted not that the said woman was the damsel of Bourton Abbas, whose image had named herself Dorothea to him in that dream.

CHAPTER 17

Richard Bringeth Tidings of Departing

Fell the talk between them at that time, and three days wore, and on the morning of the fourth day came Richard to Ralph, and said to him: "Foster-son, I am sorry for the word I must say, but Clement Chapman came within the gates this morning early, and the company with which he is riding are alboun for the road, and will depart at noon to-day, so that there are but four hours wherein we twain may be together; and thereafter whatso may betide thee, it may well be, that I shall see thy face no more; so what thou wilt tell me must be told straightway. And now I will say this to thee, that of all things I were fain to ride with thee, but I may not, because it is Blaise whom I am bound to serve in all ways. And I deem, moreover, that troublous times may be at hand here in Whitwall. For there is an Earl hight Walter the Black, a fair young man outwardly, but false at heart and a tyrant, and he had some occasion against the good town, and it was looked for that he should send his herald here to defy the Port more than a half moon ago; but about that time he was hurt in a fray as we hear, and may not back a horse in battle yet. Albeit, fristed is not forgotten, as saith the saw; and when he is whole again, we may look for him at our gates; and whereas Blaise knows me for a deft man-at-arms or something more, it is not to be looked for that he will give me to thee for this quest. Nay, of thee also it will be looked for that thou shouldest do knightly service to the Port, and even so Blaise means it to be; therefore have I lied to him on thy behalf, and bidden Clement also to lie (which forsooth he may do better than I, since he wotteth not wholly whither thou art minded), and I have said thou wouldst go with Clement no further than Cheaping Knowe, which lieth close to the further side of these mountains, and will be back again in somewhat more than a half-moon's wearing. So now thou art warned hereof."

Ralph was moved by these words of Richard, and he spake: "Forsooth, old friend, I am sorry to depart from thee; yet though I shall presently be all alone amongst aliens, yet now is manhood rising again in me. So for that cause at least shall I be glad to be on the way; and as a token that I am more whole than I was, I will now tell thee the tale of my grief, if thou wilt hearken to it, which the other day I might not tell thee."

"I will hearken it gladly," said Richard. And therewith they sat down in a window, for they were within doors in the hostel, and Ralph told all that had befallen him as plainly and shortly as he might; and when he had done, Richard said:

"Thou has had much adventure in a short space, lord, and if thou mightest now refrain thy longing for that which is gone, and set it on that which is to come, thou mayest yet harden into a famous knight and a happy man." Said Ralph: "Yea? now tell me all thy thought."

Said Richard: "My thought is that this lady who was slain,

216

was scarce wholly of the race of Adam; but that at the least there was some blending in her of the blood of the fays. Or how deemest thou?"

"I wot not," said Ralph sadly; "to me she seemed but a woman, though she were fairer and wiser than other women." Said Richard: "Well, furthermore, if I heard thee aright, there is another woman in the tale who is also fairer and wiser than other women?"

"I would she were my sister!" said Ralph. "Yea," quoth Richard, "and dost thou bear in mind what she was like? I mean the fashion of her body." "Yea, verily," said Ralph.

Again said Richard: "Doth it seem to thee as if the Lady of the Dry Tree had some inkling that thou shouldst happen upon this other woman: whereas she showed her of the road to the Well at the World's End, and gave her that pair of beads, and meant that thou also shouldest go thither? And thou sayest that she praised her,—her beauty and wisdom. In what wise did she praise her? how came the words forth from her? was it sweetly?"

"Like honey and roses for sweetness," said Ralph. "Yea," said Richard, "and she might have praised her in such wise that the words had came forth like gall and vinegar. Now I will tell thee of my thought, since we be at point of sundering, though thou take it amiss and be wroth with me: to wit, that thou wouldst have lost the love of this lady as time wore, even had she not been slain: and she being, if no fay, yet wiser than other women, and foreseeing, knew that so it would be." Ralph brake in: "Nay, nay, it is not so, it is not so!" "Hearken, youngling!" quoth Richard; "I deem that it was thus. Her love for thee was so kind that she would have thee happy after the sundering: therefore she was minded that thou shouldest find the damsel, who as I deem loveth thee, and that thou shouldest love her truly."

"O nay, nay!" said Ralph, "all this guess of thine is naught, saying that she was kind indeed. Even as heaven is kind to them who have died martyrs, and enter into its bliss after many torments."

And therewith he fell a-weeping at the very thought of her great kindness: for indeed to this young man she had seemed great, and exalted far above him.

Richard looked at him a while; and then said: "Now, I pray thee be not wroth with me for the word I have spoken. But something more shall I say, which shall like thee better. To wit, when I came back from Swevenham on Wednesday I deemed it most like that the Well at the World's End was a tale, a coloured cloud only; or that at most if it were indeed on the earth, that thou shouldest never find it. But now is my mind changed by the hearing of thy tale, and I deem both that the Well verily is, and that thou thyself shalt find it; and that the wise Lady knew this, and set the greater store by thy youth and goodliness, as a richer and more glorious gift than it had been, were it as fleeting as such things mostly be. Now of this matter will I say no more; but I think that the words that I have said, and which now seem so vain to thee, shall come into thy mind on some later day, and avail thee somewhat; and that is why I have spoken them. But this again is another word, that I have got a right good horse for thee, and other gear, such as thou mayest need for the road, and that Clement's fellowship will meet in Petergate hard by the church, and I will be thy squire till thou comest thither, and ridest thence out a-gates. Now I suppose that thou will want to bid Blaise farewell: yet thou must look to it that he will not deem thy farewell of great moment, since he swimmeth in florins and goodly wares; and moreover deemeth that thou wilt soon be back here."

"Nevertheless," said Ralph, "I must needs cast my arms about my own mother's son before I depart: so go we now, as all this talk hath worn away more than an hour of those four that were left me."

CHAPTER 18

Ralph Departeth From Whitwall
With the Fellowship of
Clement Chapman

Therewithal they went together to Blaise's house, and when Blaise saw them, he said: "Well, Ralph, so thou must needs work at a little more idling before thou fallest to in earnest. Forsooth I deem that when thou comest back thou wilt find that we have cut thee out a goodly piece of work for thy sewing. For the good town is gathering a gallant host of men; and we shall look to thee to do well in the hard hand-play, whenso that befalleth. But now come and look at my house within, how fair it is, and thou wilt see that thou wilt have somewhat to fight for, whereas I am."

Therewith he led them up a stair into the great chamber, which was all newly dight and hung with rich arras of the Story of Hercules; and there was a goodly cupboard of silver vessel, and some gold, and the cupboard was of five shelves as was but meet for a king's son. So Ralph praised all, but was wishful to depart, for his heart was sore, and he blamed himself in a manner that he must needs lie to his brother.

But Blaise brought them to the upper chamber, and showed them the goodly beds with their cloths, and hangings, and all was as fair as might be. Then Blaise bade bring wine and made them drink; and he gave Ralph a purse of gold, and an anlace very fair of fashion, and brought him to the door thereafter; and Ralph cast his arms about him, and kissed him and strained him to his breast. But Blaise was somewhat moved thereat, and said to him: "Why lad, thou art sorry to depart from me for a little while, and what would it be, were it for long? But ever wert thou a kind and tender-hearted youngling, and we twain are alone in an alien land. Forsooth, I wot that thou hast, as it were, embraced the Upmeads kindred, father, mother and all; and good is that! So now God and the Saints keep thee, and bear in mind the hosting of the good town, and the raising of the banner, that shall be no great while. Fare thee well, lad!"

So they parted, and Ralph went back to the hostel, and gathered his stuff together, and laid it on a sumpter horse, and armed him, and so went into Petergate to join himself to that company. There he found the chapmen, five of them in all, and their lads, and a score of men-at-arms, with whom was Clement, not clad like a merchant, but weaponed, and bearing a coat of proof and a bright sallet on his head.

They greeted each the other, and Ralph said: "Yea, master Clement, and be we riding to battle?" "Maybe," quoth Clement; "the way is long, and our goods worth the lifting, and there are some rough places that we must needs pass through. But if ye like not the journey, abide here in this town the onset of Walter the Black."

Therewith he laughed, and Ralph understanding the jape, laughed also; and said: "Well, master Clement, but tell me who be these that we shall meet." "Yea, and I will tell thee the whole tale of them," said Clement, "but abide till we are without the gates; I am busy man e'en now, for all is ready for the road, save what I must do. So now bid thy Upmeads squire farewell, and then to horse with thee!"

So Ralph cast his arms about Richard, and kissed him and said: "This is also a farewell to the House where I was born and bred." And as he spake the thought of the House and the garden, and the pleasant fields of Upmeads came into his heart so bitter-sweet, that it mingled with his sorrow, and well-nigh made him weep. But as for Richard he forebore words, for he was sad at heart for the sundering.

Then he gat to horse, and the whole company of them bestirred them, and they rode out a-gates. And master Clement it was that ordered them, riding up and down along the array.

But Ralph fell to speech with the chapmen and men-at-arms; and both of these were very courteous with him; for they rejoiced in his company, and especially the chapmen, who were somewhat timorous of the perils of the road.

CHAPTER 19

Master Clement Tells Ralph Concerning the Lands Whereunto They Were Riding

When they were gotten a mile or two from Whitwall, and all was going smoothly, Clement came up to Ralph and rode at his left hand, and fell to speech with him, and said: "Now, lord, will I tell thee more concerning our journey, and the folk that we are like to meet upon the road. And of the perils, whatso they may be, I told thee not before, because I knew thee desirous of seeking adventures east-away, and knew that my tales would not hinder thee."

"Yea," said Ralph, "and had not this goodly fellowship been, I had gone alone, or with any carle that I could have lightly hired."

Clement laughed and said: "Fair sir, thou wouldst have failed of hiring any one man to go with thee east-ward a many miles. For with less than a score of men well-armed the danger of death or captivity is over great, if ye ride the mountain ways unto Cheaping Knowe. Yea, and even if a poor man who hath nothing, wend that way alone, he may well fall among thieves, and be stolen himself body and bones, for lack of anything better to steal."

Hereat Ralph felt his heart rise, when he thought of battle and strife, and he made his horse to spring somewhat, and then he said: "It liketh me well, dear friend, that I ride not with thee for naught, but that I may earn my daily bread like another."

"Yea," said Clement, looking on him kindly, "I deem of all thy brethren thou hast the biggest share of the blood of Red Robert, who first won Upmeads. And now thou shalt know that this good town of Whitwall that lieth behind us is the last of the lands we shall come to wherein folk can any courtesy, or are ruled by the customs of the manor, or by due lawful Earls and Kings, or the laws of the Lineage or the Port, or have any Guilds for their guiding, and helping. And though these folks whereunto we shall come, are, some of them, Christian men by name, and have amongst them priests and religious; yet are they wild men of manners, and many heathen customs abide amongst them; as swearing on the altars of devils, and eating horse-flesh at the High-tides, and spell-raising more than enough, and such like things, even to the reddening of the doom-rings with the blood of men and of women, yea, and of babes: from such things their priests cannot withhold them. As for their towns that we shall come to, I say not but we shall find crafts amongst them, and worthy good men therein, but they have little might against the tyrants who reign over the towns, and who are of no great kindred, nor of blood better than other folk, but merely masterful and wise men who have gained their place by cunning and the high hand. Thou shalt see castles and fair strong-houses about the country-side, but the great men who dwell therein are not the natural kindly lords of the land yielding service to Earls, Dukes, and Kings, and having under them vavassors and villeins, men of the manor; but their tillers and shepherds and workmen and servants be mere thralls, whom they may sell at any market, like their horses or oxen. Forsooth these great men have with them for the more part free men waged for their service, who will not hold their hands from aught that their master biddeth, not staying to ask if it be lawful or unlawful. And that the more because whoso is a free man there, house and head must he hold on the tenure of bow and sword, and his life is like to be short if he hath not sworn himself to the service of some tyrant of a castle or a town."

"Yea, master Clement," said Ralph, "these be no peaceful lands whereto thou art bringing us, or very pleasant to dwell in."

"Little for peace, but much for profit," said Clement; "for these lands be fruitful of wine and oil and wheat, and neat and sheep; withal metals and gems are dug up out of the mountains; and on the other hand, they make but little by craftsmanship, wherefore are they the eagerer for chaffer with us merchants; whereas also there are many of them well able to pay for what they lack, if not in money, then in kind, which in a way is better. Yea, it is a goodly land for merchants."

"But I am no merchant," said Ralph.

"So it is," said Clement, "yet thou desireth something; and whither we are wending thou mayst hear tidings that shall please thee, or tidings that shall please me. To say sooth, these two may well be adverse to each other, for I would not have thee hear so much of tidings as shall lead thee on, but rather I would have thee return with me, and not throw thy young life away: for indeed I have an inkling of what thou seekest, and meseems that Death and the Devil shall be thy faring-fellows."

Ralph held his peace, and Clement said in a cheerfuller voice: "Moreover, there shall be strange and goodly things to see; and the men of these parts be mostly goodly of body, and the women goodlier yet, as we carles deem."

Ralph sighed, and answered not at once, but presently he said: "Master Clement, canst thou give me the order of our goings for these next days?" "Yea, certes," said Clement. "In three days' time we shall come to the entry of the mountains: two days thence we shall go without coming under any roof save the naked heavens; the day thereafter shall we come to the Mid-Mountain House, which is as it were an hostelry; but it was built and is upheld by the folks that dwell anigh, amongst whom be the folk of Cheaping Knowe; and that house is hallowed unto truce, and no man smiteth another therein; so that we oft come on the mountain strong-thieves there, and there we be blithe together and feast together in good fellowship. But when there be foemen in that house together, each man or each fellowship departing, hath grace of an hour before his foeman follow. Such are the customs of that house, and no man breaketh them ever. But when we depart thence we shall ride all day and sleep amidst the mountains, and if we be not beset that night or the morrow's morn thereof, safe and unfoughten shall we come to Cheaping Knowe. Doth that suffice thee as at this time?" "Yea master," quoth Ralph.

So therewith their talk dropped, for the moment; but Clement talked much with Ralph that day, and honoured him much, as did all that company.

CHAPTER 20

They Come to the Mid-Mountain Guest-House

On that night they slept in their tents which they had pitched on the field of a little thorp beside a water; and there they had meat and drink and all things as they needed them. And in likewise it befell them the next day; but the third evening they set up their tents on a little hillside by a road which led into a deep pass, even the entry of the mountains, a road which went betwixt exceeding high walls of rock. For the mountain sides went up steep from the plain. There they kept good watch and ward, and naught befell them to tell of.

The next morning they entered the pass, and rode through it up to the heaths, and rode all day by wild and stony ways and came at even to a grassy valley watered by a little stream, where they guested, watching their camp well; and again none meddled with them.

As they were departing the next morn Ralph asked of Clement if he yet looked for onset from the waylayers. Said Clement: "It is most like, lord; for we be a rich prey, and it is but seldom that such a company rideth this road. And albeit that the wild men know not to a day when we shall pass through their country, yet they know the time within a four and twenty hours or so. For we may not hide our journey from all men's hearing; and when the ear heareth, the tongue waggeth. But art thou yet anxious concerning this matter, son?" "Yea," said Ralph, "for I would fain look on these miscreants."

"It is like that ye shall see them," said Clement; "but I shall look on it as a token that they are about waylaying us if we come on none of them in the Mountain House. For they will be fearful lest their purpose leak out from unwary lips." Ralph wondered how it would be, and what might come of it, and rode on, pondering much.

The road was rough that day, and they went not above a foot-pace the more part of the time; and daylong they were going up and up, and it grew cold as the sun got low; though it was yet summer. At last at the top of a long stony ridge, which lay beneath a great spreading mountain, on the crest whereof the snow lay in plenty, Ralph saw a house, long and low, builded of great stones, both walls and roof: at sight thereof the men of the fellowship shouted for joy, and hastened on, and Clement spurred up the stony slopes all he might. But Ralph rode slowly, since he had naught to see to, save himself, so that he was presently left alone. Now he looks aside, and sees something bright-hued lying under a big stone where the last rays of the sun just caught some corner of it. So he goes thither, deeming that mayhappen one of the company had dropped something, pouch or clout, or what not, in his haste and hurry. He got off his horse to pick it up, and when he had laid hand on it found it to be a hands-breadth of fine green cloth embroidered with flowers. He held it in his hand a while wondering where he could have seen such like stuff before, that it should smite a pang into his heart, and suddenly called to mind the little hall at Bourton Abbas with the oaken benches and the rush-strewn floor, and this same flower-broidered green cloth dancing about the naked feet of a fair damsel, as she moved nimbly hither and thither dighting him his bever. But his thought stayed not there, but carried him into the days when he was abiding in desire of the love that he won at last, and lost so speedily. But as he stood pondering he heard Clement shouting to him from the garth-gate of that house. So he leapt on his horse and rode up the slope into the garth and lighted down by Clement; who fell to chiding him for tarrying, and said: "There is peril in loitering outside this garth alone; for those Sons of the Rope often lurk hard by for what they may easily pick up, and they be brisk and nimble lads." "What ailed thee?" said Ralph. "I stayed to look at a flower which called Upmeads to my mind."

"Yea lad, yea," quoth Clement, "and art thou so soft as that? But come thou into the House; it is as I deemed it might be; besides the House-warden and his wife there is no soul therein. Thou shalt yet look on Mick Hangman's sons, as thou desirest."

So they went into the House, and men had all that they might need. The warden was an old hoar man, and his wife well-stricken in years; and after supper was talk of this and that, and it fell much, as was like to be, on those strong-thieves, and Clement asked the warden what he had seen of them of late.

The old carle answered: "Nay, master Clement, much according to wont: a few beeves driven into our garth; a pack or two brought into the hall; and whiles one or two of them come in hither with empty hands for a sleep and a bellyful; and again a captive led in on the road to the market. Forsooth it is now a good few days ago three of them brought in a woman as goodly as mine eyes have ever seen; and she sat on the bench yonder, and seemed to heed little that she was a captive and had shackles on her feet after the custom of these men, though indeed her hands were unbound, so that she might eat her meat; and the carle thief told me that he took her but a little way from the garth, and that she made a stout defence with a sword before they might take her, but being taken, she made but little of it."

"Would he do her any hurt?" said Ralph. "Nay, surely," said the carle; "doth a man make a hole in a piece of cloth which he is taking to market? Nay, he was courteous to her after his fashion, and bade us give her the best of all we had."

"What like was she?" said Ralph. Said the carle: "She was somewhat tall, if I am to note such matters, grey-eyed and brown haired, and great abundance of it. Her lips very red; her cheeks tanned with the sun, but in such wise that her own white and red shone through the sun's painting, so that her face was as sweet as the best wheat-ear in a ten-acre field when the season hath been good. Her hands were not like those of a demoiselle who sitteth in a chamber to be looked at, but brown as of one who hath borne the sickle in the sun.

But when she stretched out her hand so that the wrist of her came forth from her sleeve it was as white as milk."

"Well, my man," said the carline, "thou hast a good memory for an old and outworn carle. Why dost thou not tell the young knight what she was clad withal; since save for their raiment all women of an age are much alike?"

"Nay, do thou do it," said the carle; "she was even as fair as I have said; so that there be few like her."

Said the dame: "Well, there is naught so much to be said for her raiment: her gown was green, of fine cloth enough; but not very new: welts of needle-work it had on it, and a wreath of needle-work flowers round the hem of the skirt; but a cantle was torn off from it; in the scuffle when she was taken, I suppose, so that it was somewhat ragged in one place. Furthermore——"

She had been looking at Ralph as she spoke, and now she broke off suddenly, and said, still looking at him hard; "Well, it is strange!" "What is strange?" said Clement. "O naught, naught," said the dame, "save that folk should make so much to do about this matter, when there are so many coming and going about the Midhouse of the Mountains."

But Ralph noted that she was still staring at him even after she had let the talk drop.

Waned the even, and folk began to go bedward, so that the hall grew thin of guests. Then came up the carline to Ralph and took him aside into a nook, and said to him: "Young knight, now will I tell thee what seemed to me strange e'en now; to wit, that the captive damsel should be bearing a necklace about her neck as like to thine as one lamb is to another: but I thought thou mightest be liever that I spake it not openly before all the other folk. So I held my peace."

"Dame," said he, "I thank thee: forsooth I fear sorely that this damsel is my sister; for ever we have worn the samelike pair of beads. And as for me I have come hither to find her, and evil will it be if I find her enthralled, and it may be past redemption."

And therewith he gave her a piece of the gold money of Upmeads.

"Yea," said she, "poor youth; that will be sooth indeed, for

227

thou art somewhat like unto her, yet far goodlier. But I grieve for thee, and know not what thou wilt do; whereas by this time most like she has been sold and bought and is dwelling in some lord's strong-house; some tyrant that needeth not money, and will not let his prey go for a prayer. Here, take thou thy gold again, for thou mayst well need it, and let me shear a lock of thy golden hair, and I shall be well apaid for my keeping silence concerning thy love. For I deem that it is even so, and that she is not thy sister, else hadst thou stayed at home, and prayed for her with book and priest and altar, and not gone seeking her a weary way."

Ralph reddened but said naught, and let her put scizzors amongst his curly locks, and take what of them she would. And then he went to his bed, and pondered these matters somewhat, and said to himself that it was by this damsel's means that he should find the Well at the World's End. Yet he said also, that, whether it were so or not, he was bound to seek her, and deliver her from thralldom, since he had kissed her so sweet and friendly, like a brother, for the sweetness and kindness of her, before he had fallen into the love that had brought him such joy and such grief. And therewith he took out that piece of her gown from his pouch, and it seemed dear to him. But it made him think sadly of what grief or pain she might even then be bearing, so that he longed to deliver her, and that longing was sweet to him. In such thoughts he fell asleep.

CHAPTER 21

A Battle in the Mountains

When it was morning they arose early and ate a morsel; and Clement gave freely to the Warden and his helpmate on behalf of the fellowship; and then they saddled their nags, and did on the loads and departed; and the way was evil otherwise, but it was down hill, and all waters ran east.

All day they rode, and at even when the sun had not quite set, they pitched their camp at the foot of a round knoll amidst a valley where was water and grass; and looking down thence, they had a sight of the fruitful plain, wherein lay Cheaping Knowe all goodly blue in the distance.

This was a fair place and a lovely, and great ease would they have had there, were it not that they must keep watch and ward with more pains than theretofore; for Clement deemed it as good as certain that the wild men would fall upon them that night.

But all was peaceful the night through, and in the morning they gat to the way speedily, riding with their armour on, and their bows bent: and three of the men-at-arms rode ahead to espy the way.

So it befell that they had not ridden two hours ere back came the fore-riders with the tidings that the pass next below them was thick with the Strong-thieves.

The fellowship were as then in such a place, that they were riding a high bare ridge, and could not be assailed to the advantage of the thieves if they abode where they were; whereas if they went forward, they must needs go down with the road into the dale that was beset by the wild men. Now they were three-score and two all told, but of these but a score of men-at-arms besides Ralph, and Clement, who was a stout fighter when need was. Of the others, some were but lads, and of the Chapmen were three old men, and more than one blencher besides. However, all men were armed, and they had many bows, and some of the chapmen's knaves were fell archers.

So they took counsel together, and to some it seemed better to abide the onset on their vantage ground. But to Clement and the older men-at-arms this seemed of no avail. For though they could see the plain country down below, they would have no succour of it; and Clement bade them think how the night would come at last, and that the longer they abode, the greater would be the gathering of the Strong-thieves; so that, all things considered, it were better to fall on at once and to try the adventure of the valley. And this after some talk they yea-said all, save a few who held their skins so dear that their wits wandered somewhat.

So these timorous ones they bade guard the sumpter beasts and their loads; and even so they did, and abode a little, while the men-at-arms and the bowmen went forward without more ado; and Ralph rode betwixt Clement and the captain of the men-at-arms.

Presently they were come close to the place where the way went down into the valley, cleaving through a clayey bent, so that the slippery sides of the cleft went up high to right and left; wherefore by goodhap there were no big stones anigh to roll down upon them. Moreover the way was short, and they rode six abreast down the pass and were soon through the hollow way. As he rode Ralph saw a few of the Strong-thieves at the nether end where the pass widened out, and they let fly some arrows at the chapmen which did no hurt, though some of the shafts rattled on the armour of the companions. But when Clement saw that folk, and heard the noise of their shouting he lifted up a great axe that he bore and cried, "St. Agnes for the Mercers!" and set spurs to his horse. So did they all, and came clattering and shouting down the steep road like a stone out of a sling, and drave right into the valley one and all, the wouldbe laggards following after; for they were afraid to be left behind.

The wild men, who, save for wide shields which they bore, were but evilly armed, mostly in skins of beasts, made no countenance of defence, but fled all they might towards the steep slopes of the valley, and then turned and fell to shooting; for the companions durst not pursue in haste lest they should be scattered, and overwhelmed by the multitude of foemen; but they drew up along the south side of the valley, and had the mastery of the road, so that this first bout was without blood-shedding. Albeit the thieves still shot in their weak bows from the hill-side, but scarce hurt a man. Then the bowmen of the fellowship fell to shooting at the wild men, while the men-at-arms breathed their horses, and the sumpter-beasts were gathered together behind them; for they had no dread of abiding there a while, whereas behind them the ground was broken into a steep shaly cliff, bushed here

230

and there with tough bushes, so that no man could come up it save by climbing with hand and knee, and that not easily.

Now when the archers had shot a good while, and some of the thieves had fallen before them, and men were in good heart because of the flight of the wild men, Ralph, seeing that these still hung about the slopes, cried out: "Master Clement, and thou Captain, sure it will be ill-done to leave these men unbroken behind us, lest they follow us and hang about our hindermost, slaying us both men and horses."

"Even so," quoth the captain, who was a man of few words, "let us go. But do thou, Clement, abide by the stuff with the lads and bowmen."

Then he cried out aloud: "St. Christopher to aid!" and shook his rein, and all they who were clad in armour and well mounted spurred on with him against the strong-thieves. But these, when they saw the onset of the horsemen, but drew a little up the hill-side and stood fast, and some of the horses were hurt by their shot. So the captain bade draw rein and off horse, while Clement led his bowmen nigher, and they shot well together, and hindered the thieves from closing round the men-at-arms, or falling on the horses. So then the companions went forward stoutly on foot, and entered into the battle of the thieves, and there was the thrusting and the hewing great: for the foemen bore axes, and malls, and spears, and were little afraid, having the vantage-ground; and they were lithe and strong men, though not tall.

Ralph played manfully, and was hurt by a spear above the knee, but not grievously; so he heeded it not, but cleared a space all about him with great strokes of the Upmeads' blade; then as the wild men gave back there was one of them who stood his ground and let drive a stroke of a long-handled hammer at him, but Ralph ran in under the stroke and caught him by the throat and drew him out of the press. And even therewith the wild men broke up before the onset of the all-armed carles, and fled up the hill, and the men-at-arms followed them but a little, for their armour made them unspeedy; so that they took no more of those men, though they slew some, but turned about and gathered round Ralph and made merry over his catch, for they were joyous with the happy end of battle; and Clement, who had

231

left his bowmen when the Companions were mingled with the wild-men, was there amidst the nighest.

Said Ralph to him: "Well, have I got me a servant and thrall good cheap?" "Yea," said Clement, "if thou deem a polecat a likely hound." Said the Captain: "Put thy sword through him, knight." Quoth another: "Let him run up hill, and our bowmen shall shoot a match at him."

"Nay," said Ralph, "they have done well with their shooting, let them rest. As to my thrusting my sword through the man, Captain, I had done that before, had I been so minded. At any rate, I will ask him if he will serve me truly. Otherwise he seemeth a strong carle and a handy. How sayest thou, lad, did I take thee fairly?" "Yea," said the man, "thou art a strong lad."

He seemed to fear the swords about him but little, and forsooth he was a warrior-like man, and not ill-looking. He was of middle height, strong and well-knit, with black hair like a beast's mane for shagginess, and bright blue eyes. He was clad in a short coat of grey homespun, with an ox-skin habergeon laced up over it; he had neither helm nor hat, nor shoes, but hosen made of a woollen clout tied about his legs; his shield of wood and ox-hide lay on the ground a few paces off, and his hammer beside it, which he had dropped when Ralph first handled him, but a great ugly knife was still girt to him.

Now Ralph saith to him: "Which wilt thou—be slain, or serve me?" Said the carle, grinning, yet not foully: "Guess if I would not rather serve thee!" "Wilt thou serve me truly?" said Ralph. "Why not?" quoth the carle: "yet I warn thee that if thou beat me, save in hot blood, I shall put a knife into thee when I may."

"O," said one, "thrust him through now at once, lord Ralph." "Nay, I will not," said Ralph; "he hath warned me fairly. Maybe he will serve me truly. Master Clement, wilt thou lend me a horse for my man to ride?" "Yea," said Clement; "yet I misdoubt me of thy new squire." Then he turned to the men-at-arms and said: "No tarrying, my masters! To horse and away before they gather gain!"

So they mounted and rode away from that valley of the pass, and Ralph made his man ride beside him. But the man said to him, as soon as they were riding: "Take note that I will not fight against my kindred." "None biddeth thee so," said Ralph; "but do thou take heed that if thou fight against us I will slay thee outright." Said the man: "A fair bargain!" "Well," said Ralph, "I will have thy knife of thee, lest it tempt thee, as is the wont of cold iron, and a maiden's body." "Nay, master," quoth the man, "leave me my knife, as thou art a good fellow. In two hours time we shall be past all peril of my people, and when we come down below I will slay thee as many as thou wilt, so it be out of the kindred. Forsooth down there evil they be, and unkinsome."

"So be it, lad," said Ralph, laughing, "keep thy knife; but hang this word of mine thereon, that if thou slay any man of this fellowship save me, I will rather flay thee alive than slay thee." Quoth the carle: "That is the bargain, then, and I yeasay it." "Good," said Ralph; "now tell me thy name." "Bull Shockhead," said the carle.

But now the fellowship took to riding so fast down the slopes of the mountains on a far better road, that talking together was not easy. They kept good watch, both behind and ahead, nor were they set upon again, though whiles they saw clumps of men on the hill-sides.

So after a while, when it was a little past noon, they came adown to the lower slopes of the mountains and the foot-hills, which were green and unstony; and thereon were to be seen cattle and neatherds and shepherds, and here and there the garth of a homestead, and fenced acres about it.

So now that they were come down into the peopled parts, they displayed the banners of their fellowships, to wit, the Agnes, the White Fleece, the Christopher, and the Ship and Nicholas, which last was the banner of the Faring-knights of Whitwall; but Ralph was glad to ride under the banner of St. Nicholas, his friend, and deemed that luck might the rather come to him thereby. But they displayed their banners now, because they knew that no man of the peopled parts would be so hardy as to fall upon the Chapmen, of whom they looked to have many matters for their use and pleasure.

So now that they felt themselves safe, they stayed them, and sat down by a fair little stream, and ate their dinner of such meat and drink as they had; and Ralph departed his share with his thrall, and the man was hungry and ate well;

so that Clement said mockingly: "Thou feedest thy thrall over well, lord, even for a king's son: is it so that thou art minded to fatten him and eat him?" Then some of the others took up the jest, and bade the carle refrain him of the meat, so that he might not fatten, and might live the longer. He hearkened to them, and knit his brows and looked fiercely from one to the other. But Ralph laughed aloud, and shook his finger at him and refrained him, and his wrath ran off him and he laughed, and shoved the victual into him doughtily, and sighed for pleasure when he had made an end and drunk a draught of wine.

CHAPTER 22

Ralph Talks With
Bull Shockhead

When they rode on again, Ralph rode beside Bull, who was merry and blithe now he was full of meat and drink; and he spake anon: "So thou art a king's son, master? I deemed from the first that thou wert of lineage. For as for these churls of chapmen, and the sworders whom they wage, they know not the name of their mother's mother, nor have heard one word of the beginner of their kindred; and their deeds are like unto their kinlessness."

"And are thy deeds so good?" said Ralph. "Are they ill," said Bull, "when they are done against the foemen?" Said Ralph: "And are all men your foemen who pass through these mountains?" "All," said Bull, "but they be of the kindred or their known friends."

"Well, Bull," said Ralph, "I like thy deeds little, that thou shouldest ravish men and women from their good life, and sell them for a price into toil and weariness and stripes."

Said Bull: "How much worse do we than the chapmen by his debtor, and the lord of the manor by his villein?" Said Ralph: "Far worse, if ye did but know it, poor men!" Quoth

234

Bull: "But I neither know it, nor can know it, nay, not when thou sayest it; for it is not so. And look you, master, this life of a bought thrall is not such an exceeding evil life; for oft they be dealt with softly and friendly, and have other thralls to work for them under their whips."

Ralph laughed: "Which shall I make thee, friend Bull, the upper or the under?" Bull reddened, but said naught. Said Ralph: "Or where shall I sell thee, that I may make the best penny out of my good luck and valiancy?" Bull looked chopfallen: "Nay," said he in a wheedling voice, "thou wilt not sell me, thou? For I deem that thou wilt be a good master to me: and," he broke into sudden heat hereat, "if I have another master I shall surely slay him whate'er betide."

Ralph laughed again, and said: "Seest thou what an evil craft ye follow, when thou deemest it better to be slain with bitter torments (as thou shouldest be if thou slewest thy master) than to be sold to any master save one exceeding good?"

Bull held his peace hereat, but presently he said: "Well, be our craft good or evil, it is gainful; and whiles there is prey taken right good, which, for my part, I would not sell, once I had my hand thereon." "Yea, women?" said Ralph. "Even so," said Bull, "such an one was taken by my kinsman Bull Nosy but a little while agone, whom he took down to the market at Cheaping Knowe, as I had not done if I had once my arms about her. For she was as fair as a flower; and yet so well built, that she could bear as much as a strong man in some ways; and, saith Nosy, when she was taken, there was no weeping or screeching in her, but patience rather and quietness, and intent to bear all and live. . . . Master, may I ask thee a question?" "Ask on," said Ralph. Said Bull: "The pair of beads about thy neck, whence came they?" "They were the gift of a dear friend," said Ralph. "A woman?" quoth Bull. "Yea," said Ralph.

"Now is this strange," said Bull, "and I wot not what it may betoken, but this same woman had about her neck a pair of beads as like to thine as if they had been the very same: did this woman give thee the beads? For I will say this of thee, master, that thou art well nigh as likely a man as she is a woman."

Ralph sighed, for this talk of the woman and the beads brought all the story into his mind, so that it was as if he saw it adoing again: the Lady of the Wildwood led along to death before he delivered her, and their flight together from the Water of the Oak, and that murder of her in the desert. And betwixt the diverse deeds of the day this had of late become somewhat dim to him. Yet after his grief came joy that this man also had seen the damsel, whom his dream of the night had called Dorothea, and that he knew of her captors; wherefore by his means he might come on her and deliver her.

Now he spake aloud: "Nay, it was not she that gave them to me, but yet were I fain to find this woman that thou sawest; for I look to meet a friend whenas I meet her. So tell me, dost thou think that I may cheapen her of thy kinsman?"

Bull shook his head, and said: "It may be: or it may be that he hath already sold her to one who heedeth not treasure so much as fair flesh; and fair is hers beyond most. But, lord, I will do my best to find her for thee; as thou art a king's son and no ill master, I deem."

"Do that," quoth Ralph, "and I in turn will do what more I may for thee besides making thee free." And therewith he rode forward that he might get out of earshot, for Bull's tongue seemed like to be long. And presently he heard laughter behind him, as the carle began jesting and talking with the chapman lads.

CHAPTER 23

Of the Town of Cheaping Knowe

Now when it was evening they pitched their camp down in the plain fields amidst tall elmtrees, and had their banners still flying over the tents to warn all comers of what they were. But the next morning the chapmen and their folk were up betimes to rummage their loads, and to array their wares for the market; and they gat not to the road before mid-morning. Meantime of their riding Ralph had more talk with Bull, who said to him: "Fair lord, I rede thee when thou art in the market of Cheaping Knowe, bid master Clement bring thee to the thrall-merchant, and trust me that if such a fair image as that we were speaking of hath passed through his hands within these three months, he will remember it; and then thou shalt have at least some tale of what hath befallen her but a little while ago."

That seemed good rede to Ralph, and when they went on their way he rode beside Clement, and asked him many things concerning Cheaping Knowe; and at last about the thrall-market therein. And Clement said that, though he dealt not in such wares, he had often seen them sold, and knew the master of that market. And when Ralph asked if the said master would answer questions concerning the selling of men and of women, Clement smiled and said: "Yea, yea, he will answer; for as he lives by selling thralls, and every time a thrall is sold by him he maketh some gain by it, it is to his profit that they change masters as often as may be; and when thou askest of the woman whom thou art seeking, he will be deeming that there will be some new chaffer ahead. I will bring thee to him, and thou shalt ask him of what thou wilt, and belike he will tell thee quietly over the wine-cup."

Therewith was Ralph well content, and he grew eager to enter into the town.

They came to the gates a little before sunset, after they had passed through much fair country; but nigh to the walls it was bare of trees and thickets, whereas, said Clement, they had been cut down lest they should serve as cover to strong-thieves or folk assailing the town. The walls were strong and tall, and a great castle stood high up on a hill, about which the town was builded; so that if the town were taken there would yet be another town within it to be taken also. But the town within, save for the said castle, was scarce so fairly builded as the worst of the towns which Ralph had seen erst, though there were a many houses therein.

Much people was gathered about the gate to see the merchants enter with banners displayed; and Ralph deemed many of the folk fair, such as were goodly clad; for many had but foul clouts to cover their nakedness, and seemed needy and hunger-pinched. Withal there were many warriors amongst the throng, and most of these bore a token on their sleeves, to wit, a sword reddened with blood. And Clement, speaking softly in Ralph's ear, did him to wit that this was the token of the lord who had gotten the castle in those days, and was tyrant of the town; and how that he had so many men-at-arms ready to do his bidding that none in the town was safe from him if he deemed it more for his pleasure and profit to rob or maim, or torment or slay, than to suffer them to live peaceably. "But with us chapmen," said Clement, "he will not meddle, lest there be an end of chaffer in the town; and verily the market is good."

Thus they rode through the streets into the market place, which was wide and great, and the best houses of the town were therein, and so came to the hostel of the Merchants, called the Fleece, which was a big house, and goodly enough.

The next morning Clement and the other chapmen went up into the Castle, bearing with them gifts out of their wares for the lord, and Clement bade Ralph keep close till he came back, and especially to keep his war-caught thrall, Bull Shockhead, safe at home, lest he be taken from him, and to clothe him in the guise of the chapman lads, and to dock his hair; and even so Ralph did, though Bull were loath thereto.

About noon the chapmen came back again well pleased; and Clement gave Ralph a parchment from the lord, which bade all men help and let pass Ralph of Upmeads, as a sergeant of the chapmen's guard, and said withal that now he was free to go about the town if he listed, so that he were back at the hostel of the Fleece by nightfall.

So Ralph went in company with some of the sergeants and others, and looked at this and that about the town without hindrance, save that the guard would not suffer them to pass further than the bailey of the Castle. And for the said bailey, forsooth, they had but little stomach; for they saw thence, on the slopes of the Castle-hill, tokens of the cruel justice of the said lord; for there were men and women there, yea, and babes also, hanging on gibbets and thrust through with sharp pales, and when they asked of folk why these had suffered,

238

they but looked at them as if astonished, and passed on without a word.

So they went thence, and found the master-church, and deemed it not much fairer than it was great; and it was nowise great, albeit it was strange and uncouth of fashion.

Then they came to great gardens within the town, and they were exceeding goodly, and had trees and flowers and fruits in them which Ralph had not seen hitherto, as lemons, and oranges, and pomegranates; and the waters were running through them in runnels of ashlar; and the weather was fair and hot; so they rested in those gardens till it was evening, and then gat them home to Fleece, where they had good entertainment.

CHAPTER 24

Ralph Heareth More Tidings of the Damsel

The second day, while the merchants saw to their chaffer, most of the men-at-arms, and Ralph with them, spent their time again in those goodly gardens; where, indeed, some of them made friends of fair women of the place; in which there was less risk than had been for aliens in some towns, whereas at Cheaping Knowe such women as were wedded according to law, or damsels in the care of their kindred, or slaves who were concubines, had not dared so much as to look on a man.

The third day time hung somewhat heavy on Ralph's hands, not but that the Companions were well at ease, but rather because himseemed that he was not stirring in the quest.

But the next day Clement bade him come see that thrall-merchant aforesaid, and brought him to a corner of the market-place, where was a throng looking on at the cheaping. They went through the throng, and beside a stone like a leaping-on stone saw a tall man, goodly of presence, black bearded, clad in scarlet; and this was the merchant; and by him were two of his knaves and certain weaponed men who had brought their wares to the cheaping. And some of these were arrayed like those foemen of the mountains. There was a half score and three of these chattels to be sold, who stood up one after other on the stone, that folk might cheapen them. The cheaping was long about, because they that had a mind to buy were careful to know what they were buying, like as if they had been cheapening a horse, and most of them before they bid their highest had the chattels away into the merchant's booth to strip them, lest they should buy damaged or unhandsome bodies; and this more especially if it were a woman, for the men were already well nigh naked. Of women four of them were young and goodly, and Ralph looked at them closely; but they were naught like to the woman of his quest.

Now this cheaping irked Ralph sorely, as was like to be, whereas, as hath been told, he came from a land where were no thralls, none but vavassors and good yeomen: yet he abode till all was done, hansel paid, and the thralls led off by their new masters. Then Clement led him up to the merchant, to whom he gave the sele of the day, and said: "Master, this is the young knight of whom I told thee, who deemeth that a woman who is his friend hath been brought to this market and sold there, and if he might, he would ransom her."

The merchant greeted Ralph courteously, and bade him and Clement come into his house, where they might speak more privily. So did they, and he treated them with honour, and set wine and spices before them, and bade Ralph say whatlike the woman was. Ralph did so, and wondered at himself how well and closely he could tell of her, like as a picture painted. And, moreover, he drew forth that piece of her gown which he had come on by the Mid-Mountain House.

So when he had done, the merchant, who was a man sober of aspect and somewhat slow of speech, said: "Sir, I believe surely that I have seen this damsel, but she is not with me now, nor have I sold her ever; but hither was she brought to be sold by a man of the mountain folk not very many days

240

ago. And the man's name was Bull Nosy, or the longnosed man of the kindred of the Bull, for in such wise are named the men of that unhappy folk. Now this was the cause why I might not sell her, that she was so proud and stout that men feared her, what she might do if they had her away. And when some spake to see her body naked, she denied it utterly, saying that she would do a mischief to whomsoever tried it. So I spake to him who owned her, and asked him if he thought it good to take her a while and quell her with such pains as would spoil her but little, and then bring her to market when she was meeker. But he heeded my words little, and led her away, she riding on a horse and he going afoot beside her; for the mountain-men be no horsemen."

Said Ralph: "Dost thou know at all whither he will have led her?" Said the merchant: "By my deeming, he will have gone first of all to the town of Whiteness, whither thy Fellowship will betake them ere long: for he will be minded to meet there the Lord of Utterbol, who is for such like wares; and he will either give her to him as a gift, for which he will have a gift in return, or he will sell her to my lord at a price if he dare to chaffer with him. At least so will he do if he be wise. Now if the said lord hath her, it will be somewhat more than hard for thee to get her again, till he have altogether done with her; for money and goods are naught to him beside the doing of his will. But there is this for thy comfort, that whereas she is so fair a woman, she will be well with my lord. For I warrant me that she will not dare to be proud with him, as she was with the folk here."

"Yea," said Ralph, "and what is this lord of Utterbol that all folk, men and women, fear him so?" Said the merchant: "Fair sir, thou must pardon me if I say no more of him. Belike thou mayst fall in with him; and if thou dost, take heed that thou make not thyself great with him."

So Ralph thanked the merchant and departed with Clement, of whom presently he asked if he knew aught of this lord of Utterbol. Said Clement: "God forbid that I should ever meet him, save where I were many and he few. I have never seen him; but he is deemed by all men as the worst of the tyrants who vex these lands, and, maybe, the mightiest."

So was Ralph sore at heart for the damsel, and anon he

spake to Bull again of her, who deemed somewhat, that his kinsman had been minded at the first to sell her to the lord of Utterbol. And Ralph thinks his game a hard one, yet deems that if he could but find out where the damsel was, he might deliver her, what by sleight, what by boldness.

CHAPTER 25

The Fellowship Comes to Whiteness

Two days thereafter the chapmen having done with their matters in Cheaping Knowe, whereas they must needs keep some of their wares for other places, and especially for Goldburg, they dight them to be gone and rode out a-gates of a mid-morning with banners displayed.

It was some fifty miles thence to Whiteness, which lay close underneath the mountains, and was, as it were, the door of the passes whereby men rode to Goldburg. The land which they passed through was fair, both of tillage and pasture, with much cattle therein. Everywhere they saw men and women working afield, but no houses of worthy yeomen or vavassors, or cots of good husbandmen. Here and there was a castle or strong-house, and here and there long rows of ugly hovels, or whiles houses, big tall and long, but exceeding foul and ill-favoured, such as Ralph had not yet seen the like of. And when he asked of Clement concerning all this, he said: "It is as I have told thee, that here be no freemen who work afield, nay, nor villeins either. All those whom ye have seen working have been bought and sold like to those whom we saw standing on the Stone in the market of Cheaping Knowe, or else were born of such cattle, and each one of them can be bought and sold again, and they work not save under the whip. And as for those hovels and the long and foul houses, they are the stables wherein this kind of cattle is harboured."

Then Ralph's heart sank, and he said: "Master Clement, I prithee tell me; were it possible that the damsel whom I seek may be come to such a pass as one of these?" "Nay," quoth Clement, "that is little like to be; such goodly wares are kept for the adornment of great men's houses. True it is that whiles the house-thralls be sent into the fields for their punishment; yet not such as she, unless the master be wholly wearied of them, or if their wrath outrun their wits; for it is more to the master's profit to chastise them at home; so keep a good heart I bid thee, and maybe we shall have tidings at Whiteness."

So Ralph refrained his anxious heart, though forsooth his thought was much upon the damsel and of how she was faring.

It was not till the third day at sunset that they came to Whiteness; for on the last day of their riding they came amongst the confused hills that lay before the great mountains, which were now often hidden from their sight; but whenever they appeared through the openings of the near hills, they seemed very great and terrible; dark and bare and stony; and Clement said that they were little better than they looked from afar. As to Whiteness, they saw it a long way off, as it lay on a long ridge at the end of a valley: and so long was the ridge, that behind it was nothing green; naught but the huge and bare mountains. The westering sun fell upon its walls and its houses, so that it looked white indeed against those great cliffs and crags; though, said Clement, that these were yet a good way off. Now when, after a long ride from the hither end of the valley, they drew nigh to the town, Ralph saw that the walls and towers were not very high or strong, for so steep was the hill whereon the town stood, that it needed not. Here also was no great castle within the town as at Cheaping Knowe, and the town itself nothing so big, but long and straggling along the top of the ridge. Cheaping Knowe was all builded of stone; but the houses here were of timber for the most part, done over with pargeting and whitened well. Yet was the town more cheerful of aspect than Cheaping Knowe, and the folk who came thronging about the chapmen at the gates not so woe-begone, and goodly enough.

Of the lord of Whiteness, Clement told that he paid tribute to him of Cheaping Knowe, rather for love of peace than for fear of him; for he was no ill lord, and free men lived well under him.

So the chapmen lodged in the market-place; and in two days time Ralph got speech of the Deacon of the Chapmen of the Town; who told him two matters; first that the lord of Utterbol had not been in Whiteness these six months; and next that the wild man had verily brought the damsel into the market; but he had turned away thence suddenly with her, without bringing her to the stone, and that it was most like that he would have the lord of Utterbol buy her; who, since he would be deeming that he might easily bend her to his will, would give him the better penny for her. "At the last," quoth the Deacon, "the wild man led her away toward the mountain pass that goeth to Goldburg, the damsel and he alone, and she with her hands unbound and riding a little horse." Of these tidings Ralph deemed it good that all traces of her were not lost; but his heart misgave him when he thought that by this time she must surely be in the hands of the lord of Utterbol.

CHAPTER 26

They Ride the Mountains
Toward Goldburg

Five days the Fellowship abode at Whiteness, and or ever they departed Clement waged men-at-arms of the lord of the town, besides servants to look to the beasts amongst the mountains, so that what with one, what with another, they entered the gates of the mountains a goodly company of four score and ten.

Ralph asked of Bull if any of those whom he might meet in these mountains were of his kindred; and he answered, nay, unless perchance there might be some one or two going their peaceful errands there like Bull Nosy. So Ralph armed him with a good sword and a shield, and would have given him a steel hood also, but he would not bear it, saying that if sword and shield could not keep his head he had well earned a split skull.

Seven days they rode the mountains, and the way was toilsome and weary enough, for it was naught but a stony maze of the rocks where nothing living dwelt, and nothing grew, save now and again a little dwarf willow. Yet was there naught worse to meet save toil, because they were over strong for the wild men to meddle with them, whereas the kindreds thereabout were but feeble.

But as it drew towards evening on the seventh day Ralph had ridden a little ahead with Bull alone, if he might perchance have a sight of the ending of this grievous wilderness, as Clement said might be, since now the way was down-hill, and all waters ran east. So as they rode, and it was about sunset, they saw something lying by a big stone under a cliff; so they drew nigh, and saw a man lying on his back, and they deemed he was dead. So Bull went up to him, and leapt off his horse close by him and bent over him, but straightway cast up his arms and set up a long wailing whoop, and then another and another, so that they that were behind heard it and came up upon the spur. But Ralph leapt from his horse, and ran up to Bull and said: "What aileth thee to whoop and wail? Who is it?" But Bull turned about and shook his head at him, and said: "It is a man of my kindred, even he that was leading away thy she-friend; and belike it was that slew him, or why is she not here: Ochone! ahoo! ahoo!" Therewith fire ran through Ralph's heart, and he bethought him of that other murder in the wilderness, and he fell to wringing his hands, and cried out: "Ah, and where is she, where is she? Is she also taken away from me for ever? O me unhappy!"

And he drew his sword therewith, and ran about amongst the rocks and the bushes seeking her body.

And therewith came up Clement, and others of the company, and wondered to see Bull kneeling down by the corpse, and to hear him crying out and wailing, and Ralph running about like one mad, and crying out now: "Oh! that I might find her! Mayhappen she is alive yet, and anigh here in some cleft of the rocks in this miserable wilderness. O my love that hast lain in mine arms, wouldst thou not have me find her alive? But if she be dead, then will I slay myself, for as young as I am, that I may find thee and her out of the world, since from the world both ye are gone."

Then Clement went up to Ralph, and would have a true tale out of him, and asked him what was amiss; but Ralph stared wild at him and answered not. But Bull cried out from where he knelt: "He is seeking the woman, and I would that he could find her; for then would I slay her on the howe of my kinsman: for she hath slain him; she hath slain him."

That word heard Ralph, and he ran at Bull with uplifted sword to slay him; but Clement tripped him and he fell, and his sword flew out of his hand. Then Clement and two of the others bound his hands with their girdles, till they might know what had befallen; for they deemed that a devil had entered into him, and feared that he would do a mischief to himself or some other.

And now was the whole Fellowship assembled, and stood in a ring round about Ralph and Bull, and the dead man; as for him, he had been dead some time, many days belike; but in that high and clear cold air, his carcase, whistled by the wind, had dried rather than rotted, and his face was clear to be seen with its great hooked nose and long black hair: and his skull was cloven.

Now Bull had done his wailing for his kinsman, and he seemed to wake up as from a dream, and looked about the ring of men and spake: "Here is a great to do, my masters! What will ye with me? Have ye heard, or is it your custom, that when a man cometh on the dead corpse of his brother, his own mother's son, he turneth it over with his foot, as if it were the carcase of a dog, and so goeth on his way? This I ask, that albeit I be but a war-taken thrall, I be suffered to lay my brother in earth and heap a howe over him in these mountains."

They all murmured a yeasay to this save Ralph. He had been sobered by his fall, and was standing up now betwixt Clement and the captain, who had unbound his hands, now that the others had come up; he hung his head, and was

246

ashamed of his fury by seeming. But when Bull had spoken, and the others had answered, Ralph said to Bull, wrathfully still, but like a man in his wits: "Why didst thou say that thou wouldest slay her?" "Hast thou found her?" said Bull. "Nay," quoth Ralph, sullenly. "Well, then," said Bull, "when thou dost find her, we will speak of it." Said Ralph: "Why didst thou say that she hath slain him?" "I was put out of my wits by the sight of him dead," said Bull; "But now I say mayhappen she hath slain him."

"And mayhappen not," said Clement; "look here to the cleaving of his skull right through this iron headpiece, which he will have bought at Cheaping Knowe (for I have seen suchlike in the armourers' booth there): it must have taken a strong man to do this."

"Yea," quoth the captain, "and a big sword to boot: this is the stroke of a strong man wielding a good weapon."

Said Bull: "Well, and will my master bid me forego vengeance for my brother's slaying, or that I bear him to purse? Then let him slay me now, for I am his thrall." Said Ralph: "Thou shalt do as thou wilt herein, and I also will do as I will. For if she slew him, the taking of her captive should be set against the slaying." "That is but right," said the captain; "but Sir Ralph, I bid thee take the word of an old man-at-arms for it, that she slew him not; neither she, nor any other woman."

Said Clement: "Well, let all this be. But tell me, lord Ralph, what thou wouldst do, since now thou art come to thyself again?" Said Ralph: "I would seek the wilderness hereabout, if perchance the damsel be thrust into some cleft or cavern, alive or dead."

"Well," said Clement, "this is my rede. Since Bull Shockhead would bury his brother, and lord Ralph would seek the damsel, and whereas there is water anigh, and the sun is well nigh set, let us pitch our tents and abide here till morning, and let night bring counsel unto some of us. How say ye, fellows?"

None naysaid it, and they fell to pitching the tents, and lighting the cooking-fires; but Bull at once betook him to digging a grave for his brother, whilst Ralph with the captain and four others went and sought all about the place, and

247

looked into all clefts of rocks, and found not the maiden, nor any token of her. They were long about it, and when they were come back again, and it was night, though the moon shone out, there was Bull Shockhead standing by the howe of his brother Bull Nosy, which was heaped up high over the place where they had found him.

So when Bull saw him, he turned to him and said: "King's son, I have done what needs was for this present. Now, wilt thou slay me for my fault, or shall I be thy man again, and serve thee truly unless the blood feud come between us?" Said Ralph: "Thou shalt serve me truly, and help me to find him who hath slain thy brother, and carried off the damsel; for even thus it hath been done meseemeth, since about here we have seen no signs of her alive or dead. But to-morrow we shall seek wider ere I ride on my way." "Yea," said Bull, "and I will be one in the search."

So then they gat them to their sleeping-berths, and Ralph, contrary to his wont, lay long awake, pondering these things; till at last he said to himself that this woman, whom he called Dorothea, was certainly alive, and wotted that he was seeking her. And then it seemed to him that he could behold her through the darkness of night, clad in the green flowered gown as he had first seen her, and she bewailing her captivity and the long tarrying of the deliverer as she went to and fro in a great chamber builded of marble and done about with gold and bright colours: and or ever he slept, he deemed this to be a vision of what then was, rather than a memory of what had been; and it was sweet to his very soul.

CHAPTER 27

Clement Tells of Goldburg

Now when it was morning he rose early and roused Bull and the captain, and they searched in divers places where they had not been the night before, and even a good way back about the road they had ridden yesterday, but found no tidings. And Ralph said to himself that this was naught but what he had looked for after that vision of the night.

So he rode with his fellows somewhat shamefaced that they had seen that sudden madness in him; but was presently of better cheer than he had been yet. He rode beside Clement; they went downhill speedily, and the wilderness began to better, and there was grass at whiles, and bushes here and there. A little after noon they came out of a pass cleft deep through the rocks by a swift stream which had once been far greater than then, and climbed up a steep ridge that lay across the road, and looking down from the top of it, beheld the open country again. But this was otherwise from what they had beheld from the mountain's brow above Cheaping Knowe. For thence the mountains beyond Whiteness, even those that they had just ridden, were clear to be seen like the wall of the plain country. But here, looking adown, the land below them seemed but a great spreading plain with no hills rising from it, save that far away they could see a certain break in it, and amidst that, something that was brighter than the face of the land elsewhere. Clement told Ralph that this was Goldburg and that it was built on a gathering of hills, not great, but going up steep from the plain. And the plain, said he, was not so wholly flat and even as it looked from up there, but swelled at whiles into downs and low hills. He told him that Goldburg was an exceeding fair town to behold; that the lord who had built it had brought from over the mountains masons and wood-wrights and artificers of all kinds, that they might make it as fair as might be, and that he spared on it neither wealth nor toil nor pains. For in sooth he deemed that he should find the Well at the World's End, and drink thereof, and live long and young and fair past all record; therefore had he builded this city, to be the house and home of his long-enduring joyance.

Now some said that he had found the Well, and drank thereof; others naysaid that; but all deemed that they knew how that Goldburg was not done building ere that lord was slain in a tumult, and that what was then undone was cobbled up after the uncomely fashion of the towns thereabout.

Clement said moreover that, this happy lord dead, things had not gone so well there as had been looked for. Forsooth it had been that lord's will and meaning that all folks in Goldburg should thrive, both those who wrought and those for whom they wrought. But it went not so, but there were many poor folk there, and few wealthy.

Again said Clement that though the tillers and toilers of Goldburg were not for the most part mere thralls and chattels, as in the lands beyond the mountains behind them, yet were they little more thriving for that cause; whereas they belonged not to a master, who must at worst feed them, and to no manor, whose acres they might till for their livelihood, and on whose pastures they might feed their cattle; nor had they any to help or sustain them against the oppressor and the violent man; so that they toiled and swinked and died with none heeding them, save they that had the work of their hands good cheap; and they forsooth heeded them less than their draught beasts whom they must needs buy with money, and whose bellies they must needs fill; whereas these poor wretches were slaves without a price, and if one died another took his place on the chance that thereby he might escape present death by hunger, for there was a great many of them.

CHAPTER 28

Now They Come to Goldburg

That night they slept yet amongst the mountains, or rather in the first of the hill country at their feet; but on the morrow they rode down into the lowlands, and thereby lost all sight of Goldburg, and it was yet afar off, so that they rode four days through lands well-tilled, but for the most part ill-housed, a country of little hills and hollows and rising grounds, before they came in sight of it again heaving up huge and bright under the sun. It was built partly on three hills, the buttresses of a long ridge which turned a wide river, and on the ridge itself, and partly on the flat shore of the river, on either side, hillward and plainward: but a great white wall girt it all about, which went right over the river as a bridge, and on the plain side it was exceeding high, so that its battlements might be somewhat evened with those of the hill-wall above. So that as they came up to the place they saw little of the town because of the enormity of the wall; scarce aught save a spire or a tall towering roof here and there.

So when they were come anigh the gate, they displayed their banners and rode right up to it; and people thronged the walls to see their riding. One by one they passed through the wicket of the gate: which gate itself was verily huge beyond measure, all built of great ashlar-stones; and when they were within, it was like a hall somewhat long and exceeding high, most fairly vaulted; midmost of the said hall they rode through a noble arch on their right hand, and lo another hall exceeding long, but lower than the first, with many glazen windows set in its townward wall; and when they looked through these, they saw the river running underneath; for this was naught but the lower bridge of the city; and they learned afterwards and saw, that above the vault of this long bridge rose up the castle, chamber on chamber, till its battlements were level with the highest towers of the wall on the hill top.

Thus they passed the bridge, and turning to the left at its ending, came into the Water-Street of Goldburg, where the river, with wide quays on either side thereof, ran betwixt the houses. As for these, beneath the dwellings went a fair arched passage like to the ambulatory of an abbey; and every house all along this street was a palace for its goodliness. The houses were built of white stones and red and grey; with shapely pillars to the cloister, and all about carvings of imagery and knots of flowers; goodly were the windows and all glazed, as fair as might be. On the river were great barges, and other craft such as were not sea-goers, river-ships

251

that might get them through the bridges and furnished with masts that might be lowered and shipped.

Much people was gathered to see the chapmen enter, yet scarce so many as might be looked for in so goodly a town; yea, and many of the folk were clad foully, and were haggard of countenance, and cried on the chapmen for alms. Howbeit some were clad gaily and richly enough, and were fair of favour as any that Ralph had seen since he left Upmeads: and amongst these goodly folk were women not a few, whose gear and bearing called to Ralph's mind the women of the Wheatwearers whom he had seen erst in the Burg of the Four Friths, whereas they were somewhat wantonly clad in scanty and thin raiment. And of these, though they were not all thralls, were many who were in servitude: for, as Clement did Ralph to wit, though the tillers of the soil, and the herdsmen, in short the hewers of wood and drawers of water, were men masterless, yet rich men might and did buy both men and women for servants in their houses, and for their pleasure and profit in divers wise.

So they rode to their hostel in the market place, which lay a little back from the river in an ingle of the ridge and one of its buttresses; and all round the said market were houses as fair as the first they had seen: but above, on the hill-sides, save for the castle and palace of the Queen (for a woman ruled in Goldburg), were the houses but low, poorly built of post and pan, and thatched with straw, or reed, or shingle. But the great church was all along one side of the market place; and albeit this folk was somewhat wild and strange of faith for Christian men, yet was it dainty and delicate as might be, and its steeples and bell-towers were high and well builded, and adorned exceeding richly.

So they lighted down at their hostel, and never had Ralph seen such another, for the court within was very great and with a fair garden filled with flowers and orchard-trees, and amidst it was a fountain of fresh water, built in the goodliest fashion of many-coloured marble-stones. And the arched and pillared way about the said court was as fair as the cloister of a mitred abbey; and the hall for the guests was of like fashion, vaulted with marvellous cunning, and with a row of pillars amidmost.

252

There they abode in good entertainment; yet this noted Ralph, that as goodly as was the fashion of the building of that house, yet the hangings and beds, and stools, and chairs, and other plenishing were no richer or better than might be seen in the hostelry of any good town.

So they went bedward, and Ralph slept dreamlessly, as was mostly his wont.

CHAPTER 29

Of Goldburg and the Queen Thereof

On the morrow, when Ralph and Clement met in the hall, Clement spake and said: "Lord Ralph, as I told thee in Whitwall, we chapmen are now at the end of our outward journey, and in about twenty days time we shall turn back to the mountains; but, as I deem, thou wilt be minded to follow up thy quest of the damsel, and whatsoever else thou mayst be seeking. Now this thou mayst well do whiles we are here in Goldburg, and yet come back hither in time to fare back with us: and also, if thou wilt, thou mayst have fellows in thy quest, to wit some of those our men-at-arms, who love thee well. But now, when thou hast done thy best these days during, if thou hast then found naught, I counsel thee and beseech thee to come thy ways back with us, that we twain may wend to Upmeads together, where thou shalt live well, and better all the deeds of thy father. Meseemeth this will be more meet for thee than the casting away of thy life in seeking a woman, who maybe will be naught to thee when thou hast found her; or in chasing some castle in the clouds, that shall be never the nigher to thee, how far soever thou farest. For now I tell thee that I have known this while how thou art seeking the Well at the World's End; and who knoweth that there is any such thing on the earth? Come, then, thou art fair, and young, and strong; and if ye seek wealth thou shalt have it, and my furtherance to the utmost, if that be aught worth. Bethink thee, child, there are they that love thee in Upmeads and thereabout, were it but thy gossip, my wife, dame Katherine."

Said Ralph: "Master Clement, I thank thee for all that thou hast said, and thy behest, and thy deeds. Thy rede is good, and in all ways will I follow it save one; to wit, that if I have not found the damsel ere ye turn back, I must needs abide in this land searching for her. And I pray the pardon both of thee and of thy gossip, if I answer not your love as ye would, and perchance as I should. Yea, and of Upmeads also I crave pardon. But in doing as I do, my deed shall be but according to the duty bounden on me by mine oath, when Duke Osmond made me knight last year, in the church of St. Laurence of Upmeads."

Said Clement: "I see that there is something else in it than that; I see thee to be young, and that love and desire bind thee in closer bonds than thy knightly oath. Well, so it must be, and till thou hast her, there is but one woman in the world for thee."

"Nay, it is not so, Master Clement," said Ralph, "and I will tell thee this, so that thou mayst trow my naysay; since I departed from Upmeads, I have been taken in the toils of love, and desired a fair woman, and I have won her and death hath taken her. Trowest thou my word?"

"Yea," said Clement, "but to one of thy years love is not plucked up by the root, and it soon groweth again." Then said Ralph, sadly: "Now tell my gossip of this when thou comest home." Clement nodded yeasay, and Ralph spake again in a moment: "And now will I begin my search in Goldburg by praying thee to bring me to speech of merchants and others who may have seen or heard tidings of my damsel."

He looked at Clement anxiously as he spoke; and Clement smiled, for he said to himself that looking into Ralph's heart on this matter was like looking into a chamber through an open window. But he said: "Fear not but I will look to it; I am thy friend, and not thy schoolmaster."

Therewith he departed from Ralph, and within three days he had brought him to speech of all those who were like to know anything of the matter; and one and all they said that they had seen no such woman, and that as for the Lord of Utterbol, he had not been in Goldburg these three months. But one of the merchants said: "Master Clement, if this young knight is boun for Utterbol, he beareth his life in his hand, as thou knowest full well. Now I rede thee bring him to our Queen, who is good and compassionate, and if she may not help him otherwise, yet belike she may give him in writing to show to that tyrant, which may stand him in stead: for it does not do for any man to go against the will of our Lady and Queen; who will surely pay him back for his ill-will some day or other." Said Clement: "It is well thought of, and I will surely do as thou biddest."

So wore four days, and, that time during, Ralph was going to and fro asking questions of folk that he came across, as people new come to the city and hunters from the mountain-feet and the forests of the plain, and mariners and such like, concerning the damsel and the Lord of Utterbol; and Bull also went about seeking tidings: but whereas Ralph asked downright what he wanted to know, Bull was wary, and rather led men on to talk with him concerning those things than asked them of them in such wise that they saw the question. Albeit it was all one, and no tidings came to them; indeed, the name of the Lord of Utterbol (whom forsooth Bull named not) seemed to freeze the speech of men's tongues, and they commonly went away at once when it was spoken.

On the fifth day came Clement to Ralph and said: "Now will I bring thee to the Queen, and she is young, and so fair, and withal so wise, that it seems to me not all so sure but that the sight of her will make an end of thy quest once for all. So that meseems thou mayest abide here in a life far better than wandering amongst uncouth folk, perilous and cruel. Yea, so thou mayest have it if thou wilt, being so exceeding goodly, and wise, and well-spoken, and of high lineage."

Ralph heard and reddened, but gave him back no answer; and they went together to the High House of the Queen, which was like a piece of the Kingdom of Heaven for loveliness, so many pillars as there were of bright marble

255

stone, and gilded, and the chapiters carved most excellently: not many hangings on the walls, for the walls themselves were carven, and painted with pictures in the most excellent manner; the floors withal were so dainty that they seemed as if they were made for none but the feet of the fairest of women. And all this was set amidst of gardens, the like of which they had never seen.

But they entered without more ado, and were brought by the pages to the Lady's innermost chamber; and if the rest of the house were goodly, this was goodlier, and a marvel, so that it seemed wrought rather by goldsmiths and jewellers than by masons and carvers. Yet indeed many had said with Clement that the Queen who sat there was the goodliest part thereof.

Now she spake to Clement and said: "Hail, merchant! Is this the young knight of whom thou tellest, he who seeketh his beloved that hath been borne away into thralldom by evil men?"

"Even so," said Clement. But Ralph spake: "Nay, Lady, the damsel whom I seek is not my beloved, but my friend. My beloved is dead."

The Queen looked on him smiling kindly, yet was her face somewhat troubled. She said: "Master chapman, thy time here is not over long for all that thou hast to do; so we give thee leave to depart with our thanks for bringing a friend to see us. But this knight hath no affairs to look to: so if he will abide with us for a little, it will be our pleasure."

So Clement made his obeisance and went his ways. But the Queen bade Ralph sit before her, and tell her of his griefs, and she looked so kindly and friendly upon him that the heart melted within him, and he might say no word, for the tears that brake out from him, and he wept before her; while she looked on him, the colour coming and going in her face, and her lips trembling, and let him weep on. But he thought not of her, but of himself and how kind she was to him. But after a while he mastered his passion and began, and told her all he had done and suffered. Long was the tale in the telling, for it was sweet to him to lay before her both his grief and his hope. She let him talk on, and whiles she listened to him, and whiles, not, but all the time she gazed on him, yet sometimes askance, as if she were ashamed. As for him, he saw her face how fair and lovely she was, yet was there little longing in his heart for her, more than for one of the painted women on the wall, for as kind and as dear as he deemed her.

When he had done, she kept silence a while, but at last she enforced her, and spake: "Sad it is for the mother that bore thee that thou art not in her house, wherein all things would be kind and familiar to thee. Maybe thou art seeking for what is not. Or maybe thou shalt seek and shalt find, and there may be naught in what thou findest, whereof to give thee such gifts as are meet for thy faithfulness and valiancy. But in thine home shouldst thou have all gifts which thou mayest desire."

Then was she silent awhile, and then spake: "Yet must I needs say that I would that thine home were in Goldburg."

He smiled sadly and looked on her, but with no astonishment, and indeed he still scarce thought of her as he said: "Lady and Queen, thou art good to me beyond measure. Yet, look you! One home I had, and left it; another I looked to have, and I lost it; and now I have no home. Maybe in days to come I shall go back to mine old home; and whiles I wonder with what eyes it will look on me. For merry is that land, and dear; and I have become sorrowful."

"Fear not," she said; "I say again that in thine home shall all things look kindly on thee."

Once more she sat silent, and no word did his heart bid him speak. Then she sighed and said: "Fair lord, I bid thee come and go in this house as thou wilt; but whereas there are many folk who must needs see me, and many things are appointed for me to do, therefore I pray thee to come hither in three days' space, and meanwhile I will look to the matter of thy search, that I may speed thee on the way to Utterness, which is no great way from Utterbol, and is the last town whereof we know aught. And I will write a letter for thee to give to the lord of Utterbol, which he will heed, if he heedeth aught my good-will or enmity. I beseech thee come for it in three days wearing."

Therewith she arose and took his hand and led him to the

door, and he departed, blessing her goodness, and wondering at her courtesy and gentle speech.

For those three days he was still seeking tidings everywhere, till folk began to know of him far and wide, and to talk of him. And at the time appointed he went to the Queen's House and was brought to her chamber as before, and she was alone therein. She greeted him and smiled on him exceeding kindly, but he might not fail to note of her that she looked sad and her face was worn by sorrow. She bade him sit beside her, and said: "Hast thou any tidings of the woman whom thou seekest?" "Nay, nay," said he, "and now I am minded to carry on the search out-a-gates. I have some good friends who will go with me awhile. But thou, Lady, hast thou heard aught?"

"Naught of the damsel," she said. "But there is something else. As Clement told me, thou seekest the Well at the World's End, and through Utterness and by Utterbol is a way whereby folk seek thither. Mayst thou find it, and may it profit thee more than it did my kinsman of old, who first raised up Goldburg in the wilderness. Whereas for him was naught but strife and confusion, till he was slain in a quarrel, wherein to fail was to fail, and to win the day was to win shame and misery."

She looked on him sweetly and said: "Thou art nowise such as he; and if thou drink of the Well, thou wilt go back to Upmeads, and thy father and mother, and thine own folk and thine home. But now here is the letter which thou shalt give to the Lord of Utterbol if thou meet him; and mayhappen he is naught so evil a man as the tale of him runs."

She gave him the letter into his hands, and spake again: "And now I have this to say to thee, if anything go amiss with thee, and thou be nigh enough to seek to me, come hither, and then, in whatso plight thou mayst be, or whatsoever deed thou mayst have done, here will be the open door for thee and the welcome of a friend."

Her voice shook a little as she spake, and she was silent again, mastering her trouble. Then she said: "At last I must say this to thee, that there may no lie be between us. That damsel of whom thou spakest that she was but thy friend, and not thy love—O that I might be thy friend in such-wise!

But over clearly I see that it may not be so. For thy mind looketh on thy deeds to come, that they shall be shared by some other than me. Friend, it seemeth strange and strange to me that I have come on thee so suddenly, and loved thee so sorely, and that I must needs say farewell to thee in so short a while. Farewell, farewell!"

Therewith she arose, and once more she took his hand in hers, and led him to the door. And he was sorry and all amazed: for he had not thought so much of her before, that he might see that she loved him; and he thought but that she, being happy and great, was kind to him who was hapless and homeless. And he was bewildered by her words and sore ashamed that for all his grief for her he had no speech, and scarce a look for her; he knew not what to do or say.

So he left the Queen's House and the court thereof, as though the pavement were growing red hot beneath his feet.

CHAPTER 30

Ralph Hath Hope of Tidings Concerning the Well at the World's End

Now he goes to Clement, and tells him that he deems he has no need to abide their departure from Goldburg to say farewell and follow his quest further afield; since it is clear that in Goldburg he should have no more tidings. Clement laughed and said: "Not so fast, Lord Ralph; thou mayst yet hear a word or two." "What!" said Ralph, "hast thou heard of something new?" Said Clement: "There has been a man here seeking thee, who said that he wotted of a wise man who could tell thee much concerning the Well at the World's End. And when I asked him of the Damsel and the Lord of Utterbol, if he knew anything of her, he said yea, but that he would keep it for thy privy ear. So I bade him go and come again when thou shouldst be here. And I deem that he will not tarry long."

Now they were sitting on a bench outside the hall of the hostel, with the court between them and the gate; and Ralph said: "Tell me, didst thou deem the man good or bad?" Said Clement: "He was hard to look into: but at least he looked not a fierce or cruel man; nor indeed did he seem false or sly, though I take him for one who hath lost his manhood—but lo you! here he comes across the court."

So Ralph looked, and saw in sooth a man drawing nigh, who came straight up to them and lowted to them, and then stood before them waiting for their word: he was fat and somewhat short, white-faced and pink-cheeked, with yellow hair long and curling, and with a little thin red beard and blue eyes: altogether much unlike the fashion of men of those parts. He was clad gaily in an orange-tawny coat laced with silver, and broidered with colours.

Clement spake to him and said: "This is the young knight who is minded to seek further east to wot if it be mere lies which he hath heard of the Well at the World's End."

The new-comer lowted before them again, and said in a small voice, and as one who was shy and somewhat afeared: "Lords, I can tell many a tale concerning that Well, and them who have gone on the quest thereof. And the first thing I have to tell is that the way thereto is through Utterness, and that I can be a shower of the way and a leader to any worthy knight who listeth to seek thither; and moreover, I know of a sage who dwelleth not far from the town of Utterness, and who, if he will, can put a seeker of the Well on the right road."

He looked askance on Ralph, whose face flushed and whose eyes glittered at that word. But Clement said: "Yea, that seemeth fair to look to: but hark ye! Is it not so that the way to Utterness is perilous?" Said the man: "Thou mayst rather call it deadly, to any who is not furnished with a let-pass from the Lord of Utterbol, as I am. But with such a scroll a child or a woman may wend the road unharmed." "Where hast thou the said let-pass?" said Clement. "Here," quoth the new-comer; and therewith he drew a scroll from out of his pouch, and opened it before them, and they read it together, and sure enough it was a writing charging all men so let pass and aid Morfinn the Minstrel (of whose aspect it

260

told closely), under pain of falling into the displeasure of Gandolf, Lord of Utterbol; and the date thereon was but three months old.

Said Clement: "This is good, this let-pass: see thou, Ralph, the seal of Utterbol, the Bear upon the Castle Wall. None would dare to counterfeit this seal, save one who was weary of life, and longed for torments."

Said Ralph, smiling: "Thou seest, Master Clement, that there must be a parting betwixt us, and that this man's coming furthers it: but were he or were he not, yet the parting had come. And wert thou not liefer that it should come in a way to pleasure and aid me, than that thou shouldst but leave me behind at Goldburg when thou departest: and I with naught done toward the achieving my quest, but merely dragging my deedless body about these streets; and at last, it may be, going on a perilous journey without guiding or safe-conduct?"

"Yea, lad," said Clement, "I wotted well that thou wouldst take thine own way, but fain had I been that it had been mine also." Then he pondered a while and said afterwards: "I suppose that thou wilt take thy servant Bull Shockhead with thee, for he is a stout man-at-arms, and I deem him trusty, though he be a wild man. But one man is of little avail to a traveller on a perilous road, so if thou wilt I will give leave and license to a half score of our sergeants to follow thee on the road; for, as thou wottest, I may easily wage others in their place. Or else wouldst thou ask the Queen of Goldburg to give thee a score of men-at-arms; she looked to me the other day as one who would deny thee few of thine askings."

Ralph blushed red, and said: "Nay, I will not ask her this." Then he was silent; the new-comer looked from one to the other, and said nothing. At last Ralph spake: "Look you, Clement, my friend, I wot well how thou wouldst make my goings safe, even if it were to thy loss, and I thank thee for it: but I deem I shall do no better than putting myself into this man's hands, since he has a let-pass for the lands of him of Utterbol: and meseemeth from all that I have heard, that a half score or a score, or for the matter of that an hundred men-at-arms would not be enough to fight a way to Utterbol, and their gathering together would draw folk upon them, who would not meddle with two men journeying together, even if they had no let-pass of this mighty man." Clement sighed and grunted, and then said: "Well, lord, maybe thou art right."

"Yea," said the guide, "he is as right as may be: I have not spoken before lest ye might have deemed me untrusty: but now I tell thee this, that never should a small band of men unknown win through the lands of the Lord of Utterbol, or the land debatable that lieth betwixt them and Goldburg."

Ralph nodded friendly at him as he spake; but Clement looked on him sternly; and the man beheld his scowling face innocently, and took no heed of it.

Then said Ralph: "As to Bull Shockhead, I will speak to him anon; but I will not take him with me; for indeed I fear lest his mountain-pride grow up over greenly at whiles and entangle me in some thicket of peril hard to win out of."

"Well," said Clement, "and when wilt thou depart?" "To-morrow," said Ralph, "if my faring-fellow be ready for me by then." "I am all ready," said the man: "if thou wilt ride out by the east gate about two hours before noon to-morrow, I will abide thee on a good horse with all that we may need for the journey: and now I ask leave." "Thou hast it," said Clement.

So the man departed, and those two being left alone, Master Clement said: "Well, I deemed that nothing else would come of it: and I fear that thy gossip will be ill-content with me; for great is the peril." "Yea," said Ralph, "and great the reward." Clement smiled and sighed, and said: "Well, lad, even so hath a many thought before thee, wise men as well as fools." Ralph looked at him and reddened, and departed from him a little, and went walking in the cloister there to and fro, and pondered these matters; and whatever he might do, still would that trim figure be before his eyes which he had looked on so gladly erewhile in the hostel of Bourton Abbas; and he said aloud to himself: "Surely she needeth me, and draweth me to her whether I will or no." So wore the day.

CHAPTER 31

The Beginning of the Road
To Utterbol

Early next morning Ralph arose and called Bull Shockhead
to him and said: "So it is, Bull, that thou art my war-taken
thrall." Bull nodded his head, but frowned therewithal. Said
Ralph: "If I bid thee aught that is not beyond reason thou
wilt do it, wilt thou not?" "Yea," said Bull, surlily. "Well,"
quoth Ralph, "I am going a journey east-away, and I may
not have thee with me, therefore I bid thee take this gold and
go free with my goodwill." Bull's face lighted up, and the
eyes glittered in his face; but he said: "Yea, king's son, but
why wilt thou not take me with thee?" Said Ralph: "It is a
perilous journey, and thy being with me will cast thee into
peril and make mine more. Moreover, I have an errand, as
thou wottest, which is all mine own."

Bull pondered a little and then said: "King's son, I was
thinking at first that our errands lay together, and it is so; but
belike thou sayest true that there will be less peril to each of
us if we sunder at this time. But now I will say this to thee,
that henceforth thou shalt be as a brother to me, if thou wilt
have it so, and if ever thou comest amongst our people, thou
wilt be in no danger of them: nay, they shall do all the good
they may to thee."

Then he took him by the hand and kissed him, and he set
his hand to his gear and drew forth a little purse of some
small beast's skin that was broidered in front with a pair of
bull's horns: then he stooped down and plucked a long and
tough bent from the grass at his feet (for they were talking
in the garden of the hostel) and twisted it swiftly into a
strange knot of many plies, and opening the purse laid it
therein and said: "King's son, this is the token whereby it
shall be known amongst our folk that I have made thee my

brother: were the flames roaring about thee, or the swords clashing over thine head, if thou cry out, I am the brother of Bull Shockhead, all those of my kindred who are near will be thy friends and thy helpers. And now I say to thee farewell: but it is not altogether unlike that thou mayst hear of me again in the furthest East." So Ralph departed from him, and Clement went with Ralph to the Gate of Goldburg, and bade him farewell there; and or they parted he said: "Meseems I have with me now some deal of the foreseeing of Katherine my wife, and in my mind it is that we shall yet see thee at Wulstead and Upmeads, and thou no less famous than now thou art. This is my last word to thee." Therewith they parted, and Ralph rode his ways.

He came on his way-leader about a bowshot from the gate and they greeted each other: the said guide was clad no otherwise than yesterday: he had saddle-bags on his horse, which was a strong black roadster: but he was nowise armed, and bore but a satchel with a case of knives done on to it, and on the other side a fiddle in its case. So Ralph smiled on him and said: "Thou hast no weapon, then?" "What need for weapon?" said he; "since we are not of might for battle. This is my weapon," said he, touching his fiddle, "and withal it is my field and mine acre that raiseth flesh-meat and bread for me: yea, and whiles a little drink."

So they rode on together and the man was blithe and merry: and Ralph said to him: "Since we are fellows for a good while, as I suppose, what shall I call thee?" Said he, "Morfinn the Minstrel I hight, to serve thee, fair lord. Or some call me Morfinn the Unmanned. Wilt thou not now ask me concerning that privy word that I had for thy ears?" "Yea," said Ralph reddening, "hath it to do with a woman?" "Naught less," said Morfinn. "For I heard of thee asking many questions thereof in Goldburg, and I said to myself, now may I, who am bound for Utterness, do a good turn to this fair young lord, whose face bewrayeth his heart, and telleth all men that he is kind and bounteous; so that there is no doubt but he will reward me well at once for any help I may give him; and also it may be that he will do me a good turn hereafter in memory of this that I have done him."

"Speak, wilt thou not," said Ralph, "and tell me at once if

thou hast seen this woman? Be sure that I shall reward thee."
"Nay, nay, fair sir," said Morfinn; "a woman I have seen
brought captive to the House of Utterbol. See thou to it if it
be she whom thou seekest."

He smiled therewith, but now Ralph deemed him not so
debonnaire as he had at first, for there was mocking in the
smile; therefore he was wroth, but he refrained him and said:
"Sir Minstrel, I wot not why thou hast come with a tale in
thy mouth and it will not out of it: lo you, will this open the
doors of speech to thee" (and he reached his hand out to him
with two pieces of gold lying therein) "or shall this?" and
therewith he half drew his sword from his sheath.

Said Morfinn, grinning again: "Nay, I fear not the bare
steel in thine hands, Knight; for thou hast not fool written
plain in thy face; therefore thou wilt not slay thy way-leader,
or even anger him over much. And as to thy gold, the wages
shall be paid at the journey's end. I was but seeking about in
my mind how best to tell thee my tale so that thou mightest
believe my word, which is true. Thus it goes: As I left
Utterbol a month ago, I saw a damsel brought in captive
there, and she seemed to me so exceeding fair that I looked
hard on her, and asked one of the men-at-arms who is my
friend concerning the market whereat she was cheapened;
and he told me that she had not been bought, but taken out
of the hands of the wild men from the further mountains. Is
that aught like to your story, lord?" "Yea," said Ralph,
knitting his brows in eagerness. "Well," said Morfinn, "but
there are more fair women than one in the world, and belike
this is not thy friend: so now, as well as I may, I will tell
thee what-like she was, and if thou knowest her not, thou
mayst give me those two gold pieces and go back again. She
was tall rather than short, and slim rather than bigly made.
But many women are fashioned so: and doubtless she was
worn by travel, since she has at least come from over the
mountains: but that is little to tell her by: her hands, and her
feet also (for she was a horseback and barefoot) wrought
well beyond most women: yet so might it have been with
some: yet few, methinks, of women who have worked afield,
as I deem her to have done, would have hands and feet so
shapely: her face tanned with the sun, but with fair colour

265

shining through it; her hair brown, yet with a fair bright colour shining therein, and very abundant: her cheeks smooth, round and well wrought as any imager could do them: her chin round and cloven: her lips full and red, but firm-set as if she might be both valiant and wroth. Her eyes set wide apart, grey and deep: her whole face sweet of aspect, as though she might be exceeding kind to one that pleased her; yet high and proud of demeanour also, meseemed, as though she were come of great kindred. Is this aught like to thy friend?"

He spake all this slowly and smoothly and that mocking smile came into his face now and again. Ralph grew pale as he spoke and knitted his brows as one in great wrath and grief; and he was slow to answer; but at last he said "Yea," shortly and sharply.

Then said Morfinn: "And yet after all it might not be she: for there might be another or two even in these parts of whom all this might be said. But now I will tell thee of her raiment, though there may be but little help to thee therein, as she may have shifted it many times since thou hast seen her. Thus it was: she was clad outwardly in a green gown, short of skirt as of one wont to go afoot; somewhat straight in the sleeves as of one who hath household work to do, and there was broidery many coloured on the seams thereof, and a border of flower-work round the hem: and this I noted, that a cantle of the skirt had been rent away by some hap of the journey. Now what sayest thou, fair lord? Have I done well to bring thee this tale?"

"O yea, yea," said Ralph, and he might not contain himself; but set spurs to his horse and galloped on ahead for some furlong or so: and then drew rein and gat off his horse, and made as if he would see to his saddle-girths, for he might not refrain from weeping the sweet and bitter tears of desire and fear, so stirred the soul within him.

Morfinn rode on quietly, and by then he came up, Ralph was mounting again, and when he was in the saddle he turned away his head from his fellow and said in a husky voice: "Morfinn, I command thee, or if thou wilt I beseech thee, that thou speak not to me again of this woman whom I am seeking; for it moveth me over much." "That is well, lord," said Morfinn, "I will do after thy command; and there be many other matters to speak of besides one fair woman."

Then they rode on soberly a while, and Ralph kept silence, as he rode pondering much; but the minstrel hummed snatches of rhyme as he rode the way.

But at last Ralph turned to him suddenly and said: "Tell me, way-leader, in what wise did they seem to be using that woman?" The minstrel chuckled: "Fair lord," said he, "if I had a mind for mocking I might say of thee that thou blowest both hot and cold, since it was but half an hour ago that thou badest me speak naught of her: but I deem that I know thy mind herein: so I will tell thee that they seemed to be using her courteously; as is no marvel; for who would wish to mar so fair an image? O, it will be well with her: I noted that the Lord seemed to think it good to ride beside her, and eye her all over. Yea, she shall have a merry life of it if she but do somewhat after the Lord's will."

Ralph looked askance at him fiercely, but the other heeded it naught: then said Ralph, "And how if she do not his will?" Said Morfinn, grinning: "Then hath my Lord a many servants to do his will." Ralph held his peace for a long while; at last he turned a cleared brow to Morfinn and said: "Dost thou tell of the Lord of Utterbol that he is a good lord and merciful to his folk and servants?"

"Fair sir," said the minstrel; "thou hast bidden me not speak of one woman, now will I pray thee not to speak of one man, and that is my Lord of Utterbol."

Ralph's heart fell at this word, and he asked no question as to wherefore.

So now they rode on both, rather more than soberly for a while: but the day was fair; the sun shone, the wind blew, and the sweet scents floated about them, and Ralph's heart cast off its burden somewhat and he fell to speech again; and the minstrel answered him gaily by seeming, noting many things as they rode along, as one that took delight in the fashion of the earth.

It was a fresh and bright morning of early autumn, the sheaves were on the acres, and the grapes were blackening to the vintage, and the beasts and birds at least were merry. But little merry were the husbandmen whom they met, either

267

carles or queans, and they were scantily and foully clad, and sullen-faced, if not hunger-pinched.

If they came across any somewhat joyous, it was here and there certain gangrel folk resting on the wayside grass, or coming out of woods and other passes by twos and threes, whiles with a child or two with them. These were of aspect like to the gipsies of our time and nation, and were armed all of them, and mostly well clad after their fashion. Sometimes when there were as many as four or five carles of them together, they would draw up amidst of the highway, but presently would turn aside at the sight either of Ralph's war-gear or of the minstrel's raiment. Forsooth, some of them seemed to know him, and nodded friendly to him as they passed by, but he gave them back no good day.

They had now ridden out of the lands of Goldburg, which were narrow on that side, and the day was wearing fast. This way the land was fair and rich, with no hills of any size. They crossed a big river twice by bridges, and small streams often, mostly by fords.

Some two hours before sunset they came upon a place where a byway joined the high road, and on the ingle stood a chapel of stone (whether of the heathen or Christian men Ralph wotted not, for it was uncouth of fashion), and by the door of the said chapel, on a tussock of grass, sat a knight all-armed save the head, and beside him a squire held his war-horse, and five other men-at-arms stood anigh bearing halberds and axes of strange fashion. The knight rose to his feet when he saw the wayfarers coming up the rising ground, and Ralph had his hand on his sword-hilt; but ere they met, the minstrel said,—

"Nay, nay, draw thy let-pass, not thy sword. This knight shalt bid thee to a courteous joust; but do thou nay-say it, for he is a mere felon, and shalt set his men-at-arms on thee, and then will rob thee and slay thee after, or cast thee into his prison."

So Ralph drew out his parchment which Morfinn had given into his keeping, and held it open in his hand, and when the knight called out on him in a rough voice as they drew anigh, he said: "Nay, sir, I may not stay me now, need driveth me on." Quoth the knight, smoothing out a knitted brow: "Fair

268

sir, since thou art a friend of our lord, wilt thou not come home to my house, which is hard by, and rest awhile, and eat a morsel, and drink a cup, and sleep in a fair chamber thereafter?"

"Nay, sir," said Ralph, "for time presses;" and he passed on withal, and the knight made no step to stay him, but laughed a short laugh, like a swine snorting, and sat him down on the grass again. Ralph heeded him naught, but was glad that his let-pass was shown to be good for something; but he could see that the minstrel was nigh sick for fear and was shaking like an aspen leaf, and it was long ere he found his tongue again.

Forth then they rode till dusk, when the minstrel stayed Ralph at a place where a sort of hovels lay together about a house somewhat better builded, which Ralph took for a hostelry, though it had no sign nor bush. They entered the said house, wherein was an old woman to whom the minstrel spake a word or two in a tongue that Ralph knew not, and straightway she got them victual and drink nowise ill, and showed them to beds thereafter.

In spite of both victuals and drink the minstrel fell silent and moody; it might be from weariness, Ralph deemed; and he himself had no great lust for talk, so he went bedward, and made the bed pay for all.

CHAPTER 32

Ralph Happens on Evil Days

Early on the morrow they departed, and now in the morning light and the sun the minstrel seemed glad again, and talked abundantly, even though at whiles Ralph answered him little.

As they rode, the land began to get less fertile and less, till at last there was but tillage here and there in patches: of houses there were but few, and the rest was but dark heath-land and bog, with scraggy woods scattered about the coun-try-side.

Naught happened to tell of, save that once in the after-noon, as they were riding up to the skirts of one of the woods aforesaid, weapened men came forth from it and drew up across the way; they were a dozen in all, and four were horsed. Ralph set his hand to his sword, but the minstrel cried out, "Nay, no weapons, no weapons! Pull out thy let-pass again and show it in thine hand, and then let us on."

So saying he drew a white kerchief from his hand, and tied it to the end of his riding staff, and so rode trembling by Ralph's side: therewith they rode on together towards those men, whom as they drew nearer they heard laughing and jeering at them, though in a tongue that Ralph knew not.

They came so close at last that the waylayers could see the parchment clearly, with the seal thereon, and then they made obeisance to it, as though it were the relic of a saint, and drew off quietly into the wood one by one. These were big men, and savage-looking, and their armour was utterly uncouth.

The minstrel was loud in his mirth when they were well past these men; but Ralph rode on silently, and was some-what soberly.

"'Fair sir," quoth the minstrel, "I would wager that I know thy thought." "Yea," said Ralph, "what is it then?" Said the minstrel: "Thou art thinking what thou shalt do when thou meetest suchlike folk on thy way back; but fear not, for with that same seal thou shalt pass through the land again." Said Ralph: "Yea, something like that, forsooth, was my thought. But also I was pondering who should be my guide when I leave Utterbol." The minstrel looked at him askance; quoth he: "Thou mayst leave thinking of that awhile." Ralph looked hard at him, but could make naught of the look of his face; so he said: "Why dost thou say that?" Said Morfinn: "Because I know whither thou art bound, and have been wondering this long while that thou hast asked me not about the way to WELL at the WORLD'S END: since I told thy friend the merchant that I could tell thee somewhat concerning it. But I suppose thou hast been thinking of something else?"

"Well," said Ralph, "tell me what thou hast to say of the Well." Said Morfinn: "This will I tell thee first: that if thou hast any doubt that such a place there is, thou mayst set that aside; for we of Utterness and Utterbol are sure thereof; and of all nations and peoples whereof we know, we deem that we are the nighest thereto. How sayest thou, is that not already something?" "Yea, verily," said Ralph.

"Now," said Morfinn, "the next thing to be said is that we are on the road thereto: but the third thing again is this, lord, that though few who seek it find it, yet we know that some have failed not of it, besides that lord of Goldburg, of whom I know that thou hast heard. Furthermore, there dwelleth a sage in the woods not right far from Utterbol, a hermit living by himself; and folk seek to him for divers lore, to be holpen by him in one way or other, and of him men say that he hath so much lore concerning the road to the Well (whether he hath been there himself they know not certainly), that if he will, he can put anyone on the road so surely that he will not fail to come there, but he be slain on the way, as I said to thee in Goldburg. True it is that the said sage is chary of his lore, and if he think any harm of the seeker, he will show him naught; but, fair sir, thou art so valiant and so goodly, and as meseemeth so good a knight per amours, that I deem it a certain thing that he will tell thee the uttermost of his knowledge."

Now again waxed Ralph eager concerning his quest; for true it is that since he had had that story of the damsel from the minstrel, she had stood in the way before the Well at the World's End. But now he said: "And canst thou bring me to the said sage, good minstrel?" "Without doubt," quoth Morfinn, "when we are once safe at Utterbol. From Utterbol ye may wend any road."

"Yea," said Ralph, "and there are perils yet a few on the way, is it not so?" "So it is," said the minstrel; "but to-morrow shall try all." Said Ralph: "And is there some special peril ahead to-morrow? And if it be so, what is it?" Said his fellow: "It would avail thee naught to know it. What then, doth that daunt thee?" "No," said Ralph, "by then it is nigh

271

enough to hurt us, we shall be nigh enough to see it." "Well said!" quoth the minstrel; "but now we must mend our pace, or dark night shall overtake us amid these rough ways."

Wild as the land was, they came at even to a place where were a few houses of woodmen or hunters; and they got off their horses and knocked at the door of one of these, and a great black-haired carle opened to them, who, when he saw the knight's armour, would have clapped the door to again, had not Ralph by the minstrel's rede held out the parchment to him, who when he saw it became humble indeed, and gave them such guesting as he might, which was scant indeed of victual or drink, save wild-fowl from the heath. But they had wine with them from the last guest-house, whereof they bade the carle to drink; but he would not, and in all wise seemed to be in dread of them.

When it was morning early they rode their ways, and the carle seemed glad to be rid of them. After they had ridden a few miles the land bettered somewhat; there were islands of deep green pasture amidst the blackness of the heath, with cattle grazing on them, and here and there was a little tillage: the land was little better than level, only it swelled a little this way and that. It was a bright sunny day and the air very clear, and as they rode Ralph said: "Quite clear is the sky, and yet one cloud there is in the offing; but this is strange about it, though I have been watching it this half hour, and looking to see the rack come up from that quarter, yet it changes not at all. I never saw the like of this cloud."

Said the minstrel: "Yea, fair sir, and of this cloud I must tell thee that it will change no more till the bones of the earth are tumbled together. Forsooth this is no cloud, but the topmost head of the mountain ridge which men call the Wall of the World: and if ever thou come close up to the said Wall, that shall fear thee, I deem, however fearless thou be." "Is it nigh to Utterness?" said Ralph. "Nay," said the minstrel, "not so nigh; for as huge as it seemeth thence."

Said Ralph: "Do folk tell that the Well at the World's End lieth beyond it?" "Surely," said the minstrel.

Said Ralph, his face flushing: "Forsooth, that ancient lord of Goldburg came through those mountains, and why not I?" "Yea," said the minstrel, "why not?" And therewith he looked uneasily on Ralph, who heeded his looks naught, for his mind was set on high matters.

On then they rode, and when trees or some dip in the land hid that mountain top from them, the way seemed long to Ralph.

Naught befell to tell of for some while; but at last, when it was drawing towards evening again, they had been riding through a thick pine-wood for a long while, and coming out of it they beheld before them a plain country fairly well grassed, but lo! on the field not far from the roadside a pavilion pitched and a banner on the top thereof, but the banner hung down about the staff, so that the bearing was not seen: and about this pavilion, which was great and rich of fashion, were many tents great and small, and there were horses tethered in the field, and men moving about the gleam of armour.

At this sight the minstrel drew rein and stared about him wildly; but Ralph said: "What is this, is it the peril aforesaid?" "Yea," quoth the minstrel, shivering with fear. "What aileth thee?" said Ralph; "have we not the let-pass, what then can befall us? If this be other than the Lord of Utterbol, he will see our let-pass and let us alone; or if it be he indeed, what harm shall he do to the bearers of his own pass? Come on then, or else (and therewith he half drew his sword) is this Lord of Utterbol but another name for the Devil in Hell?"

But the minstrel still stared wild and trembled; then he stammered out: "I thought I should bring thee to Utterness first, and that some other should lead thee thence, I did not look to see him. I dare not, I dare not! O look, look!"

As he spake the wind arose and ran along the wood-side, and beat back from it and stirred the canvas of the tents and raised the folds of the banner, and blew it out, so that the bearing was clear to see; yet Ralph deemed it naught dreadful, but an armoury fit for a baron, to wit, a black bear on a castle-wall on a field of gold.

But as Ralph sat on his horse gazing, himseemed that men were looking towards him, and a great horn was sounded hard by the pavilion; then Ralph looked toward the minstrel fiercely, and laughed and said: "I see now that thou art another traitor: so get thee gone; I have more to do than the slaying of thee." And therewith he turned his horse's head, and smote the spurs into the sides of him, and went a great gallop over the field on the right side of the road, away from the gay pavilion; but even therewith came a half-score of horsemen from the camp, as if they were awaiting him, and they spurred after him straightway.

The race was no long one, for Ralph's beast was wearied, and the other horses were fresh, and Ralph knew naught of the country before him, whereas those riders knew it well. Therefore it was but a few minutes till they came up with him, and he made no show of defence, but suffered them to lead him away, and he crossed the highway, where he saw no token of the minstrel.

So they brought him to the pavilion, and made him dismount and led him in. The dusk had fallen by now, but within it was all bright with candles. The pavilion was hung with rich silken cloth, and at the further end, on a carpet of the hunting, was an ivory chair, whereon sat a man, who was the only one sitting. He was clad in a gown of blue silk, broidered with roundels beaten with the Bear upon the Castle-wall.

Ralph deemed that this must be no other than the Lord of Utterbol, yet after all the tales he had heard of that lord, he seemed no such terrible man: he was short of stature, but broad across the shoulders, his hair long, strait, and dark brown of hue, and his beard scanty: he was straight-featured and smooth-faced, and had been no ill-looking man, save that his skin was sallow and for his eyes, which were brown, small, and somewhat bloodshot.

Beside him stood Morfinn bowed down with fear and not daring to look either at the Lord or at Ralph. Wherefore he knew for certain that when he had called him traitor even now, that it was no more than the very sooth, and that he had fallen into the trap; though how or why he wotted not clearly. Well then might his heart have fallen, but so it was, that when he looked into the face of this Lord, the terror of the lands, hatred of him so beset his heart that it swallowed up fear in him. Albeit he held himself well in hand, for his soul was waxing, and he deemed that he should yet do great

274

deeds, therefore he desired to live, whatsoever pains or shame of the passing day he might suffer.

Now this mighty lord spake, and his voice was harsh and squeaking, so that the sound of it was worse than the sight of his face; and he said: "Bring the man forth, that I may see him." So they brought up Ralph, till he was eye to eye with the Lord, who turned to Morfinn and said: "Is this thy catch, lucky man?" "Yea," quavered Morfinn, not lifting his eyes; "Will he do, lord?"

"Do?" said the lord, "How can I see him when he is all muffled up in steel? Ye fools! doff his wargear."

Speedily then had they stripped Ralph of hauberk, and helm, and arm and leg plates, so that he stood up in his jerkin and breeches, and the lord leaned forward to look on him as if he were cheapening a horse; and then turned to a man somewhat stricken in years, clad in scarlet, who stood on his other hand, and said to him: "Well, David the Sage, is this the sort of man? Is he goodly enough?"

Then the elder put on a pair of spectacles and eyed Ralph curiously a while, and then said: "There are no two words to be said about it; he is a goodly and well-fashioned a young man as was ever sold."

"Well," said the lord, turning towards Morfinn, "the catch is good, lucky man: David will give thee gold for it, and thou mayst go back west when thou wilt. And thou must be lucky again, moreover; because there are women needed for my house; and they must be goodly and meek, and not grievously marked with stripes, or branded, so that thou hadst best take them, luckily if thou mayst, and not buy them. Now go, for there are more than enough men under this woven roof, and we need no half-men to boot."

Said David, the old man, grinning: "He will hold him well paid if he go unscathed from before thee, lord: for he looked not to meet thee here, but thought to bring the young man to Utterness, that he might be kept there till thou camest."

The lord said, grimly: "He is not far wrong to fear me, maybe: but he shall go for this time. But if he bring me not those women within three months' wearing, and if there be but two uncomely ones amongst them, let him look to it. Give him his gold, David. Now take ye the new man, and let him rest, and give him meat and drink. And look you, David, if he be not in condition when he cometh home to Utterbol, thou shalt pay for it in one way or other, if not in thine own person, since thou art old, and deft of service, then through those that be dear to thee. Go now!"

David smiled on Ralph and led him out unto a tent not far off, and there he made much of him, and bade bring meat and drink and all he needed. Withal he bade him not to try fleeing, lest he be slain; and he showed him how nigh the guards were and how many.

Glad was the old man when he saw the captive put a good face on matters, and that he was not down-hearted. In sooth that hatred of the tyrant mingled with hope sustained Ralph's heart. He had been minded when he was brought before the lord to have shown the letter of the Queen of Goldburg, and to defy him if he still held him captive. But when he had beheld him and his fellowship a while he thought better of it. For though they had abundance of rich plenishing, and gay raiment, and good weapons and armour, howbeit of strange and uncouth fashion, yet he deemed when he looked on them that they would scarce have the souls of men in their bodies, but that they were utterly vile through and through, like the shapes of an evil dream. Therefore he thought shame of it to show the Queen's letter to them, even as if he had shown them the very naked body of her, who had been so piteous kind to him. Also he had no mind to wear his heart on his sleeve, but would keep his own counsel, and let his foemen speak and show what was in their minds. For this cause he now made himself sweet, and was of good cheer with old David, deeming him to be a great men there; as indeed he was, being the chief counsellor of the Lord of Utterbol; though forsooth not so much his counsellor as that he durst counsel otherwise than as the Lord desired to go; unless he thought that it would bring his said Lord, and therefore himself, to very present peril and damage. In short, though this man had not been bought for money, he was little better than a thrall of the higher sort, as forsooth were all the Lord's men, saving the best and trustiest of his warriors: and these were men whom the Lord somewhat feared himself: though, on the other hand, he could not but know that they understood how the dread of the Lord of Utterbol was a shield to them, and that if it were to die out amongst men, their own skins were not worth many days' purchase.

So then David spake pleasantly with Ralph, and ate and drank with him, and saw that he was well bedded for the night, and left him in the first watch. But Ralph lay down in little more trouble than the night before, when, though he were being led friendly to Utterness, yet he had not been able to think what he should do when he came there: whereas now he thought: Who knoweth what shall betide? and for me there is nought to do save to lay hold of the occasion that another may give me. And at the worst I scarce deem that I am being led to the slaughter.

CHAPTER 33

Ralph is Brought on the Road Towards Utterbol

But now when it was morning they struck the tents and laded them on wains, and went their ways the selfsame road that Ralph had been minded for yesterday; to wit the road to Utterness; but now must he ride it unarmed and guarded: other shame had he none. Indeed David, who stuck close to his side all day, was so sugary sweet with him, and praised and encouraged him so diligently, that Ralph began to have misgivings that all this kindness was but as the flower-garlands wherewith the heathen times men were wont to deck the slaughter-beasts for the blood-offering. Yea, and into his mind came certain tales of how there were heathen men yet in the world, who beguiled men and women, and offered them up to their devils, whom they called gods: but all this ran off him soon, when he bethought him how little wisdom there was in running to meet the evil, which might be on the way, and that way a rough and perilous one. So he plucked up heart, and spake freely and gaily with David and one or two others who rode anigh.

They were amidst of the company: the Lord went first after his fore-runners in a litter done about with precious cloths; and two score horsemen came next, fully armed after their manner. Then rode Ralph with David and a half dozen of the magnates: then came a sort of cooks and other serving men, but none without a weapon, and last another score of men-at-arms: so that he saw that fleeing was not to be thought of though he was not bound, and save for lack of weapons rode like a free man.

The day was clear as yesterday had been, wherefore again Ralph saw the distant mountain-top like a cloud; and he gazed at it long till David said: "I see that thou art gazing hard at the mountains, and perchance art longing to be beyond them, were it but to see what like the land is on the further side. If all tales be true thou art best this side thereof, whatever thy lot may be."

"Lieth death on the other side then?" quoth Ralph. "Yea," said David, "but that is not all, since he is not asleep elsewhere in the world: but men say that over there are things to be seen which might slay a strong man for pure fear, without stroke of sword or dint of axe."

"Yea," said Ralph, "but how was it then with him that builded Goldburg?"

"O," said David, "hast hou heard that tale? Well, they say of him, who certes went over those mountains, and drank of the Well at the World's End, that he was one of the lucky: yet for all his luck never had he drunk the draught had he not been helped by one who had learned many things, a woman to wit. For he was one of them with whom all women are in love; and thence indeed was his luck. . . . Moreover, when all is said, 'tis but a tale."

"Yea," quoth Ralph laughing, "even as the tales of the ghosts and bugs that abide the wayfarer on the other side of yonder white moveless cloud."

David laughed in his turn and said: "Thou hast me there; and whether or no, these tales are nothing to us, who shall never leave Utterbol again while we live, save in such a company as this." Then he held his peace, but presently spake

278

again: "Hast thou heard anything, then, of those tales of the Well at the World's End? I mean others beside that concerning the lord of Goldburg?"

"Yea, surely I have," said Ralph, nowise changing countenance. Said David: "Deemest thou aught of them? deemest thou that it may be true that a man may drink of the Well and recover his youth thereby?"

Ralph laughed and said: "Master, it is rather for me to ask thee hereof, than thou me, since thou dwellest so much nigher thereto than I have done heretofore."

David drew up close to him, and said softly: "Nigher? Yea, but belike not so much nigher."

"How meanest thou?" said Ralph.

Said David: "Is it so nigh that a man may leave home and come thereto in his life-time?"

"Yea," said Ralph, "in my tales it is."

Said the old man still softlier: "Had I deemed that true I had tried the adventure, whatever might lie beyond the mountains, but (and he sighed withal) I deem it untrue."

Therewith dropped the talk of that matter: and in sooth Ralph was loath to make many words thereof, lest his eagerness shine through, and all the story of him be known.

Anon it was noon, and the lord bade all men stay for meat: so his serving men busied them about his dinner, and David went with them. Then the men-at-arms bade Ralph sit among them and share their meat. So they sat down all by the wayside, and they spake kindly and friendly to Ralph, and especially their captain, a man somewhat low of stature, but long-armed like the Lord, a man of middle age, beardless and spare of body, but wiry and tough-looking, with hair of the hue of the dust of the sandstone quarry. This man fell a-talking with Ralph, and asked him of the manner of tilting and courteous jousting between knights in the countries of knighthood, till that talk dropped between them. Then Ralph looked round upon the land, which had now worsened again, and was little better than rough moorland, little fed, and not at all tilled, and he said: "This is but a sorry land for earth's increase."

"Well," said the captain, "I wot not; it beareth plover and whimbrel and conies and hares; yea, and men withal, some few. And whereas it beareth naught else, that cometh of my lord's will: for deemest thou that he should suffer a rich land betwixt him and Goldburg, that it might sustain an host big enough to deal with him?"

"But is not this his land?" said Ralph.

Said the captain: "Nay, and also yea. None shall dwell in it save as he willeth, and they shall pay him tribute, be it never so little. Yet some there are of them, who are to him as the hounds be to the hunter, and these same he even wageth, so that if aught rare and goodly cometh their way they shall bring it to his hands; as thou thyself knowest to thy cost."

"Yea," said Ralph smiling, "and is Morfinn the Unmanned one of these curs?" "Yea," said the captain, with a grin, "and one of the richest of them, in despite of his fiddle and minstrel's gear, and his lack of manhood: for he is one of the cunningest of men. But my Lord unmanned him for some good reason."

Ralph kept silence and while and then said: "Why doth the Goldburg folk suffer all this felony, robbery and confusion, so near their borders, and the land debateable?"

Said the captain, and again he grinned: "Passing for thy hard words, sir knight, why dost thou suffer me to lead thee along whither thou wouldest not?"

"Because I cannot help myself," said Ralph.

Said the captain: "Even so it is with the Goldburg folk: if they raise hand against some of these strong-thieves or man-stealers, he has but to send the war-arrow round about these deserts, as ye deem them, and he will presently have as rough a company of carles for his fellows as need be, say ten hundred of them. And the Goldburg folk are not very handy at a fray without their walls. Forsooth within them it is another matter, and beside not even our Lord of Utterbol would see Goldburg broken down, no, not for all that he might win there."

"Is it deemed a holy place in the land, then?" said Ralph.

"I wot not the meaning of holy," said the other: "but all we deem that when Goldburg shall fall, the world shall change, so that living therein shall be hard to them that have not drunk of the water of the Well at the World's End."

Ralph was silent a while and eyed the captain curiously: then he said: "Have the Goldburgers so drunk?" Said the captain: "Nay, nay; but the word goes that under each tower of Goldburg lieth a youth and a maiden that have drunk of the water, and might not die save by point and edge."

Then was Ralph silent again, for once more he fell pondering the matter if he had been led away to be offered as a blood offering to some of evil gods of the land. But as he pondered a flourish of trumpets was blown, and all men sprang up, and the captain said to Ralph: "Now hath our Lord done his dinner and we must to horse." Anon they were on the way again, and they rode long and saw little change in the aspect of the land, neither did that cloudlike token of the distant mountains grow any greater or clearer to Ralph's deeming.

CHAPTER 34

The Lord of Utterbol Will Wot of Ralph's Might and Minstrelsy

A little before sunset they made halt for the night, and Ralph was shown to a tent as erst, and had meat and drink good enough brought to him. But somewhat after he had done eating comes David to him and says: "Up, young man! and come to my lord, he asketh for thee."

"What will he want with me?" said Ralph.

"Yea, that is a proper question to ask!" quoth David; "as though the knife should ask the cutler, what wilt thou cut with me? Dost thou deem that I durst ask him of his will with thee?" "I am ready to go with thee," said Ralph.

So they went forth; but Ralph's heart fell and he sickened at the thought of seeing that man again. Nevertheless he set his face as brass, and thrust back both his fear and his hatred for a fitter occasion.

Soon they came into the pavilion of the Lord, who was

sitting there as yester eve, save that his gown was red, and done about with gold and turquoise and emerald. David brought Ralph nigh to his seat, but spake not. The mighty lord was sitting with his head drooping, and his arm hanging over his knee, with a heavy countenance as though he were brooding matters which pleased him naught. But in a while he sat up with a start, and turned about and saw David standing there with Ralph, and spake at once like a man waking up: "He that sold thee to me said that thou wert of avail for many things. Now tell me, what canst thou do?"

Ralph so hated him, that he was of half a mind to answer naught save by smiting him to slay him; but there was no weapon anigh, and life was sweet to him with all the tale that was lying ahead. So he answered coldly: "It is sooth, lord, that I can do more than one deed."

"Canst thou back a horse?" said the Lord. Said Ralph: "As well as many." Said the Lord: "Canst thou break a wild horse, and shoe him, and physic him?"

"Not worse than some," said Ralph.

"Can'st thou play with sword and spear?" said the Lord.

"Better than some few," said Ralph. "How shall I know that?" said the Lord. Said Ralph: "Try me, lord!" Indeed, he half hoped that if it came to that, he might escape in the hurley.

The Lord looked on him and said: "Well, it may be tried. But here is a cold and proud answerer, David. I misdoubt me whether it be worth while bringing him home."

David looked timidly on Ralph and said: "Thou hast paid the price for him, lord."

"Yea, that is true," said the Lord. "Thou! can'st thou play at the chess?" "Yea," said Ralph. "Can'st thou music?" said the other. "Yea," said Ralph, "when I am merry, or whiles indeed when I am sad."

The lord said: "Make thyself merry or sad, which thou wilt; but sing, or thou shalt be beaten. Ho! Bring ye the harp." Then they brought it as he bade.

But Ralph looked to right and left and saw no deliverance, and knew this for the first hour of his thralldom. Yet, as he thought of it all, he remembered that if he would do, he must needs bear and forbear; and his face cleared, and he looked

round about again and let his eyes rest calmly on all eyes
that he met till they came on the Lord's face again. Then he
let his hand fall into the strings and they fell a-tinkling
sweetly, like unto the song of the winter robin, and at last he
lifted his voice and sang:

Still now is the stithy this morning unclouded,
Nought stirs in the thorp save the yellow-haired maid
A-peeling the withy last Candlemas shrouded
From the mere where the moorhen now swims unafraid.

For over the Ford now the grass and the clover
Fly off from the tines as the wind driveth on;
And soon round the Sword-howe the swathe shall lie over,
And to-morrow at even the mead shall be won.

But the Hall of the Garden amidst the hot morning,
It drew my feet thither; I stood at the door,
And felt my heart harden 'gainst wisdom and warning
As the sun and my footsteps came on to the floor.

When the sun lay behind me, there scarce in the dimness
I say what I sought for, yet trembled to find;
But it came forth to find me, until the sleek slimness
Of the summer-clad woman made summer o'er kind.

There we the once-sundered together were blended,
We strangers, unknown once, were hidden by naught.
I kissed and I wondered how doubt was all ended,
How friendly her excellent fairness was wrought.

Round the hall of the Garden the hot sun is burning,
But no master nor minstrel goes there in the shade,
It hath never a warden till comes the returning,
When the moon shall hang high and all winds shall be laid.

Waned the day and I hied me afield, and thereafter
I sat with the mighty when daylight was done,
But with great men beside me, midst high-hearted laughter,
I deemed me of all men the gainfullest one.

To wisdom I hearkened; for there the wise father
Cast the seed of his learning abroad o'er the hall,

Till men's faces darkened, but mine gladdened rather
With the thought of the knowledge I knew over all.

Sang minstrels the story, and with the song's welling
Men looked on each other and glad were they grown,
But mine was the glory of the tale and its telling
How the loved and the lover were naught but mine own.

When he was done all kept silence till they should know
whether the lord should praise the song or blame; and he said
naught for a good while, but sat as if pondering: but at last
he spake: "Thou art young, and would that we were young
also! Thy song is sweet, and it pleaseth me, who am a man of
war, and have seen enough and to spare of rough work, and
would any day rather see a fair woman than a band of
spears. But it shall please my lady wife less: for of love, and
fair women, and their lovers she hath seen enough; but of
war nothing save its shows and pomps; wherefore she desireth to hear thereof. Now sing of battle!"

Ralph thought awhile and began to smite the harp while he
conned over a song which he had learned one yule-tide from a
chieftain who had come to Upmeads from the far-away
Northland, and had abided there till spring was waning into
summer, and meanwhile he taught Ralph this song and many
things else, and his name was Sir Karr Wood-neb. This song
now Ralph sang loud and sweet, though he were now a thrall
in an alien land:

Leave we the cup!
For the moon is up,
And bright is the gleam
Of the rippling stream,
That runneth his road
To the old abode,
Where the walls are white
In the moon and the night;
The house of the neighbour that drave us away

When strife ended labour amidst of the hay,
And no road for our riding was left us but one
Where the hill's brow is hiding that earth's ways are done,
And the sound of the billows comes up at the last
Like the wind in the willows ere autumn is past.
But oft and again
Comes the ship from the main,
And we came once more
And no lading we bore
But the point and the edge,
And the ironed ledge,
And the bolt and the bow,
And the bane of the foe.
To the House 'neath the mountain we came in the morn,
Where welleth the fountain up over the corn,
And the stream is a-running fast on to the House
Of the neighbours uncunning who quake at the mouse,
As their slumber is broken; they know not for why;
Since yestreen was not token on earth or in sky.

Come, up, then up!
Leave board and cup,
And follow the gleam
Of the glittering stream
That leadeth the road
To the old abode,
High-walled and white
In the moon and the night;
Where low lies the neighbour that drave us away
Sleep-sunk from his labour amidst of the hay.
No road for our riding is left us save one,
Where the hills' brow is hiding the city undone,
And the wind in the willows is with us at last,
And the house of the billows is done and o'er-past.

Haste! mount and haste
Ere the short night waste,
For night and day,
Late turned away,
Draw nigh again

All kissing-fain;
And the morn and the moon
Shall be married full soon.
So ride we together with wealth-winning wand,
The steel o'er the leather, the ash in the hand.
Lo! white walls before us, and high are they built;
But the luck that outwore us now lies on their guilt;
Lo! the open gate biding the first of the sun,
And to peace are we riding when slaughter is done.

When Ralph had done singing, all folk fell to praising his song, whereas the Lord had praised the other one; but the Lord said, looking at Ralph askance meanwhile: "Yea, if that pleaseth me not, and I take but little keep of it, it shall please my wife to her heart's root; and that is the first thing. Hast thou others good store, new-comer?" "Yea, lord," said Ralph. "And canst thou tell tales of yore agone, and of the fays and such-like? All that she must have." "Some deal I can of that lore," said Ralph.

Then the Lord sat silent, and seemed to be pondering: at last he said, as if to himself: "Yet there is one thing: many a blencher can sing of battle; and it hath been seen, that a fair body of a man is whiles soft amidst the hard hand-play. Thou! Morfinn's luck! art thou of any use in the tilt-yard?" "Wilt thou try me, lord?" said Ralph, looking somewhat brisker. Said the Lord: "I deem that I may find a man or two for thee, though it is not much our manner here; but now go thou! David, take the lad away to his tent, and get him a flask of wine of the best to help out thy maundering with him."

Therewith they left the tent, and Ralph walked by David sadly and with hanging head at first; but in a while he called to mind that, whatever betid, his life was safe as yet; that every day he was drawing nigher to the Well at the World's End; and that it was most like that he shall fall in with that Dorothea of his dream somewhere on the way thereto. So he lifted up his head again, and was singing to himself as he stooped down to enter into his tent.

Next day naught happed to tell of save that they journeyed on; the day was cloudy, so that Ralph saw no sign of the

286

distant mountains; ever the land was the same, but belike somewhat more beset with pinewoods; they saw no folk at all on the road. So at even Ralph slept in his tent, and none meddled with him, save that David came to talk with him or he slept, and was merry and blithe with him, and he brought with him Otter, the captain of the guard, who was good company.

Thus wore three days that were hazy and cloudy, and the Lord sent no more for Ralph, who on the road spake for the more part with Otter, and liked him not ill; howbeit it seemed of him that he would make no more of a man's life than of a rabbit's according as his lord might bid slay or let live.

The three hazy days past, it fell to rain for four days, so that Ralph could see little of the face of the land; but he noted that they went up at whiles, and never so much down as up, so that they were wending up hill on the whole.

On the ninth day of his captivity the rain ceased and it was sunny and warm but somewhat hazy, so that naught could be seen afar, but the land near-hand rose in long, low downs now, and was quite treeless, save where was a hollow here and there and a stream running through it, where grew a few willows, but alders more abundantly.

This day he rode by Otter, who said presently: "Well, youngling of the North, to-morrow we shall see a new game, thou and I, if the weather be fair." "Yea," said Ralph, "and what like shall it be?" Said Otter, "At mid-morn we shall come into a fair dale amidst the downs, where be some houses and a tower of the Lord's, so that that place is called the Dale of the Tower: there shall we abide a while to gather victual, a day or two, or three maybe: so my Lord will hold a tourney there: that is to say that I myself and some few others shall try thy manhood somewhat." "What?" said Ralph, "are the new colt's paces to be proven? And how if he fail?"

Quoth Otter, laughing: "Fail not, I rede thee, or my lord's love for thee shall be something less than nothing." "And then will he slay me?" said Ralph. Said Otter: "Nay I deem not, at least not at first: he will have thee home to Utterbol, to make the most of his bad bargain, and there shalt thou be a mere serving-thrall, either in the house or the field: where thou shalt be well-fed (save in times of scarcity), and belike well beaten withal." Said Ralph, somewhat downcast: "Yea, I am a thrall, who was once a knight. But how if thou fail before me?" Otter laughed again: "That is another matter; whatever I do my Lord will not lose me if he can help it; but as for the others who shall stand before thy valiancy, there will be some who will curse the day whereon my lord bought thee, if thou turnest out a good spear, as ye call it in your lands. Howsoever, that is not thy business; and I bid thee fear naught; for thou seemest to be a mettle lad."

So they talked, and that day wore like the others, but the haze did not clear off, and the sun went down red. In the evening David talked with Ralph in his tent, and said: "If to-morrow be clear, knight, thou shalt see a new sight when thou comest out from the canvas." Said Ralph: "I suppose thy meaning is that we shall see the mountains from hence?" "Yea," said David; "so hold up thine heart when that sight first cometh before thine eyes. As for us, we are used to the sight, and that from a place much nigher to the mountains: yet they who are soft-hearted amongst us are overcome at whiles, when there is storm and tempest, and evil tides at hand."

Said Ralph: "And how far then are we from Utterbol?" Said David: "After we have left Bull-mead in the Dale of the Tower, where to-morrow thou art to run with the spear, it is four days' ride to Utterness; and from Utterness ye may come (if my lord will) unto Utterbol in twelve hours. But tell me, knight, how deemest thou of thy tilting to-morrow?" Said Ralph: "Little should I think of it, if little lay upon it." "Yea," said David, "but art thou a good tilter?" Ralph laughed: quoth he, "That hangs on the goodness of him that tilteth against me: I have both overthrown, and been overthrown oft enough. Yet again, who shall judge me? for I must tell thee, that were I fairly judged, I should be deemed no ill spear, even when I came not uppermost: for in all these games are haps which no man may foresee."

"Well, then," said David, "all will go well with thee for his time: for my lord will judge thee, and if it be seen that thou hast spoken truly, and art more than a little deft at the play, he will be like to make the best of thee, since thou art already paid for." Ralph laughed: yet as though the jest pleased him but little; and they fell to talk of other matters. And so David departed, and Ralph slept.

CHAPTER 35

Ralph Cometh To the Vale
of the Tower

But when it was morning Ralph awoke, and saw that the sun was shining brightly; so he cast his shirt on him, and went out at once, and turned his face eastward, and, scarce awake, said to himself that the clouds lay heavy in the eastward heavens after last night's haze: but presently his eyes cleared, and he saw that what he had taken for clouds was a huge wall of mountains, black and terrible, that rose up sharp and clear into the morning air; for there was neither cloud nor mist in all the heavens.

Now Ralph, though he were but little used to the sight of great mountains, yet felt his heart rather rise than fall at the sight of them; for he said: "Surely beyond them lieth some new thing for me, life or death: fair fame or the forgetting of all men." And it was long that he could not take his eyes off them.

As he looked, came up the Captain Otter, and said: "Well, Knight, thou hast seen them this morn, even if ye die ere nightfall." Said Ralph: "What deemest thou to lie beyond them?"

"Of us none knoweth surely," said Otter; "whiles I deem that if one were to get to the other side there would be a great plain like to this: whiles that there is naught save mountains beyond, and yet again mountains, like the waves of a huge stone sea. Or whiles I think that one would come to an end of the world, to a place where is naught but a ledge, and then below it a gulf filled with nothing but the howling of winds, and the depth of darkness. Moreover this is my thought, that all we of these parts should be milder men and of better conditions, if yonder terrible wall were away. It is as if we were thralls of the great mountains."

Said Ralph, "Is this then the Wall of the World?" "It may well be so," said Otter; "but this word is at whiles said of something else, which no man alive amongst us has yet seen. It is a part of the tale of the seekers for the Well at the World's End, whereof we said a word that other day."

"And the Dry Tree," said Ralph, "knowest thou thereof?" said Ralph. "Such a tree, much beworshipped," said Otter, "we have, not very far from Utterbol, on the hither side of the mountains. Yet I have heard old men say that it is but a toy, and an image of that which is verily anigh the Well at the World's End. But now haste thee to do on thy raiment, for we must needs get to horse in a little while." "Yet one more word," said Ralph; "thou sayest that none alive amongst you have seen the Wall of the World?" "None alive," quoth Otter; "forsooth what the dead may see, that is another question." Said Ralph: "But have ye not known of any who have sought to the Well from this land, which is so nigh thereunto?" "Such there have been," said Otter; "but if they found it, they found something beyond it, or came west again by some way else than by Utterbol; for they never came back again to us."

Therewith he turned on his heel, and went his ways, and up came David and one with him bringing victual; and David said: "Now, thou lucky one, here is come thy breakfast! for we shall presently be on our way. Cast on thy raiment, and eat and strengthen thyself for the day's work. Hast thou looked well on the mountains?" "Yea," said Ralph, "and the sight of them has made me as little downhearted as thou art. For thou art joyous of mood this morning." David nodded and smiled, and looked so merry that Ralph wondered what was toward. Then he went into his tent and clad himself, and ate his breakfast, and then gat to horse and rode betwixt two of the men-at-arms, he and Otter; for David was ridden forward to speak with the Lord. Otter talked ever gaily enough; but Ralph heeded him little a while, but had his eyes ever on the mountains, and could see that for all they were so dark, and filled up so much of the eastward heaven, they were so far away that he could see but little of them save that they were dark blue and huge, and one rising up behind the other.

Thus they rode the down country, till at last, two hours before noon, coming over the brow of a long down, they had before them a shallow dale, pleasanter than aught they had yet seen. It was well-grassed, and a little river ran through it, from which went narrow leats held up by hatches, so that the more part of the valley bottom was a water-meadow, wherein as now were grazing many kine and sheep. There were willows about the banks of the river, and in an ingle of it stood a grange or homestead, with many roofs half hidden by clumps of tall old elm trees. Other houses there were in the vale; two or three cots, to wit, on the slope of the hither down, and some half-dozen about the homestead; and above and beyond all these, on a mound somewhat away from the river and the grange, a great square tower, with barriers and bailey all dight ready for war, and with a banner of the Lord's hanging out. But between the tower and the river stood as now a great pavilion of snow-white cloth striped with gold and purple; and round about it were other tents, as though a little army were come into the vale.

So when they looked into that fair place, Otter the Captain rose in the stirrups and cast up his hand for joy, and cried out aloud: "Now, young knight, now we are come home: how likest thou my Lord's land?"

"It is a fair land," said Ralph; "but is there not come some one to bid thy Lord battle for it? or what mean the tents down yonder?"

Said Otter, laughing: "Nay, nay, it hath not come to that yet. Yonder is my Lord's lady-wife, who hath come to meet him, but in love, so to say, not in battle—not yet. Though I say not that the cup of love betwixt them be brim-full. But this it behoveth me not to speak of, though thou art to be my brother-in-arms, since we are to tilt together presently: for lo! yonder the tilt-yard, my lad."

Therewith he pointed to the broad green meadow: but Ralph said: "How canst thou, a free man, be brother-in-arms to a thrall?" "Nay, lad," quoth Otter, "let not that wasp sting

291

thee: for even such was I, time was. Nay, such am I now, but that a certain habit of keeping my wits in a fray maketh me of avail to my Lord, so that I am well looked to. Forsooth in my Lord's land the free men are of little account, since they must oftenest do as my Lord and my Lord's thralls bid them. Truly, brother, it is we who have the wits and the luck to rise above the whipping-post and the shackles that are the great men hereabouts. I say we, for I deem that thou wilt do no less, whereas thou hast the lucky look in thine eyes. So let to-day try it."

As he spake came many glittering figures from out of those tents, and therewithal arose the sound of horns and clashing of cymbals, and their own horns gave back the sound of welcome. Then Ralph saw a man in golden armour of strange, outlandish fashion, sitting on a great black horse beside the Lord's litter; and Otter said: "Lo! my Lord, armed and a-horseback to meet my lady: she looketh kinder on him thus; though in thine ear be it said, he is no great man of war; nor need he be, since he hath us for his shield and his hauberk."

Herewith were they come on to the causeway above the green meadows, and presently drew rein before the pavilion, and stood about in a half-ring facing a two score of gaily clad men-at-arms, who had come with the Lady and a rout of folk of the household. Then the Lord gat off his horse, and stood in his golden armour, and all the horns and other music struck up, and forth from the pavilion came the Lady with a half-score of her women clad gaily in silken gowns of green, and blue, and yellow, broidered all about with gold and silver, but with naked feet, and having iron rings on their arms, so that Ralph saw that they were thralls. Something told him that his damsel should be amongst these, so he gazed hard on them, but though they were goodly enough there was none of them like to her.

As to the Queen, she was clad all in fine linen and gold, with gold shoes on her feet: her arms came bare from out of the linen: great they were, and the hands not small; but the arms round and fair, and the hands shapely, and all very white and rosy: her hair was as yellow as any that can be seen, and it was plenteous, and shed all down about her. Her eyes were blue and set wide apart, her nose a little snubbed, her mouth wide, full-lipped and smiling. She was very tall, a full half-head taller than any of her women: yea, as tall as a man who is above the middle height of men.

Now she came forward hastily with long strides, and knelt adown before the Lord, but even as she kneeled looked round with a laughing face. The Lord stooped down to her and took her by both hands, and raised her up, and kissed her on the cheek (and he looked but little and of no presence beside her:) and he said: "Hail to thee, my Lady; thou art come far from thine home to meet me, and I thank thee therefor. Is it well with our House?"

She spake seeming carelessly and loud; but her voice was somewhat husky: "Yea, my Lord, all is well; few have done amiss, and the harvest is plenteous." As she spake the Lord looked with knit brows at the damsels behind her, as if he were seeking something; and the Lady followed his eyes, smiling a little and flushing as if with merriment.

But the Lord was silent a while, and then let his brow clear and said: "Yea, Lady, thou art thanked for coming to meet us; and timely is thy coming, since there is game and glee for thee at hand; I have cheapened a likely thrall of Morfinn the Unmanned, and he is a gift to thee; and he hath given out that he is no ill player with the spear after the fashion of them of the west; and we are going to prove his word here in this meadow presently."

The Lady's face grew glad, and she said, looking toward the ring of new comers: "Yea, Lord, and which of these is he, if he be here?"

The Lord turned a little to point out Ralph, but even therewith the Lady's eyes met Ralph's, who reddened for shame of being so shown to a great lady; but as for her she flushed bright red all over her face and even to her bosom, and trouble came into her eyes, and she looked adown. But the Lord said: "Yonder is the youngling, the swordless one in the green coat; a likely lad, if he hath not lied about his prowess; and he can sing thee a song withal, and tell a piteous tale of old, and do all that those who be reared in the lineages of the westlands deem meet and due for men of knightly blood. Dost thou like the looks of him, lady? wilt thou have him?"

The Lady still held her head down, and tormented the grass with her foot, and murmured somewhat; for she could not come to herself again as yet. So the Lord looked sharply on her and said: "Well, when this tilting is over, thou shalt tell me thy mind of him; for if he turn out a dastard I would not ask thee to take him."

Now the lady lifted up her face, and she was grown somewhat pale; but she forced her speech to come, and said: "It is well, Lord, but now come thou into my pavilion, for thy meat is ready, and it lacketh but a minute or so of noon." So he took her hand and led her in to the pavilion, and all men got off their horses, and fell to pitching the tents and getting their meat ready; but Otter drew Ralph apart into a nook of the homestead, and there they ate their meat together.

CHAPTER 36

The Talk of Two Women Concerning Ralph

But when dinner was done, came David and a man with him bringing Ralph's war gear, and bade him do it on, while the folk were fencing the lists, which they were doing with such stuff as they had at the Tower; and the Lord had been calling for Otter that he might command him what he should tell to the marshals of the lists and how all should be duly ordered, wherefore he went up unto the Tower whither the Lord had now gone. So Ralph did on his armour, which was not right meet for tilting, being over light for such work; and his shield in especial was but a target for a sergent, which he had brought at Cheaping Knowe; but he deemed that his deftness and much use should bear him well through.

Now, the Lady had abided in her pavilion when her Lord went abroad; anon after she sent all her women away, save one whom she loved, and to whom she was wont to tell the innermost of her mind; though forsooth she mishandled her at whiles; for she was hot of temper, and over-ready with her hands when she was angry; though she was nowise cruel. But the woman aforesaid, who was sly and sleek, and somewhat past her first youth, took both her caresses and her buffets with patience, for the sake of the gifts and largesse wherewith they were bought. So now she stood by the board in the pavilion with her head drooping humbly, yet smiling to herself and heedful of whatso might betide. But the Lady walked up and down the pavilion hastily, as one much moved.

At last she spake as she walked and said: "Agatha, didst thou see him when my Lord pointed him out?" "Yea," said the woman lifting her face a little.

"And what seemed he to thee?" said the Lady. "O my Lady," quoth Agatha, "what seemed he to thee?" The lady stood and turned and looked at her; she was slender and dark and sleek; and though her lips moved not, and her eyes did not change, a smile seemed to steal over her face whether she would or not. The Lady stamped her foot and lifted her hand and cried out. "What! dost thou deem thyself meet for him?" And she caught her by the folds over her bosom. But Agatha looked up into her face with a simple smile as of a child: "Dost thou deem him meet for thee, my Lady—he a thrall, and thou so great?" The Lady took her hand from her, but her face flamed with anger and she stamped on the ground again: "What dost thou mean?" she said; "am I not great enough to have what I want when it lieth close to my hand?" Agatha looked on her sweetly, and said in a soft voice: "Stretch out thine hand for it then." The Lady looked at her grimly, and said: "I understand thy jeer; thou meanest that he will not be moved by me, he being so fair, and I being but somewhat fair. Wilt thou have me beat thee? Nay, I will send thee to the White Pillar when we come home to Utterbol."

The woman smiled again, and said: "My Lady, when thou hast sent me to the White Pillar, or the Red, or the Black, my stripes will not mend the matter for thee, or quench the fear of thine heart that by this time, since he is a grown man, he loveth some other. Yet belike he will obey thee if thou command, even to the lying in the same bed with thee; for he is a thrall." The Lady hung her head, but Agatha went on in her sweet clear voice: "The Lord will think little of it, and say nothing of it unless thou anger him otherwise; or unless, indeed, he be minded to pick a quarrel with thee, and hath baited a trap with this stripling. But that is all unlike: thou knowest why, and how that he loveth the little finger of that new-come thrall of his (whom ye left at home at Utterbol in his despite), better than all thy body, for all thy white skin and lovely limbs. Nay, now I think of it, I deem that he meaneth this gift to make an occasion for the staying of any quarrel with thee, that he may stop thy mouth from crying out at him—well, what wilt thou do? he is a mighty Lord."

The Lady looked up (for she had hung her head at first), her face all red with shame, yet smiling, though ruefully, and she said: "Well, thou art determined that if thou art punished it shall not be for naught. But thou knowest not my mind."

"Yea, Lady," said Agatha, smiling in despite of herself, "that may well be."

Now the Lady turned from her, and went and sat upon a stool that was thereby, and said nothing a while; only covering her face with her hands and rocking herself to and fro, while Agatha stood looking at her. At last she said: "Hearken, Agatha, I must tell thee what lieth in mine heart, though thou hast been unkind to me and hast tried to hurt my soul. Now, thou art self-willed, and hot-blooded, and not unlovely, so that thou mayst have loved and been loved ere now. But thou art so wily and subtle that mayhappen thou wilt not understand what I mean, when I say that love of this young man hath suddenly entered into my heart, so that I long for him more this minute than I did the last, and the next minute shall long still more. And I long for him to love me, and not alone to pleasure me."

"Mayhappen it will so betide without any pushing the matter," said Agatha.

"Nay," said the Lady, "Nay; my heart tells me that it will not be so; for I have seen him, that he is of higher kind than we be; as if he were a god come down to us, who if he might not cast his love upon a goddess, would disdain to love an earthly woman, little-minded and in whom perfection is not."

Therewith the tears began to run from her eyes; but Agatha looked on her with a subtle smile and said: "O my Lady! and thou hast scarce seen him! And yet I will not say but that I understand this. But as to the matter of a goddess, I know not. Many would say that thou sitting on thine ivory chair in thy golden raiment, with thy fair bosom and white arms and yellow hair, wert not ill done for the image of a goddess; and this young man may well think so of thee. However that may be, there is something else I will say to thee; (and thou knoest that I speak the truth to thee—most often—though I be wily). This is the word, that although thou hast time and again treated me like the thrall I am, I deem thee no ill woman, but rather something overgood for Utterbol and the dark lord thereof."

Now sat the Lady shaken with sobs, and weeping without stint; but she looked up at that word and said: "Nay, nay, Agatha, it is not so. To-day hath this man's eyes been a candle to me, that I may see myself truly; and I know that though I am a queen and not uncomely, I am but coarse and little-minded. I rage in my household when the whim takes me, and I am hot-headed, and masterful, and slothful, and should belike be untrue if there were any force to drive me thereto. And I suffer my husband to go after other women, and this new thrall is especial, so that I may take my pleasure unstayed with other men whom I love not greatly. Yea, I am foolish, and empty-headed, and unclean. And all this he will see through my queenly state, and my golden gown, and my white skin withal."

Agatha looked on her curiously, but smiling no more. At last she said: "What is to do, then? or must I think of something for thee?"

"I know not, I know not," said the Lady between her sobs; "yet if I might be in such case that he might pity me; belike it might blind his eyes to the ill part of me. Yea," she said, rising up and falling walking to and fro swiftly, "if he might hurt me and wound me himself, and I so loving him."

Said Agatha coldly: "Yea, Lady, I am not wily for naught; and I both deem that I know what is in thine heart, and that it is good for something; and moreover that I may help thee somewhat therein. So in a few days thou shalt see whether I am worth something more than hard words and beating. Only thou must promise in all wise to obey me, though I be the thrall, and thou the Lady, and to leave all the whole matter in my hands."

Quoth the Lady: "That is easy to promise; for what may I do by myself?"

Then Agatha fell pondering a while, and said thereafter: "First, thou shalt get me speech with my Lord, and cause him to swear immunity to me, whatsoever I shall say or do herein." Said the Lady: "Easy is this. What more hast thou?"

Said Agatha: "It were better for thee not to go forth to see the justing; because thou art not to be trusted that thou show not thy love openly when the youngling is in peril; and if thou put thy lord to shame openly before the people, he must needs thwart thy will, and be fierce and cruel, and then it will go hard with thy darling. So thou shalt not go from the pavilion till the night is dark, and thou mayst feign thyself sick meantime."

"Sick enough shall I be if I may not go forth to see how my love is faring in his peril: this at least is hard to me; but so be it! At least thou wilt come and tell me how he speedeth." "O yes," said Agatha, "if thou must have it so; but fear thou not, he shall do well enough."

Said the Lady: "Ah, but thou wottest how oft it goes with a chance stroke, that the point pierceth where it should not; nay, where by likelihead it could not."

"Nay," said Agatha, "what chance is there in this, when the youngling knoweth the whole manner of the play, and his foemen know naught thereof? It is as the chance betwixt Geoffrey the Minstrel and Black Anselm, when they play at chess together, that Anselm must needs be mated ere he hath time to think of his fourth move. I wot of these matters, my Lady. Now, further, I would have thy leave to marshal thy maids about the seat where thou shouldest be, and moreover there should be someone in thy seat, even if I sat in it myself." Said the Lady: "Yea, sit there if thou wilt."

"Woe's me!" said Agatha laughing, "why should I sit there? I am like to thee, am I not?" "Yea," said the Lady, "as the swan is like to the loon." "Yea, my Lady," said Agatha, "which is the swan and which the loon? Well, well, fear not; I shall set Joyce in thy seat by my Lord's leave; she is tall and fair, and forsooth somewhat like to thee." "Why wilt thou do this?" quoth the Lady; "Why should thralls sit in my seat?" Said Agatha: "O, the tale is long to tell; but I would confuse that young man's memory of thee somewhat, if his eyes fell on thee at all when ye met e'en now, which is to be doubted."

The Lady started up in sudden wrath, and cried out: "She had best not be too like to me then, and strive to draw his eyes to her, or I will have her marked for diversity betwixt us. Take heed, take heed!"

Agatha looked softly on her and said: "My Lady. ye fair-skinned, open-faced women should look to it not to show yourselves angry before men-folk. For open wrath marreth your beauty sorely. Leave scowls and fury to the dark-browed, who can use them without wrying their faces like a three months' baby with the colic. Now that is my last rede as now. For methinks I can hear the trumpets blowing for the arraying of the tourney. Wherefore I must go to see to matters, while thou hast but to be quiet. And to-night make much of my Lord, and bid him see me to-morrow, and give heed to what I shall say to him. But if I meet him without, now, as is most like, I shall bid him in to thee, that thou mayst tell him of Joyce, and her sitting in thy seat. Otherwise I will tell him as soon as he is set down in his place. Sooth to say, he is little like to quarrel with either thee or me for setting a fair woman other than thee by his side."

Therewith she lifted the tent lap and went out, stepping daintily, and her slender body swaying like a willow branch, and came at once face to face with the Lord of Utterbol, and bowed low and humbly before him, though her face, unseen of him, smiled mockingly. The Lord looked on her greedily, and let his hand and arm go over her shoulder, and about her side, and he drew her to him, and kissed her, and said: "What, Agatha! and why art thou not bringing forth thy mistress to us?" She raised her face to him, and murmured softly, as one afraid, but with a wheedling smile on her face and in her eyes: "Nay, my Lord, she will abide within

299

to-day, for she is ill at ease; if your grace goeth in, she will tell thee what she will have."

"Agatha," quoth he, "I will hear her, and I will do her pleasure if thou ask me so to do." Then Agatha cast down her eyes, and her speech was so low and sweet that it was as the cooing of a dove, as she said: "O my Lord, what is this word of thine?"

He kissed her again, and said: "Well, well, but dost thou ask it?" "O yea, yea, my Lord," said she.

"It is done then," said the Lord; and he let her go; for he had been stroking her arm and shoulder, and she hurried away, laughing inwardly, to the Lady's women. But he went into the pavilion after he had cast one look at her.

CHAPTER 37

How Ralph Justed With the Aliens

Meanwhile Captain Otter had brought Ralph into the staked-out lists, which, being hastily pitched, were but slenderly done, and now the Upmeads stripling stood there beside a good horse which they had brought to him, and Otter had been speaking to him friendly. But Ralph saw the Lord come forth from the pavilion and take his seat on an ivory chair set on a turf ridge close to the stakes of the lists: for that place was used of custom for such games as they exercised in the lands of Utterbol. Then presently the Lady's women came out of their tents, and, being marshalled by Agatha, went into the Queen's pavilion, whence they came forth again presently like a bed of garden flowers moving, having in the midst of them a woman so fair, and clad so gloriously, that Ralph must needs look on her, though he were some way off, and take note of her beauty. She went and sat her down beside the Lord, and Ralph doubted not that it was the Queen, whom he had but glanced at when they first made stay before the pavilion. Sooth to say, Joyce being well nigh as tall as the Queen, and as white of skin, was otherwise a far fairer woman.

Now spake Otter to Ralph: "I must leave thee here, lad, and go to the other side, as I am to run against thee." Said Ralph: "Art thou to run first?" "Nay, but rather last," said Otter; "they will try thee first with one of the sergeants, and if he overcome thee, then all is done, and thou art in an evil plight. Otherwise will they find another and another, and at last it will be my turn. So keep thee well, lad."

Therewith he rode away, and there came to Ralph one of the sergeants, who brought him a spear, and bade him to horse. So Ralph mounted and took the spear in hand; and the sergeant said: "Thou art to run at whatsoever meeteth thee when thou hast heard the third blast of the horn. Art thou ready?" "Yea, yea," said Ralph; "but I see that the spear-head is not rebated, so that we are to play at sharps."

"Art thou afraid, youngling?" said the sergeant, who was old and crabbed, "if that be so, go and tell the Lord: but thou wilt find that he will not have his sport wholly spoiled, but will somehow make a bolt or a shaft out of thee."

Said Ralph: "I did but jest; I deem myself not so near my death to-day as I have been twice this summer or oftener." Said the sergeant, "It is ill jesting in matters wherein my Lord hath to do. Now thou hast heard my word: do after it."

Therewith he departed, and Ralph laughed and shook the spear aloft, and deemed it not over strong; but he said to himself that the spears of the others would be much the same.

Now the horn blew up thrice, and at the latest blast Ralph pricked forth, as one well used to the tilt, but held his horse well in hand; and he saw a man come driving against him with his spear in the rest, and deemed him right big; but this withal he saw, that the man was ill arrayed, and was pulling on his horse as one not willing to trust him to the rush; and indeed he came on so ill that it was clear that he would never strike Ralph's shield fairly. So he swerved as they met, so that his spear-point was never near to Ralph, who turned his horse toward him a little, and caught his foeman by the gear

301

about his neck, and spurred on, so that he dragged him clean out of his saddle, and let him drop, and rode back quietly to his place, and got off his horse to see to his girths; and he heard great laughter rising up from the ring of men, and from the women also. But the Lord of Utterbol cried out: "Bring forth some one who doth not eat my meat for nothing: and set that wretch and dastard aside till the tilting be over, and then he shall pay a little for his wasted meat and drink."

Ralph got into his saddle again, and saw a very big man come forth at the other end of the lists, and wondered if he should be overthrown of him; but noted that his horse seemed not over good. Then the horn blew up and he spurred on, and his foeman met him fairly in the midmost of the lists: yet he laid his spear but ill, and as one who would thrust and foin with it rather than letting it drive all it might, so that Ralph turned the point with his shield that it glanced off, but he himself smote the other full on the shoulder, and the shaft brake, but the point had pierced the man's armour, and the truncheon stuck in the wound: yet since the spear was broken he kept his saddle. The Lord cried out, "Well, Black Anselm, this is better done; yet art thou a big man and a well-skilled to be beaten by a stripling."

So the man was helped away and Ralph went back to his place again.

Then another man was gotten to run against Ralph, and it went the same-like way: for Ralph smote him amidst of the shield, and the spear held, so that he fell floundering off his horse.

Six of the stoutest men of Utterbol did Ralph overthrow or hurt in this wise; and then he ran three courses with Otter, and in the first two each brake his spear fairly on the other; but in the third Otter smote not Ralph squarely, but Ralph smote full amidst of his shield, and so dight him that he well-nigh fell, and could not master his horse, but yet just barely kept his saddle.

Then the Lord cried out: "Now make we an end of it! We have no might against this youngling, man to man: or else would Otter have done it. This comes of learning a craft diligently."

So Ralph got off his horse, and did off his helm and awaited tidings; and anon comes to him the surly sergeant, and brought him a cup of wine, and said: "Youngling, thou art to drink this, and then go to my Lord; and I deem that thou art in favour with him. So if thou art not too great a man, thou mightest put in a word for poor Redhead, that first man that did so ill. For my Lord would have him set up, and head down and buttocks aloft, as a target for our bowmen. And it will be his luck if he be sped with the third shot, and last not out to the twentieth."

"Yea, certes," said Ralph, "I will do no less, even if it anger the Lord." "O thou wilt not anger him," said the man, "for I tell thee, thou art in favour. Yea, and for me also thou mightest say a word also, when thou becomest right great; for have I not brought thee a good bowl of wine?" "Doubt it not, man," said Ralph, "if I once get safe to Utterbol: weary on it and all its ways!" Said the sergeant: "That is an evil wish for one who shall do well at Utterbol. But come, tarry not."

So he brought Ralph to the Lord, who still sat in his chair beside that fair woman, and Ralph did obeysance to him; yet he had a sidelong glance also for that fair seeming-queen, and deemed her both proud-looking, and so white-skinned, that she was a wonder, like the queen of the fays: and it was just this that he had noted of the Queen as he stood before her earlier in the day when they first came into the vale; therefore he had no doubt of this damsel's queenship.

Now the Lord spake to him and said: "Well, youngling, thou hast done well, and better than thy behest: and since ye have been playing at sharps, I deem thou would'st not do ill in battle, if it came to that. So now I am like to make something other of thee than I was minded to at first: for I deem that thou art good enough to be a man. And if thou wilt now ask a boon of me, if it be not over great, I will grant it thee."

Ralph put one knee to the ground, and said: "Great Lord, I thank thee: but whereas I am in an alien land and seeking great things, I know of no gift which I may take for myself save leave to depart, which I deem thou wilt not grant me. Yet one thing thou mayst do for my asking if thou wilt. If thou be still angry with the carle whom I first unhorsed, I pray thee pardon him his ill-luck."

"Ill-luck!" said the Lord, "Why, I saw him that he was downright afraid of thee. And if my men are to grow blenchers and soft-hearts what is to do then? But tell me, Otter, what is the name of this carle?" Said Otter, "Redhead he hight, Lord." Said the Lord: "And what like a man is he in a fray?" "Naught so ill, Lord," said Otter. "This time, like the rest of us, he knew not this gear. It were scarce good to miss him at the next pinch. It were enough if he had the thongs over his back a few dozen times; it will not be the first day of such cheer to him."

"Ha!" said the Lord, "and what for, Otter, what for?" "Because he was somewhat rough-handed, Lord," said Otter. "Then shall we need him and use him some day. Let him go scot free and do better another bout. There is thy boon granted for thee, knight; and another day thou mayst ask something more. And now shall David have a care of thee. And when we come to Utterbol we shall see what is to be done with thee."

Then Ralph rose up and thanked him, and David came forward, and led him to his tent. And he was wheedling in his ways to him, as if Ralph were now become one who might do him great good if so his will were.

But the Lord went back again into the Tower.

As to the Lady, she abode in her pavilion amidst many fears and desires, till Agatha entered and said: "My Lady, so far all has gone happily." Said the Lady: "I deemed from the noise and the cry that he was doing well. But tell me, how did he?" "My Lady," quoth Agatha, "he knocked our folk about well-favouredly, and seemed to think little of it."

"And Joyce," said the Lady, "how did she?" "She looked a queen, every inch of her, and she is tall," said Agatha: "soothly some folk stared on her, but not many knew of her, since she is but new into our house. Though it is a matter of course that all save our new-come knight knew that it was not thou that sat there. And my Lord was well-pleased, and now he hath taken her by the hand and led her into the Tower."

The Lady reddened and scowled, and said: "And he ...

did he come anigh her?" "O yea," said Agatha, "whereas he stood before my Lord a good while, and then kneeled to him to pray pardon for one of our men who had done ill in the tilting: yea, he was nigh enough to her to touch her had he dared, and to smell the fragrance of her raiment. And he seemed to think it good to look out of the corners of his eyes at her; though I do not say that she smiled on him." The Lady sprang up, her cheeks burning, and walked about angrily a while, striving for words, till at last she said: "When we come home to Utterbol, my lord will see his new thrall again, and will care for Joyce no whit: then will I have my will of her; and she shall learn, she, whether I am verily the least of women at Utterbol! Ha! what sayest thou? Now why wilt thou stand and smile on me?—Yea, I know what is in thy thought; and in very sooth it is good that the dear youngling hath not seen this new thrall, this Ursula. Forsooth, I tell thee that if I durst have her in my hands I would have a true tale out of her as to why she weareth ever that pair of beads about her neck."

"Now, our Lady," said Agatha, "thou art marring the fairness of thy face again. I bid thee be at peace, for all shall be well, and other than thou deemest. Tell me, then, didst thou get our Lord to swear immunity for me?" Said the Lady: "Yea, he swore on the edge of the sword that thou mightest say what thou wouldst, and neither he nor any other should lay hand on thee."

"Good," said Agatha; "then will I go to him to-morrow morning, when Joyce has gone from him. But now hold up thine heart, and keep close for these two days that we shall yet abide in Tower Dale: and trust me this very evening I shall begin to set tidings going that shall work and grow, and shall one day rejoice thine heart."

So fell the talk betwixt them.

CHAPTER 38

A Friend Gives Ralph Warning

On the morrow Ralph wandered about the Dale where he would, and none meddled with him. And as he walked east along the stream where the valley began to narrow, he saw a man sitting on the bank fishing with an angle, and when he drew near, the man turned about, and saw him. Then he lays down his angling rod and rises to his feet, and stands facing Ralph, looking sheepish, with his hands hanging down by his sides; and Ralph, who was thinking of other folk, wondered what he would. So he said: "Hail, good fellow! What wouldst thou?" Said the man: "I would thank thee." "What for?" said Ralph, but as he looked on him he saw that it was Redhead, whose pardon he had won of the Lord yesterday; so he held out his hand, and took Redhead's, and smiled friendly on him. Redhead looked him full in the face, and though he was both big and very rough-looking, he had not altogether the look of a rascal.

He said: "Fair lord, I would that I might do something for thine avail, and perchance I may: but it is hard to do good deeds in Hell, especially for one of its devils."

"Yea, is it so bad as that?" said Ralph. "For thee not yet," said Redhead, "but it may come to it. Hearken, lord, there is none anigh us that I can see, so I will say a word to thee at once. Later on it may be over late: Go thou not to Utterbol whatever may betide."

"Yea," said Ralph, "but how if I be taken thither?" Quoth Redhead: "I can see this, that thou art so favoured that thou mayst go whither thou wilt about the camp with none to hinder thee. Therefore it will be easy for thee to depart by night and cloud, or in the grey of morning, when thou comest to a good pass, whereof I will tell thee. And still I say, go thou not to Utterbol: for thou art over good to be made a devil of, like to us, and therefore thou shalt be tormented till thy life is spoilt, and by that road shalt thou be sent to heaven."

"But thou saidst even now," said Ralph, "that I was high in the Lord's grace." "Yea," said Redhead, "that may last till thou hast command to do some dastard's deed and nay-sayest it, as thou wilt: and then farewell to thee; for I know what my Lord meaneth for thee." "Yea," said Ralph, "and what is that?" Said Redhead; "He hath bought thee to give to his wife for a toy and a minion, and if she like thee, it will be well for a while: but on the first occasion that serveth him, and she wearieth of thee (for she is a woman like a weather-cock), he will lay hand on thee and take the manhood from thee, and let thee drift about Utterbol a mock for all men. For already at heart he hateth thee."

Ralph stood pondering this word, for somehow it chimed in with the thought already in his heart. Yet how should he not go to Utterbol with the Damsel abiding deliverance of him there: and yet again, if they met there and were espied on, would not that ruin everything for her as well as for him?

At last he said: "Good fellow, this may be true, but how shall I know it for true before I run the risk of fleeing away, instead of going on to Utterbol, whereas folk deem honour awaiteth me."

Said Redhead: "There is no honour at Utterbol save for such as are unworthy of honour. But thy risk is as I say, and I shall tell thee whence I had my tale, since I love thee for thy kindness to me, and thy manliness. It was told me yester-eve by a woman who is in the very privity of the Lady of Utterbol, and is well with the Lord also: and it jumpeth with mine own thought on the matter; so I bid thee beware: for what is in me to grieve would be sore grieved wert thou cast away."

"Well," said Ralph, "let us sit down here on the bank and then tell me more; but go on with thine angling the while, lest any should see us."

So they sat down, and Redhead did as Ralph bade; and he said: "Lord, I have bidden thee to flee; but this is an ill land to flee from, and indeed there is but one pass whereby ye may well get away from this company betwixt this and Utterbol; and we shall encamp hard by it on the second day of our faring hence. Yet I must tell thee that it is no road for a dastard; for it leadeth through the forest up into the mountains: yet such as it is, for a man bold and strong like thee, I bid thee take it: and I can see to it that leaving this company shall be easy to thee: only thou must make up thy mind speedily, since the time draws so nigh, and when thou art come to Utterbol with all this rout, and the house full, and some one or other dogging each footstep of thine, fleeing will be another matter. Now thus it is: on that same second night, not only is the wood at hand to cover thee, but I shall be chief warder of the side of the camp where thou lodgest, so that I can put thee on the road: and if I were better worth, I would say, take me with thee, but as it is, I will not burden thee with that prayer."

"Yea," said Ralph, "I have had one guide in this country-side and he bewrayed me. This is a matter of life and death, so I will speak out and say how am I to know but that thou also art going about to bewray me?"

Redhead lept up to his feet, and roared out: "What shall I say? what shall I say? By the soul of my father I am not bewraying thee. May all the curses of Utterbol be sevenfold heavier on me if I am thy traitor and dastard."

"Softly lad, softly," said Ralph, "lest some one should hear thee. Content thee, I must needs believe thee if thou makest so much noise about it."

Then Redhead sat him down again, and for all that he was so rough and sturdy a carle he fell a-weeping.

"Nay, nay," said Ralph, "this is worse in all wise than the other noise. I believe thee as well as a man can who is dealing with one who is not his close friend, and who therefore spareth truth to his friend because of many years use and wont. Come to thyself again and let us look at this matter square in the face, and speedily too, lest some un-friend or busybody come on us. There now! Now, in the first place dost thou know why I am come into this perilous and tyrannous land?"

Said Redhead: "I have heard it said that thou art on the quest of the Well at the World's End."

"And that is but the sooth," said Ralph. "Well then," quoth Redhead, "there is the greater cause for thy fleeing at the time and in the manner I have bidden thee. For there is a certain sage who dwelleth in the wildwood betwixt that place and the Great Mountains, and he hath so much lore concerning the Mountains, yea, and the Well itself, that if he will tell thee what he can tell, thou art in a fair way to end thy quest happily. What sayest thou then?"

Said Ralph, "I say that the Sage is good if I may find him. But there is another cause why I have come hither from Goldburg. "What is that?" said Redhead. "This," said Ralph, "to come to Utterbol." "Heaven help us!" quoth Redhead, "and wherefore?"

Ralph said: "Belike it is neither prudent nor wise to tell thee, but I do verily trust thee; so hearken! I go to Utterbol to deliver a friend from Utterbol; and this friend is a woman— hold a minute—and this woman, as I believe, hath been of late brought to Utterbol, having been taken out of the hands of one of the men of the mountains that lie beyond Cheaping Knowe."

Redhead stared astonished, and kept silence awhile; then he said: "Now all the more I say, flee! flee! flee! Doubtless the woman is there, whom thou seekest; for it would take none less fair and noble than that new-come thrall to draw to her one so fair and noble as thou art. But what availeth it? If thou go to Utterbol thou wilt destroy both her and thee. For know, that we can all see that the Lord hath set his love on this damsel; and what better can betide, if thou come to Utterbol, but that the Lord shall at once see that there is love betwixt you two, and then there will be an end of the story."

"How so?" quoth Ralph. Said Redhead: "At Utterbol all do the will of the Lord of Utterbol, and he is so lustful and cruel, and so false withal, that his will shall be to torment the damsel to death, and to geld and maim thee; so that none hereafter shall know how goodly and gallant thou hast been."

"Redhead," quoth Ralph much moved, "though thou art in no knightly service, thou mayst understand that it is good for a friend to die with a friend."

"Yea, forsooth," said Redhead, "If he may do no more to help than that! Wouldst thou not help the damsel? Now when thou comest back from the quest of the Well at the World's End, thou wilt be too mighty and glorious for the Lord of Utterbol to thrust thee aside like to an over eager dog; and thou mayst help her then. But now I say to thee, and swear to thee, that three days after thou hast met thy beloved in Utterbol she will be dead. I would that thou couldst ask someone else nearer to the Lord than I have been. The tale would be the same as mine."

Now soothly to say it, this was even what Ralph had feared would be, and he could scarce doubt Redhead's word. So he sat there pondering the matter a good while, and at last he said: "My friend, I will trust thee with another thing; I have a mind to flee to the wildwood, and yet come to Utterbol for the damsel's deliverance." "Yea," said Redhead, "and how wilt thou work in the matter?" Said Ralph; "How would it be if I came hither in other guise than mine own, so that I should not be known either by the damsel or her tyrants?"

Said Redhead: "There were peril in that; yet hope also. Yea, and in one way thou mightest do it; to wit, if thou wert to find that Sage, and tell him thy tale: if he be of good will to thee, he might then change not thy gear only, but thy skin also; for he hath exceeding great lore."

"Well," said Ralph, "Thou mayst look upon it as certain that on that aforesaid night, I will do my best to shake off this company of tyrant and thralls, unless I hear fresh tidings, so that I must needs change my purpose. But I will ask thee to give me some token that all holds together some little time beforehand." Quoth Redhead: "Even so shall it be; thou shalt see me at latest on the eve of the night of thy departure; but on the night before that if it be anywise possible."

"Now will I go away from thee," said Ralph, "and I thank thee heartily for thine help, and deem thee my friend. And if thou think better of fleeing with me, thou wilt gladden me the more." Redhead shook his head but spake not, and Ralph went his ways down the dale.

CHAPTER 39

The Lord of Utterbol Makes
Ralph a Free Man

He went to and fro that day and the next, and none meddled with him; with Redhead he spake not again those days, but had talk with Otter and David, who were blithe enough with him. Agatha he saw not at all; nor the Lady, and still deemed that the white-skinned woman whom he had seen sitting by the Lord after the tilting was the Queen.

As for the Lady she abode in her pavilion, and whiles lay in a heap on the floor weeping, or dull and blind with grief; whiles she walked up and down mad wroth with whomsoever came in her way, even to the dealing out of stripes and blows to her women.

But on the eve before the day of departure Agatha came into her, and chid her, and bade her be merry: "I have seen the Lord and told him what I would, and found it no hard matter to get him to yeasay our plot, which were hard to carry out without his goodwill. Withal the seed that I have sowed two days or more ago is bearing fruit; so that thou mayst look to it that whatsoever plight we may be in, we shall find a deliverer."

"I wot not thy meaning," quoth the Lady, "but I deem thou wilt now tell me what thou art planning, and give me some hope, lest I lay hands on myself."

Then Agatha told her without tarrying what she was about doing for her, the tale of which will be seen hereafter; and when she had done, the Lady mended her cheer, and bade bring meat and drink, and was once more like a great and proud Lady.

On the morn of departure, when Ralph arose, David came to him and said: "My Lord is astir already, and would see thee for thy good." So Ralph went with David, who brought him to the Tower, and there they found the Lord sitting in a window, and Otter stood before him, and some others of his highest folk. But beside him sat Joyce, and it seemed that he thought it naught but good to hold her hand and play with the fingers thereof, though all those great men were by; and Ralph had no thought of her but that she was the Queen.

So Ralph made obeisance to the Lord and stood awaiting his word; and the Lord said: "We have been thinking of thee, young man, and have deemed thy lot to be somewhat of the hardest, if thou must needs be a thrall, since thou art both young and well-born, and so good a man of thine hands. Now, wilt thou be our man at Utterbol?"

Ralph delayed his answer a space and looked at Otter, who seemed to him to frame a Yea with his lips, as who should say, take it. So he said: "Lord, thou art good to me, yet mayst thou be better if thou wilt."

"Yea, man!" said the Lord knitting his brows; "What shall it be? say thy say, and be done with it."

"Lord," said Ralph, "I pray thee to give me my choice, whether I shall go with thee to Utterbol or forbear going?"

"Why, lo you!" said the Lord testily, and somewhat sourly; "thou hast the choice. Have I not told thee that thou art free?" Then Ralph knelt before him, and said: "Lord, I thank thee from a full heart, in that thou wilt suffer me to depart on mine errand, for it is a great one." The scowl deepened on the Lord's face, and he turned away from Ralph, and said presently: "Otter take the Knight away and let him have all his armour and weapons and a right good horse; and then let him do as he will, either ride with us, or depart if he will, and whither he will. And if he must needs ride into the desert, and cast himself away in the mountains, so be it. But whatever he hath a mind to, let none hinder him, but further him rather; hearest thou? take him with thee."

Then was Ralph overflowing with thanks, but the Lord heeded him naught, but looked askance at him and sourly. And he rose up withal, and led the damsel by the hand into another chamber; and she minced in her gait and leaned over to the Lord and spake softly in his ear and laughed, and he laughed in his turn and toyed with her neck and shoulders.

312

But the great men turned and went their ways from the Tower, and Ralph went with Otter and was full of glee, and as merry as a bird. But Otter looked on him, and said gruffly: "Yea now, thou art like a song-bird but newly let out of his cage. But I can see the string which is tied to thy leg, though thou feelest it not."

"Why, what now?" quoth Ralph, making as though he were astonished. "Hearken," said Otter: "there is none nigh us, so I will speak straight out; for I love thee since the justing when we tried our might together. If thou deemest that thou art verily free, ride off on the backward road when we go forward; I warrant me thou shalt presently meet with an adventure, and be brought in a captive for the second time." "How then," said Ralph, "hath not the Lord good will toward me?"

Said Otter: "I say not that he is now minded to do thee a mischief for cruelty's sake; but he is minded to get what he can out of thee. If he use thee not for the pleasuring of his wife (so long as her pleasure in thee lasteth) he will verily use thee for somewhat else. And to speak plainly, I now deem that he will make thee my mate, to use with me, or against me as occasion may serve; so thou shalt be another captain of his host." He laughed withal, and said again: "But if thou be not wary, thou wilt tumble off that giddy height, and find thyself a thrall once more, and maybe a gelding to boot." Now waxed Ralph angry and forgat his prudence, and said: "Yea, but how shall he use me when I am out of reach of his hand?" "Oho, young man," said Otter, "whither away then, to be out of his reach?"

"Why," quoth Ralph still angrily, "is thy Lord master of all the world?" "Nay," said the captain, "but of a piece there of. In short, betwixt Utterbol and Goldburg, and Utterbol and the mountains, and Utterbol and an hundred miles north, and an hundred miles south, there is no place where thou canst live, no place save the howling wilderness, and scarcely there either, where he may not lay hand on thee if he do but whistle. What, man! be not downhearted! come with us to Utterbol, since thou needs must. Be wise, and then the Lord shall have no occasion against thee; above all, beware of crossing him in any matter of a woman. Then who knows" (and here he sunk his voice well nigh to a whisper) "but thou and I together may rule in Utterbol and make better days there."

Ralph was waxen master of himself by now, and was gotten wary indeed, so he made as if he liked Otter's counsel well, and became exceeding gay; for indeed the heart within him was verily glad at the thought of his escaping from thralldom; for more than ever now he was fast in his mind to flee at the time appointed by Rednead.

So Otter said: "Well, youngling, I am glad that thou takest it thus, for I deem that if thou wert to seek to depart, the Lord would make it an occasion against thee."

"Such an occasion shall he not have, fellow in arms," quoth Ralph. "But tell me, we ride presently, and I suppose are bound for Utterness by the shortest road?" "Yea," said Otter, "and anon we shall come to the great forest which lieth along our road all the way to Utterness and beyond it; for the town is, as it were, an island in the sea of woodland which covers all, right up to the feet of the Great Mountains, and does what it may to climb them whereso the great wall or its buttresses are anywise broken down toward our country; but the end of it lieth along our road, as I said, and we do but skirt it. A woeful wood it is, and save for the hunting of the beasts, which be there in great plenty, with wolves and bears, yea, and lions to boot, which come down from the mountains, there is no gain in it. No gain, though forsooth they say that some have found it gainful."

"How so?" said Ralph. Said Otter: "That way lieth the way to the Well at the World's End, if one might find it. If at any time we were clear of Utterbol, I have a mind for the adventure along with thee, lad, and so I deem hast thou from all the questions thou hast put to me thereabout."

Ralph mastered himself so that his face changed not, and he said: "Well, Captain, that may come to pass; but tell me, are there any tokens known whereby a man shall know that he is on the right path to the Well?"

"The report of folk goeth," said Otter, "concerning one token, where is the road and the pass through the Great Mountains, to wit, that on the black rock thereby is carven the image of a Fighting Man, or monstrous giant, of the days

314

long gone by. Of other signs I can tell thee naught; and few of men are alive that can. But there is a Sage dwelleth in the wood under the mountains to whom folk seek for his diverse lore; and he, if he will, say men, can set forth all the way, and its perils, and how to escape them. Well, knight, when the time comes, thou and I will go find him together, for he at least is not hard to find, and if he be gracious to us, then will we on our quest. But as now, see ye, they have struck our tents and the Queen's pavilion also; so to horse, is the word."

"Yea," quoth Ralph, looking curiously toward the place where the Queen's pavilion had stood; "is not yonder the Queen's litter taking the road?" "Yea, surely," said Otter.

"Then the litter will be empty," said Ralph. "Maybe, or maybe not," said Otter; "but now I must get me gone hastily to my folk; doubtless we shall meet upon the road to Utterbol."

So he turned and went his ways; and Ralph also ran to his horse, whereby was David already in the saddle, and so mounted, and the whole rout moved slowly from out of Vale Turris, Ralph going ever by David. The company was now a great one, for many wains were joined to them, laden with meal, and fleeces, and other household stuff, and withal there was a great herd of neat, and of sheep, and of goats, which the Lord's men had been gathering in the fruitful country these two days; but the Lord was tarrying still in the tower.

CHAPTER 40

They Ride Toward Utterness
From Out of Vale Turris

So they rode by a good highway, well beaten, past the Tower and over the ridge of the valley, and came full upon the terrible sight of the Great Mountains, and the sea of woodland lay before them, swelling and falling, and swelling again, till it broke grey against the dark blue of the mountain wall. They went as the way led, down hill, and when they were at the bottom, thence along their highway parted the tillage and fenced pastures from the rough edges of the woodland like as a ditch sunders field from field. They had the wildwood ever on their right hand, and but a little way from where they rode the wood thickened for the more part into dark and close thicket, the trees whereof were so tall that they hid the overshadowing mountains whenso they rode the bottoms, though when the way mounted on the ridges, and the trees gave back a little, they had sight of the woodland and the mountains. On the other hand at whiles the thicket came close up to the roadside.

Now David biddeth press on past the wains and the driven beasts, which were going very slowly. So did they, and at last were well nigh at the head of the Lord's company, but when Ralph would have pressed on still, David refrained him, and said that they must by no means outgo the Queen's people, or even mingle with them; so they rode on softly. But as the afternoon was drawing toward evening they heard great noise of horns behind them, and the sound of horses galloping. Then David drew Ralph to the side of the way, and everybody about, both before and behind them, drew up in wise at the wayside, and or ever Ralph could ask any question, came a band of men-at-arms at the gallop led by Otter, and after them the Lord on his black steed, and beside him on a white palfrey the woman whom Ralph had seen in the Tower, and whom he had taken for the Queen, her light raiment streaming out from her, and her yellow hair flying loose. They passed in a moment of time, and then David and Ralph and the rest rode on after them.

Then said Ralph: "The Queen rideth well and hardily." "Yea," said David, screwing his face into a grin, would he or no. Ralph beheld him, and it came into his mind that this was not the Queen whom he had looked on when they first came into Vale Turris, and he said: "What then! this woman is not the Queen?"

David spake not for a while, and then he answered: "Sir

316

Knight, there be matters whereof we servants of my Lord say little or nothing, and thou wert best to do the like." And no more would he say thereon.

CHAPTER 41

Redhead Keeps Tryst

They rode not above a dozen miles that day, and pitched their tents and pavilions in the fair meadows by the wayside looking into the thick of the forest. There this betid to tell of, that when Ralph got off his horse, and the horse-lads were gathered about the men-at-arms and high folk, who should take Ralph's horse but Redhead, who made a sign to him by lifting his eyebrows as if he were asking him somewhat; and Ralph took it as a question as to whether his purpose held to flee on the morrow night; so he nodded a yeasay, just so much as Redhead might note it; and naught else befell betwixt them.

When it was barely dawn after that night, Ralph awoke with the sound of great stir in the camp, and shouting of men and lowing and bleating of beasts; so he looked out, and saw that the wains and the flocks and herds were being got on to the road, so that they might make good way before the company of the camp took the road. But he heeded it little and went to sleep again.

When it was fully morning he arose, and found that the men were not hastening their departure, but were resting by the wood-side and disporting them about the meadow; so he wandered about amongst the men-at-arms and serving-men, and came across Redhead and hailed him; and there was no man very nigh to them; so Redhead looked about him warily, and then spake swiftly and softly: "Fail not to-night! fail not! For yesterday again was I told by one who wotteth surely, what abideth thee at Utterbol if thou go thither. I say if thou fail, thou shalt repent but once—all thy life long to wit."

Ralph nodded his head, and said: "Fear not, I will not fail thee." And therewith they turned away from each other lest they should be noted.

About two hours before noon they got to horse again, and,

being no more encumbered with the wains and the beasts, rode at a good pace. As on the day before the road led them along the edge of the wildwood, and whiles it even went close to the very thicket. Whiles again they mounted somewhat, and looked down on the thicket, leagues and leagues thereof, which yet seemed but a little space because of the hugeness of the mountain wall which brooded over it; but oftenest the forest hid all but the near trees.

Thus they rode some twenty miles, and made stay at sunset in a place that seemed rather a clearing of the wood than a meadow; for they had trees on their left hand at a furlong's distance, as well as on their right at a stone's throw.

Ralph saw not Redhead as he got off his horse, and David according to his wont went with him to his tent. But after they had supped together, and David had made much of Ralph, and had drank many cups to his health, he said to him: "The night is yet young, yea, but new-born; yet must I depart from thee, if I may, to meet a man who will sell me a noble horse good cheap; and I may well leave thee now, seeing that thou hast become a free man; so I bid thee goodnight."

Therewith he departed, and was scarce gone out ere Redhead cometh in, and saith in his wonted rough loud voice: "Here, knight, here is the bridle thou badest me get mended; will the cobbling serve?" Then seeing no one there, he fell to speaking softer and said: "I heard the old pimp call thee a free man e'en now: I fear me that thou art not so free as he would have thee think. Anyhow, were I thou, I would be freer in two hours space. Is it to be so?"

"Yea, yea," said Ralph. Redhead nodded: "Good is that," said he; "I say in two hours' time all will be quiet, and we are as near the thicket as may be; there is no moon, but the night is fair and the stars clear; so all that thou hast to do is to walk out of this tent, and turn at once to thy right hand: come out with me now quietly, and I will show thee."

They went out together and Redhead said softly: "Lo thou that doddered oak yonder; like a piece of a hay-rick it looks under the stars; if thou seest it, come in again at once."

Ralph turned and drew Redhead in, and said when they were in the tent again: "Yea, I saw it: what then?"

318

Said Redhead: "I shall be behind it abiding thee." "Must I go afoot?" said Ralph, "or how shall I get me a horse?" "I have a horse for thee," said Redhead, "not thine own, but a better one yet, that hath not been backed to-day. Now give me a cup of wine, and let me go."

Ralph filled for him and took a cup himself, and said: "I pledge thee, friend, and wish thee better luck; and I would have thee for my fellow in this quest."

"Nay," said Redhead, "it may not be: I will not burden thy luck with my ill-luck ... and moreover I am seeking something which I may gain at Utterbol, and if I have it, I may do my best to say good-night to that evil abode."

"Yea," said Ralph, "and I wish thee well therein." Said Redhead, stammering somewhat; "It is even that woman of the Queen's whereof I told thee. And now one last word, since I must not be over long in thy tent, lest some one come upon us. But, fair sir, if thy mind misgive thee for this turning aside from Utterbol; though it is not to be doubted that the damsel whom thou seekest hath been there, it is not all so sure that thou wouldst have found her there. For of late, what with my Lord and my Lady being both away, the place hath been scant of folk; and not only is the said damsel wise and wary, but there be others who have seen her besides my Lord, and who so hath seen her is like to love her; and such is she, that whoso loveth her is like to do her will. So I bid thee in all case be earnest in thy quest; and think that if thou die on the road thy damsel would have died for thee; and if thou drink of the Well and come back whole and safe, I know not why thou shouldest not go straight to Utterbol and have the damsel away with thee, whosoever gainsay it. For they (if there be any such) who have drunk of the Well at the World's End are well looked to in this land. Now one more word yet; when I come to Utterbol, if thy damsel be there still, fear not but I will have speech of her, and tell of thee, and what thou wert looking to, and how thou deemedst of her."

Therewith he turned and departed hastily.

But Ralph left alone was sorely moved with hope and fear, and a longing that grew in him to see the damsel. For though he was firmly set on departure, and on seeking the sage aforesaid, yet his heart was drawn this way and that: and it

came into his mind how the damsel would fare when the evil
Lord came home to Utterbol; and he could not choose but
make stories of her meeting of the tyrant, and her fear and
grief and shame, and the despair of her heart. So the minutes
went slow to him, till he should be in some new place and
doing somewhat toward bringing about the deliverance of her
from thralldom, and the meeting of him and her.

END OF VOL. 1.

If you have enjoyed this PAN/
BALLANTINE Book, you may
like to choose your next book
from the titles listed on the
following pages

Hannes Bok

BEYOND THE GOLDEN STAIR   40p
'Here is a story with philosophical concepts
waiting for those who care to probe beneath its
colourful surface'

Beyond the Golden Stair reveals an imagination
as vivid and fruitful as any in the field of fantasy.

THE SORCERER'S SHIP   40p
'Tells of the adventures of a modern man
dropped into another dimension – into a world
of swordplay and sorcery; a watery world of
all-encompassing ocean broken only occasion-
ally by islands' – L. SPRAGUE DE CAMP

Since he saw with an artist's eye, Bok's prose
is prismatic, jewelled, his imagery graphically
clear.

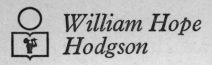

William Hope Hodgson

THE NIGHT LAND Vol. 19   40p
'*The Night Land* is a tale of the remote future –
billions of years after the death of the sun. It
is one of the most potent pieces of macabre
imagination ever written . . . there is a sense of
cosmic alienage, breathless mystery, and
terrified expectancy unrivalled in the whole
range of literature' – H. P. LOVECRAFT
A rich novel, an epic fantasy which is also a
love story, a novel of character revelation, a
dream, a nightmare, and a parable.

THE NIGHT LAND Vol. 11
'The ultimate saga of a fantasy world be-
leaguered by eternal night and by the un-
visageable spawn of darkness' – CLARK ASHTON
SMITH
A strange and beautiful fantasy.

E. R. Eddison